HIT THE GR
RUNNING

by Kate Ashwin

Cover Illustration © 2024, Ben Fleuter (benfleuter.com)

Edited by No Stone Unturned (nostoneunturnedediting.co.uk)

Email: kate@kateashwin.com

Printed in England.

First Edition 2024

ISBN: 9781068503207

ISBN 978-1-0685032-0-7

90000

9 781068 503207

To Mum, for being my biggest fan and constant support.

To Dad, for showing me I can make my own way.

CHAPTER 1

GETTING THE HELL OUT OF HERE

It was around 10 p.m. on a Thursday when Renji thought he might have a go at breaking out of prison.

This idea was terrible for several reasons. One, the prison in question was an Imperium International Forces Containment Facility, the kind widely reputed for being near-impossible to escape. Two, said facility was an airship in flight some fifty storeys above solid ground. The third, and perhaps most important reason was that he wasn't even a prisoner, he was a guard.

But to I.I. Forces Cadet Renjiro Starkweather, the young man leaning out of the mess hall kitchen's window to sneak a crafty cig, these reasons didn't seem quite good enough to not at least have a try. A shudder ran through him as the chilly coastal December wind snaked by, stealing the trail of smoke from his illicit cigarette and ruffling his thick black hair while he watched the lights of the city drift along below, lazy and slow. Just as it did every night, the ship wound its unhurried way between the immense skyscrapers shooting through each layer of the modern marvel that was the three-tiered independent city-state known as Unity. The LED advertising display along the airship's side reflected off the ranks of apartment windows, blending with the building's own billboards in a shimmer of inescapable neon.

Renji huddled into the warmth of his charcoal-grey jacket, the darkness muting the copyrighted shade of Imperium Blue that ran in stripes down its sleeves, and idly wondered what he might have otherwise been doing on a Thursday night before he'd failed to wriggle out of the responsibility of joining up. Likely he'd have been in an anonymous club downing anonymous drinks with anonymous company; a meaningless waste of time, sure, but at least a more enjoyable one than this.

For what must have been the hundredth time he turned over a few of the more traditional prison escapes in his mind. Digging a tunnel was struck off the list for practicality reasons. Slipping past the guards wouldn't be difficult since he was one, but what to do after that…? There'd not be a vehicle to thumb down, unless there was a particularly broad-minded seagull passing by. Perhaps if he could wait until shift change, then—

"—completely out of line, as usual." A haughty tone cut across Renji's daydreams, the sort of voice trapped in a state of perpetually complaining to the manager. "You'd have thought the upper brass would behave better!"

"At least it'll be a bit of excitement around here," another chirped, far too close by. Renji flung the incriminating cigarette stub out of the window and wheeled around to check if anyone had spotted it, but the kitchen he'd been lurking in was tucked neatly behind the large metallic shelving of a serving area spanning the length of the cramped little mess hall. Under the imminent threat of having to actually interact with any other cadets, he decided not to announce his presence and instead kept hidden, peering out between stacks of dirty plates to see which particular flavour of bastard was there.

The Bastards Du Jour, it turned out, came in triplicate. Three of his fellow cadets crowded around a mess hall table in a conspiratorial circle, a wiry little guy with regulation hair and mirror-shined shoes sat at the head, holding court. Renji went out of his way to forget that kind of person's name where possible, but he thought this one was probably… Simons? Simmonds? Something like that, anyway. Lounging next to Probably-Simmonds in one of the uncomfortable designer chairs I.I. insisted on stocking the place with was a round-faced, rosy-cheeked woman with chestnut hair and a smile like a knife. She was cadet… Carter? Maybe?

Probably-Simmonds huffed in annoyance. "I.I. regulations state that they're supposed to give us twelve hours' notice before they transfer any high security assets. *Twelve* hours! Not four!" He slumped on the polished table as if he'd been done a personal injustice. "It's right in the official documents and everything! I checked."

"Mm." Maybe-Carter gave him a perfunctory pat on the arm. "I'm sure you did."

"I'm just saying, the whole system falls apart if every last one of us doesn't adhere to the rules!"

Oh, shit. Narrowing his eyes, Renji remembered who Probably-Simmonds was now. He was that little stoat who kept a notebook, listing any minor infraction he happened to spy in precise detail, which he'd then present joyfully to any Upper Management who'd give him the time of day; the sort of toerag who'd try to raise himself by pulling down everyone else around him. At least once Renji had caught the pint-sized jerk writing him up for *disrespecting the cut of the uniform* because he had his hands in his pockets. If Probably-Simmonds caught someone mid-cigarette— an *actual* infraction— the sarge would have an ecstatic novelette on his desk in ten minutes flat. Considering the only reason Renji smoked in the first place was so he could get away with something, the idea of getting caught simply wouldn't do at all.

"High security assets means... Prisoners," rumbled the last man at the table, ruminating on the last word like a cow chewing its cud. "Real prisoners. For once."

That one was— he wanted to say perhaps Yates? A big bald guy with bony knuckles and a forehead to match, it was too easy to assume Perhaps-Yates had a skull too thick to house a brain, but in this at least he did have a point; in the two months Renji had been stationed at this so-called secret containment facility they had, in fact, played host to a grand total of zero captives. For a secret airship prison, the place had been remarkably dull.

"Hardly matters. It's not like we'll get to see them anyway," complained Maybe-Carter, drumming her nails on the tabletop. "They never let newbies have any fun." What her idea of *fun* might entail didn't bear thinking about— she already had a reputation as one of the more vicious cadets to have made it through training, having memorised a perfect routine of stealing credit when things went well and pointing the finger when they didn't.

Casting a glance about the room, Probably-Simmonds leaned in close. "I know *exactly* who they are," he announced in an overloud stage whisper. "The prisoners, that is. The call came in while I was on comms duty, so I heard everything."

Maybe-Carter's perfect eyebrows arched. "Well? Go on, then."

"You'll never believe it, but—"

Naturally, the little creep chose that exact moment to learn how to whisper properly. Leaning in closer to listen in meant Renji had to play a tricky game of Twister, winding between the perilous piles of kitchenware. After he'd managed to lodge himself between the dishes and bowls he could just make out the edge of a word or two; something about... Past? Vast? No, *broadcast*— and that was all he deciphered before his hand slipped on the treacherous remains of someone's beans on toast, sending two forks and a plate crashing onto the tiles at his feet.

The sounds of chairs scraping along the floor rang out instantly.

"Who's back there?" barked Probably-Simmonds, while Maybe-Carter and Perhaps-Yates advanced on the kitchen area, batons unclipped from their belts and all-too ready.

Oh well. Time to own it. Slipping into one of his best smirks, Renji sauntered around the corner. "Huh, it's only you lot. Thought there might've been something interesting happening."

"Tsch. Starkweather." sniffed Maybe-Carter, losing interest and throwing herself back into her chair.

Probably-Simmonds, however, had sniffed out a potential broken rule like a particularly determined dog tracking down a sausage. *"You!"* He stabbed out an accusatory point in Renji's direction with the end of a biro. "You were up to something, weren't you?"

"Was I? Gosh. Hope it was something fun."

"Thieving rations, I'll bet! Or using a prohibited phone! Or— or *something!*"

"That does sound fun. What else did I do? Maybe I sold company secrets to some passing pigeons. Or started an extremely localised kitchen union? Man, guess I had a real busy evening." He widened his grin, adding several extra degrees of infuriating just for the hell of it. "Shame no-one's going to believe it all happened, though. Not without proof. Which you don't have."

"I- But you—!"

"Can anyone else smell smoke?" rumbled Perhaps-Yates.

The smirk froze.

"I knew it!" hissed Probably-Simmonds, his eyes lit with petty delight, scrabbling to rip open his notebook.

Attempting to rally, Renji rolled his eyes. "Smoke? In a kitchen? Like that's rare."

"So, if the sarge were to search you," began Maybe-Carter, alight with malicious glee, "he definitely wouldn't find anything contraband, is that what you're saying?"

With a jolt Renji recalled the crumpled cigarette carton in his pocket, which ought to have joined the stub in going out of the window several minutes ago. "That's not- I didn't—!"

"Partaking in banned substances unbefitting of the Imperium brand..."

"Aw, c'mon man, there's gotta be something we can work out here..."

"...and attempting to bribe a fellow cadet." Probably-Simmonds' pen scratched over the page until it terminated in a triumphant full stop. "Disgraceful. I.I. gave us these guidelines for a reason, you know. Rules are rules."

"No matter what your surname is," added Maybe-Carter with a titter.

Renji felt his back straighten in annoyance, despite himself. "The hell is that supposed to mean?!"

"Well, it's no secret that you wouldn't have passed training if it wasn't for your connections, is it?" She was the one smiling now, altogether too many pearly white teeth on display in a blatant attempt to rile him up. It was working.

"Oh yeah, it'd be just awful to be literally anywhere else but in the Mile High Club for absolute dickheads!" snapped Renji.

"Disrespecting the Forces..." muttered Probably-Simmonds, adding to his notes with barely disguised joy.

"Fine, put me in your shitty little book! See if I care!" Renji took a step closer, gesturing at Maybe-Carter and Perhaps-Yates. "So long as you two know he'll only stick your name in there next to mine the first chance he gets!"

The frown creasing Perhaps-Yates's heavy brow deepened further.

"I- I would have no need to, obviously!" Probably-Simmonds leapt to his feet in an indignant shower of discarded biros and nervous energy. "Because we actually keep to the rules!"

"Until you're up for promotion ahead of him, then it's oops, someone's shoelaces weren't tied in the regulation knot!" Renji grinned bitterly, savouring the room's growing tension. "That's of course if she hasn't chucked you under a bus first." Maybe-Carter's own smile twisted into a snarl. "And I don't know your deal buddy, but you're probably a prick too," he added in Perhaps-Yates' direction, for equality's sake.

It was at this moment that Renji realised he'd overplayed his hand, if he'd even held one in the first place. All three of them were on their feet now, all three were pissed and worse still, all three were between him and the door. Taking a smart step backwards only served as a stark reminder of how cramped the ship was, backing into the chrome kitchen partition where the stacked plates chattered and rattled like nervous bones.

"Think we've had enough out of you," rumbled Perhaps-Yates, the crack of his knuckles adding a grim punctuation to his words.

Maybe-Carter hummed an almost musical note of sadistic joy, twirling her baton. "Bet he can't talk shit with broken teeth."

"Come and try it, then!" snapped Renji, who had precious little idea how to even throw a punch but was running out of options almost as quickly as he was running out of kitchen. Pressed up against the cold metal partition, raising his fists and cursing his lack of interest in carrying his own baton, he tensed in readiness, hoping to at least getting a few cheap shots in before going down—

"Well, well, doesn't this look absolutely bloody fascinating?"

At the sound of the voice in the doorway, every cadet froze. Striding into the mess hall as if it wasn't already at maximum bastard capacity came the worst of a bad lot, the last person Renji wanted to see at this particular moment in time; the ship's resident Upper Manager and bully-in-chief, Sergeant Flood. Surveying the room with a sneer curled under his immaculately clipped moustache, he folded his arms across his broad chest. "You lot have exactly three seconds to tell me what's going on here."

For a long, wordless moment, the cadets exchanged glares in silent debate.

"One."

The room erupted with sound.

"Starkweather had snuck in here and—"

"—I wasn't doing anything, sarge, these three—"

"—he's lying, that cadet was absolutely breaking the—"

"Two."

"—never did, he can't prove anything—"

"—had to defend ourselves against him, sarge, you saw it—"

Flood swept up a stray chair and flung it into the centre of the group, where it landed with a decisive crash that sent cadets scattering as though he'd scored a perfect first frame strike.

"Three," he snarled.

True to form, Maybe-Carter recovered first. "Starkweather was smoking, sir!" she squeaked, every syllable loaded with manufactured horror.

Some primal instinct yelled at Renji to *run, run for it!*— something more practical added *where to? You're on an airship, you dickhead*— and before he could reconcile the two impulses into something approaching useful a heavy hand had clamped onto his shoulder. Another dipped roughly into his uniform jacket pocket, where it retrieved the cigarette packet.

"Sarge, I don't know where that came from, but—" The iron grip Renji was caught in tightened, cutting him off mid-bullshit.

Flood turned his glower to the other cadets. "You three. Out."

They didn't need to be told twice, filing out of the door with barely a backward glance, leaving Renji trapped alone between the sarge and a fifty-storey drop out of a window, neither of which felt like a workable prospect.

Having been raised in a Forces household, Renji had often heard that sergeants who remained sergeants well into their thirties had either pissed someone off or were dumb as a bag of rocks, and considering he'd been assigned to an empty floating prison, in Sergeant Flood's case it might have been both. However, Imperium did like the higher-ranking Upper Management of their Forces to look the part for promotional purposes, and what Flood lacked in ability he made up for in jawline. With his sandy blond hair, those cold blue eyes and that imposing figure, he was everything I.I. loved in an Upper, a perfectly photogenic ninety-degree right Anglo-Saxon without the slightest spark of imagination. Sergeant Hugo Flood, with all of the appearance of a vintage war recruitment poster, and all the brains of the cardboard it was printed on.

"Listen sarge, I can explain absolutely everything!"

"Is that so." Underneath his groomed moustache lurked a repulsive, smug twist to Flood's mouth, the kind that made an appearance when he knew he had someone exactly where he wanted them. One hand came to rest on the hilt of the gaudy ask-me-about-my-fencing-championship-sword that was eternally clipped to his belt. "If I were you…" he intoned, "I'd think extremely carefully about my next few words."

Renji's mouth snapped shut.

"Nothing smart to say, cadet?"

"I was just thinking extremely carefully, sir."

Flood's nostrils flared, and Renji had enough time to realise his misstep before the sword's hilt slammed into his gut, driving the breath out of his lungs in one aching gasp.

Usually, he quite liked a stupid man. One of the first lessons he'd learned during two dull years of training was that he could get away with an awful lot of entertaining infractions provided he could manage an apology sincere enough to fool an Upper Manager, a task which hadn't proven to be difficult; that was, until he met this particular blue-eyed bastard. Since Flood sported the nightmare combination of a mean streak a mile wide, a regrettably sharp memory and a rock in place of his sense of humour, Renji's usual tactics for dealing with Uppers had proven to be as successful as swimming through concrete. When Renji had first been assigned to the prison ship the other month, it had taken no more than ten minutes for Flood to (quite correctly) accuse him of the crime of Getting Smart With Him, and rather than handing out some cursory overtime or adding another reprimand to the personnel file Flood had simply punched the cadet in the face so hard he couldn't see out of one eye for a week. Corporal punishment wasn't allowed under the Forces guidelines, but clearly no-one had got around to telling Flood that, as any insubordination under his watch was met with swift, brutal, and enthusiastic punishment.

All in all, it had been rather a painful few months.

"On your feet, cadet."

With a spluttering cough Renji pulled himself back upright on shaking legs, though perhaps not upright enough according to the hand that grabbed his uniform collar and yanked him sharply upwards.

"We are in the Forces, boy. Imperium's own. Do you understand what that means? Through our hard work and dedication, we have been employed by the finest company in the world, serving the finest city in the world. And what you need to remember is that when you wear that uniform, you are company property. And as your manager, I can always requisition a replacement for broken equipment."

Renji nodded with care, all too aware of Flood's manicured thumb pressing far too close to the hollow of his throat.

"Dish duty," the Sergeant rasped. "Solo."

"What?!" Renji risked a dismayed glance at the heaps of dirty crockery littering the countertops. "But—!"

"Scrub the rest of the kitchen clean too, while you're at it."

"Sarge, I—"

"You have a complaint to lodge, Starkweather?" The look in those cold blue eyes was nothing less than a challenge. *Go on, say some other line. Just give me an excuse.*

"…no, sir. Right away, sir."

#

Some hours later Renji was failing to fall asleep, staring at the sterile gunmetal grey underside of the Imperium International Force standard issue bunk above his own and feeling his hands ache with a discomfort that ran far deeper than the irritation from scrubbing away at three dozen plates and a stovetop. The midnight lights of the city seeped through the bunk's single window, casting shadows across its cold grey walls, only adding to the cold grey mood that threatened to turn the dozen cadets inside equally cold and grey. The only splashes of colour and decoration were the same style of regulation informative stickers in Imperium International branded colours scattered throughout the ship, a neglected potted plant, and since it was the season for it, one pre-approved Christmas decoration. It was a limp garland of tinsel, precisely portioned to deliver one unit of I.I.-approved holiday cheer, and if the last week of waking up to stare into that dismal yuletide omen had made anything clear it was that if Renji didn't get out of this place soon he was going to throttle someone with it. Probably himself.

When someone applied to join the Forces, they tended to be asked the standard obnoxious job interview questions. What are your greatest weaknesses, tell us a time you've worked well in a team, and the old favourite of what, exactly, do you want out of your career?

Since *I want to be paid* was apparently too obvious an answer, many waxed lyrical about their desire to safeguard and serve the city they loved so dearly and the company that ran it; that was always approved of. Others talked about their need to better themselves, to raise up from Unity's lower tiers and maybe even make it to the Imperium Court one day; an answer that was also met with approval. Some would say their only wish was to help bring about order, which was essentially code for *I would like to knock some people about please*; again, an answer that would earn entry, and possibly a note about suitability for Management training.

Having lied on his application, Renji had no idea what he wanted, at least not within the staggering structure of Imperium. It had become clear to him over the years that Unity City, or at least the top tier of Imperium Court where he lived, was a place that expected him to be a particular sort of person; and if he was not the right shape, he was to *bend*. And having failed to find a way to worm out of the family obligation of joining the Forces, he found himself stuck on the lowest rung of a ladder he had no interest in climbing.

But... it was ridiculous to even consider an alternative, since none existed. Better to keep his head down, and avoid pissing off the sarge until enough time had passed to placate Aunty L. Would it be months? Years? Ugh. It didn't bear thinking about.

In desperate need of distraction, Renji dug about in the regulation shoulder bag he'd stowed under his regulation bunk and fished out his non-regulation phone. He began scrolling through the internet mindlessly, wrapping himself in a cocoon of thin sheets to hide the tell-tale screen glare from any prying eyes, especially those with notebooks. The usual headlines flickered by on the news feed: Blah blah record profits from I.I. for a fifth year running... Something something top ten reasons it was better to live in Unity than anywhere in England... The usual boring old charity Christmas dinner at some swanky hotel in the Court this weekend... He tapped shut tab after tab until the picture at the top of one article caught his eye, leaving his thumb frozen mid-poke.

There she was, in that same freeze-frame everyone had seen thousands of times now, her white-blonde hair and grey eyes giving her the impression of having been drained of all colour, but with that snarl of righteous anger riding over her face like a lightning strike; that furious, anonymous face of the broadcast-jacker.

Just the other month, only days before he'd been assigned to this floating clown show, an unknown group calling themselves The Loose Ends had somehow broken into the emergency broadcast system, overriding all video, audio and phone alerts up and down the entire city. And this lady, this fuming-mad round-the-bend absolute nutter, she'd started ranting and raving about the complex webs of tax avoidance, wage theft, market manipulation and bribery that had allowed Imperium International to rise from a humble email provider to practically running the entire net on their servers and software. And when they'd bought the coastal city of Steelepool from the failing English government so many decades ago, it was for no other reason than to make an extraterritorial tax haven, a company town where they made all of their own laws, and enforced them too.

Developing Unity City allowed Imperium to drive profits higher and higher and hide the human cost of it all beneath the city's own rigid steel tiers, and in this woman's opinion it was time for them to pay the price.

A sting of jealousy prodded at Renji as it always did whenever he saw that grey-eyed girl, all full of flames and anger and directing it exactly where it needed to be. Now *there* was someone who knew what they wanted, her face frozen in that moment of achieving her goal. Right there on that broadcast, she'd given the details of Imperium executives and their dirty dealings and filthy laundry. She had proof too, mountains of it, blasted out over the internet for all to see: documents and signatures and emails, crooked contracts written for friends, rivals cut off at the metaphorical knees, each line more damning than the last.

As Renji hadn't left the Court at that point, he'd been treated to a front-row seat of Imperium International's top executives scrambling to work out whose boots to lick and whose back to stab. It was like nothing he'd seen before. Execs were being fired in droves, bewildered middle managers declared new department heads on the spot, teams altered, job titles vanishing. In one broadcast the blonde had put a blowtorch to the intricate webs of allegiances and rivalries that every department ran on, and it had been hours, days before the metaphorical fires were put out, throughout which Renji could only dream of how incredible it must have felt to cause that level of chaos.

There had been public outcry at first, calls for change and justice. I.I. had done their due diligence in grovelling for forgiveness, every last word committee-selected for relatable trustworthiness. Promises to take accountability and do better were repeated over and over until everyone was sick of hearing them. And with nothing left to say, the story grew fainter as it was dragged away from the public consciousness by the forever-churning rip current of topical news.

The article Renji had scrolled to wasn't a long one. It seemed that the criminals behind the broadcast had inevitably been discovered. Arrested and nameless, whoever The Loose Ends had once been, they were now no more.

Tucking his phone away, Renji rolled over in the darkness of the bunk and yawned, the kitchen work and the light snoring in the room finally catching up with him. His gaze focused hazily on the stubby shape of the potted plant, wedged onto the windowsill in the optimistic yet unlikely hope that its rubbery round leaves might catch enough light to grow.

It wasn't as though he longed to see Imperium burn, but all the same it seemed wrong that the unknown girl's fire had flickered out without leaving a mark.

A muffled crunching *clunk* of metal on metal sounded from down the corridor, jerking him awake. That noise was unmistakable; the ship's docking ramp. With all the business in the mess hall it had completely slipped his mind that midnight on Thursday was the shift change, the only time in the entire week that the airship was near anything like solid ground. A foolish plan began to take shape as Renji lay there in the dark, powerless to stop the damn thing from forming.

It would be a bad idea to desert with no destination in mind. Even worse to risk the wrath of the sarge on pulling off a desperate, spur of the moment escape attempt. Just incredibly, incoherently, weapons-grade stupid.

He was on his feet and packing his bag within seconds.

CHAPTER 2
A REALLY GOOD IDEA

Renji peered into the narrow corridor running the length of the airship's undercarriage, and found himself blissfully alone aside from the low, sleepy thrum of the ship's engines.

Skipping out of the bunk dressed in full uniform, regulation peaked cap and all, he settled into a casual swagger on the grounds that a person caught swaggering tended to be in less trouble than a person caught sneaking. Patting his bag— now loaded up with non-uniform clothes, his most-definitely-not-sanctioned phone and, for some reason, the little potted plant he'd swept up in a flurry of sympathy— he let the swagger take him towards the stairs leading down to the lower deck's docking intake.

The plan, if this loose bundle of vague ideas even counted as a plan, was simple enough; shift change meant a crowd of cadets were leaving the ship, a crowd Renji reckoned he could join unnoticed, if he was clever about it. Whatever happened after that could be a problem for later.

The swagger successfully brought him all the way to the top of the stairs, where both floors of the ship opened out and joined into the one tall, echoing space making up the docking intake. At least half a dozen cadets were busying about, filling the air with the thump of boots on the thick metal floor, the trundling of trolleys laden with supplies, and the to-and-fro shouts of people working on a tight deadline. At the room's far end the huge steel doors of the loading bay had been flung open, letting in both cargo and an occasional gust of wintery wind that threatened to rip a tablet device out from the hands of the nervous cadet who was attempting to sign for a delivery. None of that mattered, however, since standing at the top of the ramp that led down and out to freedom with his tall, wide frame casting a propaganda-poster-perfect silhouette against the spotlights of the dock, was Sergeant Flood.

The swagger fled, leaving Renji to deal with this one alone.

Back straight and voice booming, the sarge was hard at work overseeing operations in the standard manner of managers everywhere, i.e. barking out unhelpful orders and generally getting in the way.

"You! Put that over there! No, your other *there,* idiot!" he snapped at some poor bastard struggling to manoeuvre a trolley up the ramp. "Get that moving, quickly quickly *quickly!* And you!" He glowered at another cadet, who attempted to both snap to attention and bow at the same time and got herself tangled around a clipboard. "Make certain the back room is ready to receive our guests!"

Pressing his back against the wall, Renji wondered what that last order had meant— but frankly, it didn't matter. There'd be no strolling past Flood when he was this involved. *Unbe-fucking-lievable.* As Probably-Simmonds would have been happy to tell anyone who'd listen, I.I. Forces protocol stated that the on-duty Upper Manager was supposed to oversee the shift change, though everyone knew the sarge tended to bunk off that particular duty. Or at least he had, until tonight.

With his reckless half-baked idea blown, Renji needed a new reckless half-baked idea, and as luck would have it, one sprang to mind.

The now-gleaming mess hall was still helpfully empty as Renji crept in, picking through the tables and making his way back towards his old smoking buddy, the kitchen window. Turned out that fitting a ventilation system for an airship kitchen was rather a tricky and expensive affair, but a kitchen stove did need a little ventilation, otherwise the chef's special today and every day would be Greasy Clouds of Smoke with a side of Constantly Blaring Fire Alarm. The upshot was that the window by the stove opened nice and wide, offering a much more cost-effective solution than installing a ventilation system. Easy, cheap, safe, and doubled as an escape route for a suitably bold and handsome cadet with a taste for freedom.

As he reached forward to throw the window open, Renji caught a glimpse of his reflection in its surface. Against the glowing dark of the sky it was as though he were reduced to an outline of his I.I. Forces uniform, face obscured beneath the brim of the peaked cap. The outfit was regrettably stylish, in those flashy brand colours, all ironed creases and sharp tailored lines and stiff leather boots. But *uniform* was most definitely the word. The shape looking back at him from the surface of the glass was how each and every cadet was expected to be; an intimidating, elegant, faceless silhouette.

The damn thing had been handed to Renji with great reverence at the training graduation ceremony by a probably famous lieutenant with an unremarkable name and a fantastic moustache. He'd spent every second of that day hating his own stupid fake smile, shifting in discomfort on the stage amongst the rest of the beaming, proud class who had seemed to not notice the relentlessly hot sun beating down the entire goddamn time. From the crowded stands Aunty Lissa had overseen proceedings, ignoring the inevitable whispers from the other graduate's families with her usual grace. For his part, he'd played it as straight as possible, laughing and cheering his way through the presentation with a class that had disliked him about as much as he'd disliked them. After the speeches and noise and the cameras had left, Aunty L had sat with him on the stage's edge and it became immediately clear that, as usual, his acting efforts had worked on everyone but her.

"Look, I know this whole thing isn't very *you,* but—" she'd paused to flick a stray lock of straw-blonde hair out of her eyes, her sigh heavy. "Just try it out for a while, Peanut. For me." She'd given a strained smile that told him less than half of what needed to be said, and he'd returned one in kind. "All you need is to find a little direction."

Opening the kitchen window, Renji took in a lungful of cool night air, pulled off his cap, and tossed it like a frisbee out into the darkness with a bright, feral grin. Whatever his direction was, it started with out.

#

From the giant screens running up the endless height of the vast skyscrapers to the countless billboards lining the streets, Unity City was yet to meet a wall it wouldn't slap an advertisement onto. Should someone need to know which movie was currently taking the box office by storm this holiday season (it was all of them) or what toothpaste was recommended by nine out of ten dentists (again, it was all of them) they could find out by simply casting their gaze towards any given flat surface. But when a brand was above all of that common advertising, and happened to have a marketing budget big enough to be seen from space, *that* was what the airships were for.

Unity's middle tier, Central Commons, was circled by the three AirCast ships creatively named AirCast One, AirCast Two, and (wait for it) AirCast Three. Unlit they were nothing special to look at, just massive sacks of air puttering around graceful as airborne beanbags, underslung with a small metallic tin can of a cabin stuffed with around a dozen increasingly irritable crew. When the ads on the airship's sides were activated however, the whole thing would become a riot of delightful, profitable colour; millions of tiny LEDs working overtime to beam out the finest in the art of advertising over a screen the size of several houses. Twenty-four hours a day, seven days a week, the ships followed a pre-programmed path that took them winding between the famous immense skyscrapers of Unity, treating anyone living in the apartments in their paths to a compulsory light show directly outside their windows. Only once a week did the ships dock for refuelling, maintenance, and to switch out the cabin-feverish crew. This was done by each ship in turn pulling up alongside the hundred-storey tall AirCast Tower, where the open air skydock stood ready to do the supply run shuffle.

One of these ships, AirCast Two, to be precise, also just so happened to run a neat side business in squirrelling away anyone that Imperium really didn't want to see the light of day any time soon, such as anti-I.I protestors, general dissidents, or people who had too many thoughts about the word *union*. And as a neat bonus, it also provided them with a dull duty in which to sequester any particularly hopeless Force cadets, motivating them to find their ambition by fighting each other tooth and claw for promotion in order to escape the blasted place.

Renji, on the other hand, had a more direct route in mind.

The freezing December air slapped him in the face as if it had a point to make about his cool and sensible idea, but from this new vantage point with his back pressed against the side of the airship's carriage, he was too close to freedom to pay too much attention to small considerations like gravity.

AirCast Tower was among the tallest buildings in Unity City, one of the few that shot from the depths of the buried town of Steelepool, up through Central Commons and all the way out to support the heights of Imperium Court, some hundred and fifty storeys tall in total. The skydock itself was a hive of activity scattered with engineers and I.I Force cadets, a busy platform carved into the building's side around ninety storeys up; high enough that it was closer to the gleaming metal and glass underside of Imperium Court than the cluttered streets of the Commons.

At this moment and with any luck, for a few moments more, AirCast Two hovered alongside AirCast Tower with its ramp extended, lined with blinking red lights and forming the only point of contact between ship and building. Said ramp was currently being stomped across by the boots of a half dozen cadets, loading and unloading whatever the hell it was they needed to load and unload and generally trudging about getting in each other's way; in other words, the perfect cover. All he would need to do would be to shimmy around the ship's outside to the ramp, hop on while no-one was paying attention, and stroll on out of there in the crowd before anyone realised he wasn't meant to be there. There were even a set of helpful ledge-like ridges running decoratively along the carriage's sides, providing just enough inches of metal to grip onto and shuffle along. Granted, he was only a single slip away from a much faster and more fatal way off the ship, but since he had no intention of slipping Renji was confident he'd be fine. Plus, he'd seen more than enough movies to know that all he had to do was avoid the classic mistake of looking down, which couldn't possibly be so difficult as all that.

Eyes locked on the lights of the skydock, he began his shuffling progress forwards; but at once, a yell froze him to the spot. Ice shot through his veins as he clung in place, craning his neck to discover that for once, the shout wasn't aimed at him.

As it turned out, Probably-Simmonds hadn't been bullshitting in the mess earlier, as a group of actual factual prisoners were being marched over the ramp and into the ship. To Renji, all three seemed to be your standard Forces definition of troublemakers; a scowling woman with a trembling lip and a scattering of facial piercings, her black hair chopped into a rough bob; another with long blue hair drifting ragged and wild in the wind about her shivering shoulders; and lastly a shorter guy with wide, thoughtful eyes that would have been quite attractive if they hadn't been ringed with vivid bruises marring his dark skin. All sported matching handcuffs, beige prison jumpsuits, a grab-bag of injuries, and a defeated air of grim resignation as they were propelled up the ramp by a whack or gruff bark from one of the armed cadets surrounding them. Nothing about the group seemed to shout *High Security Prison Required*, except… There was something about them, something in the shade of blue in that one lady's hair that seemed oddly familiar… But before Renji could get a better view, the poor bastards had already been swallowed up into the belly of AirCast Two, most likely to never see the light of day again.

Despite being mere metres away from victory, Renji found himself hesitating. The thought of leaving the exhausted captives at the sarge's mercy was uncomfortable, to say the least. But even if he wanted to help, what the hell could he *do?* It wasn't as though he could hop back in and crack a door open for them. Hell, he didn't even know what they'd done to end up here! Just because they appeared pathetic now didn't mean that they couldn't have been doing some murders or whatever yesterday.

He dithered on the ledge, achieving nothing except the waste of several precious seconds, and just when he'd nearly maybe begun to perhaps approach an approximation of a possible decision it no longer mattered, because out of nowhere, a hand had clamped itself around his ankle.

Somehow, he didn't scream.

The Forces would say there was no medal for not screaming when grabbed by a hand that had no right to be there, but in Renji's recently over-informed opinion, there ought to have been such a thing and he should have twelve.

Rather, he stared down at his boot and the black-gloved appendage grasping it, then farther down to where the attached arm ran out of his sight below the ship and presumably along to an owner of some kind. Lacking a better option he kicked the hand with his other heel and it let go, retreating under the curved base of the airship's carriage; and before he could stop himself it was too late, his eyes had kept travelling past the edge of the ship and down, down all the way down to endless amounts of *down*.

Beneath lay the night-dark streets of Central Commons, peppered with thousands, or hundreds of thousands, maybe millions of lights. Street lights, apartment windows, car headlights, even some holly jolly Christmas lights, all twinkling and pretty and far, far away and they were moving now, swirling, like the tacky strobe lighting in a bar after having a few too many to keep things still without concentrating *really hard.* The unceasing hum of the ship's great engine seemed to be keeping time with the undulating motion of the lights and forming some kind of head-crushingly horrible pressure, until Renji realised what he was hearing was the sickening throbbing of his pulse in his own ears, loud enough that it felt as though the sound alone would propel him straight off the edge. At the mere thought of falling he buckled, knees trembling, fingers scrabbling to hold onto the metal ridge that had felt so much wider mere seconds ago.

Perhaps, just perhaps, he could admit that he'd made a teensy mistake here. Just a small one.

Clinging to the side of the ship with his breath running rapid, he wasn't surprised to find he had zero clue what to do when a face appeared over the edge of the carriage just below his feet. The majority of said face was hidden behind a woollen balaclava but what was visible seemed pretty shocked, as if they too hadn't expected company out here. *Well, same here, buddy,* Renji thought furiously. Whoever the figure was, they had overcome their own shock and were advancing now, climbing with their hands flat against the surface of the wall like a spider that had left half of its legs at home.

Finally locating his voice, Renji had just enough time to blurt out "What the *actual* fuck?!" as the intruder drew level with his more and more cramped ledge, positioning themselves between him and the skydock, but no explanation seemed to be on offer as to what the actual fuck.

Now the figure was closer Renji could see it was some kind of guy hanging onto the metallic siding using a pair of magnetic clamps, one in each hand. Moving via pull up alone couldn't have been easy, but he seemed to have the muscle for it under all of the black tactical crap he was wearing. Black *only,* in fact, not a hint of the I.I. brand-permitted grey or blue, which meant he was more likely to be an intruder than an extremely committed patrolman. Between the kit and the getup this man looked like a professional killer got into a fight with an army surplus store, and when those well-worn boots began to pace towards Renji he reached for his usual best defence; high-speed negotiations.

"Hey hey, woah, let's not do anything hasty, buddy! We can talk about this!" he tried, backing up towards the window as fast as he dared. As a reply, Army Surplus leant back while hanging onto just one of his magnetic clamps and gave a precise flick of the wrist. A short but practical knife appeared in his free hand.

"Not much of a talker, huh? More of an action guy, I can respect that!" Renji babbled as he groped around for the still-open kitchen window with one shaking hand. "Listen, you're breaking in, I'm breaking out, seems best if we just go our separate ways, yeah? Act like we never even saw each other! There's no need to—"

Before Renji could finish the knife cut a neat arc through the air, only missing his neck due to a wobbly backstep that felt quite a lot like cashing in a last chip of luck. At last his grasping fingers locked onto the frame of the kitchen window behind him; but he had been slow, too slow to move before the next lunge of the grim little blade that came driving towards his ribs.

Slamming his eyes shut and wishing he could bunk off this class on what being stabbed felt like, it came as something of a surprise when instead of the expected jolt of cold pain, there was only a rush of movement skimming past his chest. The knife had somehow missed, falling short of its target by a few inches and instead claiming a slice of paint from the ship's flank. Grunting in apparent frustration, Army Surplus slammed a fist into his left knee before moving forward with a strange stiff motion; but before he'd regained his momentum Renji had already used his grip on the window frame to haul himself over to and in through the kitchen window to relative safety. While mid-scramble he caught a glimpse of some poor cadet standing against the lights of the skydock, staring at the scuffle with mouth agape and radio dangling from his hands as he failed to remember the Official Forces Code number for *Dudes On The Side Of The Airship, Please Send Help*. It seemed sensible to file that one away under trouble for later however, since trouble for now was wearing a balaclava and still advancing along the wall like a knife-wielding spider from hell. Less Army Surplus, more Army Excess.

Only a few seconds after Renji cleared the window that black gloved hand made an appearance on the window frame, but a few seconds was all he needed to snag a freshly scrubbed iron skillet and bring it down onto the guy's fingers with a crunch he could feel straight through his own finger-bones. The digits disappeared, and then… nothing.

With an inhale of shock Renji dropped the skillet, the adrenaline draining out of him and leaving a hollowness in its wake. *Shit.* If the guy hadn't been hanging onto anything else, then— then…

 But he hadn't made a sound. Renji was by no means an expert on what someone falling to their death from the side of a secret prison airship might sound like, but he reasoned there'd be something. A blood-curdling scream, or, if the universe was feeling lighthearted today, maybe even a cartoon slide whistle. Not *nothing.* Carefully, he crept up to the window and peeked over the edge, dreading what he might or might not see.

Apparently— thankfully— it took more than kitchen utensils to kill a guy like that since the hardcore bastard was still hanging in there, his stubborn fingers wrapped around the handle of one of those magnetic clamps. The good news was that his knife was absent; the bad news was that judging from the blood dripping between the fingers of the hand that had met Renji's skillet, it wasn't going to be of much use in getting him out of this one. With a noise of exertion the intruder attempted to execute a one-armed pull up that didn't seem as though it was going to happen, leaving him dangling hopelessly over a fifty-storey drop. As Renji stared down in dumb shock, the man's eyes met his own; they were a serious, storm-cloud grey, softened at the edges by those fine, familiar wrinkles he'd seen on older people who smiled often.

What a good Forces cadet ought to do here was obvious. The sarge would have barked phrases like *deadly force* and *acceptable loss,* since the protocols for dealing with an armed intruder on I.I. property were both brutal and clear. And good cadets were, after all, expected to follow protocol to the letter.

"C'mere!" he shouted, reaching his hand out.

The intruder hesitated; then his bleeding hand closed around Renji's in silent acceptance.

After some amount of painful hauling and protesting shoulder muscles, both of them tumbled into the kitchen. Rolling into an awkward crouch, the intruder clutched at his left knee and winced, but while he didn't seem good, exactly, he was sure as hell not dead. Meanwhile, Renji's own legs came to the conclusion that they were no longer needed to keep him upright and decided to take some time off, sending him slumping to the linoleum in a boneless pile. Drifting in through the open window came a furious clanking, a racket that could have only been the sound of the docking ramp being retracted and the intensifying hum of the ship's engine that followed meant they were leaving AirCast Tower, and any hope of escape, behind.

"Well, damn." Renji rolled his head sideways to meet the intruder's gaze once more. "Dunno about you, but I'm at my knife fight limit for tonight. We good?"

This was met with the briefest of nods and, almost lost by the muffling effect of the balaclava, a gruff whisper. "Thanks, kid."

"Oh, don't thank me yet, buddy." Renji gave an exhausted floor-height grin as the mess hall door clattered open with the sound of a dozen pairs of approaching boots. "We're *both* screwed now."

#

The intruder was hauled off at once. Renji, on the other hand, got to enjoy the mess hall floor for a little longer, guarded by a gaggle of unsympathetic cadets with a silently gloating Maybe-Carter at the head. He'd not even had time to assess his current level of Utterly Done For before Flood stomped in, tore Renji's bag from his shoulder and upended it, sending his belongings tumbling onto the tiles where they couldn't have screamed *Renji was absolutely one hundred percent trying to desert* any louder unless it had been printed on one of the T-shirts.

There was a moment of silence, undercut by a soft, Maybe-Carter-esque giggle.

"Now I know what you're thinking, Sarge," began Renji, because anything's worth a try, "but I—"

"Do you know what the penalty for desertion is, Starkweather?" Flood asked, tone worryingly pleasant.

Renji paused, mouth open. "Uh… no, actually."

"It doesn't come up often, you see, so neither did I." The sergeant's perfect smile was a cold crescent beneath his clipped moustache. "And since I have only the highest regard for our city's rules, I thought it best to call the commander to make certain."

"T-the commander, sarge—?" stuttered Renji in disbelief. Nearly getting knifed off the side of an airship was nothing compared to the dread he was feeling in this moment.

"The one and only. And do you know what she said?" Flood's voice was syrupy sweet, smug as a cat with a bird between its claws. "She said she'll be over directly to *personally* oversee the matter."

For once, Renji was speechless. On her way here, now, was the leader of the entire Imperium International Forces; Commander Lissa Starkweather. Or, as he'd always known her, Aunty Lissa. His mother's sister. The woman who'd raised him, and as soon as she found out what he'd been up to, the woman who was going to end him too.

Flood swept out of the room, radiating a level of malicious glee only achievable after having played the ultimate I'm-telling-your-mum card.

A bony elbow bumped Renji in the ribs. "You're proper fucked, aren't you?" snorted Maybe-Carter.

She wasn't wrong.

CHAPTER 3

CALL WAITING

If Renji had to leave a review for the cells of AirCast Two, it wouldn't be a very complimentary one. A disgrace really, lacking any of the standard facilities he'd been led to believe would be in any decent prison. No bedsheets to knot into a rope, no loose pieces of convenient lockpick-shaped metal, not even a sleepy guard sat within arm's reach with an oversized ring of keys on his belt. Zero out of five stars, would not recommend.

Before now, he'd only peeked into what was labelled as the Asset Confinement Area once and found nothing of interest, thus hadn't bothered checking it again since. It didn't seem much more interesting from the inside either; an enclosed room with high steel walls, containing a row of six barred cells. On an average day, each cramped yet state-of-the-art cell contained nothing more than gathering dust and a championship contender for the world's least comfortable bench, but since it had been anything but an average day, there were three other people in here besides Renji; the black-clad intruder, curled into a corner and unwilling to talk, and two others from the group who had being marched in earlier. One, the smaller guy with the big eyes, was quite thoroughly passed out. The colourful patchwork of bruises across his face had only grown since Renji had seen him out on the docking ramp, and now there was fresh blood matting in his thick, tight curls. In the cell next to his, pressed against the bars between them as though she could pass through them with enough effort, was a ghostly pale girl with sharp features and black hair cut into a choppy bob. Hugging her bony knees in her prison-issue jumpsuit, she seemed to be putting all of her remaining energy into giving Renji a seriously dirty look. Much like her friend, poor old

Choppy Bob had also been knocked around some, judging by the blood caked around her hooped lip piercing. There were in fact a variety of metal loops and studs dotted about her face, and even the occasional symbol tattooed onto the skin of her fingers and neck. The third member of their gang, the one with the familiar blue hair, was nowhere to be seen.

"Don't suppose you've found a way out of here yet?" Renji asked his new neighbours optimistically.

Choppy Bob's eyes widened in surprise as though she hadn't expected to be addressed. She took a moment to gather herself, before settling back into the belligerent sneer that seemed to be her face's default mode. "I don't talk to cops."

"Cops? I'm not a—" Renji paused, mid-sentence. Huh. Was he a cop?

Having done such a terrible job during training, Renji had never had to interact with the public while in uniform yet. No matter how many classes he'd skipped and performance reviews he tanked he was still the commander's nephew, so the ancient mummy's curse of nepotism meant that some poor bastard in some office somewhere must have spent a lot of overtime finding places to store him where he might do the least amount of damage. Essentially, he'd managed to bounce from training to posting without having to deal with anyone not being paid by Imperium and thus had never had cause to do his actual damn job before. Hell, he'd barely even thought about what that job meant. It was impossible to avoid hearing the mumblings of violence and unjust treatment by Forces, complaints by disaffected crowds of protestors and whispered online in anonymity, but those hardly seemed connected to Renji himself.

Or at least, that was how he'd always seen it. The look Bob was giving him, with her split lip and concussed friend, very much expressed her opinion on the matter. Those narrowed eyes were defiant, but the way her thin fingers trembled as she shielded her unconscious friend gave away the fact that she was terrified.

A bolt of something nauseating twisted right through Renji's core. No-one had ever been scared of him before. Annoyed by or angry at, sure, but he'd never seen anyone *frightened* by his presence. It felt singularly, completely, gut-wrenchingly wrong.

"I, uh… I'm a pretty bent cop, if that helps?" he tried.

Her only response was the furrowing of pierced eyebrows into a silent glower.

"Yeah, alright." He nodded, still a little dazed. "Fair enough."

Intending to leave her alone for a moment, Renji turned to the former intruder turned inmate in the next cell along only to find the man was already on his feet and listening.

Admittedly, when not climbing up an airship the guy didn't look quite so terrifying. A few more injuries had piled up to add to the bleeding fingers Renji had given him, including a fresh cut to the cheek and a nasty red welt near his eye that suggested he'd had a welcoming fist-to-face meeting with Sergeant Flood. He was still avoiding putting weight on that tricky left leg of his too, for whatever reason. Having been de-balaclava'd, the tactical terror was revealed to be not particularly tall and somewhat good looking in a square-jawed, craggy old white guy sort of way, with startling gunmetal grey eyes that seemed pale against the rapid bruising blooming on his weathered cheek. Going by the fine lines his scowl had carved into his skin and the silvery threads in his dark, close-cropped hair the man must have been in his forties, or perhaps fifties, Renji had never been much good at guessing that sort of thing. One thing he didn't need to guess was that the guy was military as all hell, from the tip of his broken nose down to the soles of his ruthlessly practical boots.

"Where's Harlow?" the intruder rasped.

Renji had barely got out a note of confusion before he realised the question hadn't been aimed at him. In the next cell over, suspicion curled Choppy Bob's pierced lip as she surveyed the intruder. "You know Harlow?"

Quick and intent, he nodded. "She's my—" he hesitated for a moment, folding his mouth into a thin line as though the words didn't want to leave him. "I'm her father."

"Her *father?!* But, but she said you'd never get involved, she… She…" Gnawing at her lip ring in indecision, Bob looked to her unconscious teammate as if for guidance. When no answer came her shoulders slumped, and she let out a sigh of resignation. "She isn't here." she told the intruder, in a little more than a whisper. "Bastards moved her out somewhere before they transferred us from holding, but I- I don't know where to. They didn't say."

"She ain't here?" The intruder repeated the words in apparent disbelief.

"Wait, who's what now?" asked Renji, feeling as though he'd skipped a step in the conversation.

"She ain't here," he echoed again, his rough voice heavy with exhaustion. It was hard to reconcile this tired old guy with the person who'd been doing thousand foot-high pull-ups on the side of the ship.

A deep breath that seemed to contain the last of something important left him, and he slid down to lie on the slim bench, throwing his arm over his face in a manner that suggested he was very much done talking.

Unfortunately for him, Renji was never done talking.

"Soooo… If the person you're looking for isn't here, then you've gotta break out and find her, right?" he started hopefully, leaning against the bars separating their cells. Nodding at Bob, he continued. "Kinda seems like all of us want the same thing, here, in fact! Maybe we can help each other out?"

The intruder barked out a dismissive laugh without so much as a glance in his direction, which seemed like a bad opening to negotiations. For her part, Bob didn't seem won over either.

"Don't be stupid, cop. There's no way out of this place." She wrinkled her studded nose. "Not unless pigs can fly."

Renji decided to ignore that dig in the name of diplomacy. "Bullshit!" he snorted, cheerfully. "There's always some kinda way out of any situation, you just gotta fuckin' find it!"

The intruder tutted at that, actually *tutted*, like a grandmother assessing subpar work at the local knitting circle. "No need for language like that, kid."

Biting back his surprise at being admonished for cursing by a guy who'd been attempting to drive a knife into his ribs not twenty minutes ago, Renji continued. "C'mon, I bet a guy like you has gotta have some kinda idea about how to get out of here."

"A guy like me, huh."

"Yeah! Hell, I saw you out there, you clearly know your shi— your *stuff.* And you were trying to break in to find someone, right? Gonna guess you didn't plan on sticking around too long after you found her, so you gotta have had an exit in mind!"

That got him a one-shouldered shrug. "Guess all you like."

"Fine, fine." Renji took a seat on the floor with a dramatic sigh. "Then I *guess* we're all boned when the commander gets here."

A suspicious eye appeared from underneath an elbow. "The commander..?"

"Mm-hm. The head honcho herself, Commander Starkweather. Leader of the Forces, one of the most powerful people in Unity, so on and so forth." Renji shrugged in feigned ambivalence. "Kind of a big deal."

"Why would she be coming here?" The man was sat bolt upright now, tense as a taut rope. In the next cell along the girl was pretending not to pay attention, but had shuffled forward to listen closer. *Bingo.*

"Weeell—" Renji began arranging his sentence with great care to avoid letting on that she was coming here less in her capacity of commander and more to drag her wayward nephew home by the ear, "—I didn't hear any details, exactly. But whatever it is, this can't be good for any of us, right?"

"Hm." Squinting, the intruder surveyed Renji critically. "What exactly was a kid like you doing out there on the side of the ship, anyway?"

"I wanted out." Renji shrugged.

"Most dropouts use the door, not the window." The older man seemed less than impressed. "Coulda just quit."

"It's- it's not that simple."

"Yeah, it is. Ain't like service in the Forces is mandatory."

"Sometimes it *is,* alright?" snapped Renji, feeling the conversation angling in a direction he didn't care for. The intruder opened his mouth as if to ask something else awkward; but a sudden sound, a quiet but insistent beeping, caught the both of them off-guard, staring at each other in mute confusion for a long moment.

"Your, uh… leg is ringing." Renji informed him.

With a blink of realisation the guy shifted position to face the wall, his hands darting to hitch up the hem of his combat trousers and roll it back to reveal not the expected knobbly old man knee, but scarred, pitted metal. His left leg, at least as much of it as was on display, was artificial.

He'd heard they were more common in Central Commons or down in Steelepool, but bionic limbs were something of a rarity up in Imperium Court. The Court was made of luxury offices and boutique shops, with little room for messy things like factories, yards or farms, thus there was less chance of a catastrophic workplace accident; not unless something went terribly awry in the office kitchen. Even in the Forces most injuries were minor, as the majority of Unity City's criminals were unlikely to wield anything with much more firepower than a broken bottle, and the state-of-the-art patrol gear offered to those on the front lines of any brewing protest was more than up to task.

There had, however, been a growing trend among Forces Upper Management and I.I. Executives alike for carrying a bladed weapon as both status symbol and warning, much like the one Flood carted about everywhere, and that had inevitably let some of the more overzealous among them to challenge each other to duels. A nasty combination of overpaid and undertrained meant that thanks to this fad prosthetics weren't unheard of, and were even seen as something of a mark of honour on occasion. The type Renji had seen once or twice were more of a stylish affair, all covered in plates of patterned or painted rare metals, sleek hyper-deluxe designs featuring name-brand labels and glittering precious stones.

The one before him now seemed like it had been jammed into a garbage disposal. Several times.

Going by the grim twitch flickering over the intruder's face, it must have worn as ugly as it looked; dents and scratches littered the drab grey surface of the covering plates, criss-crossed with welding lines that suggested it must have been taken apart and put back together more times than had ever been intended. Just below his knee lay the intersection where hardware met flesh in an ill-fitting disagreement of swollen skin, a sticky red trickle seeping from underneath the joint.

When Renji was able to drag his eyes up and away from the battered limb he found the guy giving him a pained glare, as if daring him to say something about it. He didn't.

With the sort of precise, quick movements usually seen from someone field-stripping a rifle, the man popped open a narrow hatch on his calf no wider than a centimetre across, and withdrew something rather like a tiny cell phone with a stubby antenna that let out an incessant beeping and buzzing.

"Is that a phone? You put a phone in your leg?!"

"Radio."

"You put a radio in your leg," began Renji incredulously, "and you didn't leave it on silent?"

But the intruder was too focused on the device to reply, stabbing at the fingerprint recognition plate with a calloused thumb. After a short burst of white noise, the speaker crackled to life.

"Merry Christmas." came a voice over the airwaves in a sing-song drawl. "Or, well. Christmas-adjacent week, anyway. Eh, close enough."

#

As far as 1 a.m. on a Thursday went, Renji had to admit there were worse things to be doing than watching a professional killer argue with a mystery voice coming out of his leg radio. Glancing at Renji, he raised a finger to his lips in the universally recognised gesture of *shut up and let me do the talking,* which was met with the equally well-known rolled eyes of *fine, whatever.*

"Who's this? How d'ya get this frequency?" the intruder growled into the radio, his stubbled jaw tense.

"Right now, I'm Santa," the radio voice said, the sounds of furious typing suggesting she was preoccupied by something else. Her keystrokes seemed to almost be keeping time with a tinny, poppy tune drifting by in the background that was most definitely not Christmas-themed. "Ho ho ho and all that. Got a present for you."

"What kinda present?"

"A way out of that cell. Dead good, right? Better than a gift card, anyway."

"Melo…?" whispered the bob-haired girl in the other cell, pierced eyebrows arched high as her hands gripped the bars in white-knuckled intensity. "Melody! It's me!"

The sounds of typing ceased. "Alright, Sugar," replied Melody flatly. Her tone made it quite clear that wasn't an adorable pet name.

Sugar visibly winced. "I- I know we messed up, but you gotta help us, please—!"

"Don't be daft," sighed Melody. "O'course we're getting you out of there. Though I guess how is up to Weaver. That's you, right?"

The intruder Weaver stiffened, before grunting a reluctant affirmative.

"Cool, cool," hummed Melody, unphased, returning to hammering her keyboard. "The boss wants a word. I'll send you over now."

"Who—" Weaver began, but the muffled pop track cut off in an abrupt burst of static, replaced with the ambient hum of a much quieter room.

A different voice came crackling over the radio; older, wearier and firmer than the previous. "I have to admit," the second stranger began, breathing out a husky sigh, "that I had hoped it would not come to this. Yet, I feel we may still make this work, hm?"

"Boss!" yelped Sugar, all of a sudden very animated. "Get us out of here! Trig's not moving, and they already took Kiki who knows where, and—"

"Breathe deep, dear girl. I am working on it," the voice responded, with patience. "Mr Weaver, my name is Ms Cellanea. I have a proposition for you. Are you willing to hear me out?"

Weaver's glare deepened. "This frequency. Only Harlow knows it."

"And she gave it to us for this very reason. A smart girl, is she not?" Cellanea said. Her tone was soft yet controlled, a hint of some tuneful accent playing about its edges.

"Fine." Weaver clicked his tongue in irritation. "Whatever you're gonna say, hurry up an' say it."

"Mr Weaver… David. If you only believe one thing I will tell you tonight, make it this; I want to bring my team home. Safe. Alive. This includes your daughter."

"You're that group she was with. The ones that put out that broadcast," he said it evenly, but his injured fingers had tensed into a fist. "The Loose Ends."

Holy shit. Renji's hand flew to his mouth just in time to muffle his sound of surprise. It was them, it was actually them. At once, it clicked into place; the grey of the old man's eyes, the blue of the other rebel's hair, both shades he'd seen repeated on that video that'd disrupted the entire Court. That weasel Probably-Simmonds had said it too hadn't he, whispering it to his cronies right before Renji's little dish-based slip-up; broadcast.

"Indeed, though I assure you I did not approve of that particular task."

Over in her cell, Sugar was pulling the exact sort of expression Renji was certain he'd done himself at the idea of Aunty L dropping by for a visit.

"Regardless," continued Cellanea, "you cannot help her from in there, and I am out of people to send after her. Thus it is in our best interests to work together. Are we in agreement?"

From the twisting of his face Weaver didn't seem certain, but soon enough he let out another reluctant yet affirmative grumble.

"Glad to hear your enthusiasm. But before we begin, would you care to tell me exactly why there is a Forces cadet listening in on this call?"

Renji's head snapped up. So much for staying quiet. "The hell?"

Sugar tittered. "Melody's got the cameras. Melody's *always* got the cameras."

"What cameras?!" he hissed, looking around the room wildly. In his entire time on AirCast Two he hadn't seen hide nor hair of a security camera.

Weaver nodded to the corner of the ceiling near the door, where an all-too-innocent light fixture hung.

"Quite," added Cellanea. "As you must know, I.I. wish to have their eyes everywhere. So sad for them that we have been looping the feed for the last few minutes. Now, who are you?"

"Well… For starters, don't let the uniform fool you cus I'm not exactly a cadet any more. Probably." His heart was thumping now, so loud he thought she may have been able to hear it through the radio. *"Definitely.* I'm done with Imperium. Whatever it is you're doing here, I want in."

"That did not answer my question," she replied. "I will ask one more time. Who are you?"

No good answers were presenting themselves, so Renji settled on his favourite standby of the truth, told vaguely. "I'm soon-to-be ex-cadet Renjiro Hayakawa, ma'am."

The family name had belonged to his father, long since deported back to Japan, so he reasoned it wasn't a lie. And it wasn't as if he could give them the same surname as the commander and expect any kind of positive reaction, so really he was doing everyone a favour by simplifying matters.

There followed a brief but significant pause of the exact right length for Renji to worry that he'd been made, before Ms Cellanea responded.

"Hayakawa. I see. You say you want *in*, Mr Hayakawa. In on what, exactly?" she asked, each syllable cut with clipped precision.

"Your whole rebellion against Imperium thing, like the lady in that broadcast! I mean, you just said you're out of people? *I'm* people! Hell, I'm people with a head fulla Forces knowledge, that's gotta be pretty useful, right?" Addressing the vague direction of the camera, he waved in Weaver's direction. "Listen, the old man here's obviously got skills, but him and the rest of your people here are all busted up. They're gonna need help, and I've been stuck here long enough that I know this tin can like the back of my hand! It's a perfect fit!"

"We don't need help from a *cop!*" protested Sugar, but her boss ignored her.

"So you would dissent, yes?" she asked. "Just like that?"

"Hell yeah, just like that!"

"Hmm." Another long moment of silence hung in the air, punctuated only by the crackle of the radio, until… "You are clearly in no small amount of trouble. How do we know you will not sabotage this escape to regain your position?"

"What position, lowest-rung cadet on a shit-tier posting?! No fuckin' chance!" Renji grinned, buzzing with excitement. "Let me level with you, I've been looking for a way out of here, and it looks like you're it. Do us both a favour, huh?"

She hummed a note of discontent, soured further by the crackle of the radio. "Mr Weaver. Do you think you can trust this boy?"

Weaver grunted. "Kid's full of it."

"Alright, rude." noted Renji.

"But—" Weaver shook his head with a sigh. "—he ain't the backstabbing kind, I'll give you that much."

The brief flicker of approval caught Renji off guard. "Thanks, I think!" His beam was met with a scowl.

"Then that shall have to suffice for the meantime. It is settled," Ms Cellanea said, a smile creeping into her voice. "Now, let us get you out of there."

CHAPTER 4

EXIT STRATEGY

From what Ms Cellanea knew– and with Melody running wild in ship's network, that seemed to be a lot– AirCast Two had requested an unscheduled visit back at the skydock where it would be taking onboard a passenger of the sort whose security clearance was so high the radio operator had to redact their own shocked cursing from the official logs. This request had been approved and booked in for half an hour from now, during which time the ship would be slowly moseying its way back over to AirCast Tower, a slow mosey being high speed for an airship.

That, Weaver determined, would be their best opportunity to get off the ship one stop early.

"Tower next door is some luxury high rise. Apartments ain't ever sold, so it's pretty near empty. Airship slows down on approach to the dock and draws level for just long enough to zipline on over. That's what I did to get in, anyhow," he said, as though ziplining over onto a secret government airship prison was just one of those things people often did of a Thursday night. Sugar nodded, apparently unfazed and also a member of the Thursday Zipline club. As the only one to not immediately nod, Renji was met with a steady grey glare.

"Y'ever use one of those before, kid?"

"I mean, y'know… Not *exactly,* but how hard can it be?"

"Hm."

With that decided, Cellanea brought up the small yet pertinent fact that their current lack of zipline might prove to be an issue with the zipline plan. Along with the rest of his gear, the line that Weaver had intended to use for his return route had been confiscated before he'd been thrown into the cell.

"No friggin' way is the sarge gonna pass up a chance to dig through shit that isn't his. Bet you anything it'll be in his quarters." said Renji.

Weaver nodded. "Right. Goin' off the blueprints, there's a room at the back end of the ship, furthest away from the stairs down to the dock. Figure we make ourselves a distraction there, pick up the gear and our injured, then get out through the loading bay doors."

The back room—the one Flood had mentioned had needed to be readied in that foreboding command he'd given back before the prisoners had arrived. The place was a restricted access type area, the sort of thing Renji would have stolen a peek into out of curiosity, but even just approaching the suspicious, unmarked door had felt off in a way he couldn't quite put his finger on. There had just been something strange about the plainness of it, the starkness, the coldness. He'd told himself it wasn't worth the bother, and had never approached it since.

Now however, with a potential way out of the Forces and into The Loose Ends on the line, there was no chance Renji could let some vague sense of dread get in the way.

Ms Cellanea's strong hints that Sugar ought to stay in place to guard her injured teammate and prepare for the escape were met with no small amount of complaint, but eventual agreement. With only Renji and Weaver moving, plus Melody keeping an eye on their virtual backs via the cameras, it should be simple enough to get into the back room without being seen, find the missing teammate Kiki, trigger whatever distraction Weaver seemed to be planning yet not sharing, and zip on over to the empty apartment block quite literally under the commander's nose.

"Risky," grumbled Weaver.

"Fun, too." Renji beamed. The sole downside was that he'd miss seeing Flood explain to Aunty Lissa how he'd wasted her time *and* misplaced her nephew.

"I believe that is the most amount of planning we are going to manage in the time we have. I shall pass you back over to Melody, she will oversee you from here." Cellanea sighed. "Good luck, gentlemen, I fear we shall all need it."

"Hiya, Sugar. Hiya, Mr Weaver. Hiya, other bloke." The muted pop tune and typing chimed back in over the little radio, and with them the leisurely tones of Cellanea's hacker. Now he was listening for it, Renji noted an English accent; full-on northern English too, none of that telltale Unity City twang of American both he and Weaver had in spades. Much like Ms Cellanea and her European lilt, this one must have been from beyond Unity's borders. That wasn't a rare thing; Imperium International lived up to that second part of their name with offices around the globe, and transfers to the Unity headquarters were common. That plus the tax breaks the city offered had always made for some strong incentives to apply for citizenship.

"You can call me Melody. Or Melo. Not Mel though, I hate that one. What's your name again, other bloke?"

"Renjiro," he said slowly, bracing himself for the usual failed attempts at pronunciation.

"Ren-ji-row…" To his surprise she sounded it out a few times, drawing out the syllables. "Renjiro. I get it right?"

"Actually… yeah," he said, delighted to hear someone put in the effort. "Just Renji's good, though."

"Renji! Sound. Gimme a minute while I finish popping your locks," she said, raising her voice over the sound of her clattering keyboard. Wherever Melody was situated, it was filled with the strains of a boy-band harmonising some lyrical crimes. "You alright, Sugar? How's Trig holding up?"

Still curled up in the corner of her cell, Sugar traced a finger along the shoulder of her unconscious friend through the cell's bars. "Been better."

"Silly bloody business you lot pulled," Melody chided gently. "Just wish you'd actually told me what you wanted that Emergency Broadcast System hack for. I'd have done a cleaner job of it."

"You wouldn't have done it at all."

"Yeah, no… Probably not. Still, no wonder they nabbed you so easily."

"We had to tell everyone! That information—"

"—didn't change owt." A pause in typing just long enough to hear an exhale, low and slow. "Just like Ms Cellanea said it wouldn't."

There was no reply from Sugar, just a wilting of the shoulders.

"Gotta admit though…" Melody added after a thoughtful pause, "It was pretty cool."

Burying her face in her hands, Sugar snorted out an exhausted laugh. "Yeah… Yeah, it was."

A definitive tap at the keyboard rang out with finality. "Rightio! Let's get cracking." The cell doors' locks let out a muted, simultaneous *click* of success. "Good news, your security sucks. Bad news, there's a guard out in the corridor. A biggun, too. He's not facing you though, so I reckon if you're quick enough you can— oh, there he goes."

Already Weaver was moving, advancing towards and through the door in a determined, limping charge.

"Woah hey, old man!" Renji leapt forward. "Lemme help you with… that…?" His words guttered out as Weaver shuffled back into the room dragging a surprised cadet, one arm locked around his neck. The guard must have been a head taller than Weaver and at least half his age, yet after a few seconds of kicking and choking he went down all the same, toppling down to the tiles with a muted thump.

"Damn, alright," muttered Renji, trying not to appear too impressed.

"Bloody hell," agreed Melody reverently.

Seeing as they were wearing the same uniform and all, Renji couldn't help but feel a pang of sympathy for the hapless cadet as Weaver deposited his unconscious body into a cell, though that dissipated on seeing who it was.

"Well well well. 'Scuse me!" Reaching down, Renji plucked the access card from Perhaps-Yate's belt, and after a moment, his uniform cap. "Thanks for the rental, you huge bastard!" he chirped with a little too much glee, flipping the cap onto his head with a pointless flourish. "This is already extremely fun, y'know?"

Weaver's head turned, the briefest glimpse of exertion and pain falling back into a frowning granite mask as if it had never been there. "Let's go," he muttered.

"Hey... Are you really Harlow's dad?" asked Sugar, as they made for the exit. Fixing her with his tired frown Weaver nodded cautiously.

"Please find Kiki for us, yeah? She's— I don't think she'll—" Her voice cracked and guttered out. Shaking her head, she pulled herself together. "Uh. She's got blue hair. Kinda tall." She wiped her nose with the back of her hand, then added "Really good at pinball."

The creases of Weaver's frown deepened. "Gonna do what we can. But—"

"Hey, no worries. We're gonna find your girl," Renji told her, ignoring the look this got him from Weaver.

Pulling his purloined hat's peak down to hide his eyes, Renji peered out into the east corridor he'd so recently been swaggering down. The idea wasn't much different; this time, he would pretend to be escorting the captured intruder to the back room, which ought to allow the both of them to bustle past any other guards easily enough, provided they didn't notice which cadet was doing the escorting. The corridor itself, with its glossy white walls peppered with notices and I.I. lingo leading up into a bowed ceiling, was designed to be modern and sleek; a rounded and unthreatening interior for what was once meant to be an advertising hub. In this moment though it seemed cold, almost bleached, shot through at regular intervals with sturdy steel beams with a curve to them that reminded Renji all too much of some great ribcage. He shook the unsettling idea away, instead dialling back into the comfortable swagger he'd employed earlier.

"Alright, lads," piped up Melody over the radio now nestled in one of Weaver's many tactical pockets. "You've got two on the way."

Seconds later she was proven correct as a pair of the newer cadets came around a corner to walk down the same passage, their low whispered conversation halting at the sight of a prisoner. Straightening his back and keeping his pace steady, Renji nodded at them in a brusque, places-to-be sort of way but as planned, both were too busy gawking at the limping, bloodied intruder to give him much regard. As they passed by, one let his gaze hang on Renji a little too long for comfort. *Gotta sell this one better.*

He gave Weaver's shoulder a rough shove, sending him stumbling forward with a hiss of pain that didn't seem entirely faked, earning them a mean little giggle from one of the cadets. Without further incident they rounded the corner, towards the mess and out of sight.

"They seemed nice," Melody said after they were well out of earshot.

"Sorry 'bout that, man." Renji winced, offering Weaver an arm to help him straighten up. He brushed it aside with a noncommittal grumble.

The radio gave out a pop that sounded a lot like a bag of crisps being opened. "You're alright at that," Melody told him around a mouthful of crunching. "The blagging, I mean. Useful skill, that."

Renji blinked. He'd never seen lying as a skill, exactly. It was just something that had to be done around the Court, building camouflage, hiding parts of himself that could be used against him. "Pretty standard, really. I mean, you just gotta show someone what they expect to see and they fill in the rest for you." He shrugged. "It's not like it's hard or anything."

"When you ain't the one bein' shoved around, sure." muttered Weaver, righting his limping steps.

"Gotta have the nerve for it, though." The keyboard tapping had slowed, with just the occasional clack of keys cutting across her languid tones. Even elite hackers could only type so well with one hand in a bag of crisps. "Seems difficult."

"Says the computer witch."

She snorted. "Nothing magic about this. Not when that sergeant of yours has got an unsecured wireless printer sat in his office, anyway." Despite her flippant words, there was a glimmer of warmth in her voice, as though she were enjoying the chance to show her skills. "After that it's just a bit of poking about and using the right this and that to get into the network, then the CCTV and locks and whatever. No audio on them cameras though, so keep that radio about, please and thank you."

"Provide the soundtrack. Can do."

"Good lad."

At the end of the corridor a quick turn to the left took the pair towards the ominous unmarked door, tucked away in the ship's dimmest corner. The place was as eerie and empty as Renji had remembered it, unsettling in its starkness.

"Hm. No branding." noted Weaver. He was right; this corner was perhaps the only one in the ship that was empty of I.I. notices covered in their sharp logo and copyrighted font. There wasn't even a plate on the door announcing its purpose, almost as if I.I. would rather not admit it was part of their facility.

Renji swallowed. "Uh, hey, Melody? Can you use your crystal ball and see what's in there?"

"Yeah... Bit of an issue on that 'un," she replied distractedly. "So, right, that whole room's not on the same network as everything else, yeah? There's an air gap, no connection to the rest of the ship, or owt else, for that matter. Total dead zone. Means I can't see in."

Renji wished she'd used a less ominous term than *dead zone.* "What's that for?"

"Extra security." She crinkled her crisp bag in thoughtful contemplation. "You use it for something really important. Or really bad."

"Or both." He hummed, tapping the access key card against his palm.

The warm weight of Weaver's gloved hand settled on Renji's arm. "Gimme that." he said, nodding at the card.

"What? Why?"

"You did your part. You got me over here, I got the rest. Go on back to the cells."

"The hell? No way, man."

Storm-cloud eyes met Renji's, solemn beneath the lines of Weaver's permanent frown. "Just go, willya? Get fired and leave. Stay outta Imperium. Stay outta all this."

"Three more coming," warned Melody, as the distant thump of boots on linoleum made its way down the west corridor.

"Go home. Last chance," Weaver said softly, moving to tug the card out of Renji's grip— but Renji stepped back, running the key through the door's lock and opening it with a clipped *click.*

"Time's wasting," Renji said with a confident wink he didn't quite feel, gesturing towards the opening door. For a split second he saw some kind of look flickering over Weaver's face, an odd mix of annoyance and apology; before the approach of footsteps drove it away, and they both slipped into the silence of the dead zone, leaving that last chance of his behind for good.

#

Passing from the sterile white lighting of AirCast Two's corridors into the mysterious room's unknown darkness was as smothering and sudden to Renji as having a heavy woollen sheet drawn over his head. As he stood there trying to blink away the gloom, it was precious little comfort when he realised he'd been right. Something was most definitely wrong in here.

A small monitor flickered in the far corner opposite the chamber's only door, its nauseating green-tinged display serving as the room's sole, unenthusiastic source of illumination. Its jade glow cast out to reflecting off the dull chrome cabinets lining the walls, and light the edges of *something* in the centre of the room that Renji couldn't make out the specifics of. It was a shadowed form upon a central table, an unfamiliar shape partially covered in a sheet, a mix of angles and curves making up some sort of visual puzzle he wasn't quite certain he wanted to solve.

Yet he was drawn to look all the same, and a chill rippled through his guts as he spotted something peeking out of the sheet, by the head of the table. A spray of thin, messy strands of an unnatural, sickly hue in the monitor's light.

Hair.

Renji took in a breath, and held it.

"Not being funny, but I'm missing that soundtrack I was promised," piped up Melody, a touch of strain seeping into her calming tone. "You find something?"

"Not sure yet." came Weaver's voice from behind him in the shadows. "Gonna hit the light."

That last statement was aimed in Renji's direction. A warning. He bit back the immediate impulse to snap that he didn't need the concern *thank you very much,* electing to instead hang onto that inhaled breath for all he was worth.

It escaped him all the same, sputtering out as soon as the overhead lights flickered on.

The first thing that Renji noticed, before the blood, before the pale, torn skin, was her hair. It was long with a slight wave, dyed that shade of electric blue he'd seen in the broadcast's background, but the colour had begun to fade to a mossy green at the tips, with another half-inch band of light brown at the root where it had begun to grow out. It wouldn't grow again. She'd probably planned on re-dyeing it soon. She'd have planned on all sorts of normal things, like everyone did. Where to pick up dinner, what to wear tomorrow, and now none of those plans were going to happen for Kiki, who was kind of tall and good at pinball.

Renji thought about that look of furious anger Sugar had given, back in the cells. He felt sick.

Shaking his head, Weaver spoke into the radio. "Bad news, Miss."

"Alright... Yeah." Melody inhaled, a sucking sound of acrimony and regret and a total lack of surprise, all being pushed aside to be dealt with later. "Right then. Right. Borrowed time, and all. Tell me what you're looking at."

Keep it together. Answer her. Renji cleared his throat, determined to still be useful. "It's- she's on a table..."

Leather straps cutting into skin, binding her arms and legs to a gurney.

"There's... there's... tools—"

A small tray beside her littered with them; syringe, scalpel, *drill.* Glistening drops of ruby-red blood. Maybe still warm.

"And in her head—coming *out* of her head... there's... t-this... this *thing—"*

A metallic nightmare of sharp edges, jutting out from pale skin and matted, slick hair. A thick, invading cable snaking from the base of her skull away into the cold mechanical depths.

"Cranial port," muttered Weaver, brushing a lock of blue away from empty eyes. "Ain't done professionally. Or kindly."

"It's— there's a fucking *plug* in her head!" Renji blurted out, losing his last shred of decorum. "What the hell is happening here?!"

Melody cut across him, level and direct. "Is there a cable? Maybe leading into a server with a terminal attached?"

Peering at a small screen with a keyboard, Weaver nodded. "Looks like."

"Brilliant," she said, with a note of savage triumph. "Renji, you're Imperium, you use Collabor8tr much?"

"I'm not... uh..." he stammered in useless reply, eyes locked on red and metal. Catching his breath, Renji forced himself to turn away and concentrate on the monitor and the rather simple question he'd just been asked. Collabor8tr was an Imperium standard, the simple, lightweight command line interface installed on all their devices and terminals. Training had included a course on its common commands, every last one of which had vacated Renji's head at this particular moment. On the display a black window sat like a void, a flat green cursor blinking out at him guilelessly. He blinked back.

Once more the soft pressure of Weaver's hand fell on his arm, pulling him away from the screen. He let it.

"I know it." Weaver took a seat at the terminal.

"Shouldn't ask why, I take it." said Melody.

"Good call. What d'ya need?"

Her own keyboard fell silent as she guided Weaver's own quick staccato typing through a series of lines. "...Then forward slash, dot, and then history. It'll output some stuff."

"File zero two four three dot base saved to external memory drive J."

"Sound, that's what we like. Forward slash dot eject external memory drive J."

A tiny click of release sounded and a thin rectangle no bigger than a phone slipped smoothly out of the terminal's side. Melody sighed in clear relief as Weaver pocketed the thing.

"A data drive… What's on there?"

"Bit of a story, that. I'll tell you later, when you've not got a distraction to set up."

With an affirmative grunt, Weaver limped back towards the gurney. "Get ready to move," he told Renji, picking up a neat little saw from the tray and testing the blade's strength with his fingertips. Renji nodded, barely paying attention as Weaver clambered onto one of the tall cabinets and began working at a patch of ceiling with his stolen blade.

Standing useless in the centre of the room, staring resolutely at the cabinet's drawers to avoid having to look at what was behind him, Renji found a few things seemed to be coming into focus. The glare of hatred from Sugar. The cold words from Cellanea. Weaver's warning, just minutes ago. All signs that he was dancing on the edge of a far deeper pit than he'd ever reckoned with.

"Let's go." A thump of boots hit the floor, followed by the compact dark shape of Weaver crossing the room to begin steering Renji toward the exit.

"What'd you do?" Melody asked Weaver.

"Hm. Gonna be a gas leak alert in a few seconds."

"How come?"

"Cus I made one."

"Aye alright, that'd do it."

A thin hiss of gas was indeed emanating from the corner of the room, rippling the torn material that had until now formed a protective seal around the cabin's ceiling. Above them, the fuel cells seemed to hum a little louder than they had previously.

"Isn't that, like… really dangerous though?" said Melody slowly. "Y'know, where it's bad to breathe it in, or it's explosive or whatever?"

"It's helium, not hydrogen. It ain't gonna explode."

"And breathing it?"

"Mm… Dunno. Let's not find out." Weaver peered around the door before flinging it open. "Coast's clear, kid. Which way?"

That last question seemed to be addressed to Renji, although he wasn't quite able to parse it. The bare white corridor yawned open, girded by its beams of clean white bone. He shuddered. "Uh. What, sorry?"

"Sergeant's quarters," prompted Weaver. "Gotta get my gear back."

"Oh. Yeah." Keep it together. *Keep it together.* Tugging the cap's brim back down to shield his eyes, Renji gestured in something like the correct direction and tried to convince his legs of the benefits of getting the hell out of there. "T-this way."

CHAPTER 5

CHEMISTRY, OR WHATEVER

Luckily for everyone aboard AirCast Two, the use of hydrogen as a lifting gas for airships had gone out of fashion some time ago due its explosive properties falling on the side of being just a little too spectacular for comfort. It had been replaced by the less economical but safer option of helium; the same helium that was in the process of flooding the back of the ship. AirCast had lobbied to use the cheaper, more volatile option when they'd designed the ships, with arrays of cells containing the fuel lined the inside of the ship's balloon, kept safely away from the crew's cabin by a sealed roof which was considered to be tear-proof. It was not, as it turned out, Weaver-proof, and whichever exec had decided that avoiding the optics of a flaming billboard ship colliding with a local school in favour of spending a little extra on helium would be earning their Christmas bonus this year.

Nevertheless, a gas leak was a gas leak, and the alarm began blaring away, to be met with the same joy any alarm sounding at just past one in morning might provoke. Confused cadets came piling out of the bunk room groaning in frustration, only to find themselves bowled aside by the pyjama-clad form of Sergeant Flood, who came roaring out of his quarters wielding his sword and radiating the groggy yet livid aura of a man who'd been awake for ten seconds and furious for every single one of them. Cursing and stomping and flicking his blade in the direction of anyone fool enough to get in his way, he stormed down the corridor and towards the offending back room, dragging the rest of the bewildered troops in his wake. As the cadet who'd drawn the short straw for today attempted to unfasten the biometric lock on the safety emergency welding torch, in all the fuss no-one seemed to notice the sole guard with his cap pulled down low, escorting a limping prisoner in the opposite direction.

Weaver led the way as they slipped into the sergeant's quarters, a room Renji had never bothered sneaking into on the assumption it would be as dull as the cadets' bunks but with the possibility of getting caught snooping and summarily punched in the teeth. Having made it inside, however, he rather wished he'd made the effort to break in sooner.

Flood's room bore so little resemblance to the cadets' bare quarters that it may as well have been on another planet. The furniture— yes, actual *furniture*— was of a fine dark wood, the surface of a spacious varnished desk littered with paperwork and a high-end laptop, the leather office chair behind it pristine and gleaming. A downy soft bed with luxurious sheets lay disturbed, having been so recently vacated. Above it hung a large Unity City flag in thick, expensive material that must have cost an appropriately patriotic amount of money. There were even curtains.

"Is that a fucking mini fridge?!" spluttered Renji. Without so much as a glance at the offensive appliance, Weaver stalked forward to search through a large polished oak closet.

"Bit of an issue, lads," piped up Melody, over the sound of the still-wailing alarms. "Looks like the alert tripped some kind of reset, kicked me right out of the security system. No more cameras, and the loops I've been running are shot. Reckon you'll be out of there before they notice, but I'd get a wiggle on if I were you. I'll try to hop back in to wipe their footage before I'm out for good, alright?"

"There's a liquor cabinet and everything," mumbled Renji, still staring around. Between the howling alarm and the sudden change in scenery, he was beginning to get the distinct sense he was on the brink of Problems. Head swimming, he watched Weaver retrieve the blue and grey bulk of his own regulation shoulder bag, still packed with everything he owned on the whole ship.

"Gonna get ready." Weaver told him, passing Renji his luggage. "You wait there an' try not t'break anything."

Quickly and methodically he began to retrieve his own things from the closet and clip them back onto his belt, stowing mysterious tactical-looking items back into the pockets they'd been confiscated from. Still a little shaken, Renji clung to his bag and waited in stunned silence.

"Fancy in there, is it?" asked Melody, in a wry, slow tone. Her keyboard was silent, even the music straining in the background was muted to a low hum. "What d'you think?"

Blinking, Renji took in the decorative detailing on the desk's edges. It might have even been hand-carved. Probably took someone somewhere days, no, *weeks* of work, chipping away with a chisel, a millimetre at a time. And just down the corridor, behind that unmarked door, a very different table containing a very different kind of work stood. As small as it was, this ship was somehow able to contain both of these things, and the thought of that made Renji's fingers tense.

Again, he was reminded of that expression of mingled fear and hatred from Sugar, the casual brutality from the sergeant, and connected the dots. That look of terror that had sickened him to his core; that was what a person like Flood thrived on.

"What do I think?" He glared at the delicate woodwork and bit his lip. "I think I wanna come back in here with a baseball bat."

"Good answer, mate. Good answer."

Behind him rang out the sound of metal clicking into place with a *snap* of resolve, and Renji turned to see Weaver, his face set in a grim grey line, wielding a very deliberate little device loaded with a sharply hooked grapple.

"You ready?" he asked, that softer tone of his edging in again, just as it had in the corridor not a few minutes ago.

This time, Renji had to think about it. The word ready sure seemed a lot bigger all of a sudden. In a daze, he opened his bag and peered inside. Within sat the reassuring shape of the stubby houseplant he'd

58

stolen, still intact, its round little leaves desperate for the sun.

He zipped the bag back up, and nodded. "Now or never."

"Hm." Weaver returned the nod, then turned to his radio. "How long til we're level with our exit?"

"Five minutes." came Melody's cool reply. "Plenty o' time, right?"

"Hell yeah." Shrugging the bag back onto his shoulder, Renji mentally shoved aside the contents of both rooms for now and let a confident grin take over his features, hoping that it at least knew what it was doing. "Plenty."

#

While someone had thankfully put the alarm out of its misery, that hadn't prevented the back end of the ship from turning into a perfect chaotic mess. Every last cadet on the ship, all now as awake as it was possible to be, had sensed an opportunity to display the goal-oriented teamwork they'd been told would lead to *opportunities,* hopefully of the salaried kind, but judging from the helium-distorted snarls of the sergeant, most of them hadn't quite managed "teamwork" so much as "getting in the bloody way", and the ruckus continued to roll on.

Of course, had any of them thought to check on the cells at that exact moment in time, they'd have earned themselves that promotion on the spot.

"Helium is a colourless, odourless, tasteless, non-toxic, inert, monatomic gas, the first in the noble gas group in the periodic table."

Renji frowned, shifting the weight of the semi-conscious Trig between his and Sugar's shoulders as they made their way towards the docks at the fastest manageable hobble. "Yeah? So…?"

"Its boiling and melting point are the lowest among all the elements," continued Melody, ignoring his interjection.

"You're just reading this off Wikipedia, aren't you?"

"Might be. Its atomic number is two. Two doesn't sound very high, so that's probably good."

"Can you skip to the bit about breathing it in?"

"Let's see... funny voice, light head... burst lungs..."

On the other side of Trig's bowed head, Sugar's eyes widened. "Burst what?"

"Oh wait, that's only if you huff it from a canister. Hmm... Nah, looks like you're good, probably."

"'Probably'?!" she squeaked.

"And more importantly, it's also fully one hundred percent certified non-explosive. So if you happen to explode any time in the next few minutes, it wasn't the helium's fault," Melody concluded, with the finality of someone who had imparted deep wisdom for which her listeners ought to be grateful.

Renji nodded. "Dunno if it's just the fumes, but that was kinda reassuring."

Wrinkling her pierced nose, Sugar scowled. "Definitely the fumes."

"That's gratitude for you," tutted Melody. "Gonna disconnect now, security's getting dodgy and I've done all I can from here. See you on the other side. Usual place, Sugar."

"Got it. Thanks, Melo."

"Dock's clear, kids," came Weaver's tired voice from the end of the corridor where he stood overlooking the stairs that lead down to the exit below, wincing at the twitch in his left leg. "Get movin'."

As suggested they got moving, manoeuvring an unconscious man down the clanging metal steps and through the docking intake's jumble of unsorted supply crates and displaying all the subtlety of a one-man band where the one man in question was an elephant. It didn't matter though, not anymore; stealth had ceased to be the plan the instant the alarm had sounded, which was quite lucky considering the wrenching squeal of under-oiled emanating from the bay door's manual release as the heavy doors parted with an agonising, shuddering slowness that suggested they didn't care to be disturbed at such an hour. The instant they were open a gust of frozen December wind bustled in and busied itself with scattering loose papers, knocking over some of the emptier crates and attempting to jostle the zipline harness out of Weaver's gloved hands. Gritting his teeth, he adjusted his grip and clicked the final clip into place around Trig's midsection.

"Listen, you're all strapped in there, but you're gonna need to hang onto the handle all the same, you hear me? Only got two of these with me and there's four of us, so you lady friend is gonna have to hang onto you."

Despite the way his eyes were still a little unfocused, Trig nodded, though a frown creased his bruised features. "S-she's not, uh, my—"

"We'll be fine," said Sugar, with conviction.

Weaver produced the grapple gun again from the infinite depths of his tactical storage and advanced through the wind to the very edge of the open hatch and took aim at his target; the husk of an apartment block neighbouring AirCast tower, its luxury penthouses standing dark and empty, too expensive for their neighbourhood but just the right price for a quick exit. The dim red lights and eternally active sounds of the AirCast skydock seemed too close now, only metres and minutes away from disaster.

Shuffling a little awkwardly, Renji felt compelled to address the two remaining rebels. "Uh. Sorry, by the way. About your friend."

Neither he nor Weaver had needed to say what had happened when they'd shown up at the cells to collect them. The simple fact that Kiki wasn't with them had been enough. Sugar's mouth had folded into a grim line of determination, Trig had given a blank little nod as though he'd known from the start, and somehow the lack of shock and fury had made the whole thing even bleaker.

"Yeah, well. Can't think about it right now," Sugar said, avoiding his gaze.

"That's right. Get out first, think later," agreed Trig, placing his hand on her shoulder and giving it a gentle squeeze. He wasn't a big guy; rather, he was quiet and slight to the point where the bulky safety harness all but swamped him, but Sugar's reassurance by his presence was all too clear.

"Not *your* fault anyway, copper," she added hurriedly as if she wanted the words out and away from her at high speed. Renji beamed, always happy to catch a compliment no matter how awkward the throw.

From the open docking bay doors came a series of promising sounds— the hollow *thump* of the grapple gun firing followed by the long spooling zipping of the nylon rope fading into the distance— then a satisfying solid crunch of metal biting concrete. With a brisk, practised movement Weaver anchored the line's other end in the thick metal frame of the door. *"Go."* he growled, and neither rebel needed telling twice. Sugar hopped onto Trig's back, locking her knees about his waist and slipping her skinny arms under his shoulders to grasp his hands in hers, anchoring the both of them to the handlebar. Then with nothing more than the silken sound of metal on nylon they were away, sailing along the taut line to land on what a realtor had no doubt once called a deceptively spacious balcony area.

"Holy shit, it worked!" Renji felt almost dizzy with relief. "It actually *worked!* We're really gonna do this!"

"Looks like," Weaver grunted, ironing out his own expression and picking up the second harness. "Hold still while I get this on you. Ain't got much time to…" He trailed off into a significant silence, eyes focused over Renji's shoulder and towards the dock's entrance at the top of the stairs. Before Renji could turn around, an all-too familiar and unwelcome reedy tone sang out across the echoing room.

"Ah, look look look, see?! I told you they were in here!" Probably-Simmonds bleated with terrible glee, stabbing at his snitches' notebook with an accusatory biro. "This is *exactly* why emergency security protocol means regular checks of the cameras!"

"That's right, we told you they were here, sarge." Maybe-Carter, a sly sneer on her face and a nightstick in her hand. Both were descending the metal steps, lurking in the shadow of one exceptionally pissed-off Sergeant Flood. The sarge ought to have looked ridiculous in his nightclothes and slippers, but a furious man of that size and breadth can find a way to be terrifying, no matter how striped his pyjamas. The gleaming pistol in his hand wasn't helping matters, either.

Renji felt his breath catch. Out of the corner of his eye, he could see Weaver shift his footing with a wince. Behind them the whistle of wind still rolled in from the docking hatch, joined in chorus by the creaking strain of the zipline as the ship's slow yet inevitable drifting brought it farther from the line's other side and towards the terrible point where the grapple would no longer hold.

"I knew it. Knew you were never committed to the cause, *cadet.* Someone like you could never serve Unity the way it deserves." Flood's broad chest heaved as he closed the distance towards them. "No, bad blood will always show itself, sooner or later."

Renji twitched, torn between the sudden need to launch his fist at that leering grin and the knowledge of what would happen if he did.

The sergeant chuckled darkly, enjoying his cadet's discomfort. "Now, we're going to wait right here until we land and I can hand the both of you directly to the commander. If either you or that trespasser so much as move an inch…" Flood didn't finish the threat. He didn't need to. The gun was conclusion enough.

Weaver's hand was making its way towards his belt, but too slow, too obvious; anything he was about to try seemed unlikely to be as fast as a bullet. Just a few steps away, Maybe-Carter tittered that mocking little laugh of hers, while Probably-Simmonds radiated all the smug delight of a dog that had pulled off a complex trick.

It was, in short, time for another stupid idea.

"Sarge, listen," Renji forced some calm into his voice, raising his hands in a pleading gesture. "You know you can't fire that in here, right?"

"If you think you have any say in what I do on my own goddamn ship—"

"No, that's not it!" he interrupted, layering on the dramatic sincerity with a trowel. "The leak, sarge, the gas leak! That's *flammable* gas, coursing all through the ship as we speak! Just one spark, one shot, and this whole balloon goes up in flames!"

Flood paused. "That's not... No." He shook his head. "Wasn't in the brief. Captain would have told me if it was flammable." The scowl stayed fixed in place, but his tone rose a notch on the word *flammable,* just enough to dance on the line between statement and question.

Renji was more than happy to provide an answer. "Oh but it *is,* it definitely is!" he insisted in a horrified whisper. "You know, like that one airship disaster in the old pictures! The whatsit!"

"Hindenburg," supplied Weaver, giving him a strange look.

"Yeah, that's the one! The big fiery explosion where everyone died horribly! You *must* have seen it, sarge!"

There was a pause as each of them pictured that famed black and white image of disaster, this time in vivid technicolour, then stared at the gun in Flood's hand.

"That— that wasn't the same gas, was it?" said Probably-Simmonds slowly. "Unless— *was* it?"

"Of course not! This is helium, that was... some other H-word, I'm sure of it!" Maybe-Carter scoffed. "Helium is *not* explosive! They put it in kids' balloons!"

Renji met her with a baleful gaze. "Trust me, I've done my research. Helium's boiling and melting point are the lowest among all the elements," he recited, to Probably-Simmonds' increasing horror. "It has an atomic number of two, and it is fully, one hundred percent certified *explosive.*"

"What if he's right?!" Probably-Simmonds' eyes bulged, flipping through his notebook in alarm as though it might contain the answers. "H-he might be right! And I don't know about you, but *I* don't want to explode!"

Maybe-Carter let out a snarl of exasperation. "You idiot, he's bullshitting!"

"But if he isn't…!"

"It's a pretty big risk to take, but if you want to gamble with your life, then I can't stop you," lamented Renji, earning him a fresh round of cursing from both parties.

"Shut up, the lot of you!" Flood's order snapped out like a whip, dropping the docking bay into uncertain silence. The tortured groans of the zipline were the only sounds as underneath that neat moustache, the sergeant's mouth twitched in indecision once, twice; then twisted into a frustrated grimace as he flung the gun aside, sending it clattering away into some unknown corner.

"Blast it!" he roared in frustration. "I don't even need a bloody gun for the likes of you!"

And before Renji knew what was happening Flood's fist had already slammed into his jaw, dropping him with all the inevitability of a speeding truck.

"Think you can get away with anything, don't you, you little brat? Think you're so bloody *clever.*" Looming over Renji, Flood drew that ever-present sword from its sheath in a smooth, practised movement. "I'll show you what *clever* gets you around here," he sneered, raising the weapon— which was when Weaver seized his chance and lunged, hand sweeping up from his belt in a blur of shining surgical silver as he brought the stolen saw down onto Flood's wrist. With a yelp more of shock than pain, the blade clattered to the floor. Infuriated beyond words and bellowing like a bull, Flood charged towards Weaver, Maybe-Carter following his lead with her baton clutched tight.

From his excellent vantage point on the floor Renji realised three things at once; The first being that while Weaver seemed more capable than your average older gent, he was injured, limping, and facing two vicious bastards half his age, one of whom was around a foot taller than him. The second thing Renji noticed was that, judging from the angry squeal of metal from the zipline's anchor point, their time was very nearly up. The third and perhaps most important thing was that there was now a convenient sword lying less than two metres away.

Unfortunately he wasn't alone in this realisation. Having broken out of his terrified stupor Probably-Simmonds was already scurrying towards the weapon, his grasping little fingers outstretched. With no chance of reaching it before him but no desire to see what a fully armed Probably-Simmonds would be capable of, Renji lunged forward and grabbed at the only possible target within reach; the little weasel's ankle. A squawk of surprise rang out as Probably-Simmonds hit the floor face-first in a shower of loose biros, accompanied by a rather satisfying *crunch.*

Nearby, Weaver was living up to his name, ducking around a heavy right hook from Flood and dodging the following jab from the left with increasingly sluggish movements. Pain creased his ever-present frown further as he was forced to shift his weight to his bad leg, stepping back to line up a return blow, then tripped over a smirking Maybe-Carter's outstretched foot. A sharp elbow drove underneath his ribs and sent him sprawling backwards, too far backwards, towards the howling nothingness of the open cargo bay door. His hand shot out lightning fast and closed around the straining zipline without a second to spare, those battered boots of his mere millimetres away from the open air and a fifty-storey drop.

"You!" Weaver looked up as a furious Flood came bearing down in his direction, eyes alight with rage, one huge fist back pulled to deliver an unavoidable, final shove. "Nobody makes a mockery of the Forces, you little—"

Sadly, the sergeant never managed to express his exact opinion of Weaver as the weight of a fencing championship award sabre came slamming down on the back of his head. For a moment he swayed in confusion; then slowly, he folded onto the floor in an unconscious heap.

"In my defence," Renji stepped forward over the sergeant's pyjama-clad prone form, still clutching the sword, "he was already dressed for a nap."

Glancing at her unconscious Upper Manager and the bloody-nosed crumple of Probably-Simmonds, Maybe-Carter's face twisted as she ran a mental calculation; then having come to a conclusion about her odds of winning this one, she turned on her heel and fled up the stairs out of the docking bay without so much as a backward glance.

"Hngh." Weaver grunted, rolling his shoulders stiffly as he surveyed the scene. Renji nodded in dazed agreement. *Hngh* about seemed to sum it up.

Almost as though it had been waiting for a polite moment to say something, a loud creak rang out from the direction of the open bay doors. The angle of the zipline to the building was by now so strained there could be only seconds before the rope gave way to the pull of the airship's great engines, and as Renji blinked at it with less than no idea what to do next, he felt his feet leave the floor. With a grunt of exertion Weaver hefted the stunned cadet onto his shoulder, gripped the zipline's remaining handle, clicked it into place and without a moment's hesitation, plunged forward and out into the cold night air, sending the both of them hurtling along the doomed line.

Too overwhelmed to do anything other than cling to Weaver's shoulder, Renji stared back at the ship in awe as they flew through the air, speeding away from the yawning mouth of the docking bay, from the receding bulk of the airship carriage that had been his home for months, from the bright LEDs running along the balloon's surface to display a frankly adorable advert for cat food that he was in no real state to appreciate. As the ship itself grew smaller, his gaze instead fell on the imposing grey form of AirCast Tower and the blinking lights of the skydock, where someone waited in the centre of the crowd for a meeting that had just been cancelled; a tall, slender figure in the Imperium Blue uniform of the Force's most senior Management. Pale blonde hair whipped about her face in the frigid December wind, one hand resting carelessly at the blade buckled to her hip as she stood in a casual contrast to the straight backs and nervous shuffling from those around her.

It seemed unlikely, but all the same, at the last fleeting second Renji could have sworn that his aunt's head tilted, her sharp eyes meeting his own for one heart-jolting stab of guilt; then the moment was lost as they landed on the balcony with a jolt and a suppressed grunt of pain from Weaver, retreating towards the dark emptiness of the apartment and whatever else might come next.

CHAPTER 6

GOING DOWN

It wasn't until they'd been on the elevator for several minutes that Renji remembered he was still holding a sword.

Blinking at the golden curve of elegant guard all decorated with fine scrollwork, the fine leather of the grip and the thin blade that ran as sharp as the creases in the sergeant's uniform, he found that despite having no clue how to use the thing he was more than a little satisfied to have taken it from the utter bastard who did.

The presence of the sword at least went some way to explaining why he had a seat all to himself in the otherwise packed cabin, and it seemed likely that the grim grey and blue of his Forces uniform was doing the rest of the work, leaving several clear feet of nervous space between him and the crowd. He stuffed the blade under his chair and out of sight, but since no-one present had the object permanence of a newborn it didn't do much to change the frosty atmosphere. Considering their destination, none of this should have been much of a surprise.

Unity's three-tiered layout meant its public transit had rather unique requirements. Much like any other large city it has its share of snarled roads and buses for the traditional horizontal style of transport, but quite often its residents needed to travel in a much more vertical fashion. Numerous immense skyscrapers stretched up throughout the city, piercing through all three layers; from their dark roots in the buried city of Steelepool, to their trunks in Central Commons running endlessly from floor to ceiling, to their peaks among the shining spires of Imperium Court, both literally and figuratively holding the city aloft. While these towering structures housed countless offices and apartments, many were also home to the mass transit elevators that were part of the great arteries of the city. Twenty-four hours a day, seven days a week, commuting citizens had the unparalleled pleasure of stuffing themselves into the overcrowded, under-ventilated elevator carriages; once to ascend to the gleaming glass of their workplace, then again to drop back into the relative gloom of their neighbourhoods. I.I. offered this particular service at a discount to all workers, and this being their city, that included most people.

Everyone else, well… they could always pick up an application form.

As Renji and the rest of their limping ragtag group had boarded an elevator that was heading downward there'd been no real security checkpoints, since no ID or clearance was required to descend from one tier to another. Ascending would have been a very different matter, and given the probable state of Sugar and Trig's IDs (or lack thereof), damn near impossible. Weaver's clearance, much like the man himself, remained a mystery, but Renji's Court-level ID was a distinct privilege that could have taken him anywhere he fancied at any time, even with registered guests if required.

Or at least, that *had* been the case, up until he'd got up to a little light assault and prison breakery, and left Aunty L stood on the docks probably wondering what the hell kind of nephew she'd ended up with.

Propelled by a pang of remorse, he rooted around in his shoulder bag until he withdrew his mobile phone; and felt his stomach sink at the sight of the little white light in the corner, whose lazy blinks reported a new unread message. Surreptitiously, Renji glanced around. Most of the people present seemed like tired late shift workers, all of whom were avoiding eye contact with what he was coming to recognise as an *I just want to get home please don't start anything officer* look in their eyes. A few seats back Sugar and Trig sat huddled together, his head resting on her shoulder as they whispered back and forth in hushed tones of relief and exhaustion, too absorbed with each other to notice much of anything else. Weaver had taken up position one seat ahead at the carriage's front and was staring fixedly out of the window at the descending skyline, doing an admirable job of ignoring the way the tiny elderly man next to him had managed to take up a good three quarters of their seat with bags of Christmas shopping.

Sensing the coast was about as clear as it was going to get, Renji swallowed his guilt and checked his messages. Two new, received a few minutes ago.

> **L. Starkweather (Private number, emergencies only):**
> Heya, Peanut.
> This a kidnapping or an AWOL? Your sergeant certainly has an opinion, but I thought I might check with you.

Their previous conversation was still on the screen above, though it was less a conversation and more a gallery of his aunt's beloved flat-faced pedigree cats wearing tiny felt Christmas hats. Renji had replied with an emoji of a cat barfing, which seemed a lot funnier at the time.

> ✨ *it's ya boy renjiiii!:*
> heya
> well i guess the good news is that i haven't been kidnapped
> so there's that

> **L. Starkweather (Private number, emergencies only):**
> Glad to hear it. I'll have a little word with the sergeant, I'm sure I can smooth things over.
> I should have known that post was a wrong fit for you.
> My bad. We'll get you a more interesting one next time.

The reply came in quick, which was a relief, but… next time? She couldn't be serious. Perhaps she hadn't been fully briefed yet? Frowning, Renji's fingers tip-tapped at the screen in response.

> 💫 **it's ya boy renjiiii!**:
> i don't think they're gonna let me have a next time
> even if i wanted one
> which i don't

L. Starkweather (Private number, emergencies only):
Oh please, it's just one upset Manager. I can deal with him.

> 💫 **it's ya boy renjiiii!:**
> you don't have to
> i'm not coming back.

L. Starkweather (Private number, emergencies only):
We've been here before enough times, haven't we?
Look, you just take some time and pull yourself together.
Try to do it before the holidays if you can, it'd be nice to see you.
Leaving your ID active so you can get back. I'll be out avoiding the Christmas party all evening tomorrow, feed the cats if you're in before six, okay?

Renji stared at the phone in disbelief. Raging, yelling, a full on guilt-trip of sheer disappointment, he'd expected any or all of that, but this casual dismissal felt far worse than he could have anticipated. Somehow after everything he'd done tonight, she assumed he would come sloping back home again as though he were still a moody teenager sneaking in through his bedroom window at four in the morning. Too exhausted to piece together an articulate response he instead settled on resending the cat vomit emoji and glaring out of the window at nothing whatsoever, all the while feeling his face burn a mortifying shade of scarlet.

"Y'oughta turn that off, y'know."

Weaver hadn't turned around in his seat. A sliver of his face was visible, framed in that harsh yet grubby light that could only be found on late-night public transit. "They can track you down with it, easy."

"Gimme some credit, man. It's not like I left the GPS on or anything." Renji sniffed, rubbing at his cheeks as if that might return them to normal; but Weaver's gaze never left the window ahead.

"That don't matter, kid. It's an Imperium-made OS. If they want your location on, it's on."

He was most likely right. Renji glowered at the back of his regulation haircut all the same. "Whatever." he muttered, jabbing at the phone's power button with a vengeful finger. "And quit calling me 'kid'."

"You're what, twenty?"

"Twenty-*two.*"

"Mm, yep." Grimacing a little, Weaver gave the knee above his false leg a rub, moving carefully to not dislodge anything from his seat neighbour's mountain of grocery bags. "That's a kid, kid."

"If you reckon, old man."

With that established, they sat in the silence of the rumbling elevator carriage, letting the other passengers' conversation roll over them as the minutes dragged by. Beyond the window the pitch black of a 2 a.m. December night began to merge with the still-burning lights of Unity's lowest city, forming a murky halo overlain by the unfamiliar shapes of derelict buildings, so jarringly different to the shining modernity of the Court that Renji found himself wondering for the first time tonight whether this had been such a great idea after all.

"You, uh… you trust them?" he asked, in little more than a whisper, aware that Sugar and Trig were close behind. "The people we're meeting, I mean."

"Hm. Trust is a big word to throw about. But it ain't like I got much of a choice here." In the reflection of the glass, something hard and dark settled over Weaver's features, deepening his scowl into something more absolute. "I'm gonna find my daughter. And if this is what it takes t'get her back, then this is what I'm doing."

"Right." Renji nodded. It was hard to argue with an expression like that. "Sorry," he found himself adding after a pause.

"Mm?"

"That you didn't find her."

"Oh." Weaver's heavy brow unknotted, the tension lifting from his face and shoulders as if the scowl had been bearing their weight. He peered back over his shoulder at Renji. "Sorry I tried t'stab you."

"Yeah, well. Sorry I broke your fingers with a skillet."

"Hrm." He flexed his bleeding fingers experimentally. "You didn't. They're just busted, not broke."

"In that case I'm not sorry at all." Renji grinned, and while he didn't exactly get a *smile* in return, the fine lines at the corners of the old man's eyes deepened just enough for him to mark it as a win.

#

The elevator carriage's doors rolled open to spill its passengers out into the ground floor station, and where they went after that seemed to be their own problem. The station, which had been jammed into the repurposed lobby of what used to be a towering hotel block named The Portside Inns, was one of those places that felt empty no matter how many people were inside. On the opposite side of the walkway, separated by a sturdy steel fence and an automated checkpoint, a scant and yawning few waited to board the upward ride. He was thankful to be leaving the place behind as they moved along with the crowd toward the exit, shuffling in a tired swarm.

Even when they were outside the air felt strange and thick, its stillness a little unsettling to Renji, who was used to the Court's brisk breezes and airy sunlight. All around them the hulks of buildings pressed in, tall and foreboding, historic stone-carved architecture rammed up alongside brutal metal and glass modernity with no apparent interest in consistency. Along their implausible lengths lights burned away despite the late hour, trapped behind a haphazard scattering of identical apartment windows made individual by bright patterned curtains, lines of washing, some Christmas lights and at least one carrier bag hanging from a nail where it served as a makeshift fridge for a small bottle of milk. Advertisement hoarding screens pushed right up against some windows, practically covering others, their thick curtains were drawn tight in a futile effort to hold back the invading glare.

The streets below were quiet but not silent, as cars busied their way along the winding and narrow streets; original, English-styled streets, seemingly more strewn about at random than designed with a purpose, a complete contrast to the ordered grids of Unity's upper levels. Along the roadside traditional hand-painted pub signs mingled with neon-lit bar logos, battered office markings and guttering fluorescent takeaway signs, all humming away with activity amongst the boarded-up frontages and rotting To Let signs of their emptier neighbours. Silhouettes of late-night stragglers wound their way through a mismatched maze of alleys lit by unenthusiastic streetlights, some hurrying by at a determined pace, heads down as to not draw attention from others who were staggering from a pubwards direction in rowdy, scattered gangs. One of the latter was wearing a pair of plastic reindeer antlers and howling his way through most of a Christmas song, though he'd apparently dropped most of the lyrics in the gutter before the chorus came around.

After a brief glance it was clear that Buried didn't see much value in order or propriety, a notion that filled Renji with a strange, nervous thrill; a wobbly sense of fascinated unease that left him torn between exploring every corner of the place, or dashing right back into the elevator and never coming back.

The rest of the commuters dispersed, disappearing into the city away from Renji and his uniform at the fastest a walk could be before it counts as a run. This left him, Weaver, Sugar and Trig alone outside the station, waiting in a square that contained nothing more than a flickering streetlight, a large yet woefully under-decorated Christmas tree, and the awkward silence that had settled in between them all.

"This your first time downstairs, Mr Weaver?" Sugar asked after some time.

"Nope." No further elaboration was offered.

"What about you, copper?"

"Well, it's the first time anyone's given me an invitation."

"Pffh, no surprise there." She smirked, the relief at their escape having evidently revived her interest in ribbing Renji where possible. "What d'you reckon?"

"Uh…" He hesitated, wanting to fire back a taunt of his own yet finding himself unable to scrounge up the words. Glancing around, he felt something in particular nagging at him, an unfamiliar sort of wrongness, as though something vital were missing he couldn't quite place.

"You'll adjust." Still leaning on Sugar's shoulder for support, Trig threw him a tired yet welcoming smile. "It, ah… takes a while to get used to it." he added, pointing upwards. Frowning, Renji followed his gesture; and, with effort, caught the gasp before it jumped out of his throat.

Overhead where the night sky ought to be loomed an endless overwhelming expanse of metal coated with a dense thicket of intertwining beams, wiring and even more advertising billboards written in fonts the size of cars; the underside of Central Commons, hanging above the whole of the lowest city like a threat. While he hadn't spent much time on the Commons itself, it'd been enough to know that this was nothing like the upward view from there; Imperium Court's great glittering floor of thick, tempered glass let both sun and stars filter through to the tier below, allowing the Court

76

to sparkle in the sky as if it were a great golden crown, one anyone could imagine being able to touch if they only stretched their fingers high enough.

From down here, reaching would achieve nothing.

"S'not exactly subtle, is it?" A familiar voice with a northern twang dragged Renji back down to ground level. "'Course it keeps the rain out, so there's that at least."

From a nearby street's shadows a figure strolled over to join them near the depressing excuse for a Christmas tree, moving with all the urgency of a sleeping cat in a sunbeam. The first thing to notice about Melody was, quite simply, *colour.* As if to stand out from the general gloom around her, she'd taken care to stack up least four layers of clothing in the wildest clashing colours she could find; her hands were shoved into the pockets of an acid-green denim jacket, covered in an indecipherable riot of patches and buttons and thrown over a thick black hoodie printed with skeleton bones, all of it quite clearly from the bargain rack. Her torn jeans were the startling blue of a raspberry ice pop, and her pink platform trainers must have been at least three decades out of style. The whole look was topped off with a tangle of plastic and stainless steel jewellery so varied and numerous it was as though someone had given a six-year-old a debit card and three pounds of sugar and pointed them at Claire's Accessories.

Digging past the ensemble to see the actual person wearing took some effort, but having done so Renji found Melody was not much older than himself, though most of a foot shorter. At a guess she had Indian or Pakistani roots, with her skin a cool, sandy tone, dark against the amplified colour of her clothing. Loose locks of brown-black hair framed her narrow features, their ends fading into a greenish-blue about her shoulders. Having caught him watching she flashed Renji a brief, abstract little smile, one that seemed to be keeping its distance until some unknown condition was met. She turned to Weaver.

"Alright, Harlow's dad. You got that drive?"

With a nod, he tossed her the thin rectangular device poached from the room with the wires and blood, and pocketed it with a note of thanks.

That done, Melody turned to face her forlorn teammates. Sugar shifted under her silent scrutiny, seemingly doing her best to not meet her eyes. Having let them squirm for several long moments, she shook her head with a fond little tut of acceptance. "Alright, you two?"

The tension dissolved. "Melo..." croaked Sugar. "Look, I know you're pissed with us, but—"

"I'm not pissed."

"...You're not?"

"What's done is done." Melody shrugged. "Cade is right pissed, but that's her problem, not mine."

"Then let's enjoy the calm before the storm while it lasts." Trig gave Melody's elbow a gentle bump with his own, a fond and familiar motion that mellowed her expression into something far warmer.

"If past ventures are anything to go by, I expect that shan't be long," came a clipped voice from the shadows. Stepping out from the shadows behind Melody came a short, stout man with a round face and a practical haircut, the sort of person who couldn't have been older than his early thirties but via the alchemical mix of a thick jumper, sensible shoes and a stern gaze managed to carry with him the air of being The Only Adult In The Room. Like Melody, his clothes were cheap yet patched with care, and a hint of an unfamiliar accent flitted about his speech; from what he remembered of his father's language Renji ruled out Japanese, but the man's features suggested the answer wouldn't be too many countries over.

"Christ!" yelped Sugar. "How long were you hiding back there, Min?!"

"Eons," he replied, expression impassive. "I'm sure I needn't tell you that Ms Cellanea would like a word with you both."

"Oh." Her face twisted in slow realisation. "Oh god..."

"Aw, buck up," Melody said, with all the sympathy of the person who isn't in trouble. "She might do the thing where she swears in French, if you're lucky."

"Luck hasn't really been our thing tonight…" Trig smiled sadly. "Not until these guys came along, anyway." He nodded at Weaver and Renji.

From the lamppost he was leaning against for support, Weaver grunted noncommittally. "No problem."

"Yeah yeah, no problem." echoed Renji, aware the instant he did that it sounded far less cool coming from him.

"I really do mean it though. Thanks for all your help." Trig's round eyes brimmed with sincerity. "I... thought none of us were walking out of there."

"Kiki didn't," the other man said, snapping that line of conversation shut like a briefcase at the conclusion of a meeting. "Since no-one here has the manners to introduce me after having summoned me out here at this absurd hour, I'll do so myself." Ignoring Trig's stammered apology, he gave a curt little bow of his head towards Weaver and Renji in turn. "Minjun Jeong, Ms Cellanea's assistant. She would like to request an immediate meeting with Mr Weaver."

A Korean name, then. That made sense. Still, Renji frowned at his words. "Wait, just the old man? What about me?"

"As useful as it would be were it otherwise, we only have one Ms Cellanea, thus she is only capable of one meeting at a time. She'll see you afterwards, Mr Hayakawa. Perhaps in an hour or so."

"Alright, but…" He glanced around at the unfamiliar buildings. "What do I do til then?"

"You hungry?" Melody cocked her head. "Was gonna go find dinner anyway. You can tag along, if you've nowt better to do."

"Dinner? You haven't had *dinner* yet?" Minjun gave her an exhausted look of reprimand. "What time is it, exactly?"

"Half past chips o'clock," she replied matter-of-factly, as he peered at his phone's clock.

"Otherwise known as two in the morning. I believe it legally counts as breakfast at that point." With a sigh, Minjun shook his head. "Well, you enjoy your… *breakfast chips*. Do you have any, ah," He paused, eyeing the sword that Renji was still clutching. "luggage that you would like me to take?"

"Oh! Yeah, I guess this is a bit much for chips, huh." Renji handed the weapon over to Minjun, who received it in a delicate yet assured grasp.

"Thank you. Melody, Ms Cellanea will message you when she'd like Mr Hayakawa escorted back to base, by which point I very much hope to be asleep. Shall we?" The last was addressed to the others, who began to wearily pick themselves up and get moving. Without intending to, Renji found himself glancing towards Weaver as they left. He had been mostly silent since leaving the elevator station. Catching Renji's gaze, he gave a small nod before turning to leave; an almost imperceivable gesture, but a reassuring one all the same. Then the old man joined the others, following Minjun into the night and leaving Melody, Renji and the pathetic Christmas tree alone in the flickering lamplight.

"So, which way to chips?"

"That'd be…" The girl span lazily on her shoe's chunky heel, coming to a stop with a gesture along one of the crooked streets. "… This way. But unless you want yours spat in, we're making a stop first."

CHAPTER 7

FISH AND/OR CHIPS

While it may be true that there was no such thing as a nice public toilet, many places tried to do their best all the same. This one had not. Dirt and mould coated every surface, brightened by countless duelling political stickers and home-printed posters advertising everything from an online anarchist erotica writing collective to a ska revival concert in a car park. The windows and mirrors were a spiderweb of cracks, the smell was indescribable, and only one stall door still clung to its hinges, holding a thin line of defence against the outside world. On it, some poetic soul had written *LOVE URSELF* in red paint, complete with a drawing of a heart. Someone with a better sense of realism had scribbled a dick over it.

Still, it was a step up from changing in the middle of the street, so Renji made do with trying not to breathe in too frequently. Thankfully for once, he'd thought ahead enough to have brought some spare clothes in his escape bag: red sneakers, fashionably faded jeans, a favourite T-shirt, and a now rather concerning total lack of jacket.

"Well shit." he muttered.

"Problem?" Melody's voice drifted in through the broken window.

"Nah, it's nothing." On the way here his new hacker friend had made it quite clear that while an Imperium International Forces uniform would open a lot of doors around here— usually with a battering ram— it'd also draw more than its fair share of unwelcome attention from the locals, so risking a chill seemed like a more sensible prospect than wearing the thick woollen uniform jacket. Besides, after everything he'd seen tonight, crumpling the perfectly ironed garments into a ball and stuffing them as far into his bag as possible gave him no small sense of malevolent satisfaction.

"So do Forces come down here often?" he asked, attempting to find a clear spot in the mirror to assess the look.

"Not if you *call* 'em. They'll come and chuck their weight around sometimes, though."

"What, really?"

"Mm. Everyone here knows if there's a table full of uniforms you don't bother sending them the bill, not if you wanna keep your windows. Or maybe they'll knock someone about a bit and say it's cus they looked at 'em funny. Confiscate your money and stuff as 'evidence'. The usual sort of arseholery."

"Oh." Renji frowned, running a finger along the red welt on the underside of his chin where Flood's fist had left its mark. For the last few months he'd thought people like the sergeant were a rarity, but it was beginning to seem there may be more Floods at I.I. than he'd assumed.

Still, inspecting his injuries showed there hadn't been too much damage done; the bruise was sore but not immediately noticeable, and the rest of his face was as well put together as it always had been. Renji hadn't known his parents for long, but should he ever get the chance he'd have to thank his mother for the cheekbones and his father for the eyes, a strikingly handsome combination that had brought him a lot of luck in the clubs and a lot of trouble at I.I.; and one he wouldn't trade it for the world. He swept his ink-black hair back into a stylish, casual wave, taking a little extra time and effort to make it seem effortless.

"You fall in or what?" called Melody eventually, forcing him to stop mid-preen.

"Alright, coming...!"

Leaving the bathrooms did mean leaving the wretched toilet stink behind, but the downside of stepping back out into the night was that the December chill caught up with Renji at once, prickling the bare skin of his forearms into goose-pimples before he'd even cleared the door.

From her perch on a low wall, Melody gave him a long look. "Better," she concluded, hopping down from the wall with her hands still stuffed into her hoodie pockets. "Nice shirt."

Renji glanced down at himself as if he hadn't seen that particular shirt a thousand times before. It was ancient as far as clothes went, a souvenir from a visit his father had once made back to his home village somewhere west of Tokyo. The logo on the front featured the prefecture's mascot— the adorably marketable fox Susu-kun, with a cheeky wink on his face and fishbone in his mouth, dashing away from a hopping mad little old man whose bins had been rifled through. Supposedly, that area had so much trouble with urban foxes stealing from their trash that they decided to name one as their mascot, hoping to make it seen as more of a fun little quirk than a sanitation problem. Whether that plan had worked was debatable, but it had at least sold a couple of T-shirts. The thing had fit like a tent when Renji's dad had first bought it for him but now, so many years later, it was just about the right size.

Tugging at the fabric's edge for a moment Renji swallowed something difficult back down before looking up at Melody, putting on a smile. "Thanks."

Fortunately, she hadn't seemed to notice the pause before his answer. "Hang on, didn't you bring a coat? It's December, mate, you're gonna freeze your arse off."

"Oh, yeah, no. S'fine. I'm fine." He danced from one foot to the other to keep warmer. "It's nothing chips can't deal with."

"Eh, alright then. If you reckon." She hummed, picking what seemed like a random direction to head off in. "Chipwards we go."

#

Despite her short stature and impractical shoes, Melody carried herself through Buried's tangled streets with an admirable lack of fear of what might lurk in their shadows. Her confident, loping stride led

Renji on a route that seemed so certain on her part, but left him unsure of where they'd begun besides a vague notion of backward and to the right, somewhere past where that one lady was throwing up on a discarded pizza box.

Before long they came upon their apparent destination; an area standing empty among the otherwise incessant press of buildings, ringed by low stone walls on which someone had done their absolute best with several strings of mostly operational Christmas lights. A wrought iron gate hung open, signifying an entrance leading into a bleak expanse of barren dirt, littered with the sorts of paths that only the consistent tread of hundreds of feet per day could make. Gravel and rocks mingled with the dry, dead soil, converging into peaks and mounds along the sides of the trail they followed, giving the whole area the feeling of a building site for a project long since abandoned. It wasn't until Renji saw the gnarled, long dead trunks of trees in the distance that he understood what sort of place this was supposed to be.

"Hang on… Was this a park?" he asked incredulously.

"Still is."

"*Is* it?!"

Imperium Court was famed for its parks, especially the Fringe Gardens that ran along the tier's edge; wide green spaces surrounded by lush trees, alive with the scent of fresh grass that shone with dew and bordered by flower beds sculpted with care, laid out like a scattered floral rainbow in the sunlight. Here, the only non-dirt colour came from the occasional discarded crisp bags and coffee cups.

"Don't be a snob, mate. I'd like to see you do any better at growing owt with that bloody great bin lid of yours up there." Melody bobbed her head up towards the oppressive shape of Central Commons above, and before he could protest that it wasn't *his* bin lid actually, she continued. "Besides, no-one comes to Temperley Park for the daisies."

And as they cleared the hill they'd been ascending, he saw what she meant.

Right at the centre of the destitute gardens lay a circular paved plaza that served as host to a rather stunning outdoor kitchen. Half a dozen or so food trucks were humming with activity, dotted around the dry crumbling bowl that must have once been a stately water feature. Each one had their hatch propped open to let their spicy, sharp, delicious scents drift out into the night and lure in unsuspecting customers who could swear they weren't hungry a minute ago. It being two in the morning the place wasn't experiencing rush hour, yet still they had customers filing in from the surrounding pubs, looking to soak up tonight's sins. Whoever had been stringing up fairy lights had done a number on this area too; row upon row of warm orange bulbs cast a friendly, welcoming glow, and there were even some plastic tables and chairs set out to complete the picture of an inviting little oasis of life in the otherwise depressing landscape.

"There. Now tell me you're not impressed," smirked Melody.

"I could, but I'd be lying," Renji replied, feeling his stomach start paying attention to where the rest of him was.

"Riley does decent coffee over there, if that's your thing." She nodded at a small trolley with a French press and the name *The Bitter End* displayed across its front. Glancing up from a phone, the black-clad goth proprietor returned the nod with a shy little smile behind a thatch of scruffy dark hair. "Their cakes are incredible but they always sell out early, so good luck getting any this late," Melody added.

Renji nodded, distractedly. "Alright, but that pizza smells *amazing.*"

"Oh aye, that'd be Pete and Linda's," she said, nodding towards a red and green truck with *Speedy Pete's Reet Pizza* emblazoned across the front. Within, an elderly couple were assembling food at lightning speed, while their customer waited with a slight drunken wobble and a look of mild concern. "They're good and all but a bit *too* fast, really. Don't expect them to actually give you what you ordered, is all I'm saying," added Melody in a low whisper as they passed the truck.

"Evening, Linda."

The bespectacled old lady handed her customer a ham and mushroom pizza that he had in no way ordered, and waved at them.

"Evenin'…" There was a pause as Linda peered at Melody, adjusting her glasses, then "…Melody?" she finished, as if hazarding a guess.

"That's me," Melody replied with her standard slow smile, but her steps quickened, clearing the length of the pizza truck at a faster pace than she had gone all evening. "Linda can be a bit forgetful sometimes," she explained in a whisper, an obvious lie Renji stored away to decipher later.

The promised chip van smelled exactly how a fish and chip shop ought to smell after midnight. It hit its customers right in the face, overwhelming them with a cloying yet glorious soup of airborne grease, cut through with a waft of nose-tingling sharp vinegar tang that set mouths watering as if it had been engineered in a lab for that very purpose. The heat of the fryers radiated from the van in welcoming waves, to an increasingly chilly Renji's eternal gratitude. Yet, for all that the *Steelepool Fish Shop* had got right, there was one drawback; one who was lurking behind the counter wearing a Santa hat and giving Renji the most intimidating glare he'd been treated to all evening. The chef wasn't tall, but made up for a lack of height in breadth and eyebrows. Broad arms were folded over a broader chest, lank greasy curls of hair were plastered to a wide forehead, and a fryer's gentle but insistent beeping went ignored in favour of putting out as much glower per second as was humanly possible.

"Chiiiips pleeeease," Melody warbled, slumping on the food truck's counter as though she'd been journeying through a desert for hours rather than taking a stroll through the streets. "And curry sauce. And vinegar. And—"

"Mushy peas." Turning his back, he jabbed a thick finger at the fryer to silence its beeping. "As if I don't know your order by now," grumbled the man, a hint of a Welsh accent making itself known through the gruffness. He couldn't have been out of his twenties from the look of him, but when it came to grousing he was clearly very advanced for his age.

"Chips Darren, you're a bloody lifesaver when you want to be. Oi Renji, what're you having?"

Renji hesitated, having not yet given a second glance to the menu board and its neat little handwriting properly as the name Chips Darren had taken him like a left hook to the face. "Uh—"

A sharp bang of metal on metal rang out as *Chips Darren* tipped a fresh pile of golden potato out of the frying basket and into the warmer. "And does *sir* plan on paying for his order tonight?" he asked with a scowl.

Well, that hadn't taken long. But how the hell had this guy worked it out already? Was it something in Renji's accent? His stance? Was the subtle poison of the Court that obvious to an outsider? "Listen man, I'm not still part of Imperium, I—"

"Give over, Chips Darren. I'm vouching for him. There's no going back upstairs for this one, trust me on that." Melody rested her head on her forearms, eyes fixed on the chips that were in the process of being aggressively salted.

"Yeah, what she said," Renji finished lamely.

"Hrm." With a practised hand, the man popped a Styrofoam container out from a package and began shovelling it full of fresh hot chips. "Wouldn't trust any Forces as far as I could throw 'em. And I know *exactly* how far I can throw 'em, like," he added, throwing a meaningful squint over his shoulder as he hefted a bottle of vinegar with menace. "Watch your back with this one, Mel."

"You know I hate it when you call me Mel."

"And I hate it when you call me Chips Darren, so."

"Don't let Darren bother you, dears! He's been soaking in his own vinegar too long," called a cheerful lady from the neighbouring truck, which was adorned with a hand-painted sign that featured the Sri Lankan flag and the words *Roti Queen.* The queen herself was an older lady with the kind of face that was built for beaming, her dark cheeks round and dimpled, and the sizzle from the flat griddle in front of her cloaked the entire truck in a pleasant aura of cumin and oil.

"Evening, Sarasi," Melody greeted her. "Any chance you'll feed my mate here without being a total bellend about it?"

"Oh, every chance." Sarasi gave Renji a wide smile. "How do you like kottu roti, boy?"

"Ma'am, I honestly don't know what the hell that is," he admitted. "But I'd really like to find out."

"Good boy, very good!" Sarasi let out a hoot of delight, sweeping up a handful of cabbage and tossing it onto the hot griddle before her with an appetising hiss. "You found a real skinny one here, Melo! Let's get some meat on those bones." She tossed some onions into the mix with reckless abandon. "Why're you all bare-armed out here, fishing to catch a chill like that? Don't you have a coat, new boy?"

"I, uh… left in kind of a hurry," he said, huddling his arms closer to his chest at the reminder.

"So it goes, so it goes. Well, that's nothing that extra chilli can't cure!" Sarasi added more mysterious handfuls and pinches and spoonfuls to whatever the hell she was making, sweeping and chopping at the dish with a pair of wide and flat yet sharp blades.

"No sense wasting words on the likes o' him," grumbled the chip shop chef, sloshing curry sauce into a Styrofoam pot with a face like thunder.

"Oh, Darren. With customer service like that, it's no wonder I steal all your business!" chirped Sarasi, cracking an egg onto her grill with another wink at Renji.

"He going to pay you for that food, then?"

"Since you asked so nicely, Chips Darren, no he isn't paying for his dinner, cus *I'm* paying for it." Melody yawned, still slouching on her elbows on the countertop. "We owe him that much, since he helped us find Trig and Sugar."

Darren paused while reaching for the peas. "…you got 'em back, like?"

"Just about. Might not have managed without Renji, if I'm being honest," she replied levelly. "So let's try to be a bit civil, alright?"

"So Cellanea is taking in some new strays, eh? It's about time!" Sarasi drummed her flat blades against the grill, chopping a fresh roti into thin strips with satisfaction. "They need the help down there, that's for sure!"

"Keep it down, woman!" chided Darren, narrowing his eyes at Renji. "Don't tell the whole bleedin' world where she's at, will you?"

"Oh pish posh, I told nothing!" With a final mixing motion, she threw in what looked like enough dried chilli flakes to level a horse, and tipped the dish into a foil container. "There, new boy. Kottu roti. You'll love it."

It certainly smelled like he would. As she attached a paper lid, Darren threw Renji one last glower for old time's sakes. "Yeah, well. We'll see how long he lasts before he runs back up home," he rumbled, handing Melody her dinner.

She rolled her eyes. "Leave it be."

"Sure. Enjoy your chips and impending betrayal, Mel."

"Shut your face, Chips Darren," she replied with a fond smile, sliding a handful of loose change over the counter.

Something in Renji's guts ached. The man was of course, right, though he couldn't have known how right he'd been; unlike any other cadet in his position, Renji *could* still go back to the Court. Despite what he'd done, despite what certain other people in his family might have done, as long as he stayed in his Aunty Lissa's seemingly endless good graces a cover-up of even the wild events of tonight could be arranged, should she will it so. I.I. could always find space in its machine for a piece with the right name, even if it was a non-standard fit.

But of course, he couldn't go back. *Wouldn't*. Which meant that it was fine that he was misleading Melody and the rest, just a touch. *Somewhat*. It was only a different surname after all, another of those little Court lies, told to make life easier.

Renji picked up the parcel of food before the guilt devoured his appetite out from under him.

A little way beyond the plaza yet more lights burned bright in the doorway of what must have once been the manor house of someone rather important, judging by the stately pillars, lead-piped windows and general size of the place. Above the doorway, the words *Temperley Park Manor House* were carved into what might have been marble, but now it was covered by a time-worn banner that read *Temperley Sanctuary—Community Food Bank and Feeding Centre.* A smaller notice, printed out on A4 paper and taped beneath in a plastic sleeve, apologised for the lack of available beds and wished all a happy holiday. The hall's courtyard held a small play park with woodchip flooring clear of stray garbage, the pretty, painted climbing frames and chain-link swings gleaming from the sort of maintenance that only someone who cared deeply could provide.

Melody threw herself down onto the hard plastic swing seat with a sigh, though whether it was one of contentment or exhaustion was difficult to tell.

"You didn't have to pay for mine," said Renji, settling onto the swing next to hers.

"Kinda did. How much paper money do you have on you?"

"Uh… None?" No-one in Court or Commons used actual physical cash. For convenience, bank accounts were connected to a person's ID, stored on their phone and used as a sort of virtual wallet. "Oh. Right," he said, thinking of his dormant phone, and the clear trail he might leave from something so simple as paying for dinner. Right now and for as long as he stayed in Buried he was flat broke, an unfortunate fact that hadn't occurred to him until this very second. "Thanks…"

"Aye, well." Melody tugged her own Styrofoam container open, sending the steam from the hot food billowing out onto the breeze and breathing out a note of relief to join it. Opening his own box, Renji found a delicious golden mess of egg, sliced roti, flaky fish and vegetables, all generously spiced and warming.

Digging a plastic fork into the pile, he threw out one of the many questions he'd been working on over the last few hours. "So, how'd you get started on the, uh... computer stuff?"

"Dug some bits out of a bin at the charity shop. Put 'em together for fun."

"Lucky find!"

She wrinkled her nose. "Worked there. You get first pick that way. Why d'you care?"

"Just being polite, y'know? Getting to know you! It's the sort of thing you're meant to do. Like, hey; where are you from?"

Melody gave him a flat look. "England."

"No shit." He matched her look with one of his own. "I meant where in England, duh. Your accent isn't Unity, so..."

"Oh." She selected a chip and sniffed it. Apparently satisfied, she popped it into her mouth. "Right," she said, chewing. "It's just normally when people ask that they mean— Eh, look who I'm telling."

"Yeah." Renji grinned in sympathy, cradling the foil around his food closer to heat his hands. "Been *there* before."

"Always a fun time. It's Manchester, anyway, is where we're from."

"We?"

Melody cursed under her breath as she opened the pot of curry sauce and spilled some onto her fingers. "Ugh. Yeah, *us*. You'll meet my sister eventually, if I can't help it," she added with a frown, dumping the sauce onto the chips as if to drown them. "Can't avoid it forever, I s'pose."

"What's the problem? I can make a good first impression with the best of 'em!" He paused before adding, "Maybe not with Mr Chips back there, but usually."

"No such thing for some people," she muttered, which would have been more ominous had it not been muttered around her finger, which she'd stuck into her mouth to lick off the curry sauce.

Renji blinked, plastic fork halting halfway to his own mouth. He hadn't noticed it until now, but Melody's fingers— no, her whole hand? Wait, *both* hands— were nearly entirely prosthetic, aside from a scarred thumb and two fingers on her left, one of which was at present having curry sauce removed from it noisily. The cuffs of her hoodie's sleeves had been pulled up to obscure the interlocking plates that made up her palms, though now in the playground's ample lighting they were unmissable; tiny metallic joints clicked together in a neat design, much better-maintained than the kind Weaver had been sporting, despite their current layer of curry sauce.

Still, sleek engineering or no, whatever must have happened to cause that kind of injury must have been drastic to say the least, and the careful sleeve placement couldn't have said *don't ask about it* any louder. As laid-back as Melody was she had her guard up, so before Renji could start asking stupid questions he stuffed a forkful of kottu into his mouth and they instead sat in a pleasant tired haze of quiet, shoes skimming the wood chips of the playground floor as the kitchens continued to work away nearby.

Digging into the charitably large dinner Renji found that the fish was delicate, the roti was a chewy yet tasty delight, and the amount of chilli flakes verged on assault.

"You're making a right go of that," Melody said, eventually.

"I-I'm fine!" Renji coughed, fighting back the chilli-induced tears. "It's just a little, uh… Whew. I-I can handle it though!"

"Uh huh." She watched him sneeze away his dignity while she finished off her chips. "If it helps, the extra chilli means she likes you."

"Great." He gave a weak sniff. "At least I'm not cold any more."

"Except you are, cus it's December."

She wasn't wrong. Without the open sky there was very little breeze, but an English winter was still winter enough to turn Renji's arms the blotchy red and white that meant it was long past time to go indoors. Besides which, it was an obscene hour in the morning following what had been a rather eventful night, a realisation that had him stifling a yawn.

Melody balled up the paper from her chip dinner. "I've still not had owt from Cellanea, so I can't take you back to hers yet. Probably we should get you somewhere though, before you freeze to death and I get blamed for it." She pitched the paper ball towards a nearby bin and frowned as the shot missed horribly, thumping into the plastic siding and rolling onto the floor. "Bugger," she mumbled.

Once again Renji chose to not push his luck, and made no comment. "Any ideas?" he instead asked, as she hopped up and off the swing.

"Well, I did have a delivery to make," she mused, scooping the trash into the bin. "How d'you feel about hitting up the club?"

"A club?" Renji's exhaustion melted away in an instant. "What kinda club?"

CHAPTER 8
A CHANCE ENCOUNTER

The entrance for Static Void didn't give much away. Sandwiched between derelict buildings and beneath a Turkish barbershop, only a small arrow underlit in vivid pink indicated there was any reason to venture down the foreboding, dark stairwell which descended beneath the street. Once below however, Renji found himself being led down a mirror-panelled corridor towards the familiar sound of muffled bass thrumming through the walls and floor, beckoning him closer.

With another of those inscrutable little half smiles Melody pushed open the door to the club, allowing the music to roll over them as if it had been waiting at the entrance to rush forward in greeting. Whatever was playing was a chill tune underlaid with light electronic strains that loped along at a pleasant, easy pace for a late Thursday night, but with a rhythm steady enough that it would take a strong test of will to not bop along in time to the beat.

Static Void was an industrial-style place that made the most of its exposed brickwork and visible metal girders, framed with low ceilings and even lower lights in pink, purple and blue hues that danced over the small crowd within. The few dozen patrons were ignoring the late hour in favour of swaying together on the dancefloor in delightful, thoughtless bliss. A decked-out stage area for live music lay empty to one side, and to the other sat several booths with tables, much less empty and shadowed in cosy seclusion. The centrepiece of the place however, was the chrome-topped bar which took point at the back of the room. Much of it was the standard bar top; at the front shone an array of beer taps decorated with labels he'd never seen before, and at the back dwelled a wide array of bottles in noxious colours that promised an endless quantity of delicious headaches to come. Above those hung something less usual; from the bar top to the ceiling, the back wall of the entire club was covered in an artfully tangled mess of PC monitors, all scrolling through line upon line of complex code whose meaning was likely lost on most viewers, though no knowledge was needed to enjoy their flashy effect against the backlighting.

Breathing out a deep sigh, Renji paused on the dancefloor to drink in the atmosphere. Back in Imperium Court, most social events were nothing more than a glitzy showcase, a gilded frame to position yourself in and be *seen*. Every conversation was a trial of wits, every drink bought for either enemy or friend a calculated move. As the commander's nephew his reputation and more importantly Aunty L's would rest on his performance, and the least Renji could do for her was to play his part. He'd always risen to the occasion, neatly snipping off the parts of himself that didn't fit into the template and performing in the shallow little pageants to the best of his ability.

Static Void, though, was more like the sort of tiny unnamed bar he'd sought out on his own time. Here dancers unashamedly weaved around the floor and around each other regardless of their respective genders, sometimes colliding with each other and spilling their drinks with a burst of easy, intoxicated laughter. The crowd was keen, the floor was sticky, and no-one here knew his name.

In other words, it was perfect.

Already Melody had strolled across the length of the club as comfortable as if she were in her own living room and come to a stop on a barstool, where she was greeted by an absolute vision of a bartender. It was hard to discern the particulars of this person from a distance, though the clothes were a statement of intent to be seen. An impeccably neat silver-blue toned bob haircut and a huge white fluffy coat dotted with patches of sky-blue, worn with pants in pearlescent ivory and little to no shirt, a bright bubbling bombshell of an outfit, which made a stunning contrast to its wearer's beautifully deep brown skin. Melody beckoned Renji over with a languid wave.

"Renji, this here's Allegro." she indicated the bartender with a bob of her head. "They own the place, so be nice."

They, huh? Alright, neat. He'd heard of the notion of doing away with the whole gender thing, but never met anyone with the opportunity to live it before. Renji made a few mental adjustments, then offered them a wide smile and an outstretched hand. "Oh please, I'm always nice."

"You sure look it." They took a moment to run an eye over Renji before matching his grin with their own in a flash of perfect white teeth, taking his hand in an affectionate grip. "Welcome to Static Void, darlin'. We like people who play nice here." Allegro's accent was pure Unity City, thick with that same Central Commons drawl Weaver sported, though he hadn't thrown in quite so many sly little winks as punctuation.

"'fraid we're here on business. Came over to drop something off." Melody dug a compact little rectangle out of the recesses of her lime green jacket. "Or someone, really."

With a sharp inhale, Allegro let go of Renji's hand and looked from Melody to the data drive. Their face fell in realisation. "Oh, hell… Who is it?"

"Kiki." She handed it over to Allegro, who accepted the thing with a joyless reverence.

Renji could feel the mood souring as he stared at the device they'd pilfered from AirCast Two. "What do you mean, it's… it's *her?* There's a whole-ass person on that thing? That doesn't make sense."

"Why not?" Melody said. "It's all just data, if you think about it. Brains, drives, it's only storage."

"But— so it's like her thoughts, or—?"

"It's whatever they lifted out of her with that dodgy headjack you saw. Tends to be a full disk image, if they have the time. Memories are usually what they're after from us criminal types, but since Imperium don't want anything unnecessary data like, y'know, *personality,* they usually automatically filter it out and…" She mimed a flippant tap of an imaginary button. "...delete it."

"*'Delete it'?!*"

"Delete it." Her expression hardened. "Might be they haven't. Dunno yet. Can't tell which bits are still there til we open it up and have a poke about. Either way we're kinda lucky it was an air-gapped machine. No network means that since you lifted the drive, they got nothing from her."

"But- But-!" Renji stuttered, aghast. "You can't just copy a person's everything, not just like that!"

"Not copy, darlin', *stole*. It's a fucking ransack. They take what they can grab outta you and don't leave nothing behind. Just a shell." Allegro ran a delicate finger along the drive's edge. "Bless your heart, Kiki. You didn't deserve this."

"Not many do," Melody added.

"Oh, I can think of a few." Despite their soft tone, Allegro's words bore an undeniable edge that reflected in their dark, glittering eyes.

Renji's mind reeled. "Wait, then— So, say we're lucky and all of her is on there... Then what? What could you actually *do* with it all?"

"Sorry to say we ain't worked that part out yet." Allegro sighed. "For now we just gotta store them away safe til we do."

"Them? As in, *plural* 'them'?" Renji spluttered. "This has happened before? Like, how often?!"

"More than you'd think," said Melody.

"Well shit, we gotta go back and get her body! If it's a full copy, can't you... I dunno, upload the data? Put it back into her brain?"

Biting their painted lip Allegro shot Melody a worried glance, but she shrugged, detached as ever.

"Body's dead, mate," she said quietly.

"But—"

"The good news," Melo cut across him, "is we got Trig and Sugar back in one piece."

"Well thank heaven for small mercies!" Allegro drummed their pearl-white nails on the bar's counter. "And my girl Harlow?"

"Still nowt on her. No bloody idea where they've taken her, or why, or much of anything at all if we're being honest."

"Poor lil Cellanea's gonna run out of merry men at this rate." Shaking their head, Allegro turned and busied themself with fishing a couple of random beers out of a nearby fridge. "Well, nothing more you can do tonight, anyhow. Tell you what, Melo darlin', you fancy taking over on the tunes for a spell? Let your hair down some, sounds like you earned it."

She squirmed on the bar stool in contemplation, then nodded. "Yeah actually, that does sound good. Think I might just do that."

Despite everything he'd just heard, Renji still had it in him to blink in surprise at that. "You're a DJ?"

Tittering, Allegro cracked open both bottles. "Hell yeah she is! Best in Unity!"

Melody snorted in amusement, but didn't disagree. "You have to say that. I work for you."

"And I know you wouldn't doubt my taste in talent, so there we have it," they concluded with another wink, slipping the drive into the recesses of their furred jacket. "Right then, I'm gonna go get my girl here somewhere safe. Here, on the house, for getting back Celly's nerds." Allegro handed a beer to Melody. "You, go spin up somethin' good for Kiki." The second beer went to Renji. "And you, go have some fun. I'd avoid the booth at the back though, they ah… ain't paying customers, if you catch my meaning." They cast a nasty glare in the direction of a table towards the far corner of the club where four Forces Upper Managers sat in all their uniformed glory, swigging their drinks and barking out jeers at passing patrons.

Renji nodded in a daze as Allegro departed. Taking a long gulp of beer, Melody eyed him silently.

"What? I'm fine!" he spluttered after several long unbearable seconds of scrutiny.

"Uh huh."

"Obviously I'm fine!"

"So I see."

"A-okay."

"Right."

"Right then."

Having run out of acceptable words he squirmed in place, attempting to hold back the unacceptable ones. They came blurting out anyway. "It's just— What the fuck, man?! Downloading brains is some mad science shit! I didn't know that was something we— *they* could do. *Would* do! I knew they're not like... good people or anything, but... *fuck!* I- I didn't know." Renji sighed, running his fingers through his hair in frustration. "I swear, I didn't know."

"Course not. They didn't want you to know. But now you do." Melody hopped off the barstool and gave him a fleeting half-smile. "What you do with it is up to you, mate." And with a lazy, cat-like stretch she trotted off in the direction of the dance floor, leaving Renji alone to stare at the flickering screens of complex code he could never begin to understand, while trying not to think too hard about the word *delete.*

#

It didn't take long for Melody to show she was as skilled at the mixing table as she was at the keyboard. Having stepped up to the DJ booth and slipped on the headphones, she'd stood for a moment to survey the crowd, intent as a ship's captain stood at her prow, taking in the direction of the wind and temperament of the waves. Her course set, she'd rolled up her sleeve with a workmanlike air, slotted an aux cable into a port at her wrist and tapped something into her phone; then with a few mysterious twiddles at the mixer deck she'd gently, lovingly set Static Void's dancefloor on fire.

Following Melody's lead her audience whooped and yelled and dived into the dance, and as tempting as it was to join the melee, Renji found he didn't have the stomach for it.

Even now, two tracks into Melody's set and counting, he was lurking in the sullen shadows of a booth and frowning at nothing in particular. The only empty seat had been close to the table of Uppers, which hadn't exactly improved his mood. A furtive glance revealed them to be a gaggle of corporals, the lowest Upper Management rank usually reserved for young bullish types whose parents knew people, and these four seemed to fit the mould. While Renji didn't know any of them personally, that didn't stop their presence from being both disconcerting and just plain obnoxious, from their constant jeering and guffawing to their general aura of having had five too many. The rest of the club's patrons had by now learned to give them a wide berth, so with a lack of direct targets to holler at they'd started to complain about the club itself, then the music, not to mention the quality of the drinks that they weren't even planning on paying for.

Yawning through gritted teeth, Renji huddled into the booth's faux-leather seats, arms still raw and pink from the winter chill, while next to him the table of stubble-headed idiot Uppers guffawed at nothing in particular. The sound of it twisted his guts into sickened knots, and he began to pick at the label of his now empty bottle in irritation, fussing at the edges with cold, shaking fingers. Did they know about what was being done in those secret, unmarked rooms? A few hours ago in that cell he'd been so ready to join in with Ms Cellanea and Melody, ready to help that wild-eyed girl in the broadcast send the Court running scared; but right now all he felt was exhausted and uncertain and cold and alone. Aunty L's apartment may have never felt like his home, but right now he ached for it, it and the simplicity of not *knowing*.

Face twisting into a frown, he hunched further into his seat in an attempt to fight the shivering coursing through his bones and continued to maul the bottle's label, ripping and picking at the disintegrating paper under his fingernails. This whole time, how much of the Forces knew they'd been digging around inside people's skulls, stealing, *deleting*—

"Rather cold to be out without a jacket, don't you think?"

A honey-slick voice cut straight across Renji's thoughts, leaving them more scattered than the papery ruins strewn about the table. "Though I must admit, that shirt is rather adorable."

A shape had detached from the club's shadows, sliding into his booth as though given a gilded invitation, but with one glance at the stranger Renji knew he wasn't about to protest the intrusion; whoever the hell this guy was, he was devastatingly good-looking, with clever green eyes that locked onto Renji's own and all but pinned him to his seat. In one hand the stranger held a glass of some rich, dark liquor that seemed like the choice of someone older than his apparent twenty-something years, and while his clothing may have been casual it was chosen with care; plain jeans and a simple button-down shirt, made unique by a leather biker jacket in a striking cherry red.

As the man's lips curved into a knowing smile, Renji realised he'd been staring.

"This place *does* have a cloakroom, you know," he pointed out, while sweeping the beer label's remains off the table in what he hoped seemed like a casual manner.

The stranger let out a soft chuckle. "It does indeed, but since you entered the club wearing neither cloak nor coat I'm unsure how much use it would have been to you."

Now that was intriguing. "So you've been watching me?"

"From the moment you walked in."

Extremely intriguing. While up in the Court, even in the more discreet bars a certain amount of caution had been required when approaching an attractive man; not, as the HR execs would hastily declare, that I.I. saw anything wrong with same-gender relationships, *haha oh heavens no, we're champions of diversity and employees can do what they like— in their own homes of course, not in public, what if children saw, I'm sure you understand,* and any promotions that were turned down or jobs that were lost following certain accusations were of course for *other* reasons. His own interest in other men had always been an edge he had to blunt, an awkward angle he was expected to sand down until he better fit the approved profile.

Down here, though, that all seemed quite distant. The dancefloor's lights caught the edges of the stranger's almost unfairly attractive features, highlighting in their purple-pink a classical, captivating combination of a straight nose and a sharp jawline, with just enough stubble to be interesting. The man's smile widened, pearl-bright against his tanned skin, and all thoughts of discretion left the building.

"Gonna assume you liked what you saw, then," Renji asked with playful nonchalance, leaning ever-so-slightly forward.

Another laugh. "Most definitely. Though I'd like to make just one adjustment, if I may." Without waiting for a response, the man shrugged off his jacket and slipped it around a surprised Renji's shoulders. "There. Much better."

Renji pulled the coat tighter about himself with a sigh, burying his frozen limbs in the unexpected yet welcome heat. A rich, intriguing scent hung on the leather, lending it an earthy, peppery heat. Cologne, or perhaps aftershave. "W-wow. Uh, you didn't have to—"

"And yet. It's yours for now, at least until you're trembling a little less." The stranger settled back into his seat, running an appreciative eye over his work. "It may suit you better, anyway."

"You're not wrong there." Renji replied, sliding his arms into the jacket's sleeves. It fit perfectly. "On any other night I'd buy you a drink in return, but I'm kinda broke right now."

"Quite alright. Though if you're offering recompense, I'd be more than happy to accept your name."

"Uh—" He attempted to summon something, but found himself too tired to piece together a worthwhile lie in time. "Listen, that's a whole… thing. A whole complicated thing, and right now I'm really more into simple."

"Straightforward." The man smiled.

"Easy." Renji grinned.

"Then I must ask," murmured the handsome stranger, a wonderful glimmer of something shameless in his eyes, "what brings an easy man like yourself out here tonight, without even a jacket to his non-existent name?"

"That's… also kinda complicated."

"Ah."

"Let's call it a job interview."

"I see, I see. And how is that going?"

"Pretty good, but…" Renji hesitated.

"Complicated?"

"Y-yeah. More than I thought it was gonna be." Absently, he worried at the beer bottle with his thumbnail, loosening the sticky remains of the label. That earned him a questioning look. "Uh. Anyway." Pulling himself back into the moment, Renji shoved the bottle out of reach. "So how about you? Seems like you know this place pretty well. What's your deal?"

"Oh, I come to the Void often. Let's say my reasons are also… *easy.*" Eyes still locked onto Renji's, the man gave his glass a lazy swirl, melting ice clinking against its edges. "And what could be simpler than this? Just two attractive people, both looking for the same thing. Isn't that right?"

Somewhere a million miles away the dance floor had been steered towards chiptune metal, melodies overlaid with the whirring and beeping of ancient hard drive systems that were whipping the crowd into a frenzy, yet deep underneath all the clamour and the increasing beat of his own heart it was as though the music was blaring like a siren, a warning against the mounting risk of being lost in the depths of those too-clever emerald eyes. The man's smirk widened wolfishly, and as he parted his lips, whatever he said next was lost underneath the sound of breaking glass.

"Fuck these fucking shit tunes!" came a drunken wail from one of the uniformed men in the booth nearby, plucking another empty bottle from the dozens on their table and tossing it at the wall to explode in another burst of sound. "Beep boop *bullshit!* Here's a proper bleedin' rhythm for you!"

Looking past his new companion, Renji had a clear view of the other three Uppers braying with laughter, drumming their approval onto the tabletop and tunelessly chanting in indistinct fervour that only built as their apparent leader hefted another bottle.

"Well, shit," Renji sighed, moving to stand— but the stranger's hand settled on his arm.

"Oh please, ignore those idiots. They're hardly worth your time." He shot a disdainful glare in the direction of the rowdy booth. "Look, the owner's here now. It's their problem, not yours."

And sure enough Allegro had burst out of a back door in a flash of agitated silver fluff, marching towards the trouble and donning the grim smile that was the tried and tested battle armour of customer service workers everywhere.

"There, now. All taken care of." The stranger gave a dismissive wave of his glass to indicate it was no longer their business.

"I- I guess." Somewhat relieved, Renji gave in to the warm weight of the hand guiding him back down to slump into his seat. He wasn't certain why he'd tried to get up in the first place; despite his sneaky little takedown on Flood earlier he'd never been much of a fighter, especially against four corporals on his own. Besides which, he found he was losing interest in anything except the motion of the stranger's fingers along the leather of the borrowed jacket.

"Now." The man's hand traced up Renji's arm, a leisurely line that curved upward to hook around his shoulders and draw him closer, "where were we?"

Out of habit Renji found himself glancing around, but again the realisation dawned that no-one in this whole blessed bar cared what they were doing as long as flying glass wasn't involved. Quirking a smile, he allowed himself to give in to the stranger's gentle pull until he was close enough to feel the heat of breath on skin. "Here seems good."

"It rather does, doesn't it?"

Having lost any reason to hold back they drew together into an inexorable kiss, sending a blissful shot of adrenaline coursing through Renji's veins that he had no idea how much he'd needed until that very second. Hands tangled in his hair, holding him steady and close; as if he'd want to be anywhere else in that moment. Despite knowing it was acceptable here, the audacity of kissing a guy so brazenly out in the open was so thrilling he found himself pausing to breathe out a soft chuckle against those shameless lips.

"Something funny?" asked the stranger, a smirk playing across his face once more.

Renji laughed again, running a finger along that perfect jawline in something like disbelief. "It's just been a hell of a night, is all."

"One that isn't quite over yet." The man's voice was low, soft, intense. "If you'd like, you could come with me. It just so happens I have a rather fine hotel room waiting upstairs."

"What, over the club?"

It was the stranger's turn to laugh. "No. I mean…" He pointed towards the ceiling, spreading his fingers. "…upstairs."

Oh. "Gonna guess you don't mean Central Commons."

"Let's just say…" A hand came to rest on Renji's knee. "I could take you much higher than that."

Several things clicked into place at once. The fancy clothes, the pricey cologne, the lack of Commons accent, of *course* this guy was Court. If he were to recognise Renji, things could get awkward, fast. All the same, he had to admit that the thought of sneaking into a cushy Court-level suite made him shiver with pleasure. A hot shower, a soft bed, a wildly attractive partner; more than enough glorious distractions to leave an unfortunate night like tonight far, far in the past. Turn his back, shut that door. *Forget.*

He bit his lip, drew in a breath.

"Y'know, I—"

This time, the sound of smashing glass was accompanied by a scream.

Without pausing to think, Renji leapt to his feet. Stopping to throw out a quick apology, he caught only the briefest glimpse of those handsome features curling in irritation— but had no time to ponder it as he threw himself in the direction of the disturbance.

Beside the Uppers' table, Allegro was unfolding from a crouch and taking a shaky step backwards. They didn't seem to be injured, at least not visibly; their fluffy coat must have taken the brunt of the blow from the tossed bottle, judging by the shards of glass glittering in the beer-dampened strands of faux-fur.

Stepping between the bedraggled bartender and the booth of assholes, Renji went for the play that sprung to mind.

"What in blue hell are you horrible lot playing at?" he thundered, summoning his best impersonation of Sergeant Flood. "Is that any way for the Upper Management of the Forces to behave, eh? I bloody well think not! You lads are a disgrace to the uniform, is what you are!"

Three of the table's occupants had the reaction he had been hoping for; overtaken by the instinctual shame of being caught in the act they were reduced to cadets, cowering and cringing into their seats. One of them, a guy who seemed to be mostly eyebrows, looked like he was about to throw up. A particularly bulldoggish man however, one who Renji recognised as the primary bottle-chucker, drew himself up into a swaying stance that suggested he was a little too pissed to have picked up on the subtleties.

"What's this, then?" jeered The Bulldog, jutting a drink-reddened chin in Renji's direction. "You tryin' it on? We're the fuckin' *Forces,* mate! Who the fuck are you?" The Bulldog swept a beefy arm to encompass the entire club and all of its occupants. *"No-one,* that's fuckin' who!" he spat.

Another Upper, a lanky one with a long, mean face, thumped his glass on the wood over and over in roaring agreement, prompting a braying chortle from the giggler. Even the nervous guy was buoyed by the sheer volume of his companions, the concerned frown ironing out of his huge eyebrows.

"Might wanna speak up, corp," one of them sniggered. "Doesn't look like this one knows much English."

Renji sighed in feigned disappointment. "Listen. Might be you're right. Might be I'm no-one. Or *might* be you don't recognise me because I work in another department. Somewhere quieter. Somewhere out of the way. Somewhere like…" *Pause for dramatic effect…* "Internal Affairs."

The thrum of the beat from the dancefloor seemed to build louder and louder at the mention of the most feared department in all of the Forces. Pausing mid-table-thump, Lanky gave a slow, horrified blink of realisation. Laughing Boy fell silent. Mr Eyebrows seemed to be making rapid progress along the path towards wetting himself.

"Fuck, oh fuck, oh—"

"What did he say?!"

"Shit… Shit, I- I can't take another mark on my record, I *can't*—"

"Alright fellas, let's just call it there, huh?" With a wince Allegro shook the loose glass out of their coat, letting it scatter to the floor unheard beneath the steady increase of Melody's bassline. "Y'all go on home now, and no more needs t'be said to *no-one.* "

The tilt of their head towards Renji on that last note was perfectly unsubtle. A murmur of agreement rose up around the table based on the general principle that getting the hell out of there sounded like a good idea.

"Decent move, slick." Allegro murmured to Renji through the mask of another Customer Service Grimace. "Whose jacket you got there?"

"It's—" Renji looked back towards the booth he'd shared with the stranger. It was empty. "—mine now, I guess." He frowned, fingering the lapels.

But even as three of the panicked Uppers were shuffling to stand and leave, the Bulldog stood his ground.

"Nope." he grunted. "No way this little shit is in Internal Affairs."

Renji chanced a step towards the man, who seemed even larger and redder up close. "Is that really a risk you're willing to take…" He took an exaggerated glance at the numberplate affixed to the man's uniform as though committing it to memory. "…Corporal 2256?"

Unwavering, the Bulldog nodded. "Yeah, actually. It is."

"O-oh?" said Renji, feeling the ground beneath his hastily constructed lie rumble in time with the beat. "And why's that?"

As the music rose to a crescendo of smothering sound, a gleeful leer spread across the man's jowls. "'Cus my dad is the Chief of Internal Affairs."

"…Ah."

A huge hand fastened around the collar of the borrowed jacket, and just as the Bulldog's other paw curled into a meaty fist that seemed quite intent on introducing itself to Renji's face; that was the exact moment that the power cut out, plunging all of Static Void into sudden darkness.

CHAPTER 9

IN THE DARK

The blackout settled in all around the club, making itself at home like an unwelcome guest. A bewildered silence took the place of Melody's playlist, backed by confused muttering as the mob on the dancefloor began to realise that this wasn't part of the show. Soon enough, a small rectangle of light flicked on from somewhere in the direction of the DJ table; Melody's phone, highlighting her frown in the light of her lock screen. The rest of the crowd followed her lead and pulled out their own phones to use the torch setting, lending the room just enough of an ambient glow to give Renji a closeup view of the panicked snarl plastered across the Bulldog's face.

"The hell's going on here?!" he snarled in alarm, staring wildly about the room before settling his accusatory gaze on Renji.

"Like *I* know!" Renji squirmed, trying in vain to get out of the man's iron grasp. "This isn't exactly my idea of a good time either, is it?!"

"If you're trying somethin' funny, I swear I'm gonna—"

"Alright alright, everyone calm down!" Allegro's face was underlit by a retro flip-phone they must have had stashed somewhere in the fluffy depths of their coat. The murmur of confusion quieted to a whisper. "It's just a power cut. Y'all wanna head towards that there green emergency exit sign over there in the corner to get outside, okay?"

Ushered along by Allegro the nervous crowd began to shuffle their way towards the green sign above the door, yet the guy holding Renji by the collar tightened his grip. "Nah, I've seen this shit before!

They're fucking with us, doin' it on purpose!"

Nodding, the others rumbled in the sort of bleary yet assertive agreement that could only come from drunk people at four in the morning.

"This is how they chuck you out when they don't wanna serve you no more!"

"If this has happened multiple times then that really sounds like a *you* problem, buddy." Renji snapped without thinking.

Even in the dull light the flare of drunken rage in the Bulldog's eyes was clear. He had just enough time for a sliver of regret before he found himself being tossed underarm like a ragdoll to slam into the back of a bundle of fluff and shouting that must have been Allegro, the impact bringing them both down to sprawl dazed in the darkness of the concerningly sticky dancefloor.

In a shocked wave of murmuring the crowd parted, turning their phone torches to get a better look at what was happening and half-blinding Renji with their glare as he attempted to disentangle himself from the bartender. Alarming sounds broke out from unseen places— a shriek, an angry shout, what might have been breaking glass— but all he could see were a dozen dazzling lights, framing the advance of a menacing, wide shadow.

"Well, fuck." Renji shuffled backwards as much as he was able, which didn't feel like much at all. "Don't suppose we can talk about this…?"

"Like I wanna hear another bloody *word* out of you." snarled the Bulldog. Behind him, the bleary shapes of the other Uppers swam into view, accompanied by a horrible giggle from Laughing Boy. Was that something in one of their hands? Another bottle, perhaps. In the darkness, it was impossible to tell. Either way, this particular fight felt even less winnable than before.

"A-alright, fair enough!" Lacking a better option, Renji continued to deploy his usual defensive yammering. "No more talking, gotcha! I feel that, really I do, and you've clearly got a plan in mind here, but instead of you having to go to all the trouble of kicking my face in, how about—"

"How about…" A pair of pastel pink platform trainers placed their owner between Renji and the mob. "…you leave this to a *professional.*" That final word came along with a grunt of effort and the unmistakable sound of fist colliding with face. A gasp went up around the crowd as the Bulldog staggered backwards, colliding with his table in a clattering shower of empties and protesting hollers from his colleagues.

Renji squinted up as an unmistakeable lime green denim jacket hit the floor beside him. "Melody…?"

"Nah." A soft thump of material suggested that the hoodie joined the discarded jacket. Now she was without sleeves, the full extent of her cybernetics was visible in the purple-pink glow of a strip of light that ran up a right arm made of plastic and metal, from wrist to elbow. Above the elbow joint was bare, scarred skin over a rippling bicep and strong back that, even in this light, seemed far too toned to belong to the languid hacker Renji could have sworn he'd been talking to all night. Unlike her right arm, her left was made of unscarred and whole muscle all the way along to the wrist, where two of her fingers and most of her hand had been replaced with shining metal and plastic attached to something like a robotic glove. As she cracked her remaining knuckles on her left against the plated palm of her right, in the light of her forearm it was clear the detached and distant smile was gone, replaced by a scowl of barely contained fury that only deepened further under the attention of a dozen phones that seemed to form an arena around her.

"Aren't you lot meant to be pissing off by now?" she addressed the crowd, waving towards the exit sign which featured the traditional little glowing green man doing a runner. "Go on! Get to it!"

The crowd replied with a muttering shuffle of feet that seemed to suggest they'd rather stay for the show, actually, if it was all the same to her. Some of the more enterprising had already flipped their phone from torch to camera.

"Fine. Whatever." she grumbled, dropping into a fighting stance. "Stick a good filter on before you upload it, at least."

And with one neat step backwards, the punch shooting out of the shadows missed her face by inches. Mr Eyebrows, who'd summoned up just enough courage to attempt landing a cheap shot, stumbled forward into the circle of phone lights under the momentum of his wild, missed swing. Underneath his thick brow, he blinked in surprise — then let out a yelp as a mechanical elbow was driven solidly into his back. A murmur of appreciation shot through the club's patrons. Some even applauded.

She rocked on her heels for a moment to regain her balance and curse the platform soles of her shoes, but rallied in an instant. "Two choices!" she barked at the gloom around her, where Lanky, Laughing Boy and the Bulldog must have been lurking. "Either we get this over with, or you follow the little green man and *fuck directly off.* What's it to be?" A howl of anger cut through with the tinkling of broken bottles came bellowing in her direction, and by her pale purple light it seemed as though the corner of her mouth twitched upwards. "Yeah. That's what I'd have picked too."

From the floor, a bewildered Renji felt a shuddering thumping of feet, then a sharp tug at his elbow as Allegro yanked him out of the path of the charging Bulldog, dragging him across the room to the relative safety of the bar.

"Well, hell. This ain't quite how I saw tonight going." Allegro sighed, retrieving something from underneath the bar top. "That's club life, I s'pose."

"Shouldn't we help her?!"

"Oh no no, best not to get in her way, slick." A click sounded out, and a torch sprang to life in their hands. "Cadence has her own way of doing things."

Back on the dancefloor there was a crunch of a nose being flattened by a mechanical palm, followed by the crowd's jeers of approval.

"Cadence?" Renji frowned, utterly lost. "Who the hell is Cadence?"

"Ah. She ain't told you yet, huh. Gee, thanks Melo, I sure do love explainin' *this* one." Sighing, Allegro picked a piece of stray glass out of their coat by the light of the torch and flicked it away in irritation. "That, there…" With a bob of the torch they indicated the woman who was busy elbowing a man in the throat. "…is Melo's sister."

"Sister?" Renji blinked in confusion. "But that's *her*, that's just Melody! Same face, same hair, same cool robot hands, same— Well, she threw away the jacket, but she *did* have the same clothes. Oh, unless—!" Dredging up a vague memory of some terrible thriller he'd seen with Aunty L one bored rainy evening, he snapped his fingers in realisation. "Unless this is like some kinda, whaddya call it! Multiple personality type of thing!"

"Naw, it ain't like that." interrupted Allegro testily. "Cade and Melo, they're whole entire separate people with separate bodies. Or they *were,* anyhow. Still are, just not physically anymore."

"Not following."

"They're two people in one body, y'see? It's kinda like… the rest of us get to have an apartment each, but they're stuck havin' to split rent."

"You're saying they're *housemates?* "

"Yep. And their landlord is a real piece of shit." They gave him a hopeful look. "Don't s'pose you know much about hard drive partitions, do you?"

Renji replied with a blank stare.

"Shame. Look, there's a whole history to it, but it's a long and complicated story and it ain't mine to tell. Main point is; Melo's signed out right now, and Cadence has logged the hell in. Got it?"

Barely. Still, he nodded and placed this information in the rapidly growing mental pile marked *Just Deal With This Later, Alright?*

"Good." With their face underlit by the torch, the smile Allegro shot him seemed particularly grim. "Word of advice, slick. Get on Cade's good side. If you can find it."

Surrounded by cheering dancers in the eerie spotlight of the screens of a dozen phones, Cadence dipped and weaved around the Uppers' furious drunken blows as though moving in time to her own playlist. Another swift jab ensured Laughing Boy wouldn't be giggling at much of anything else tonight, and the press of the jeering crowd parted to allow him to topple backwards out of the fight, leaving the Bulldog with only one friend remaining on his feet. Behind Cadence, a gangly silhouette moved, and just as Renji realised what was about to happen and jolted up from behind the bar to shout a warning, it was too late; Lanky had already made his move, lunging forward to snake an arm around her neck. Struggling in the tall man's grasp, she seemed unable to throw enough power into a backwards blow to wrest herself free, and the Bulldog took his chance for vengeance. Guffawing with triumph, he strode forward and drove a brutal fist into her unprotected ribs.

A gasp rippled through the onlookers as Cadence writhed in pain, snarling out a gasping curse in aggressive Mancunian until another drunken blow caught her on the side of the head.

"Useless fuckin' civvies!" spat the Bulldog, turning to face the crowd. "The fuck's wrong with you, cheering for her?"

The crowd fell silent, shuffling, mumbling.

"The Forces are here to protect you from criminals like this jumped-up little tart!" Facing their cameras, he jabbed a finger towards a spluttering Cadence, pinned with a spindly arm across her throat. "So get them bloody cameras and watch close, you ungrateful shits, and just you make sure an' show everyone what you get for fucking with *the law.*"

"Yeah," snarled Cadence, laying her metallic palm against her assailant's forearm. "Watch close."

And in an abrupt burst of static and a smell of ozone, Lanky let out a scream of shock. A rictus of pain twisted his face and arched his back and already in one lightning-fast second Cadence was throwing off his stiff, useless arm, spinning around to knock him off his feet by delivering a solid hook to the jaw.

An arc of electricity, white-blue and frantic, danced across her left palm as she turned her gaze to her only remaining foe. For his part, the Bulldog managed to throw off his surprise long enough to swoop up a broken bottle, the desperate arc of which Cade slid under with ease, swatting it out of his paw with an effortless swipe while rising in one smooth, clean motion. In a move Renji would have loved to see the slow-mo footage of, Cadence's ascending, unstoppable electric fist caught the Bulldog under his wide chin in a resounding final blow, toppling him out of the crowd's circle and into the welcoming darkness beyond.

Once the filmable fight was over, it didn't take Allegro too long to clear the still-darkened Static Void of chattering, shocked stragglers. The Upper Management cleared out even quicker, slinking away nursing their bruises and muttering darkly about unfair advantages.

"Oh aye, fine advantage I had outnumbered four to one in shoes like *this*, you bag of absolute arseholes." Cadence muttered. She had claimed a barstool to perch on, straight-backed and stern, inspecting the bruise forming on her temple by the light of her phone. "Had she been drinking? Feels like she was drinking." This was addressed to Allegro, who was making their way back over to the bar, still wielding the torch.

"Only the one beer. You know Melo doesn't go too wild if she's at the deck."

"Tsch. Told her not to booze it at all if she's on official business. Proper slows us down."

"You seemed fast enough to me!" Renji shot her a friendly grin, which bounced off an armoured glare. "And in her defence, we really did think the job was over for the night."

As Cade turned to face him, Renji suddenly had a notion of what it might be like to stare down a charging rhinoceros. "The *job,*" she spat, "is never *over.* Not that I'd expect someone like you to know that."

Holding his palms out, Renji took a conciliatory step back. "Woah, alright, back up a sec. I'm tired and I'm messing this up, so lemme take another run at the first impressions thing, yeah?" He extended a hopeful hand and the best, most genuine smile he had in his arsenal. "Nice to meet you, I'm Renji Haya—"

"I already know who you are." Cadence remained unmoved, arms folded.

"Oh. Well, great!"

"You're Imperium."

Finding his own stocks of patience running low Renji tried a different approach, folding his arms to mirror hers. "Alright, I know you only just got here and all, but you missed a whole fuckin' lot back there. It's been a real long night fulla ziplines and gas leaks and guns pointed right at me and whatever, and while I don't know much of anything right now I sure as shit *do* know I'm not Imperium anymore." He stood his ground, a little miffed that the solid bar top between them was ruining the gesture's effect. "If I ever was."

Cadence leaned forward slowly, her expression as serious as a four car pile-up. With great effort Renji forced himself not to back away as she drew uncomfortably closer in the darkness, accompanied by the scrape of metal on metal; her elbow, digging into the bar top.

"Saw the whole thing, mate," she growled, her fury mere inches from his face, "and I'm not exactly what you'd call *impressed.* You think tonight was a long night? Wait til tomorrow. And the day after. And the day after that. And after it's all stacked up, all of those long bloody nights in a row?" Her words were dagger-sharp, aimed at his throat. Unable to help himself, Renji swallowed, nervously.

She let out a harsh chuckle. "Yeah. *Then* we'll see who belongs where." And in a swift movement Cadence had already left the barstool, snatching up her phone and its light to leave Renji alone in the darkness as though he weren't there at all.

"We're done here," she called to Allegro, who had been keeping out of it in favour of attempting to sweep the floors by torchlight. "May as well knock the lights back on."

"Would if I could, darlin'." They shrugged. "I wasn't lying to wideboy back there, this here's a genuine power cut. Take a look outside, half of Steelepool's gone dark."

Cadence tensed. "Shit."

"Could be bad weather, maybe. Or..."

"Fuck."

"You, ah... don't reckon they cut us off, do you?" Allegro fiddled with the broom handle. "I mean, I know they said they would if we didn't pay up but that bill was just stupid-high, no-one coulda paid that much! And if folks don't have power and heat, this time of year-"

"Shitting *fuck*." Cade paused, drawing a deep breath. In the silence as she exhaled, she seemed to draw herself together, placing a steady hand on Allegro's shoulder. "It's going to be okay. Ms Cellanea will know what's going on."

Allegro seemed less certain, but they slid their hand over Cade's all the same, and smiled. "Yeah, she might, at that."

"She will. And whatever's happened, we'll take care of it."

"That, I don't doubt."

Nodding, Cadence broke away from the bartender. "Oi, idiot. Follow me," she barked in the direction of the bar.

With little choice in the matter, Renji did as he was told. In the torchlight, Allegro gave him one last wink as he passed by. "Good luck, slick."

"Thanks. I, uh... think I'm gonna need it."

#

It was odd, Renji thought to himself as he fought away yet another yawn, that what had made him really, truly believe Cadence was a separate person to Melody hadn't been the crazy high kicks or the nasty attitude. It was how she walked.

While both sisters may have carried themselves with a similar air of confidence, Melody had strolled along, taking her time at a fearless, calm pace. A natural born saunterer, that one. Cadence, on the other hand, *marched*. Stiff-limbed and radiating impatience from every pore, the soles of her ridiculous shoes pounding the ground as though she held a personal grudge against each individual centimetre of concrete.

She led Renji through the dimly lit streets without sparing a glance in his direction, and even if attempting conversation would have been a good idea he was far too exhausted to have made a decent job of it. At this point he was pretty sure he'd have given pretty much anything for a decent sleep in a comfortable bed— the same one the handsome stranger had invited him into, for preference— but there seemed to be a stubborn lack of either beds or gorgeous men magically appearing before him.

Forcing back another yawn, he stepped around a pile of abandoned coats on the pavement, and all but leapt out of his skin when they sat up. An old man with lank grey hair framing his face, huddled in as many layers of frayed, filthy clothing as he likely owned, rose to a sitting position from his thin cardboard mattress to peer around the dark streets in curiosity. As exhausted as Renji was, he knew for a fact he'd never been half so tired as that guy seemed, and the sting of guilt at that realisation drove him to keep moving without complaint.

Despite the late hour, the rest of Buried had also blearily begun to realise something was wrong. Confused faces were pressed against dark windows, some bumbling out of their pitch-black apartment buildings by the light of their phones or torches to find their neighbours had already made their way outside and had no more answers than they did. Much like Static Void the various clubs and pubs had turfed out their patrons, who milled about in tipsy bewilderment underneath the dim street lights. Now Renji knew to look for them, he saw other people sleeping on the streets, bundled in layers of coats against the winter chill and roused from their huddles in derelict shop fronts by the commotion.

Concerned murmurings followed them as they wound between buildings, some remaining alive with light, most of them pitch dark. More than one pair of eyes fell on Cadence, full of recognition and hope as though asking her what she planned to do about it. Rather than respond to their silent pleas she continued her grim advance with her own gaze fixed firmly ahead, only faltering when an electronic buzz sounded from the pocket of Melody's retrieved hoodie. Dipping her hand inside she retrieved a hair scrunchie in the same yellow of a highlighter pen and her phone, vibrating away in silent mode. Subjecting the scrunchie to a glare of pure disdain, she slipped it onto her wrist with great reluctance and answered the phone.

"Yes, ma'am. That's right, it's me." Holding the phone between her shoulder and ear, she gathered up a messy handful of hair. "On this side too, ma'am. Looks like everyone on the community bill got hit." Whoever she was speaking to, Renji noticed her responses were clipped, her otherwise broad Manchester accent receding into something plainer. Twisting her long brown-and-teal locks into a loose bun, she listened to the phone for a moment before frowning in Renji's direction.

"...he's still here, but haven't we got more important matters to—" Her expression faltered. "Yes ma'am, of course. Right away."

She secured her hair with the ugly scrunchie, hung up the phone, and turned a sudden, sharp left.

Renji trailed after her warily. "Change of plans?"

"We're going this way."

"Instead of...?"

"The other way."

No further information seemed to be forthcoming.

Without meaning to, Renji squirmed. Something seemed off in a way he didn't like, something to do with the way Cadence kept peering back at him now where she hadn't bothered looking at him at all before the phone call.

But… it was a tense situation after all, so it wasn't as though extra scrutiny would be out of the question. And Melody was still in there somewhere, sharing that body with her terrifying sister; chill, thoughtful Melody, who'd seemed to like him well enough. Perhaps she could talk Cadence down, if that sort of thing was even a possibility. All the same, it wasn't as if he had anywhere else to go, not anymore, not unless he wanted to swallow his pride and go back to Aunty L's. No way, fat chance of *that* happening, thank you very much.

Brushing the stray worries aside, he quickened his pace to catch up to Cadence, and as he drew nearer he spotted something strange; a flash of silver at the nape of her neck, just visible below the messy knot of hair she'd thrown together. A sort of input plug, of the kind he'd seen stuck in the back of a desktop computer, metal and plastic. Embedded into the base of her skull.

A tangle of faded blue hair and blood dragged itself across Renji's skin, and suddenly he had to work very hard to keep himself upright. *A cranial port,* Weaver had called the thing back in that gleaming room, *not professional or kind.* As far as Renji could tell in his limited experience this one seemed much cleaner, edged as it was with healed skin; still, it was far beyond any body modifications he'd seen before. The sight of it turned his stomach.

"You're staring." A suspicious eye glowered at him over a tensed shoulder.

"I mean yeah, obviously." He forced some casual into his shrug. "Never seen anyone tie up their hair with a radioactive lemon before."

120

Scoffing, Cadence turned her gaze back to the street ahead, her stride never faltering. "Save the fashion advice for Melody. She's the one that needs it."

Dropping into silence, Renji lagged several paces behind, trying not to peer too hard at what jutted out of his guide's flesh as Melody's earlier words about the unfortunate, downloaded remains of Kiki floated to the surface of his memory; *It was all just data. Brains, drives, it's only storage.*

With a shudder, he continued to follow one of the strangest strangers he'd met tonight deeper into the unfamiliar city's shadowed heart.

#

It seemed to Renji that while he had no idea where one would traditionally have secret meetings with leaders of criminal gangs, the correct answer was probably not a condemned leisure centre. Yet here they were all the same, passing through long-abandoned corridors whose walls were lined with damp tile, coated in a grimy, sticky film of dust. Even if the floors hadn't sagged like a sponge with every step they took forward, the wood rot would have been obvious from the dank, earthy stench that seemed to seep through the floorboards, intent on besieging the senses of any unfortunate passers-by. As Cadence strode along the halls, the strip light on her arm picked out more depressing details; laminated sheets of paper still clinging to peeling felt noticeboards, and over the flyers advertising years-past coffee mornings and five-a-side clubs and swimming lessons for under tens every Thursday at 6 p.m. was pinned a series of multicoloured A4 sheets printed with care and stuck together to read *Save Our Sports!* Beneath that, in faded felt tip marker pen someone had handwritten a plea for donations towards the upkeep of the Steelepool Leisure Centre, which apparently hadn't been convincing enough.

The sturdy lock and chains that had been removed from the entrance just before their own arrival must have done a decent job of keeping the public out, as there was no evidence of anyone using the place as a shelter or ill-advised party location. There were, in fact, no signs of life at all. Renji pulled the borrowed jacket tight about himself in an attempt to ward off the chill. It didn't quite work.

Cadence led him to a pair of double doors, and before she'd even finished pushing them open the lingering odour of chlorine gave away what sort of place they were heading into.

From the size of the building this pool must have once been a popular destination, yet now it was as abandoned as the rest of the leisure centre. A stark white ceiling curved overhead, its angle accompanied by a huge arched window that took up most of the back wall where night filtered in through its frosted panes. The steady dripping of some unknown leakage served as the only hint of liquid present, the pool itself standing dry and purposeless; a void in the centre of the room, empty and moulding, the paint marking its once bold lanes now barely visible. Shabby rubber rings and other safety devices were scattered on the benches running along the edges of the room, casting shadows onto the pitted stone walls in the light of a small electric lantern sitting on the pool's edge.

A figure rose from one of the benches, drawing herself up to a height not much taller than Cadence's petite frame. Stepping forward into the lantern's soft light came a woman with the kindest face Renji had ever seen. Her skin was a warm, dark brown, lined with just enough age to give her an air of gentle authority, her hair worn with natural curls piled on top of her head in a burst of black peppered with grey. Under her worn no-nonsense khaki jumpsuit she wore a floral blouse in elegant purples and pinks that matched the deep plum frames of her glasses. She would have made the perfect picture of someone's favourite primary school teacher, if it hadn't been for the intricate black tattoos of stylised geometric waves running from below her elbows upwards to vanish under her rolled-up shirt sleeves.

Thankfully, she seemed to be free of weapons, unless you were to count the rather heavy duty thermos flask she had tucked under one arm.

"Thank you, Cadence dear. I shall take things from here."

Cadence's nod of response was so low and emphatic it almost became a bow. The woman chuckled with a shake of her head, slipping on an affectionate smile as easily as one might wear their best coat. Something about that struck Renji as rather odd. Almost practiced. Kind of a Court move, in fact.

Still, no backing down now. "You'd be Ms Cellanea, then." he said.

Her eyes met his with apparent ease as she twisted the lid off the flask. "And you would be Mr… Hayakawa, was it not?" A question that wasn't a question, but before he could untangle that phrasing she'd already moved on. "Coffee? It is only instant, I am afraid to say."

"Nah, I'm good."

"More for me, then." Cellanea retook her place on the bench, cradling the small plastic cup between worn hands, free of jewellery. "You have already met our friends, of course."

Leaning up against a tall stack of children's pool floats and wielding a matching tiny mug was Weaver's unmistakeable tactical silhouette. Fixing Renji with a serious look— the only kind he had, it seemed— he nodded in greeting.

"Alright, copper?" Sugar had taken up a spot on a low diving board, her feet dangling over the empty pool. She seemed in much better shape already; having already found her way into a pair of chunky combat boots, she'd also adopted her prison coverall as a fashion statement, pulling it down to her waist and tying the sleeves in a knot to reveal a cropped shirt and assorted tattoos that seemed to have been placed with no real rhyme or reason. Her cuts and bruises had been tended to and, somewhat worryingly, a short yet vicious little knife flickered in the light as she flipped it between her fingers.

"Alright yourself," Renji greeted her, trying not to stare at the flashing blade. "How's Trig?"

"Not bad. He's off getting patched up at the docs." She tossed the knife to her other hand, and raised a pierced eyebrow. "He looks better than you right now, anyway. You need a *nap,* mate."

"Psh, you're telling me. No sign of your other friend?"

"We are monitoring what we can for any signs of Harlow, but I am afraid nothing has shown up yet, and our resources in that area are, ah… limited." Cellanea sighed, with an apologetic look in Weaver's direction. "To be honest, it was pure luck that we happened to chance upon locating any of our team at all. If Melody had not happened to notice that someone was broadcasting on Harlow's frequency…"

"Ugh..." Sugar shuddered. "Say no more, boss."

"Ma'am, about this blackout," Cadence cut in. "Allegro said maybe we'd been cut off by the power company. Is that true?"

"Of course they said that. God forbid we control the panic somewhat, hm?" Cellanea exhaled slowly, the motion sending the steam from her coffee curling and dancing through the derelict pool's still air. "I awoke Minjun before we left. After much complaint about his sleep schedule, he is looking into it."

Cadence stood straight as an iron pike, ignoring Cellanea's gentle patting to indicate a spare seat on the bench. "So you think they *did* cut us off."

"It is a distinct possibility, yes."

"They can't!" said Sugar, with such force the diving board wobbled beneath her. "I mean, they *could* but… they can't, though! Not in the middle of winter!"

"Dear girl, I am afraid they can and will." Cellanea offered her a sad smile. "As you well know."

"But— but—!"

"Why'd so many places go dark at once?" rumbled Weaver suddenly, causing Sugar to wobble a little more in surprise. "Ain't like you're all on the same bill."

"Actually, we are." Cellanea took in a long gulp of her coffee, savouring it for a moment before continuing. "Some years ago at the behest of our council, much of Steelepool's community made a rather unorthodox agreement with the power company Thermosurge. They enjoyed an exclusive contract to provide every home who chooses to take part with gas and electricity. They also provided us with a particularly large bill. Sharing this equally works out cheaper for all, especially when it is buoyed by any... *donations* that The Loose Ends may procure." At that, a snicker sounded out from the direction of the diving board. Unphased, Cellanea took another sip and continued. "This, my dears, is intended to keep down costs to the individual and prevent those of us who are less fortunate to go without. Or at least it did, until Imperium became aware of what we were doing."

"Why would they have a problem with that?" interrupted Renji. "Why not just let you keep handling your bills however you want?"

"They wish to make a point, I suspect. The line is set, and we are to walk along it as we are told. Though I am quite sure the extra money suits them well also."

"Alright, but what could Imperium even *do* about it?"

"While they did not own Thermosurge, much of the city's energy is provided by Imperium-held companies."

There was a creak as Weaver leaned back, settling into the corner with the pool floats. "Price fixing."

"Mm. That is a bingo, Mr Weaver. It is not a difficulty to raise the prices of a market you mostly own, nor to target one tier of the city specifically. And when the laws that would prevent this are yours also, well..." With a delicate motion, Cellanea drained her cup. "Inutile de discuter. What more is there to say?"

Cadence scowled. "I'd bloody well 'ave a thing or two to say to the pricks—" Looking abashed, she waved away a proffered cup from Cellanea and continued, accent receding once more. "Ah, ahem... No thank you, ma'am."

"Wouldn't that mean Thermosurge woulda had to play along with it? Raise their prices to match Imperium's?" asked Weaver.

"Indeed. And they of course did. No company will leave that sort of money on the table, hm? And then once the prices were at an all-time high, well… I am sure you can guess which company just so happened to acquire Thermosurge this year." Cellanea replaced the lid of her flask, giving it a final, firm twist. "All have paid what they can of this bill of course, but with our own group's resources diminished…" A glance in the direction of the pool, where Sugar squirmed uncomfortably, "we find ourselves unable to raise the extra funds required. Without power, without heat, in the depths of December, well… I am sure I do not need to explain how terribly long a winter this would be."

Shuddering, Renji thought of the people who had been out on the darkened streets, full of confusion and worry. The elderly man he'd seen sleeping on a thin cardboard bed. The full-to-capacity homeless shelter in the park. A long winter, indeed.

"And now you understand the situation," Cellanea said, with a nod towards Cadence, "I am sure you understand why we must resort to such extreme measures."

"Measures?" With a sinking feeling in his stomach, Renji watched Cadence stride back over towards the double entrance doors. "What kinda measures?"

"I believe we would be able to raise the funds we need if we were to, ah… How best to say it?" Cellanea drummed her fingers on the thermos lid thoughtfully. "Yes, this is good phrasing, I think. We shall be requesting a ransom from Commander Starkweather."

"For what?" asked Weaver, with a frown.

She gave a last tap on her lid and looked up at Renji, her smile never faltering. "For the safe return of her nephew."

CHAPTER 10

WELL, SHIT

For a long few seconds the entire hall was silent, save for the echo of that faint, constant, *drip... drip... drip...* until the spell was broken by the solid *thunk* of Sugar's knife driving into the diving board.

"You're her fuckin' *what?!"* she shrieked, and the rest of her words were lost in the sudden clamour; Cadence's hissed threats ran up against Sugar's indignant cries, both ignoring Weaver's pleas for calm. None of that mattered to Renji, however, not while he was so thoroughly pinned by Ms Cellanea's steady gaze.

"When...?" he managed to croak out.

"Immediately, I am afraid. You lie well, Starkweather, but I have done enough research on the commander to know of her family, and there are not so many with the name Renjiro in this city."

"Right. Yeah. That makes sense." He took in a deep breath, and let it out as a curse.

"Your mother was the commander's sister Paige, both rumoured to have been in the same covert Forces squad for a time, though where she is at present, I am afraid I do not know. And your father, Junpei Hayakawa— also not a very hidden name, I am afraid— was a systems security analyst for I.I.'s digital interests, until he was accused of selling data to a rival corporation some years ago and deported back to his native country of Japan. At this point, your aunt Lissa took you in. Do I have this all correct?"

Renji felt his stomach drop. It sounded so much worse, laid out bare like that. Despite the understandable hole in the information about his mother, she had him through and through. What an absolute idiot he'd been.

"I thought… But I could still be useful on your side, couldn't I…?" he said, his voice a mortified waver.

"While I am sure that may be true, dear boy, I fear you may be more trouble to keep than you are to return."

Visibly torn between sticking to her ordered position and leaping forwards to throttle him, Cade's metallic fingers twitched and curled. "I knew it. I knew there was something off about you!" she seethed. "Fuck me, I nearly let a bloody spy walk right into base!"

"A spy? *Me?!*"

"That ain't a spy." With a sigh, Weaver leaned back against the pool floats. Brow creasing, he looked Renji over once more; then shook his head. "He's just a dumb kid."

"Mr Weaver, sir, you can't *know* that!" Cadence began, but she stilled as Ms Cellanea raised a hand.

"At first, I had similar suspicions, Cadence dear, but… I think Harlow's father may be correct. This is only a boy who has waded into waters deeper than he expected."

Renji flinched at her words, but found he had none of his own to counter them.

Rising to her feet, Ms Cellanea brushed the loose dust of the room from her clothes with a finality that suggested their business here was completed. "We shall arrange things promptly, of course. I am quite certain Commander Starkweather will comply."

Heart sinking into the floor, Renji nodded glumly. "Yeah… She will."

"Then let this transaction be a painless one." Her smile this time had a sadness about it. "This is the simplest way that we shall all get what we wish for, yes?"

Ms Cellanea would. Aunty L would too, and since they were likely after no more than a nibble at her vast pension fund, she'd barely be put out at all. What Renji wanted didn't seem to factor into the equation.

Cadence took a deep breath. "Ma'am, we do have one problem." she said. "He's... He's seen your face. *Our* faces. He knows too much."

The way she was avoiding his eyes held far too many implications for Renji's liking. His head began to spin. "H-hang on! I'm not gonna say anything!"

"Cadence..." began Ms Cellanea, her tone a warning.

"Of course you won't!" Cade span around, turning to face Renji with a snarl. "Not until the next time you need a favour from Aunty dearest! That's how you Court types work, isn't it? Well fuck *that*. I'm not going to be some bloody bargaining chip the next time you want a new pony."

"Holy shit." Sugar stared between Cadence and Renji in mounting horror. "Holy *shit* that's cold, Cade! He helped me and Trig break out!"

"And the second we send him home, we'll all be right back in again." She ran a hand across the back of her neck, lip curling. "I dunno about you, but I don't plan on joining Kiki in Allegro's junk drawer any time soon."

"Oh my god, *Cade!*"

Ignoring Sugar's protests Cadence turned to her superior, almost pleadingly. "Look, I- I'm sorry, but *someone* had to have the bollocks to say it!"

"Mm. And say it, you certainly did."

Her face fell at the lack of approval, but she pressed on regardless. "I mean, whatever you say is best, obviously. But you can't say you hadn't thought it too."

Without meaning to, Renji stumbled back a step. He watched Ms Cellanea's kindly face as she surveyed him for a long moment. Too long a moment.

Sickening dread gripped him like a vice, his pulse racing almost as rapid as his mind. Cadence still stood between him and the exit; fast, furious Cadence, whose electric fists had already taken down men twice Renji's size. The only other way out of the hall was a dark archway lined with a couple of doors whose signs had long since fallen away, but even if he could have reached them before Cadence, there was no telling what lay beyond them.

Out of options, Renji opened his mouth in the hopes of piecing together some sort of plea; then slammed it shut again as an abrupt series of thudding crashes sounded, dragging everyone's attention to the far corner.

"Hnh. Sorry." grumbled Weaver, one hand clutching his knee, the other on the displaced container of pool floats that now littered the floor around him. His eyes met Renji's, and the look that passed between them hit like a bucket of cold water. *Run, kid.*

Pure fear ripped straight through exhaustion and before Cadence could turn back in his direction, Renji had already darted for the archway.

His sneakers squeaked on the tiles as he made a break for it, barrelling through the closest door without even stopping to work out where it may lead. A snarl of annoyance sounded from the direction of the pool, the bark of an order, a shocked cry; all followed by the heavy tread of approaching pink platform trainers. Slamming the door shut behind him, Renji realised he'd careened into some sort of changing room lined with nothing more than coat hooks and empty rusted locker cabinets. With no time to think it over he summoned up the sort of terrified strength that only comes along with pure adrenaline, put his back to the wall, and gave a cabinet a clumsy kick, sending the thing crashing down in front of the door. The immediate thud of the door rattling against the makeshift barricade combined with the harsh Mancunian cursing told him two things; firstly that he'd only just made it in time, and secondly that it wasn't going to hold Cadence back for long.

Backing away from the door and trying not to skid on the grime-slick floor, he searched wildly for some semblance of a clever idea. The far end of the room turned a hopeful corner, around which a hint of grubby white tile was visible. A shower room, perhaps? Lacking a better option, he flung himself in its direction, hoping for a miracle; and receiving one in the form of a series of high windows situated above the showerheads, just large enough for a person to fit through, their frosted panes hanging loose in damp, rotted frames.

The crash of the metal locker dislodging from the door sent him scrambling up to the window by way of the shower fixtures before they were able to take enough offense to detach from the wall, and with a quick shove the windowpane tumbled away to smash on the ground below. He squirmed and squeezed in a desperate scrabble to post himself through the too-small space while still holding onto the shoulder bag that contained all he owned; until with one last particularly effective wriggle he managed to work himself free, dropping onto the concrete. Unsure of what else to do next, and too terrified to find out what would happen if he took too long to think about it, he fled into the unknown maze that was the shaded streets of Buried, not daring to look back once.

#

Renji had often heard about the benefits of an adrenaline rush, but no-one had seen fit to mention how incomparably shitty it felt once the stuff wore off. After several minutes of running down blind alleys and similar streets his legs began to give way, turning his sprint into a stagger, his stagger into a stumble, and before long even the stumble gave way into a slump that took him down onto the nearest flat surface he could find.

Hollow and drained, he glanced around in an attempt to make sense of where he'd ended up; a dimly lit backstreet, the kind that sidled along between boxy blocks of concrete flats, their windows empty and dark. It was a cramped and unwelcoming little road, at least it had the decency to be deserted. He'd collapsed onto a set of stone stairs littered with elderly bags of rubbish, leading to a door coated so covered in aged posters and graffiti that it probably couldn't have opened even if it needed to. An abandoned set of scaffolding enveloped the walls of the building, smothering stone beneath a tangle of rusted piping that had been there long enough to become part of the structure, growing over its walls like decaying ivy. Yet the doorway itself was strangely beautiful beneath the mess, an intricate, carved botanical design laid out in chipped stone fashioned by hand and with pride, set into place long, long before Buried had become quite so... well, *buried.* Blearily, he wondered what else had been left hidden away to rot down here under countless boards and fences and broken things.

Either unable or unwilling to stop himself, Renji found himself tipping backwards until he was laid out on the steps, staring up at the twisted metal underside of Central Commons and waiting for the thudding in his chest to slow its sickening pace.

That meeting... hadn't gone how he'd hoped. He had expected a few days, perhaps even weeks to prove himself useful before his little lie wormed its way out, time to settle in, make friends; prove himself to Ms Cellanea, party with Melody, hang out with Trig and Sugar, talk Cadence into tolerating him, maybe even work out what the hell Weaver's whole deal was. Instead, it turned out that had never been an option. This whole time he'd only been setting himself up as a chip to play against his own aunt, one too risky to hold onto for too long.

So now what? Even contemplating that question sent another wave of fatigue rolling over him, heavy as though it were pressing him down into the cold stone beneath his back. Obviously, he couldn't go back to Aunty L's place. That would be unthinkable; just thoroughly humiliating, especially after he'd made such a show of his departure. That meant he'd have no access to the money in his bank account, too, since it had all been hers. And the idea of re-enlisting in the

Forces was out of the question after what he'd seen and wished he could forget...

So what did that leave him with besides a borrowed jacket, a stolen potted plant, and zero ideas?

Renji blinked up at Buried's steel sky as if looking for a clue, but all it had for him were immense ever-changing boards advertising movies, or perhaps brands of beer, or cars? Hard to tell. It didn't matter, though; the blurred words swam too much to be read anyway. All those colours and lights, dotted around the mute grey pillars of skyscrapers piercing the great and terrible structure that was Unity City, all the way up, to the very top of everything.

He hadn't even realised he'd drifted off until he was wrenched awake.

"Well well, look at this, lads! It's Mr Internal Affairs!" came a drunken chortle, bouncing off the street's close walls. As Renji sat up groggily, he could just make out four distinct silhouettes approaching through the darkness; one short, one medium, one tall, and one stocky... rather like a bulldog.

"Ah, *fuck.*" He scrambled to his feet and turned to run— but stumbled, too slow to avoid the wide palm that slammed into his back and sent him toppling back down to the cold flagstones.

"Fancy runnin' into you again, mate!" A regulation boot collided sharply with Renji's ribs. "Just when we thought tonight was gettin' borin'!"

Even if he'd wanted to, he couldn't have held back the yelp of pain as a second heavy kick slammed into his side, all too close to where Flood's sword hilt had caught him only hours ago. The blow left him gasping for air, trapped in the circle of Uppers hooting and hollering in vicious delight.

"Your freak of a robo-girlfriend leave you already?" snorted the Bulldog. "What a shame. Means she won't get to see what we're gonna do to you."

The threat prompted a round of sinister little giggles from Laughing Boy, though he and the others were glancing around in case Cadence was lurking in the shadows.

"W-wait!" Renji rasped, hoarsely. "Y-you don't— you don't wanna do this…!'"

"Pretty sure I do." As if to make his point he booted Renji in the ribs once more, to a fresh round of jeering laughter.

"The commander! Commander Starkweather!" The words came out of him in a desperate babble. "I-I'm her n-nephew!"

The laughter paused. A look of utter horror creased the face of Mr Eyebrows all but in half; yet The Bulldog shook his head.

"Hear that, lads? Not only is he Internal Affairs, he's the bloody commander's family!" He gave an unpleasant chuckle. "S'a wonder he's got the time to be the King of England alongside all that other shit, isn't it?"

With a groan of pure dismay, Renji curled up into a ball, folding in on himself as though they'd leave him alone if he could only make himself small enough. He'd always supposed his various lies would catch up with him at some point, but really, it would've been nice if they'd not done it all at once.

Alongside a backing chorus of encouragement from Lanky and Eyebrows, Renji squeezed his eyes shut as the Bulldog wound back for another kick, this time aimed straight for his target's face—

But rather than the expected crunch of boot meeting bone, a hollow *clang* sounded out. A startling, bright little *donk!* cutting through the still night air, accompanied by a spray of acrid liquid and a yelp. Warily, Renji opened his eyes and peered up to see all four Uppers blinking in shock. From the way they were peering about the empty alley, they had no idea what had just happened either, until they saw it; a half empty beer can lay by Lanky's feet, and judging by the stain on his uniform, it had hit its target.

"What the piss was that?!" The Bulldog roared, in no particular direction.

"Wasn't piss!" shouted a distant voice. "No guarantees on the next one, though!"

A peel of laughter rang out from one of the flats' many windows, and another, and *another,* the sound bouncing from the walls and making its exact origin impossible to determine.

"Fuck off out our street!" came an anonymous cry from another anonymous window, to the general agreement of their neighbours.

"Go home, pigs!"

"Yeah, no-one wants you 'ere!"

Something else arced towards them— a jar of marmalade or perhaps jam— that missed Laughing Boy by inches, smashing into the wall behind them and causing Mr Eyebrows to let out a very undignified yelp. The Bulldog craned his neck upwards to squint at the pitch-black windows of the flats that boxed them in.

"When I find out which one of you threw that…!" But his threat was lost in the rounds of laughter that followed, a chorus that only gained more voices by the second.

"Oooooh, Sherlock says he's gonna find you out! Oh noooo!"

"Cadet Cockhead's on the case of the flyin' jam!"

"Gonna arrest the whole building, tosser?"

And while all four Uppers fumed and threatened and spat curses at their hidden, mocking audience, Renji seized his chance. He scrambled to his feet and bolted, not especially caring in which direction he was heading besides *away.* The aftermath of the kicking he'd just received made itself known at once; an insistent ache thrummed through his torso causing his frantic steps to falter, but the speed of sheer panic alone was enough to carry him out of the alley. Over the pounding of his pulse in his ears he could just about make out the sounds of encouraging whoops from the windows, triumphant calls of *Off he goes!*, and *Run, mate, run!* followed by indignant bellowing as the Bulldog realised his prey was loose.

Tearing blindly through the darkened streets pursued by the sounds of four pairs of uniform boots, not for the first time tonight Renji found himself wishing he had the slightest idea of where he was heading. His phone was still in his bag, but what was he going to do, call the cops? These *were* the fucking cops. As the tightly packed buildings flew by around him he caught sight of something hopeful; a glow of light, not too distant, rising up from a rare clearing between buildings. He threw himself in its direction, past a gate, through a hole in a wall, over a fence; and before long the pavement beneath his sneakers gave way to soil-soft, bone-dry dead grass.

The park. Somehow he'd made it to Temperley Park, and there surrounded by the familiar shape of dozens of darkened fairy lights, right in the central plaza—

With little air left in his lungs, Renji came skidding and crashing into the circle of food trucks, just about avoiding a collision with the fountain. By now the previous handful of customers had cleared out, yet not quite everyone had finished closing up shop. The window of Roti Queen was still open, generator humming away as its proprietor and chilli-based weapons expert Sarasi scrubbed her spatulas clean by the warm light. A few others also remained; the elderly couple that ran the pizza place bagged up trash while bickering lightly, the scruffy-haired coffee-slinger lounged on a bench engaged in the very important twin tasks of chewing gum and checking their phone, and, waiting by Roti Queen and still wearing the Santa hat he had been wearing earlier, glowered the tangle of greasy hair and width known as Chips Darren. Every one of them had turned to stare at Renji, standing breathless and shaking in the middle of the square.

"Oh! Melody's new friend!" Frowning, Sarasi wrung out her cloth and set it down on the newly-scrubbed grill. "What happened to you, boy?"

Despite his best efforts, Renji's knees gave way and he crumpled downwards, clinging to the low stone wall of the fountain as if it were a life raft in the ocean. "I'm- there's—!"

Before he could finish stammering out a reply, the boots that had been following his steps caught up. In an instant, the still night air grew thick with tension as the chefs looked from the uniformed gang of Forces Upper Management to Renji, and did the maths. The Bulldog's lip curled into a sneer and he glared back, sizing each of them up and evidently reaching an unkind conclusion.

"Forces business." He lifted his wide chin, where the fresh bruise from Cadence's fist had left its mark. "Clear the fuckin' way, we're makin' an arrest."

A terse silence hung over the square for long enough for Renji to worry that he'd lost his last gamble, until at last, someone spoke.

"Still on the beat at this time o'night, like? Blimey, you Forces lads don't half work hard." With a heavy sigh, Chips Darren pushed away from the side of the van he'd been leaning against. In surprisingly few strides he cleared the plaza, coming to a stop between the furious officers and the empty water feature Renji was cowering against. Even from behind the counter of the fish and chips truck Chips Darren had been an imposing figure, but now he was out in the open it was as though he'd become even wider; ropes of muscle flexed along thick arms mottled with heat scars from the fryer. He folded those impressive arms across his broad chest, giving every impression of an immoveable brick wall. The novelty Santa hat somehow only added to the menace.

Lanky and Laughing Boy took an instinctive step backwards, but Chips Darren simply nodded a greeting at the shorter Upper, the one with the thick bushy eyebrows. "Alright, Ian. Been a while."

Avoiding his gaze, Eyebrows mumbled something like a greeting, his hint of Welsh lilt matching the chip shop proprietor's own. Chips Darren waved a large, greasy hand in Renji's direction. "Out of interest, what's this fella done, like?"

"Er. Uhm. Well—"

"Impersonatin' Upper Management, for starters. Interferin' with our ability to conduct our duties." The Bulldog leered at Chips

Darren, unintimidated. "And resistin' arrest."

"That so?" Darren peered down at the quaking, battered shape of Renji. "Well, it looks like he's learned his lesson, doesn't it. Whatever it was, you shan't be doing it again, will you?"

With absolute sincerity, Renji gave a frantic shake of his head.

"There you have it." Said Chips Darren, levelly. "Let's leave it at that then, shall we."

The Bulldog started forward. "'ang on, you can't just—"

Ignoring him, Darren nodded towards Eyebrows once more. "Your mum's been asking after you, Ian. I know you're right busy with your *career* and all these days, but you know how Auntie Sue worries when her boy doesn't check in."

"Um. Yeah, Darren. Sorry, Darren." Eyebrows Ian cleared his throat, throwing a pleading look at the Bulldog, who halted in his steps with a hiss of derision.

"There now. All sorted." Apparently satisfied, Chips Darren treated the group to a cold, brittle smile that ran at odds with his pleasant words. "Now, it's late, we're all of us tired and I'm sure you'll be needed back at your barracks or station or what-have-you. Got a lot of important things to do, I'd wager."

"Yeah. We should... We should really go," mumbled Eyebrows Ian, fidgeting for all he was worth. The Bulldog opened his mouth as if to protest, but caught a bony elbow to the ribs from Lanky, who indicated back towards the trucks where Riley sat with their phone out, camera light on. Back within the Roti Queen, Sarasi gave a meaningful tap of her wide, sharp spatulas against the now spotless griddle.

The Bulldog curled his lip as he weighed up his options, then rolled his eyes. *"Whatever,"* he grumbled, turning away. "Dunno why we bother coming down to this shithole anyway." And with a brief, almost apologetic backwards glance from Eyebrows Ian, the Uppers took their leave, retreating back into the darkness of the park.

"Oh my days, they certainly had a try at you, didn't they?" Gently but firmly Sarasi had guided Renji to sit in the open back door of Roti Queen near the warm, humming generator, to inspect his injuries by the amber hued light of her truck. "Looks like no bones broken, lucky boy!"

Renji didn't feel especially lucky at that moment, huddling into the scant warmth of the borrowed leather jacket. Linda, an older lady he remembered as being one half of the pizza truck couple, adjusted her thick-lensed glasses and frowned down at him with concern. "You look proper knackered, pet." Now *that* one, he could agree with.

"Sorry to disappoint, ladies. I promise next time I'll show up looking my best for ya!" He shot them both one of his best grins, leaving Sarasi chuckling and Linda a little flushed. "For real, though... thanks. For the help."

He'd meant to address the square at large, but his gaze had fallen on Chips Darren, who'd hunched over a seat at one of the bench tables. "I- I, uh, appreciate it."

The big man answered with a shrug. "S'nothin'."

Renji thought for a moment. There was something he'd been turning over in his mind for a while now, and it seemed like the only chance he'd have to ask. "Look, um... There's this one thing I wanna know. Earlier, when I was round here with Melody, you knew I was Imperium right away. How?"

Chips Darren regarded him. "You really want to know?"

He squirmed, dreading the answer. "Yeah."

Darren clicked his tongue, and nodded at Renji's shoulder bag. "Had a bit of a clue, like."

Renji looked at his bag, with its Imperium blue stripe and blindingly obvious branding. "Oh." He said, then "Ah." Followed by "Alright." Then he sank his head into his hands and deflated into a puddle of idiot.

"Back there, that was the cousin you mentioned, Darren? Your auntie's boy?" Sarasi asked, her disapproval clear.

"Yeah. Don't get me wrong, like, he always was a toady little shite, but since he joined up he's been a real prick to his mum and dad. Acts like that stick up his arse makes him better than us."

Next to him on the bench Pizza Van Pete tutted, his feet resting on the trash bag he'd previously been in the process of throwing out. "Ach, that's just how it is, mate." he sympathised in a Newcastle patter. "Any bastard what joins up t'the Forces reckons they're a wee big man all a'sudden. Then they've nee time for them that raised 'em."

"Little bastard said he's *elevating* himself." Darren's heavy brow creased into a scowl. "He can elevate right off the edge of the Court, like."

A coffee appeared in front of Renji's face, jolting him back to life.

"It's black." Riley told him, in whisper-quiet Scots-tinged tones, tapping the paper cup with a chipped, black painted nail. "Ran outta milk. Hope that's alright."

Before Renji could reply the coffee had already been pressed into his hands, its deliverer scuttling back to the safety of their bench. Usually he took coffee with more milk and sugar than actual caffeine, but right now it was a gift from heaven no matter the dairy content. He managed to stutter out a word of thanks toward Riley, though they had already pulled out their phone and hidden behind it. Taking a cue from them, he sunk back into the food truck's doorway where he could stay hidden for a much needed quiet moment, sipping his bitter coffee and trying not to think about how utterly screwed he was.

"Right then. Still want walking home, Sarasi?" rumbled Darren as he rose from his seat.

"You know I'd never turn down your company." she giggled, pulling on a thick woollen jacket. Linking her arm in Darren's with a playful little curtsey, Sarasi leaned in and lowered her voice. "Though we'd better get Ms Cellanea's new recruit back down to her." Her gaze turned upwards, past the strings of dead lights and towards the darkened, freezing skyline of Steelepool. "I have a feeling she's going to need all the help she can get to fix this one."

"You're not wrong." Sighing, Darren pulled a smudge-screened phone out of his pocket. "Pete, Linda, do us a favour and keep an eye out for those lads coming back." The couple nodded in the affirmative, though Linda's squawk of outrage as she spotted the trash bag that still hadn't found its way to the bin and the subsequent bickering that followed suggested they may not be the most attentive lookouts.

"I'll just give Mel a ring. She can come pick her lad up, like."

Hidden in the doorway, Renji clamped a hand over his mouth to cover the sound of the coffee he'd just inhaled into his nose; then quietly, reluctantly, he pulled himself up on shaking legs and slipped away from the warmth of the food court to flee once more into the bleak darkness.

#

The sun hadn't quite risen yet, the thin grey night still clinging to the skies as long as it could. It occurred to Renji, in a bleary sort of way, that what with Buried's construction-choked skyline and the low forbidding metal ceiling, he had no idea if the sunrise was even visible from all the way down here.

Thanks to the coffee his feet were still somehow dragging him forward, though where forward may lead to he had no idea. Not a single good destination came to mind; none, except for his warm and comfortable bed back in Aunty L's apartment. Probably at least two cats would have taken up permanent residence on it, but that didn't matter. Right now, he would fight any number of cats for a mattress as soft as that.

In an attempt to keep himself awake he began to make a mental list of which exact parts of him felt like shit, starting at his aching feet which were protesting every lurching step, following up to his bruised ribs that were howling their discontent, and finally to the welt on his jaw that was beginning to make itself heard among the clamour. Even his shoulder had begun to lodge some strongly worded complaints on the topic of having to carry around his goddamn bag all night.

Far too lost in the foggy depths of exhaustion to even begin caring about GPS signals and evading tracking and trails and other paranoid nutso bullshit like that he unslung his bag and dug out his phone, the last lifeline he had to anything he knew. As he did so, a waft of some delicious scent teased by his nose, something peppery and exciting; that beautiful stranger's cologne, still clinging to the lining of that cherry red jacket and bringing with it a memory of warm lips, fingers threading through his hair, and enthralling hints at the sort of night he bloody well *could* have enjoyed if he'd only minded his own fucking business.

Without fanfare, the phone booted up. No new messages.

Though he had no clue what result he'd been hoping for, Renji's heart sank all the same. Peering up from the empty screen he found that his feet had brought him right back to where he'd entered into this whole fucking mess, into this horrible midnight-dark town with its dead grass parks, trash-strewn streets and abundance of arseholes trying to kick his head in on every corner. Above loomed the bulk of Portside Inns Station, the lights along its grimy length still shining in the surrounding darkness all the way up to its polished counterparts in the Court. As alive, active, and in order as ever.

Much like the ID on his phone that would let him take the elevator out of this nightmare.

The look Melody had given him was slow and considered, as though she guessed it might end up somewhat like this. "They didn't want you to know. But now you do." she'd said, without judgement. "What you do with it is up to you, mate."

She'd said he was a good liar. Lying to yourself couldn't be so difficult. And so, shouldering his bag and swallowing his pride, Renji went home.

CHAPTER 11
A RUDE AWAKENING

He woke up at 2 p.m. with a headache and a cat standing on his hair. An attempt to roll over and disappear into the soft, welcoming sheets was thwarted before it even began by the considerable weight of a second cat sitting on his chest. Inches above his face, two big blue eyes blinked down at him guilelessly.

"Harps, you lil fucker." Renji mumbled at the interloper. "Does it *look* like I've got any food?"

Undeterred, Harpier mewed and began to knead his paws on both pillow and hair alike in an apparent attempt to make the lack of food more the human's problem than his own. Grumbling, Renji pushed the little seal point scrounger away so he could embark on the much more complex feat of getting out from underneath the hulking form of Grimalkin, a mighty beast who was snoring the afternoon away safe in the knowledge that her nice warm mattress wouldn't dare move under threat of a thorough chomping. Deciding he'd had enough injuries for one week, Renji settled on his usual anti-Grim technique of sweeping up both cat and bedding into one outraged bundle and depositing it gently onto the floor. A furious flat face framed in perfect ivory fur poked out of the duvet to spit and hiss, but it was too late; her prey was out of clawing range. Rather than admit defeat, she took the usual feline measure of curling into an implacable circle, settling in as though this had been her plan all along.

Left alone to stare up at the room's high ceiling, Renji found himself having some regrets about sacrificing his duvet. It seemed, at least, that the night's rest had lowered yesterday's aches and bruises from a boil down to a simmer. He was still wearing at least some of yesterday's clothes, and the way his jeans and the borrowed red leather jacket were hanging on a desk chair rather than on Renji himself suggested he'd probably struggled out of them before collapsing into bed, though the memory of doing so had vanished. That wide balcony window, still just about reachable from the outside by a quick shimmy up and along the garden's prize imported Indian sandalwood tree, was now shut tight against the December draft despite having been left obligingly unlocked during the night. On his bedside cabinet stood an expectant glass of water, and a packet of paracetamol.

While the heavy colour-block blinds did their best to prevent it, the clear grey light still filtered in through the room's huge windows, scattering along the stark white walls. On one of the windowsills sat the potted plant he'd inexplicably taken with him on his exit from AirCast Two; perhaps a little worse for wear and missing a few leaves, yet as alive as ever. Despite having reached the sunny spot it so clearly needed, it still seemed to not quite fit the space, standing out as an awkward burst of ragged colour against the perfect, spotless backdrop of the room.

Aunty L's brutal minimalism had somehow always managed to win out over Renji's ability to make a huge mess, though how that actually physically *happened* was something he'd never considered until now. She hired cleaning staff, right? He seemed to recall something about a maid or two. Having spent so little time in the apartment in recent years he'd never got around to thinking about it, let alone meeting one of the people who kept the place together. Looking at his jeans and jacket, neatly folded and placed on the chair by hands that were all but invisible to him, he was reminded of the tired, drawn faces he'd seen coming down on the elevator yesterday. At least one of them had been an older lady wearing what may have been a cleaner's tunic, all wrapped up in a quilted coat whose shiny, cheap fabric reflected the city's lights as they'd descended to Steelepool. He wondered if she'd been one of those who would have woken up this morning to a house with no electric or heating.

With a shiver that had nothing to do with the cold, he downed the painkillers and rolled out of bed.

Staying in the shower all afternoon seemed like a viable idea for the first thirty minutes, after which hunger kicked him out of the underfloor-heated comfort of the bathroom and steered him in more of a kitchenwards direction. Despite Harpier's best and loudest efforts Renji managed to dance all the way down the apartment's long corridor without once treading on anything feline, until he was brought to a sudden halt just before the kitchen door by a horribly familiar voice.

"No. Absolutely *not.*" A clinking sound rang out from the direction of the kitchen, perhaps a cup or a spoon, followed by a sigh so loaded it was at risk of collapsing under the weight of its own exasperation. "We're both busy women, captain. I'm sure you'll understand that if I am forced to repeat myself once more, matters will go extremely poorly for you."

Ah. Aunty L was working from home today. That made things a little more awkward. Still, as cavernous as the apartment was, he couldn't hide from his aunt forever. Plus if he wanted something to eat— and he very much did— there was no other option. Carefully, he inched open the saloon-style doors, and crept through.

Always a fan of being able to see everything all at once, Aunty Lissa had designed her apartment to be as open plan as possible. The kitchen, dining room and living room all shared the same large space, one made bright and airy by the huge, impressive windows running from floor to ceiling. Sleek modernity dominated the room, from the perfect pale leather sofas to the glossy, pristine kitchen fixtures. The majority of the reclaimed driftwood coffee table was taken up by massive and well-arranged hardcover books of modern art, the insides of which Renji suspected had never seen the light of day. Above the wide faux fireplace with its ivory and cream marble surround hung a pair of elegant crossed swords, the ornamentation on their basketed hilts so fine it almost looked like silver lace. If it weren't for the somewhat ratty yet beloved cat tree in the corner and the half-empty tray of takeout sushi left on the breakfast bar, the place could have sprung right out of the pages of a home styling magazine. No Christmas decorations were present, which wasn't a surprise.

Sitting at the glass dining table with a phone in her hand and a scowl on her face was Aunty Lissa herself, wearing her traditional *the commander gets to work from home whenever she says she gets to work from home* outfit of leggings and a faded Unity University T-shirt, her short blonde hair more ruffled and spiked than its usual uniform-ready sleekness, that rarely seen scar of hers disappearing underneath the shirt's neckline. A pair of frameless designer reading glasses was perched on her nose, and her non-phone hand was buried in the soft ginger fur of Paddock, the stupidest and most beloved of her three cats, who was sprawled out over her work laptop and purring like a contented motor. Nearby sat a mug, tragically empty of coffee.

"Perhaps I'm not speaking clearly enough, captain," Aunty L enunciated each word to within an inch of its life. *"No* seems like a simple enough word to me, but if you're having trouble understanding its complexities I'm sure I can be along shortly to demonstrate them for you."

Not wanting to risk being caught in the crossfire Renji made his way across the kitchen as quiet as possible, targeting the sushi tray; but before he'd even made it halfway there his aunt had spotted him, throwing him a wink over her shoulder. By the time he'd mustered up a weak smile in response, she'd already returned her attention to the phone.

"Yes, that's the ticket. Glad to hear you agree, captain. I knew you were smarter than they said." Her words and smile were laced with the same brittle ice. "Take care."

With a precise stab of her finger and a tut she ended the call, then turned her attention to Renji, her expression growing more genuine. "Hello, trouble. Was beginning to think you'd sleep all day. Help yourself to lunch, if you're not too hungover for fish."

"Y-yeah, thanks." He dipped into the paper bag from the upmarket takeout sushi place Aunty L favoured, pushing aside far too many napkins until he found a spare pair of chopsticks.

Lissa snatched up her mug— her favourite, the *World's Okayest Aunt* one Renji had made for her some years ago— and frowned at the lack of coffee within. "So!" she said brightly. "Any chance you wanna talk about what you got up to yesterday? No need to tell me about whatever party you ended up at of course, but we should probably talk about the way you left."

"Uh…"

"No rush, Peanut, you tell me whenever you're ready." Paddock let out a mewl of complaint at the sudden lack of fuss as Aunty L left the dining table, mug in hand. "Whatever you did, it sure as hell riled up that sergeant of yours."

"Guess he was kinda pissed, huh?"

"Face like a baboon's arse, yes."

At the thought of Sergeant Flood's face and the murderous look he'd last seen stretched across it, Renji winced and busied himself with poking through what remained of the sushi tray. As expected, all of the sashimi was long gone. "So… What exactly did the sarge say?" he asked, experimentally.

Aunty L rolled her eyes and poured herself a fresh cup from the coffee maker, the only appliance in the kitchen that saw regular use. "He had rather a lot to say, though most of it sounded like utter tosh. Some bullshit about explosive helium, or something? Not exactly our best or brightest, that one."

Renji said nothing, concentrating on the food in front of him as though the nigiri was about to do something fascinating.

"Oh, and he also claimed you stole a sword of his. Any comment on that?" she asked.

Ah, now they were on better ground to plant a lie. "Aw, c'mon, Aunty L." He snapped up a piece of salmon, popping it into his mouth with a shrug. "What the fuck am *I* gonna do with a sword?"

That earned Renji a small chuckle; his total lack of interest in duelling and fencing was just another thing that set him apart from the rest of his mother's family. Aunty Lissa had always excelled at swordsmanship and was rarely seen in public without her own blade at her hip, and Renji's own mother had been even better, but given how that whole thing had turned out he couldn't say he found the fact especially inspiring.

Lissa slid him a mug loaded with milk and sugar and a trace amount of coffee, then took a seat opposite at the breakfast bar, her eyes twinkling. "Oh go on, you can tell me. Was it that one he's always carrying about, the championship sabre with the big ugly golden guard? You *have* to tell me if it was that one, I always wanted to see how badly balanced that thing was."

He speared some tuna maki and gave his chopsticks a dismissive wave. "I swear, I don't have the stupid sword." Truth, technically. "Silly bastard probably just left it in his golf bag or something." Lie, absolutely.

"Tut tut." Amused, she raised a thin eyebrow. "Is that any way to talk about your Upper Management?"

"You're the one who said he was an idiot." he grumbled around a mouthful of rice.

"Ah, but that's one of the benefits of being *the* Upper Management." Aunty L regarded her nephew for a moment before shaking her head with a contented sigh. "Still, like I always say, you're old enough now that I don't need the details of whatever it is you get up to. The important thing is that you're back home in one piece, despite your former sergeant's best wishes." She ruffled his hair fondly. "We'll work out what comes next later, huh? Maybe after New Year."

Swallowing awkwardly, Renji couldn't help but wonder why this was going so damn *well*. Bending the truth around Aunty Lissa had always been a trickier prospect than most; ever since he could remember, she'd been sharper than her sword and twice as cutting.

Yet, she'd also been a casual enough guardian that he'd not had to make the attempt too often, and they'd settled into a comfortable, unspoken routine of half-truths and questions gone unasked, a ritual which seemed to be holding up despite last night's events being rather more questionable than Renji's usual.

Something twisted in his guts, something that had little to do with the scavenged sushi.

A jingle of bells heralded the arrival of Harpier clambering onto the kitchen counter, his little black nose scrunching with interest in the direction of the fish. Aunty L gave the cat an indulgent smile and a scratch behind the ears. "Though, I do have to wonder... I only ask because something seemed to go wrong with AirCast Two's cameras, but those prisoners, the three that made their escape at the same time as you were having your... *incident.* You didn't happen to talk with them at all, did you?"

"N-not really." Renji poked at another piece of salmon nigiri, scattering loose rice around the tray. "Not much, I mean."

"Ah. So you *did* talk to them, at least a little."

The unfortunate nigiri had all but fallen in half. "Well..." he began, slowly picking up the mauled piece of sushi as though it might offer him a better answer than the ones he had. "We ran into each other, yeah."

"They didn't happen to mention anything interesting, did they?" Aunty L continued, resting her chin on her hands with a serene smile. "Particularly, anything about the little gang they work for. It'd be really helpful if you could remember any specifics for me, Peanut. Perhaps a name or two, hm?"

While Harpier's rapt gaze followed the salmon, the look Renji's aunt was giving him was twice as intense. Suddenly feeling a little nauseous, he set down his chopsticks.

"Nope, sorry." Renji replied, picking the salmon off the rice. "Wasn't paying much attention, I guess."

He tossed the piece of fish towards Harpier, where it vanished in a flurry of small white teeth and fur.

Her mouth a thin line, Lissa regarded him for another long moment. "Ah well. Perhaps something will come to you, in time." She relaxed and took a sip of her coffee. "Hell, for now I'm just glad you've given me an excuse to avoid tonight's godawful Christmas party."

"Aunty L, you're the boss. You don't need an excuse, just tell 'em to shove it."

"Oh please. It's only good manners to reel out some line of bullshit or another, especially for charity events, and you, nephew dearest, have given me a particularly good one. How about I find us a movie to watch tonight? If we dig past all the stale Christmas shit there's probably something worth a laugh in there. Maybe one of those cheapo alien movies with the crap effects and fake guts flying everywhere." She grinned over her coffee at the thought. "You up for pizza? Tonight feels like a prime candidate for pizza night."

Enjoying a stupid movie and a greasy takeaway dinner with Aunty Lissa sounded like just what Renji needed, and it almost felt like an option he could happily take, except... A memory of blood-matted blue hair caught up with him once more, and the knots in his stomach gave way to a deep hollowness that he knew wouldn't go away until he asked.

"Listen, I, uh... I gotta know something. About the airship." Renji fixed his hands around his mug, more to stop himself fidgeting than anything else.

"Oh? What about it?"

"I- I mean, you'd said it was a secret prison and all—"

"Ah-ah." she waggled a finger. "Monitored containment facility."

"Sure, yeah, whatever. But— and I know I wasn't meant to go there, but... at the back, there was this room, with this machine..."

"Ah." The playful tone dropped away, concern knotting her brow.

"Yeah." His gaze flicked back down to his mug, and held there, as he forced the words to come fumbling out. "And last night, I saw… On it, *attached* to it, there was this, this person, and she… she…"

"Renji." She leaned in, her voice soft yet insistent. "Renji, dear. Let me stop you there."

"But she was *dead."*

"Yes, well." Aunty Lissa placed her own mug down with a sigh. "That's an unfortunate side-effect of the Limbic Imagers that we haven't quite worked out yet."

Renji had thought he couldn't have felt worse. He'd been wrong. "The- the *what?* You know about those?!"

"Peanut… Of course I do." Knotting her fingers together, she faced him across the breakfast bar with the air of a teacher explaining something to a particularly slow student. "I oversee everything the Forces does, even the more unpleasant aspects. I assure you, no-one takes any joy in it, least of all me. Solutions like this are simply a necessity that we need to employ every so often in the name of keeping the peace."

"Necessity?!" His coffee mug hit the counter so hard the cat sprang away. "They hollowed out her brain! Fuckin' pulled out all of her insides and just *left* her there, on some table, alone!"

"I know it might seem a little cold, but that was a criminal, Renji. A dangerous one, at that. The Forces needed more information about her group in order to prevent further incidents. Save *lives. "* Her smile was sad, almost wistful. "I forget how young you are, sometimes. I know this feels like it's all a little much, but one day you'll understand that certain unpleasant things simply need to be done so that the rest of the city can thrive and grow. As the ones who have to deal with the sharp end of things, we need to use all of the tools at our disposal, and the Limbics are simply a cleaner, faster and far more accurate method of extracting the knowledge we need to do our jobs."

Renji didn't want to ask what method they'd replaced. "All they did was hijack the fucking telly, how does that make her dangerous enough that she had to be murdered?!"

"Murder is a rather loaded word, isn't it? Not one we tend to use." She patted his hand. "Look, it's no problem. I'll make sure you're posted somewhere a little safer next time, yeah? Something more low-key."

Renji stared at his aunt in horror as she took a sip of her coffee. "Just stop looking and forget about it, that's what you're saying?!"

"Really, Peanut, you need to let this go. You'll understand in time, there's no use in taking on sympathy for every last delinquent you see, or you'll never get anything done. That girl had made her choice to break the law, and the consequences were hers to deal with, not yours."

He drew in a sharp breath. "Kiki."

"I—" She frowned. "Sorry, what?"

"That girl. Her name was Kiki."

"Oh." A shoulder raised in a shrug. "If you say so."

"You… You had her executed, and you didn't even know her name." The chair squeaked across the hardwood floor as he pushed away from the counter. "Hey, you know what? Fuck this. I'm going for a walk."

"Do what you gotta do, Peanut. I'll see you later." Aunty Lissa pushed her glasses back along the bridge of her nose. "Though… One last thing, before you go."

Halting in the doorway Renji turned back to face his aunt, and wished he hadn't. The glint of scrutiny in Lissa's eyes was one he'd seen before on occasion; whenever he'd gone a little too far, broken something too expensive, gone a bit overboard on a night out where someone could have recognised him. The same look she'd aimed over the side of the skydock only hours ago.

"That man, the one who broke into AirCast last night after the prisoners were brought aboard. The footage of him had been erased from the cameras, but I saw him. I saw him with *you.* And I need you to think very carefully before you answer this one." While the commander's smile was calm and steady, her words were nothing less than an order. "Who was he?"

Luckily, Renji had never quite got the hang of following orders. "No idea, Aunty L." he said over his shoulder as pushed the door open. "Guess neither of us are much good with names today, huh?"

#

Making a dramatic exit had seemed like a good idea at the time, until it quickly became apparent that it left him trailing through the winter streets, cold and pissed-off, with nowhere in particular to be. At least he'd remembered to bring a coat this time.

Despite the early hour the sun had decided to clock out for the day, slipping behind the drab grey clouds and sneaking towards the horizon before anyone could notice what it was up to. The grey afternoon was something of a pity; it'd been months since Renji had been among the gleaming spires of Imperium Court, which had always looked their best in brilliant sunlight. Still, even on a dull day the Court was a sight to behold, standing tall and proud with each block of buildings a deliberate, neat row carefully placed to craft the perfect skyline. Large-scale works of modern art dotted the streets, yet every one of the soaring towers was a work of art of its own, each a display of sublime cutting-edge architecture packed to the reclaimed antique rafters with luxury boutiques, hotels, and condo apartments, all glassy grace and razor-sharp angles seeming to pierce the very sky. The tallest of all, and home to the city-state's central government, was Panopticon Tower; an immense cylindrical pillar which pierced the very heart of Unity City, running through Buried and Commons to emerge in the Court as a glittering centrepiece of a citadel. From the opaque crystalline plate that served as the tier's ground to the very tip of Panopticon, Imperium Court was, to quote the city's Tourist Experience Primer app, *a shining beacon of the future, and a monument to modernity and progress.*

Since Renji had been here last the famed Christmas displays had been brought out in full force, with hundreds of rows of elegant ice-blue lights arranged in beautiful delicate snowflake patterns strung between the streetlights, lining the roads and bobbing in the lightly salted coastal breeze. In no mood to care about any of that Renji picked through the modest midday crowd of leisurely shoppers and hustling executives until he spotted what he was looking for—the leafy, arched entrance to one of the Fringe Gardens.

The gardens ran around the edge of the Court to encircle the whole tier in what the Tourist Experience Primer app called *a bright emerald spray of foliage, the manicured flowerbeds and grassy plains a welcome breath of fresh air in the bustle of the city.* Right now though, it was nice and quiet, which was all Renji needed it for. This close to both the city's hundred-storey high edge and England's coast, the winds could become harsh when they had a mind to do so, driving away most of the park's potential visitors, leaving it an empty spot in which someone could have a real good mope.

As soon as Renji cleared the gate he headed straight off the path, towards the line of trees running up against the thick wall of reinforced safety glass that was the Court's great rim. Enough wandering brought him to the sort of a tree that a guy could really slouch against, and as he did so he let his head drop backwards to hit the bark with a quiet *thunk.* Some scouting of the pockets of his winter coat turned up a crumpled cigarette packet with a few remaining smokes, and while the Tourist Experience Primer may have had strong sentiments about smoking in the otherwise pristine Fringe Gardens it was only an app and thus powerless to stop Renji from moodily lighting one up.

He'd never considered himself to be a stupid person; nevertheless it hadn't been until the words *Limbic Imagers* had left his aunt's lips that he'd even considered she would have anything to do with them. The idea that cool, fun Aunty L even existed in the same universe as those nightmarish machines hidden away in blood-stained back rooms felt alien, wrong.

But… How could she *not* know? She was in charge. Head of the Forces, overseer of the whole operation, and every grisly little detail that entailed.

Until now, nothing about his aunt had driven him to leave the apartment, overcome with that same sick unease he'd felt looking at Sergeant Flood's hand-carved antique desk. Until now, he'd never known the cost of what she did all day. Until now, it had never been quite so *real*.

He hadn't met Kiki. All he knew was that once she was branded a criminal, she had been reduced to something less than human, someone who had to be held accountable for her actions. Yet no-one seemed interested in holding Imperium accountable for theirs.

No-one up here, at least.

Perhaps that had been why he'd held back on telling her about his meeting with Ms Cellanea and The Loose Ends. How long could he string along that particular lie? Cadence's snarl of anger rose up in his mind, *Not until the next time you need a favour from Aunty dearest,* she had said. *That's how you Court types work, isn't it?*

Shivering, Renji took a harsh drag on the cigarette and thumbed through his phone, seeking out a distraction. To his surprise, there was little to no coverage of the massive blackout in Buried; only a brief news article mentioning a number of homes had been left without power last night due to an "ongoing payment dispute". A quick scan of social media turned up some pleas from people with dwindling phone batteries and no ability to recharge them, drowned out by messages of derisive scorn for those Buried scroungers who were now reaping the results of a failure to plan their budget. For a moment Renji was so preoccupied with tapping out a reply with an anatomically impossible suggestion about where they could shove their budget, he almost failed to notice someone calling to him from the direction of the path.

"—excuse me, sir? Mr Starkweather?"

"Huh?" Renji looked up from his impending ban to see someone picking their way through the trees in his direction, hopping across the muddy carpet of leaf mulch with the gait of a person who knows exactly how much their shoes cost.

"It *is* you, I thought it was!" The young besuited man with the bland face seemed only vaguely familiar to Renji, though he was beaming as though they were long-lost friends reunited at last.

"Um. Sorry, do I know you?"

"Haha, of course, I wouldn't expect you to remember, Mr Starkweather. We met at your Aunt's birthday do last year?" His smile was a strained blend of anxiety, hope and apology that was becoming rather difficult to watch. "I'm Jeremy, from Marketing? In the event planning team?"

Renji blinked, bewildered. "Okay…?"

"So how's your aunt doing? Good, I hope? I'm sure she's very busy, haha, though aren't we all at the moment, eh? Holidays, am I right? Haha!"

"Oh. Yeah, right." sighed Renji, shifting from confusion into a more familiar state of low-key annoyance. While most of the people working for I.I. were just trying to pay the rent and get by, it had more than its fair share of climbing little bastards who'd step over their own grandmothers and anyone else's if they thought it might get them ahead. Many took the offensive approach, like Probably-Simmonds and his notebook, but from time to time this other sort would pop up instead, the type who'd seek to get in good with the commander via her young and hopefully impressionable nephew, and would have no problem with dashing across the length of a park to give it a try.

That was why the guy seemed familiar; he'd met dozens of Jeremy from Marketings before, all brimming with that same nervous too-much-coffee energy and spending every last iota of it on seeking out a quick path to success by any means necessary. Usually he'd pretend to listen if only to play along for his Aunt's sakes, but since this particular Jeremy from Marketing had turned up on a bad day, Renji took a long wordless drag on his cigarette and waited for the conversation to die of natural causes.

Unfortunately, Jeremy from Marketing seemed determined to keep the dialogue shambling along. "Will she be coming tonight, do you think? The commander. To the Christmas party, I mean?" His eyes followed the lit cigarette end, straining with sheer desperation to not mention just how considerate he was being to overlook this breach of the gardens' no smoking policy. "She, ah, never replied to the invitation email, too busy I'm sure haha, but we really did put an awful lot into it this year, I'm sure she'll be impressed! It'll be a real return to form after the other month's, ah… unpleasantness, yes?" A twitch of unease at the memory of the broadcast and the chaos it left in its wake was snuffed out as soon as it began. "And, ah, if you happen to notice the table centrepieces in particular, that was little ol' me, haha!"

In the face of Renji's total lack of engagement Jeremy from Marketing bravely soldiered forward, bombarding the wall of silence with full-force minutiae about the party arrangements, reinforced by volleys of insincere chuckles. "The hotel that's hosting us this year is simply divine, too! Such a fabulous setting, all these incredible views over the coast, and the food is just to die for! It's that new hotel Il Coccodrillo, have you heard of it? You know, they actually have a real live *crocodile* there? Isn't that just so quirky? Fun, but with that little added soupcon of *danger,* yes? The top brass and their kiddos will just adore it, won't they?"

The amount of questions that the man could ask without waiting for an answer was rather impressive. Without realising what was happening, Renji found himself so caught up in the flow of constant inquiry that he gave a slight nod; a mistake he realised the instant he made it.

Renewed by the distant glimmer of engagement, Jeremy from Marketing plunged ahead cheerfully. "Yes, that's right! And of course, we'll be giving a record-breaking amount to charity again! So good to do that, don't you think, especially at this time of year, haha! And did I mention the food? Oh the menu is just *incredible,* the starter will be a light little number from—"

"Which charity?" asked Renji.

"Beg pardon?"

"The whole big money rah-rah donation thing. You're doing the usual, yeah? With the Santa sleigh and that." It had been the same performance every year, ever since Renji could remember; some lucky interns dressed as Santa's elves would roam through the party, making a show of collecting up charity donations of cash in big sacks and allowing the attendees to display how generous they were being while at the same time judging the contributions of others. It was pretty much the only time paper money was seen in the Court, since making a bank transfer via app didn't quite have the showy appeal that was required. Then, towards the end of the night, Santa himself would appear to make a lap of the room, his sleigh loaded down with gifts for any brats who happened to be in attendance. When he'd been one of said brats, Renji had found the whole thing exciting, but now it seemed more than a little forced.

Jeremy from Marketing laughed in what he probably thought was a casual manner. "Naturally, it's an I.I. tradition, after all! For the kids, you know?"

"Alright. So like… All those bags of money. Which charity are they actually going to?"

"Oh. Um. Well, one of our approved partner charities, of course! Can't quite recall which one right now, haha, but it's all for a good cause, right?"

"Right, right." *Just not one you care enough to remember the name of.*

"And if you look at how much we're likely to raise this year compared to last, you'll see the numbers are really going to be—"

"Hey, Jeremy? Don't suppose you happened to hear about that big power cut down in Buried last night, did you?"

"Wha… In Buried?" The smile faltered, his lip twitching up into something legally distinct from a grimace. "No, why would I—"

"Yeah. Whole streets are out. No light, no power. Right in the middle of December."

He thought for a moment. "Come to think of it, I do think I read something about a bill not paid… But I don't see what that has to do with—"

"It's real fuckin' cold in December, Jeremy," Renji said, exhaling a cloud of smoke.

"Terribly sad, I'm sure." Jeremy from Marketing lamented, with a polite little wafting gesture. "Though, haha, what can you do? I'm sure the power company gave them every chance to pay their due. I know I certainly snap to attention when the bills start to arrive in red envelopes, eh?" Another burst of false laughter, and the smile had made a sly comeback. "It really is just so good of you to care though, Mr Starkweather, it is! So telling of your character, to have such a big heart even for those that don't deserve it. Haha, I'm sure you can sympathise with that sort on a quite personal level, after all."

"Hey, Jeremy?" Renji tossed the cigarette's remains to the ground and, quite deliberately, trod on them. "I'd *really* love for you to explain what you mean by that."

"I mean to say, you'd understand that people aren't always, uh— Say if you're, uh haha, *related* to someone who perhaps did something a little outside the law—"

"Criminals, y'mean. Obviously, I'm gonna feel bad for those terrible people who didn't pay some messed-up gas bill cus everyone knows my dad broke the law, and not just because it's gonna drop below freezing tonight."

"Haha, I didn't exactly mean to insinuate that— uh, I mean, it's all just rumours of course, haha, years ago, doesn't reflect on yourself or a-any other member of your family, so, er—" Jeremy from Marketing had begun to turn a little purple. "Um. Look, I should really head off, we've got a lot to do before tonight..!"

"I bet. Run along, Jeremy."

Jeremy from Marketing did not need telling twice.

With little else to do besides avoid further Jeremys, Renji decided to take himself deeper into the treeline to stomp through dead leaves and duck under branches in search of some Jeremyless spot where he could finish his last remaining cigarette in peace. Soon enough he could go no further as between the tree's bare branches, the thick glass of the Court's rim came into view, looming against the grey winter sky. The great, implacable wall was ice-cold to the touch, yet he laid a hand on it anyway as he frowned out over the horizon. From here, the outer edge of the Central Commons was visible, the ring-road motorways running along the curve of its own wall bustling with afternoon commuter traffic. Below that lay the careless sprawl of Buried, its roaming roads and scattered enclaves unrestricted by rims or walls until it met the uncompromising border of the coastline, where the port and shipbuilding yard that had once been the beating heart of Steelepool lay motionless, a husk rusting the years away in isolation.

The early afternoon light was so dull it had already brought a few stray streetlights to flicker to life in Buried, though despite the oncoming gloom, many buildings remained dark. *Too* many. As a few scant flakes of snow began to drift down it was impossible not to think of those apartments from last night, the ones whose anonymous occupants had saved him from a thorough kicking at the hands of people who would have been his fellow Forces members only hours before, and wonder if those windows would be among those that remained cold and dark tonight. How long the petrol generators on the food trucks in that other, very different park, might last.

Though he wasn't supposed to care, was he? Like Jeremy from Marketing had said, the people down there were *criminals*. Ones who'd tried to stab him, kidnap him, or if Cadence had her way, far worse.

Criminals like Kiki had been. Like his own father had been.

The reminder of Jeremy sent Renji's fingers twitching over his phone screen, and five seconds of searching the internet told him what the event planner hadn't been interested enough to remember; the official charity for tonight's Christmas party was the SparkBright Imperium Internship program, which promised to help Unity's disadvantaged youth by finding entry-level roles within the company. Dozens of otherwise bare sites and recently written articles with nothing but adulation filled the first few pages of search results, though a little deeper digging led to some rather more interesting headlines, ones like 'Imperium Intern Placement Charity Among Named In Fraud Investigation'.

It seemed that SparkBright had been on the list which Harlow and the others had blasted out over the internet the other month, along with details and more than a little evidence of the ways that scheme and others like it had been used to take in large amounts of money and deposit it cleanly here there and everywhere. 'Internal Investigation Clears Charities of Wrongdoing' came hot on the heels of the other headline, far quicker than one might think a thorough investigation might take.

Again, there was Melody's tired smile; *They didn't want you to know. But now you do. What you do with it is up to you, mate.*

Once more an idea was forming; another terrible, stupid idea, somehow even more terrible and stupid than the last. Renji dropped his cigarette end, and before he had finished stamping the embers out into the leafy mulch, he knew what he was going to do next.

CHAPTER 12

YET ANOTHER REALLY GOOD IDEA

The outside of the Portside Inns elevator station looked a little more cheerful in Buried's dim daylight, but only a little. Just beyond the concerned commuters and the dismal, darkened Christmas tree, Renji had parked himself on a low wall that ran around the square, his sneakers scuffing the pavement as he waited impatiently.

Much like the nearby station building, Weaver seemed less intimidating when not cloaked in shadow, to the point where it took Renji a moment to even recognise the figure shuffling towards him. Now clad in the traditional Someone's Dad attire of a sweater and tan sheepskin jacket, both as battered and worn as their wearer, paired with the noticeable limp and scruff of extra stubble he'd gained overnight, Weaver seemed no more lethal than any other passer-by.

Renji hopped down from the wall and greeted him with a nod. "Yo, old man. You good?"

"Mm. Been better." Weaver said, throwing a glare at his stiff left leg.

"Yeah, I hear that."

For a few seconds they stood in awkward silence, Renji keeping his face still in an attempt to outlast Weaver's taciturn stare; until finally the older man let out a sigh of resignation.

"So. Boss sends her apologies for how everything went down back in the pool." he rumbled. "Says things got outta hand, and they never intended to harm you."

"D'you believe her?"

"Mm. If you still wanna put forward whatever this plan of yours is, you got her word that you'll be safe from her and hers while you're doing that."

"And…?"

Weaver regarded him for a long moment, one gloved finger tapping on his crossed arms. "You got my word, too."

"Great!" Renji said a little too brightly before remembering his audience and dialling the enthusiasm down a few notches. "I mean, y'know. Alright, I guess. Got an idea that might help with the money problem, is all. Think it's worth a try." He shrugged, throwing in as much casual as possible.

That heavy brow furrowed as Weaver eyed Renji over one more time. "Don't suppose there's a chance I can still talk you out o'this?"

"Not a one."

Letting loose another deep sigh, he turned to walk away. "C'mon, then."

Together they headed in the direction of the park, Renji trailing in the wake of Weaver's slower steps. This time out at least, he knew he was much better prepared; not only did he have an actual real plan, the bag he carried was a much larger one without Imperium branding on it— thank you, Chips Darren— and contained exactly what he needed. That said, while he *had* brought a coat along this time, he'd left behind his warm winter parka in favour of the stolen red leather jacket, on the basis that if he was going to do something stupid he may as well look cool while he was doing it.

As they made their way through the near-freezing streets there was a distinct tension in the air, one that hadn't been present last night. Many more people were outside their homes, huddled in worried conversation with neighbours, wrapped in layers upon layers of clothing. Others were hustling back and forth with tarps and planks, scaling ladders to see how much weatherproofing could be done to their windows and roofs before the fast-approaching night fell. When Renji had left the Court the snow had already begun to come down in fat, thick flakes, and while few of those could make their way down into Buried intact, the chill they brought along with them would seep into everything and everyone before long.

"Still think you shouldn't be here," said Weaver. "But at least you had enough brains to set up a meet in public. If you're making a mistake, you might as well make it properly."

Renji let himself bask in the flicker of approval for a moment. While his confidence had taken a bit of a mauling last night, he had still been rather proud of the delicate relay of phone calls that had led to this meeting; Static Void's number was listed on their website and a delighted Allegro had been more than happy to pass a message onto Ms Cellanea, then once a tense half-hour of waiting had passed a time and place were negotiated. Now with Weaver escorting him to the open grounds of the park, and with the likely backup of the old man in case things went south, he ought to be able to avoid an ambush.

All that was left was the simple matter of convincing a notorious terrorist leader that the plan he was going to propose would be a much better prospect than letting Cadence stuff him into one of the leisure centre's old lockers and throw away the key.

Weaver scowled down at a discarded soda can on the pavement, kicking it into the gutter. "Wondering why you asked for me in particular."

Renji shrugged. "Given the options, you just seemed like someone I could trust, y'know?"

"Kid... I appreciate the vote of confidence and all, but I did absolutely try to stab you last night."

"What, that little scuffle out on the side of the airship? Pfsh, that was nothing! You hadn't even *met* me then! Besides, I saw you back there in that pool. You knocked over all that shit on purpose so I could make a run for it." While Renji may have been trailing too far behind to see the look on Weaver's face, the tense shift of the man's shoulders was all the confirmation he needed. "Heh. Can't fool me." smirked Renji, escalating his stroll to more of a swagger. "Not that

I'm complaining, but why *did* you help me out like that, anyway?"

Weaver's steps slowed to a stop by the side of the road. For a moment, Renji thought the old man was waiting for a break in traffic to cross, but when he drew level with him by the kerb, Weaver spoke. "You're Paige's kid."

"...yeah?"

"Mhm." He jabbed at the button on the pedestrian crossing.

Renji stared at him. *"And?!* You really can't just leave it at that, man, c'mon! You know my mom?"

"Now I'm looking for it, it's obvious you're her's. No wonder I can't convince you to back off of a bad idea. Never could with her, either."

The light changed from red to green, but Renji hadn't moved. "How... How do you know her?" he asked, over the crossing's insistent beeping.

"Was on her squad, back in the day. Long time ago now. I dropped out when Harlow was born. That musta been just before she met your dad, I s'pose." Weaver said, limping his way across the street. Once he'd remembered that he also needed to move Renji darted over the road as the lights changed back to red, earning a reproachful honk from a waiting taxi.

"Then you're ex-Forces!" he said breathlessly, drawing level with Weaver. "Man, I figured it was something like that, what with all the cool stealth ninja moves and all! Holy *shit.*"

"Language," Weaver muttered, without venom.

"Wait a minute, if you were Imperium too then how come Cadence wasn't going for *your* throat?"

"I've been out more'n two decades, kid. You'd barely been out two hours."

"Jeez... Alright, fine. I'll work on it, I guess. And hey, if I can't talk her round, I'll just dodge her punches for the next twenty years or so." This was met with the noncommittal grunt it deserved. Renji shook his head, awestruck. "Man... Mom's team, huh. That's wild!

Hey, Aunty L was in that squad, that mean you know her, too?"

"Mm."

As Renji opened his mouth to ask about a hundred further questions, Weaver cut him off before he could begin. "How's Paige doing, anyway? Ain't caught up with her for years."

"She's, uh…" Renji paused, trying to work out how much to say. "She's out of the picture right now," he muttered.

"Hm. Shame."

And with that, they both walked on in the stiff silence of two people united in their need to elaborate no further. Soon enough their steps led them to the iron-gated entrance to Temperley Park, which Weaver looked over with a critical sniff.

"So, what's this plan of yours, anyway?" he asked.

Renji grinned.

"That… is a most interesting idea." Cellanea blinked. "Yes, very interesting indeed."

"You have got to be joking," growled Cadence, the aura of menace she was radiating somewhat dulled by the bright red children's climbing frame she was perched upon.

Despite mid-afternoon being the usual prime time for kids to run about a park yelling at the top of their lungs, the tension simmering in the air meant that the tiny well-kept playground in Temperley was abandoned, except for the current impromptu Loose Ends meeting. The only crowds nearby were the clusters of people around the Sanctuary shelter, forming a loose yet long queue weaving out of the old building's door and around the plaza with its bone-dry fountain. Volunteers busied back and forth, attempting to set up a borrowed and beaten-up old gas generator in a hastily constructed tarp-covered hut beside the building.

Ms Cellanea appeared to be deep in thought, which Renji chose to see as a good sign considering the alternative was to let Cadence pull off the flying elbow drop onto his head that she was so clearly itching to launch herself into. While Cade may not be getting the joy of punching Renji in the face she must have at least been the one in charge of her wardrobe this time; the current tight black strappy fishnet-laden getup she was in was quite distinct from the colourful yet shapeless mess that Melody favoured, and the pink platform trainers had been very much replaced by well-worn black leather ankle boots. Cellanea had also brought her assistant Minjun along with her, though the neat little man seemed quite content to stay out of the way and take a seat on the swings for the time being, brow furrowed and tapping away at his phone with a quiet urgency. Weaver had stationed himself by the play-park's entrance, lurking as much as it is possible to lurk while resting on a bench.

"It is certainly a *bold* plan." mused Cellanea, hugging her padded winter coat about herself to counter the chill of the climbing frame she was leaning against.

"C'mon, it's perfect! The Christmas party's tonight, and timing like that has gotta be like *fate,* or something!" Renji beamed at each of them in turn. "And it's not as if it'll even be hard to get in, I'm on the friggin' guest list! Think about it; all that paper cash, just sitting in those big stupid sacks, ready for us! We can just, y'know… repurpose it, for *actual* charity! I've got the basic idea together but we gotta work on the details before—"

"'We'?! Who's 'we'?" snapped Cadence, planting her feet on the climbing frame and drawing herself up to her full height. "Last *I* heard it, *we* were going to sell you back to that psycho aunt of yours, and I don't see what's changed since then!"

Reaching over her shoulder, Cellanea rapped the heel of Cade's boot lightly with a knuckle. "Now now, take a moment, dear girl. What has changed is that Mr Starkweather has returned to us of his own accord, at no small risk to himself. A most interesting move."

Renji shifted in discomfort under Cade's glower. "Uh, d'you mind if we stick with Hayakawa? Not really feeling that other one right now."

"Of course, Mr Hayakawa. Though perhaps you will satisfy Cadence's curiosity. Despite everything that has occurred, you are set upon joining us. Why is that?"

Renji grimaced. He hadn't been looking forward to this part; wrangling lies was easy, but the truth was a different beast. Best to just let it all out and deal with the consequences later.

"Look, it's just— I- I think I'm starting to get it, alright? I never liked I.I. in the first place, but I didn't know just how bad shit was. Like really, *actually* bad. Stealing-people's-brains-for-information bad. People-freezing-in-the-streets bad. You know in a vague way that things feel wrong, but the details are kinda hard to see from up there. Especially if… you're not actually looking for them." he sighed. "But now I have looked— or at least, I *saw,* anyway— and I can't stop fuckin' seeing it everywhere! Nothing's fair and everyone's a dickhead and I don't know how to deal with it because while I'm up there all I can do is make things worse! And… And here's you guys, actually properly helping people. So if there's even a chance I can do that too, well… How could I not at least *try,* y'know?"

That had been more of a flood of words than he'd intended. In the following silence, Cellanea and Minjun exchanged a glance.

"You're actually considering this, aren't you." Flipping his phone's case shut, Minjun raised his eyebrows a fraction as he took in the thoughtful smirk spreading over his bosses' face.

"May I hear your thoughts, my friend?" she asked, rather than giving him an answer.

"It's a gamble." For a moment, his smirk matched hers. "And you never could turn down a gamble."

"Oh wah wah, sad little rich boy looked at the poors and had an emotion," Cade snapped. In a single neat movement she slipped between the climbing frame's bars to land with a crunch of woodchips beneath the soles of her boots. "You already had a plan, ma'am! Ransoming him is way less risky than this Christmas party crap! Why don't we just stick to that?"

"You were the one who was worried about sending me home alive, weren't you?" Renji cut in. "If I help you with this robbery thing, even Aunty L couldn't pull enough strings to keep me outta trouble. If I do this I don't get to go home. Ever! Not without handcuffs, anyway. So that's that solved, huh?" Pausing to consider that unexpectedly heavy thought, he shrugged it off and continued. "Hell, this way it'd even mean you don't have to get your hands dirty by murdering me, too! Bonus, right?"

The look Cade gave him suggested that wasn't something she'd been particularly worried about. "Ma'am," she began, through gritted teeth, "Mind if I say something?"

"I would never wish to stop you, darling girl."

"Cus what it is, right, is that walking directly into the flippin' middle of the Court's flippin' Christmas do on the say-so of the actual commander's actual flippin' relative, to do a job with about four hours prep, maximum? That's bananas, that is."

"And yet you have to admit, we've had worse plans," conceded Minjun. "Often from you, Cade."

"Oh, give over."

Raising his hands defensively as if that had a hope of keeping Cadence at bay, Renji plastered on his best smile and kept going. "Listen, I know it's kinda wild, but this is the sort of thing you guys do isn't it? Crime and shit?"

"Crime and shit." Cellanea mulled that one over. "That is not exactly how I would say it, but… I suppose it is not incorrect, yes. The purpose of The Loose Ends is indeed to gather extra funds to help our community, and often that involves a little crime."

"And shit." added Minjun.

"Alright!" Allowing a little more confidence to settle in, Renji fell back into a casual sprawl on one of the nearby roundabout's seats. "Then this is the shit! And you gotta admit, it's pretty good shit too!"

"Ma'am—!"

"This would be the highest jackpot we've ever played for," Ms Cellanea mused. "Though I suppose we needed to raise the stakes sooner or later."

"It could work," Weaver said abruptly. All turned to face him, and he shifted in discomfort at the sudden attention. "Just saying. The idea ain't a bad one," he grumbled. "Kid's gonna find some sorta way to get into trouble, might as well be the kind that pays your bills. Plus it'd be one in the eye for Lissa if her own dang nephew robbed the place on her watch. If that's the sorta thing you care about, that is."

"It is not," Ms Cellanea replied, though the expression on Minjun's face suggested that may not have been entirely true.

"Mental," groaned Cadence. "This is *mental.*"

"Oh yes." Something wicked shone in Ms Cellanea's dark eyes. "Though perhaps mental is what is required today."

"Hell yeah!" Renji looked up from the important business of spinning the roundabout with the toes of his sneakers. "Then let's go make some trouble!"

Before Cadence could protest further, Ms Cellanea had placed her hands upon her shoulders. "I understand why you do not like this, my dear. If you do not wish to join us on this, I would never dream of forcing you. But I am sure *you* understand, in turn, that I cannot simply sit by and do nothing about what is being done to us." The older woman smiled, tracing a soft thumb along the studs embedded into the girl's black leather jacket. "The invitation is extended to you, my brave and beautiful girl, to help us. To help everybody. What do you say?"

Amazingly, some of that permanent tension seemed to drain from Cadence all at once. Renji watched with interest. Last night the enigmatic Ms Cellanea had struck him as someone who knew how to wield both her words and her kindness to her advantage, and it seemed he'd been right on the money. If this lady *was* former Court, she must have been pretty terrifying back in the day.

"You already know what I think," grumbled Cade. "I'm not here to show some flippin' tourist around on his holiday from being rich."

"Noted." Ms Cellanea nodded.

She shot Renji a warning glare. "And I'm not apologising for what I said back at the leisure centre."

"Noted, also."

"I don't trust him." She gave a large woodchip a vindictive kick across the playground. "But... I trust *you*, ma'am. Whatever you reckon is best, I'll do."

"I am so very glad to hear it." Cellanea's smile was radiant. "Besides, if I know you as I believe I do, then I am quite sure you will enjoy this one."

"Mm." A faint smile in return flickered across Cade's lips. "Messing up a swanky party *does* sound pretty fun."

"That's my girl." Squeezing her shoulder, she took a step back. "Now, perhaps we may speak with Melody for a moment? I should like to hear her opinion also."

"Really?" Cadence gave her a wretched look. "Now?"

"If you please."

Quickly, Renji spun the roundabout to get himself the best view; having missed the changeover between sisters in the darkness of the club the last time, he was curious to see what the hell the process of switching minds was like in action, not to mention quite eager to trade the abrasive bloodthirsty jerk for her far chiller counterpart. Sensing his attention on her, Cade threw him another filthy scowl, and he gave her a cheeky little wave goodbye in response. She snorted, squeezed her eyes shut, and... changed. Renji had half been expecting sparks and lights, some sort of showy transformation sequence like one of those old magical girl anime shows, so when it turned out to appear more like a silent sneeze, it was a little disappointing. A dozen tiny changes in her posture registered all over her body as her shoulders relaxed, her taut muscles loosened, and her face fell into the intrigued frown of someone who had just been told some fascinating news.

"Thanks, Ms C." Sniffing, she wiped her nose on the back of her sleeve and nodded at Cellanea, then at Renji. "Alright, mate."

"Hi! Uh, you should know, I wasn't like… one hundred percent truthful about a couple of things yesterday—" Renji began hesitantly, but Melody cut him off with a wave of her hand.

"S'cool, I got it. Memory's in a shared bit of the brain, or summat. Everything Cade knows, I know." She strolled over to the roundabout, then flopped into the seat next to Renji's.

"Sorry." he mumbled.

Melody patted down her jacket as if searching for something. "Nah. It's whatever, isn't it? No big deal."

"You, uh… Don't mind that I didn't tell you I'm literally related to the head of the Forces?"

She withdrew a pair of black gloves from the depths of her pocket with satisfaction. "Not really. You don't get to pick where you're from." And that seemed to be that. Slipping the gloves on, she let out a note of irritation as her mechanical fingers poked through their unexpected fingerless openings. "Mad plan though, mate."

"Can't disagree."

"Absolutely bonkers." She leaned back and kicked the floor to spin the roundabout in a slow, thoughtful circle. After it completed its rotation, she gave a lazy snap of her fingers and a bob of her head. "I'm in. Let's rob the bastards."

"Hell yeah!" he whooped, giving the roundabout a kick-off to pick up speed. *"We're gonna fuck up a party!"* Snorting out the first laugh he'd heard from her yet, Melody gave another shove to help them pick up more speed, dragging her boot along the ground to send up a spinning spray of woodchips.

"Interesting that part of stepping up our criminal ventures seems to involve announcing our plans loudly in the middle of town." Minjun said over the clatter of playground equipment and sniggering.

"Kids." grumbled Weaver.

"Let them enjoy themselves for a moment, hm?" The winter wind tousled Cellanea's salt and pepper curls as she smiled coolly. "After all, it seems we have a rather long night ahead of us."

CHAPTER 13

MAINTENANCE MODE

The dull December sun had all but vanished by the time they left the park. Only a few hours remained until the Imperium Christmas party opened its glitzy doors, and despite Renji's insistence he had everything covered, a lot of the plan had yet to be planned.

"Unfortunately, Melody and I have another matter we must attend to before we can discuss details." Cellanea told them, over the hacker's groan of complaint. "A council meeting. Even down here, the bureaucracy is inescapable. I shall make it as brief as possible."

"A council? Like a secret crime council?" Renji asked.

"Like a regular city council. In the meantime, both of you must be checked over by our doctor friends."

"Pfsh, it's just a couple of bruises."

"For you, perhaps." Minjun raised his eyebrows in Weaver's direction.

Looking over him again, between the stiff fingers from the skillet-bashing, the limp, and the greying scruff of stubble peppering his chin, Weaver did seem somewhat worse for wear. "You are looking kinda rough, old man," said Renji, helpfully. "Didn't pack a razor, or what?"

A scowl.

"Now now, you know that is not what I meant," Cellanea chuckled. "Besides, a beard would look rather handsome on him, do you not think?"

To his credit, Weaver's granite glare twitched only a touch.

"Facial hair preferences aside, that leg needs attention," noted Minjun.

"Lucky for you that our doctor and mechanic are available today, then. Melody can attest to their skills," Ms Cellanea said. Melody gave a mechanical thumbs up as confirmation.

Another uncomfortable shuffle from Weaver. "I can't afford to—"

"That is not a problem," Cellanea interrupted Weaver's protests with a dismissive wave. "I have a favour or two to cash in. It will be done."

After a considered pause, he gave a slow nod. "Appreciate it, ma'am."

"My pleasure."

And with that decided, Ms Cellanea took her leave with Melody trailing behind her seeming for all the world like someone's kid being dragged along on a boring errand.

"This way, gentlemen." Tugging up the sensible collar of his soft yet worn brown cord jacket, Minjun led the way along a series of confounding backstreets, moving at a brisk stride that almost seemed faster than should be possible for a man with legs that short. With each covert little alleyway of worn brick and boarded-up windows, their path took them further and further from the city's crowds until even the roar of the constant traffic was dialled down to a distant hum. When Minjun slowed his pace to a stop, the place they found themselves in front of seemed unobtrusive enough; parked between a grocers and a tired-looking second-hand clothes shop sat a squat little building, its graffiti-strewn cracked tile front and illegible signage no different to the neighbouring buildings. Yet unlike the others, it featured a large open doorway barred by a large locked lattice metal gate, beyond which a staircase descended below street level.

Nothing about this particular arrangement was familiar to Renji and his Court-level experience, but it tugged at the corner of a memory all the same, something he'd seen in one of the countless dull

Unity City History lessons at school. "This is…"

"A station." Weaver finished, his faltering steps catching up to the group. "For the ol' Grid trains. Didn't think they were still runnin'."

"They aren't. This doesn't mean a series of networked underground tunnels can't be useful." Minjun scanned the empty streets for a long moment, then fished a hefty bundle of keys from the depths of his coat and picked out one that seemed indistinguishable from the others. It turned in the rusted gate's padlock with a smooth, obliging *click*.

"Quickly. Best to not let anyone see you come here." he cautioned, pushing the gate to swing open without a fuss on what must have been well-oiled hinges, and slipping past. Taking a deep breath, Renji turned the confidence dial up to eleven, brushed aside any concerns with what he chose to think of as determination, and strode after the receding sound of Minjun's footsteps.

It was… *dark* down there. That had been expected to a degree; abandoned underground tunnels aren't usually known for being welcoming. Still, the sheer quantity of darkness was far higher than he'd been expecting.

The way ahead seemed to stretch out for miles, the twin parallel sets of debris-strewn tracks on the ground leading the way off into the unknown blackness, the walls reaching up to arch into a rounded ceiling lined with rough bricks and half a dozen arm-thick cables, gnarled as the roots of an ancient tree. Those must have been humming with electricity once, enough to power a whole transport that would have been the arterial system of Steelepool back when it was alive before it was Buried. Now they lay dormant, their rubber coating rotting unobserved in the silent shadows beneath Unity City.

Biting his lip, Renji attempted to concentrate on the soft glow of Minjun's flashlight bobbing along the rusted tracks at their feet. He'd never been afraid of the dark before, but something in the texture of this place felt different than any darkness he'd encountered before. There was an endless amount of it pressing in from all sides, shadows seeming to take up space where air ought to have been. It was as though the entire weight of the rest of the city was bearing down on them. The flashlight's beam held steady along endless stretches of tunnel, identical but for the occasional paint or chalk scrawl from some engineer or electrician countless years ago, the markings long since faded and past any use.

Smoothing the uncertainty out of his expression, Renji hurried his pace to match Minjun's. Perhaps it was just because he was the only one holding the flashlight, but Renji had already begun to find the stocky little man to be a soothing presence. While the guy wasn't actively wearing a tweed jacket and glasses he seemed to embody their spirit, and though the buttoned-up Responsible Young Man sort of look had never been Renji's thing there was still an undeniable charm in the certainty of Minjun's stride, and that firm set to his delicate jaw.

"So hey," Renji began, because filling the silence had always made him feel better, "What's your deal, then?"

"My deal," repeated Minjun.

"Yeah, y'know!" Renji beamed at him. "How'd you end up down here anyway? And don't say *hm Mr Hayakawa, why I simply unlocked the door and walked downwards*, cus that shit ain't flyin'."

Whether the noise that Minjun made at the back of his throat was a cough or a laugh was impossible to tell. "Well. I suppose I would say that I'm relatively new to Buried. I had a position within I.I. which I lost some years ago rather, ah… suddenly."

"Fired, huh? Sucks."

"That's putting it lightly, yes."

"Which department?"

"Marketing."

"…Huh."

"Oh yes. Graphic design is my passion," he intoned wryly.

Renji tried to picture quiet, precise Minjun occupying the same office as the grating intensity of Jeremy, and could see how that sarcastic tone had been honed to such an edge.

"It was actually Harlow who introduced me to Ms Cellanea," Minjun continued. "I'd had something of an eventful year, and meeting the both of them was a much-appreciated break in the clouds. In fact, I am quite certain I would never have got myself back onto my feet without Harlow's intervention, nor found my way into The Loose Ends." He aimed the last comment over his shoulder, towards the shuffling sound of Weaver's uneven tread.

A grumble rolled out of the gloom in reply. "She talk you into it, huh?"

"Your daughter can make herself rather difficult to disagree with," Minjun said, with clear fondness. "Though I don't regret taking this position. This work can certainly be rewarding, as I suppose you're both about to discover."

"Don't get used to me being around. I'm only here to find my kid. Once she's safe, I'm retiring," Weaver muttered. "Again."

"I perhaps owe you an apology. Over the last few years, Harlow mentioned that she hadn't been entirely truthful with you about what she's been up to, and I can't say I discouraged her from that."

"Tsch. Volunteer work, she told me."

"Not entirely inaccurate."

"Ain't exactly what I had in mind," grumbled Weaver.

"I caught that broadcast of hers, y'know." said Renji. "Pretty great show!"

By the pale light of the torch, Minjun's mouth set into a thin line. "I daresay everybody did. That rather seemed to be the purpose."

"How'd they even pull off a stunt like that, anyhow?" asked Weaver.

"Hacked the emergency broadcast system. Melody had an exploit for that particular system set aside in case we needed it. Evidently, Harlow decided she needed it."

From further behind in the darkness, Weaver watched the back of Minjun's head carefully. "You don't approve."

"I…" Minjun paused, a flicker of uncertainty disrupting his usual composure. After a slow exhale, he continued. "It took a long time to gather up the store of information that she gave away. Years of poking and prying and stealing and saving what we could when we could, all filed away until we could work out how best to use it, and now it's just… out there. Useless. Harlow was so certain that releasing it to the public would make a difference, that people would hear it and, I don't know, rise up somehow. Overthrow the villains. Dismantle the machine. *Win.* I suppose I understand why she needed to believe that; it's a comforting fiction."

"Fiction?!" Renji blurted out in surprise. "But she's right, isn't she? I mean not with *that* plan exactly, but surely that's the point of this whole thing! Fighting back! Taking down Imperium! *Stopping them!"*

"Stopping them." The tired look in Minjun's dark eyes seemed as though it came from a much older man. "This isn't a fable with some terrible dragon for the heroes to hunt down, or a magic combination of words that will break the overlords' evil spell. This is a city, a society, an ecosystem with problems embedded in its very roots. How exactly do you *stop* a society?"

"Well—" Renji shook his head. "Look, I don't know yet! But it *has* to be possible!"

Minjun shrugged, the motion lending the torch's beam an erratic curve. "I would very much like to believe that, but…"

"You don't," finished Weaver.

Another pause. "Ms Cellanea believes we should concentrate on preventing things from becoming worse. Maintaining what we have."

Renji considered the streets of Buried that would be used by too many people as an ice-cold bed that night, the casual cruelty at every level of the Forces, the lack of interest from the Jeremys in Marketing, and found himself wondering what part of that was worth maintaining.

"Harlow came to us first with her broadcast plan, of course, but Ms Cellanea turned it down. It was rather beyond our capabilities; usually we make our money through hacking operations and information brokering. Shadow tactics. But what Harlow wanted to do… That was a declaration of war. Ms Cellanea said it was too risky, that it would amount to nothing." Minjun said, his voice tight. "And she was right. The machine rolls on, regardless. *Nothing* is precisely what happened."

"I dunno about that, man." Renji piped up. "I know they played the response real smooth, but I was in the Court when that broadcast dropped and it was fuckin' chaos up there."

"Is that so." Minjun's expression was unreadable in the tunnel's shadows, but the lilt of curiosity in his voice was impossible to disguise.

"Oh yeah, never seen anything like it! All-night meetings and shit, everyone out of their minds on way too much coffee, thinking they might lose their job any minute? Whole departments turning on each other like a goddamn free for all! They were barely holding it together, even in the Forces!" Renji grinned at the memory. "I swear the whole of the Court didn't sleep, they just had one big collective headache for like, a solid week. Fuckin' hilarious."

Minjun hummed. "Interesting. Not a dismantling, but perhaps… a ripple."

Renji's grin widened. "A start!"

"Ah. Optimism. I remember that well."

From Weaver's direction a snort of amusement echoed off the tunnel walls, and they made the rest of their way in amiable silence.

#

Their trek led them winding through so many identical turns that Renji had begun to wonder if their guide had become lost several minutes back and was simply hiding it very well; until he noticed that the number of rails on the ground was multiplying at each junction. More and more tracks joined the set they'd been following, appearing from other tunnels to join the flow of their path, which soon widened from a small dingy tunnel into something that more resembled an underground version of the motorways in Central Commons. The glow of a faltering red signal light and the hum of a distant generator greeted them at the tunnel's exit, where they emerged into one of the oddest, oldest buildings Renji had ever seen.

It was wide and open like a warehouse, with crumbling graffiti'd red brick walls that curved into a circular space peppered at intervals with the dark mouths of at least a dozen other entrance tunnels just like the one they had exited. While there were no windows on the walls, the grey afternoon light still filtered in through a vast clouded dome of glass in the centre of the ceiling, one decorated with the sort of curling floral patterns of black leading that suggested this structure had been around for a very, very long time. While the ground was thick with rubble and trash the tracks that emerged from the tunnels were still very much visible, flowing and joining together until they coalesced underneath the dome into ranks upon ranks of neat lines. Upon them stood the sort of sight that would have driven the average six-year-old round the bend with glee; rows of abandoned train carriages, dozens of them, their blue and purple Steelepool TransGrid livery faded yet proud.

"Huh." Weaver peered around. "Carriage yard."

Minjun hummed in confirmation, clicking off his torch in the dusty half-light. "This is the Roundhouse, supposedly named for the turntable that had once been in the central circle there, to turn about the steam trains. Much later, it was used as storage for the TransGrid. And now that the Grid is no more…"

"It's like a fuckin' train cemetery." Renji said. He'd never seen anything like these carriages before outside of picture books; the Court's own sleek transport system ran suspended above the streets, zipping through the crisp air as an unstoppable, punctual bullet, whereas these stocky box-like beasts before him must have once rumbled along like a cratered old herd of dinosaurs.

"A depressingly accurate way to frame it, but yes." Minjun strolled over to flip a switch attached to a puttering generator, bringing to life the strings of lightbulbs dotted about the girders. There was another device attached to the same wall, a compact tangle of makeshift wires and a keypad into which he tapped a quick series of numbers. An electronic beep signalled something that he apparently found satisfactory. "This way."

To Renji's confusion, Minjun began to walk into the cluster of carriages. "What, into those rust buckets?"

"Ms Cellanea requested that you see the base, and for now, the Roundhouse and its 'rust buckets' are it."

"Holy shit. You live in here? Like, literally *in* the train carriages?"

Now he was looking for it, Renji could see one of the windows wasn't simply dark, it was covered in fabric. Curtains. In fact, several of the nearby cab windows were lined with material of all types, some heavy and patterned, some plain and black, some spray-painted into false darkness. One even boasted a window lined edge-to-edge with beautiful, thriving plants, their thick green foliage lit in an ultraviolet neon-purple glow, prompting Renji to think about his own little ailing houseplant that he'd once again stuffed into his bag. He wondered who the resident gardener was, and if they'd have any tips.

"A carriage can be converted to an adequate living space, though it does take some effort." Minjun told them. "But this way, everyone gets their own space, and we can move them through the tunnels to a different station if needed. It is an adequate solution, if perhaps a little draughty."

"A little? Dude, it's freezing here!" Renji wrinkled his nose as he gave the ice-cold siding of a nearby carriage an experimental poke. His fingers came back filthy.

"Mobile base, huh." muttered Weaver, nudging a wheel with the toe of his boot. "Not bad."

"Except for the bugs and dirt, yeah."

Heaving a sigh, Minjun continued ahead, picking out a winding path forwards. "You may choose one for yourselves and keep it as clean as you wish, though you'll need to find a bed somewhere. I have placed your, ah… *luggage* in that one there, Mr Hayakawa." He nodded towards a carriage.

Renji trod up the creaking steps, wincing in case they gave way, to peer in at what would be his new makeshift home. It was indeed an unaltered commuter carriage, with the uncomfortable plastic seats, peeling flooring and faded insurance ads above the cracked windows to prove it. This was less of a step down from the comfort of Aunty L's apartment and more of a cliff-edge plummet into the abyss.

Still, something caught his eye within the carriage; that sword he'd stolen from Sergeant Flood, propped up against a seat. Everything that happened last night almost seemed like something of a dream, yet there was the proof of it all, its shining gold handle and brilliant blade gleaming almost nervously against that grubby, patchy public transit fabric.

Renji's grin reflected back at him in the window's glass. Perhaps this could work out after all.

"Come along. We've a schedule to keep." Minjun led Renji and a limping Weaver through the clutter of carriages and towards a squat bunker-like structure hunched against the Roundhouse's wall like a sullen, loitering teenager. Hadn't Ms C said they were going to visit a doctor? This wasn't quite what Renji pictured when he thought about medical facilities. An array of warning signs hung on the door, promising that *TRESPASSERS WILL BE PROSECUTED* and *TRESPASSERS WILL BE SHOT*, though they neglected to mention in which order those would happen. Minjun rapped on the wood below them regardless.

He hadn't even lowered his hand before the door swung open to let out a high-pitched sound that made Renji think they'd tripped some kind of alarm. Even Weaver took a step back in surprise, but not far back enough to avoid the short-range ballistic hug that shot out of the doorway to cannon into both him and Renji, and just as that ache in his ribs was beginning to make itself known again over the mounting pressure of the embrace, the siren wail resolved itself into a whoop of joy.

"Well here you are, you absolute bloody angels! Let me get a good look at you!" She released the hug to hold the both of them at arm's length, and Renji got to see the force that had swept them off their feet. The lady in question was perhaps in her forties or so, either not quite as old as Weaver or perhaps wearing her years in a way that suited her well. Her height, width, and manner were all equally overwhelming, her hair a spray of short fire-engine red curls that matched the ruddiness of her cheeks to give her a lively, almost overpowering glow. A lens covered one of her eyes like a tinted monocle, the iris below it startling wide and black compared to the pale blue of its twin. Her powerful forearms were covered in colourful tattoos seemingly chosen at random like stickers covering a teenager's notebook, and she beamed at both him and Weaver as though they were here to gift her a massive cheque and a unicorn.

"Couple of handsome lads you've brought us, Min! Ah, where the hell are my manners? Come in, I've just put the kettle on for a cuppa!" She ushered them through the door without waiting for a reply, Minjun trailing behind them while sensibly remaining outside hug radius.

The small room beyond was piled high with boxes, some stacked high on the peeling linoleum floor, others perched on fold-out trestle tables, all suggesting that whatever arrangement was occurring here must have been either new or temporary. Several boxes were open, spilling out an assortment of what looked to Renji like random junk; springs, wires, and tiny screwdrivers with baggies full of matching tiny screws.

She led them to a boxless, neat corner, where a patched yet clean medical bench sat surrounded by gleaming trolleys. A kettle boiled away merrily on a counter nearby, beside a chipped sunshine-yellow teapot with a smiley face drawn on it.

"'Scuse the mess, we're not set up here yet. Got our own clinic, o'course, but Ms C likes to make a spot for us! Speaking of, you tell that boss of yours that this one's on the house!" The lady's large hands were an affectionate vice grip on each of their shoulders. "No way in hell are we charging anyone, not after you saved our Trig and Sugar!"

"Hey, any time!" Renji matched her grin and threw in a wink, much to the woman's delight. "Right, old man?"

Weaver grumbled, clearly unhappy with the quantity of attention he found himself receiving.

"Oh please." croaked a hoarse voice from the far corner. "We're all doomed eventually. Some of us more than others."

Minjun cleared his throat. "Mr Hayakawa, Mr Weaver, these are the Aunties. Auntie Biotic—" The large lady waved again cheerfully. "And over there somewhere is Auntie Septic."

A suspicious glower peered from behind a dense wall of cardboard to squint at the room at large. Having assessed her guests and apparently found them as dissatisfying as she'd expected, Auntie Septic sidled out from the stacks of junk. She was the precise opposite of the double helping of sunshine who had greeted them at the door; a short, scrawny figure of a woman about the same age as Biotic, her cool dark skin pitted with scars across hollow cheeks. Between the greying dreadlocks piled high on her head and the sharp features outlined in black makeup she gave every impression of a sullen storm cloud, like a scowl given human form. A spare prosthetic leg was tucked under one of her skinny arms, its plating and joints of a similar make to Melody and Cadence's arms.

"Auntie Septic is a roboticist and limb expert. Auntie Biotic is a more traditional style of doctor," said Minjun, who was helping himself to a cup of tea.

"He means I look after the squishy human bits." Biotic beamed, "Seppy does the metal ones."

"For what good it'll do." Auntie Septic snapped her fingers and pointed at Weaver. "You. Leg."

Weaver limped over to sit by Septic's workbench as though glad to meet someone more on his conversational level.

"Ain't much to look at," he grumbled, gingerly pulling off his boot and rolling back his pants leg to reveal the scarred metal beneath.

Auntie Septic stared at it, her black-painted lip curling more with each passing second. "What the fuck is this," she said. "What the *fuck* is that. Let me see that." She grabbed Weaver's false shin, pulling it forward into her lap as he wobbled to stay on his seat. "Are you joking. Were you actually walking about on this insult to my profession? How long for?"

Weaver shifted stiffly in the tiny fold-out chair. "Couple years," he muttered. "Still paying out for the emergency op to have the damn thing put on. Between that and Harlow's meds, there wasn't enough left for the maintenance subscription."

"They're still doing that pay monthly shit? Vultures." Her mouth set into a thin, bleak line. "Home repairs, then?"

"Did what I could."

"Tsch. Hold that cuppa, Bio." Septic snatched up her tool kit with purpose. "This is gonna take some doing."

"That means I get *you* all to myself, love!" Auntie Biotic beamed at Renji, patting the medical bench. He hopped onto it, and she set to work inspecting the various cuts and scrapes he'd acquired yesterday.

"Seppy doesn't approve of people doing home repairs." Biotic confided in a voice a little too loud to be a whisper. "Unless she's the one doing them."

186

"S'not what you say when *your* repairs need done." muttered Septic, not looking up from her work.

"She does keep me ticking over, it's true!" Biotic winked her one monocled eye, and having realised what it was, Renji found it impossible not to stare; he'd never seen a cybernetic eye before. As Biotic ran a finger along her temple, the monocle device set before her eye lit up into a tiny display that must have appeared over her vision. "Now, let's see what ails you!"

"I'm fine, really!" he said, full of false bravado as she tilted his chin to inspect a scrape on the underside of his jaw. "Nothing I can't deal with!"

"Oh aye?" Eyeing his torso, she gave him a friendly poke in the ribs right where one of the Uppers' boots had struck, and it became a difficult endeavour to not whimper like a tiny kitten.

"Dealing with it is all you can do for now. Nowt else for it with bruised ribs, I'm afraid!" Auntie Biotic turned to fish through one of her gleaming drawers. "It's painkillers for you, my lad. And these, to bring the swelling down." She handed him a couple of assorted pills and a cup of tea. "Honestly, from what I'd heard about what you lot got up to, I was hoping for some more interesting injuries than that."

"Sorry, I'll try harder next time." Renji grinned.

"See that you do! Give me something nasty and complicated. Messy and gory!" She sighed, dreamy as a schoolkid thinking about their first crush. "Have something torn up real nice, and then we'll talk."

"Ma'am, I promise that the second I get any part of myself bitten off by a monster, you'll be my first stop."

"You, I like." Biotic pinched his cheek fondly. "And you, I have meds for!" She tossed a paper bag to Minjun, who almost dropped his tea in a fumble to catch it.

"Appreciated." His nod was curt, but there was real gratitude in his voice as he slipped the bag into his jacket. "Mr Hayakawa, we ought to be going. Auntie Septic, if you'd please help Mr Weaver to find the usual council rooms once you're done?"

"Yeah sure, whatever." Septic said around the screwdriver stuck between her teeth. "This is only a temp replacement to get you through whatever stupid shit you're planning tonight," she told Weaver. "I'll measure you up for a proper replacement. Get that done next week."

"Thanks, ma'am."

"Don't *ma'am* me yet." Weaver held back a grunt of pain as she uncoupled his prosthetic from the raw-red joint below, inspecting the wound with a critic's eye. "Ergh. Hey Bio, come look at this fucked-up knee."

"Ooh, let's see! Ohoho, crushed fingers, too? *Lovely!*"

"Good luck, old man!" Renji called over his shoulder as they left the delighted medic cooing over an increasingly frazzled Weaver's fascinating array of injuries.

CHAPTER 14
BAR ROOM POLITICS

One more tunnel and another of Minjun's keys later, Renji found himself being led down a winding street packed shoulder-to-shoulder with rundown shops. They passed the dim windows and shuttered doors of grocers, second-hand clothes shops and several of those places that do questionably legal things to phones before stopping outside a shabby local tavern of the kind that seemed to occur naturally on most English streets. It even came with the traditional hand-painted pub sign, though this one had undergone a few modifications.

"The… Arms." Renji read out loud, as Minjun rapped on the door. "Just The Arms? Isn't it meant to be like The King's Arms or The Queen's Arms or something?"

"No monarchists in 'ere, pal." The door cracked open, and the round face of an extremely bald man loomed against the pub's dark interior like a crimson, surly moon. He regarded Renji and his friendly grin with the sort of deep suspicion reserved for the sorts of people who knock on the door with pamphlets before his gaze swept down towards the more diminutive figure of Minjun, and softened in recognition. "Afternoon, Jeong."

"Arthur. May we come in?"

"Aye, you better had." The door swung open to reveal the rest of the landlord, who turned out to be one of those older British men who were so white they had wrapped around to being a sort of mottled pinkish red. He also seemed to let out a grumbling noise as a matter of course, muttering out a stream of low-key annoyance at nothing in particular under his breath as he shut the heavy door after they had filed into the pub. Much like the landlord himself the building's narrow leaded windows were very selective about what they'd let in, and most of the fading daylight had been denied entry. With the electrics cut off, the only remaining source of light was a camping lantern that looked as though it had been excavated from a forgotten box in a basement and was doing the best it could in a bad situation. A tinsel garland in festive red and green drooped from the ceiling, and a faded plastic Santa whose missing eye did not seem to affect his cheer level sat beside the empty till behind the bar. Between the poor light and the shabby decor the place seemed like an abandoned relic of decades past, as though a thick layer of dust ought to be coating the worn bar top or the cracked leather of the unoccupied barstools.

Arthur took up a position behind the counter, arms folded and stern, fitting in as though he were part of the traditional pub decor. "In't exactly a full house today. 'cept them downstairs, the useless shower. Must be near done now, only so long you can bloody well bleat on about how there's nothing you can possibly do t'help."

"The usual council meeting, then." nodded Minjun.

"Same as per. No bloody council funding allocated, no leg t'stand on in negotiations, no bloody accountability on a societal level. An' all that means for the likes o'working class sods like me is no bloody customers." Arthur snorted, glaring around his empty establishment.

"Ah, the wheels of government."

"Rusted to fuck, as usual. Between you an' me an' whoever this arsehole is," a wide sweep of a beefy arm indicated Renji, "fuck the red tape. An' fuck payin' them parasites at the power company. The sooner you lot do what needs done, the better." This last statement came accompanied by a large, obvious wink.

The corner of Minjun's mouth twitched into an unavoidable smile. "The vote of confidence is appreciated."

"*Voting!*" he groaned. "Don't get me bloody started on the bloody futility of voting…"

"I shall spare us both from doing so. See you later, Arthur."

"He seems nice." Renji said as they left the bar.

Behind them, the barman retrieved a thick book of furious political thought from underneath the counter and flipped to his bookmarked page with glum determination.

"Arthur's heart is in the right place." said Minjun, quietly. "His mouth, however, seems to have established its own nation state."

Leading Renji to the farthest of the pub's endless dark corners, Minjun pushed open an unobtrusive door hidden behind a dartboard.

"Secret passage!" whispered a delighted Renji.

"It's a beer cellar."

"Secret passage to a beer cellar!"

Minjun withdrew his torch from the depths of his jacket, clicking it on with a weary look at Renji. "If I were you, I'd temper my expectations."

Renji nodded sagely, and did not do that.

Minjun had, of course, been correct. While Renji had never set foot in a pub cellar and had no idea what one ought to smell like, the basement of The Arms had what the Unity Tourist Experience Primer App would have called *a distinctly traditional, workmanlike aroma.* Awkward steps of irregular, unyielding stone led their way down into the sour darkness beneath the pub, towards the rolling mutter of voices in debate.

"…have already diverted all possible funds." A male voice, speaking with the affected calm of someone who has repeated themselves for what they hope is the last time. "As I've stated repeatedly, what little remains is earmarked for other purposes, and under no circumstances can be misappropriated."

"Misappropriated?!"

A flurry of annoyed grumbles mounted. "We've still got a little left in the pot for waste disposal!" someone snapped. "We could just move some from there and—"

"Those funds are meant for the new disposal unit." The false calm was fraying at the edges now.

"A garbage truck, you mean. People're gonna freeze in their own homes tonight, and y'all are prioritising a new goddamn garbage truck?"

A fresh round of complaining broke out from all sides, and while there was still a door between them and the meeting Renji recognised the distinctive twang in that last voice all the same. "Allegro?"

Minjun raised a finger to his own lips, tapping them lightly. "Indeed," he confirmed in a low mutter. "They're one of the Community Council's volunteer members, there to represent Steelepool's collective entertainment facilities and the interests of its workers. Though personally, I suspect they simply like to argue."

The basement room Renji and he had arrived in was little more than an unfinished dirt-floor corridor lined with bare plasterboard. A door coated in thick layers of peeling gloss must have led to the rest of the basement and to the meeting room itself, but Minjun ignored it in favour of approaching one of the walls.

He shot Renji a warning glance. "Don't get excited." he muttered, then gave the plasterboard a shove with his shoulder to reveal a space within the wall.

"Another secret passage!" hissed Renji, scrambling inside; but the narrow cavity within was empty except for dust and loose insulation, plus a couple of barstools that looked even older than the ones upstairs. Slumped onto one of them and tapping at her phone was a bored DJ.

"Alright?" Melody yawned in greeting.

Renji pouted. "Increasingly disappointed in the quality of the secret passages around here, if we're being honest."

"You're telling me." Melody glared at her phone. "Signal's shocking down here."

"What did I say?" Minjun gestured towards a tiny, eye-height opening on the wall, from which emanated a sliver of warm light and the sounds of more furious debate. "Still, at least it has a front row seat."

"To an admin meeting," finished Melody, sliding her phone into her pocket.

Renji deflated as Minjun stepped back out of the nook and slid the plasterboard back into place. Evidently he wasn't so sold on the entertainment either. All the same, with little else to do, Renji's curiosity took no time in getting the better of him, and he stepped forward to peer through the peephole.

Aside from the secrecy, Steelepool Community Council's choice of venue left a lot to be desired. Every inch of the place not full of the near dozen councillors was stuffed with a variety of pub junk; an old pool table with mouldy felt, the hollow corpse of a trivia quiz machine, and countless empty kegs were littered about, bathed in the light of however many candles Arthur had been able to dig out at short notice. Despite the mess, because Unity was at least England-adjacent, someone had taken the time to set aside a neat little table with a kettle and tea-making facilities.

The council itself was in the centre of the room, huddled around the bleached skeleton of a table that must have taken up residence in a beer garden in some past life, every last council member talking at once and creating the sort of useless wall of empty unproductive noise that could only be summoned into being during an important meeting.

A greying man in a well-kept suit and red tie, the one who had been keeping up that front of false calm, raised his voice in an attempt to maintain some semblance of order. "As the honourable councilperson is aware," he began, addressing Allegro directly, "every last penny of our budget has already been accounted for at a governmental level. This money is, indeed, for a disposal unit."

"A bin lorry," someone muttered, and Mr Red Tie glared in the complaint's direction.

"Yes. A bin lorry," he repeated, voice straining with the effort of keeping his temper. "They want us to buy a bin lorry. I am quite certain I don't need to remind any of you that all of the funds assigned for the upkeep of Steelepool are *non-discretionary.* So when that money comes in, it has a bloody great big label on it that says Bin Lorry, and it'd damn well better be spent on that bin lorry, because if it's not there will be no further label and no further *money. "*

The grumbles of complaint faded into a sullen silence. Even Allegro, who was this time sporting shoulder-length powder blue ringlets and a sharp, professional blazer, grudgingly accepted his point with a roll of their painted eyes. His cheeks flushed almost as red as his tie, the fraught councilman let out a sigh of genuine exhaustion. "I understand the impulse to help in the immediate, I really do," he said, "but setting ourselves up for far worse problems in the future is not the way we solve the immediate one."

"So what else do you suggest?" This was the strident snapper from before, a short woman with a round face framed by a fiery orange hijab and a voice still quivering with fury. "All you've done today is tell us what we cannot do, councilman, and not what we *can* do. We need solutions, and we need them now!"

A mumble of agreement rumbled about the room, raising the volume once more, and as Mr Red Tie's stores of patience visibly ran out and he gathered himself for what was likely to be a poorly considered reply, a pleasant voice rose over the clamour.

"Perhaps I may have a little something in mind that could help, hm?"

All turned to face a darkened corner where Ms Cellanea had been sitting on an upended keg, unnoticed until this very moment. As the room's attention focused on her, she raised the takeaway coffee cup in her hand in salute. "Bonne après-midi, my friends. Shall we get to work?"

Renji leaned back from the peephole and gave a quiet whistle in the dark. "Solid nine outta ten entrance, there! Them's some good dramatics."

"Eh. I give it a seven," whispered Melody, standing on tiptoe to take a look for herself. "She's done better."

In the now silent council room, Mr Red Tie was the first to pull himself together. "It's good of you to join us, Ms Cellanea, though we were lead to believe that your…" he cleared his throat, *"contributions* would be minimal for the time being."

"Because half of her mob got arrested, you mean," muttered the Snapper.

Ms Cellanea took a sip of coffee. "Let us simply say that a new opportunity has presented itself."

"Yeah, I'm thinking me and your opportunity might have met." Allegro's sly smile seemed to flicker in the direction of the peephole. "So how sure a thing are we talking, here?"

"I am quietly confident of our success."

"Oh please. You're playing around, the lot of you!" The Snapper slammed her hands onto the beer garden table, risking the poor thing's destruction in the process. "Swapping your coy little lines like you're in the movies! There are actual *people* out there, people who don't know if they're going to be able to make it through the week, and what've your little squad brought us for months now? A load of police attention and nothing else! Here's the only way your Loose Ends can help us now!" She pulled something out of her jacket pocket and held it up for all to see. It was a flyer in I.I.-branded colours, with a heading in serious bold uppercase. *FelonyFreezers: Do You Have Any Information To Share?*

Melody took a sharp breath. Renji knew why; FelonyFreezers was a public phone number for reporting criminal activity to the Forces in exchange for reward money. A snitch hotline. And from the way the council had erupted into a muddle of sound at the sight of the flyer, they knew what it was too.

"Oh come on!" the Snapper growled, standing firm at the head of the table as Cellanea took another sip of coffee. "Did you know the reward for handing over information about The Loose Ends has *doubled* in the last month? Doubled! The longer we cover for them, the more the risk is going to outweigh whatever they can do for us!"

The tension in the council room was palpable now, an unhealthy brew of uneasiness and outright hostility that threatened to boil over at any moment. Mr Red Tie's diplomatic appeals for calm sank without a trace, and just as Renji was starting to wonder if they were going to need to launch a rescue for his new boss, Allegro stepped up to the plate in full nightclub manager mode.

"Hey! Everyone shut up a moment, huh?!" they bellowed in a voice honed by years of shouting over thumping bass, silencing the shocked council.

"Alright, enough bullshit," they sighed, turning to the Snapper. "Haji, you gotta cool it. I get where you're coming from, we all do. Ain't none of us here wanna see y'all at the shelter going through this! We're as pissed as you are, right?" At Allegro's little verbal nudge, the rest of the council muttered in agreement. "Thing is... I hate to admit it, but Roberts had a point earlier." They nodded at Mr Red Tie in recognition.

Red Tie Roberts rolled his eyes, but let them continue uninterrupted.

"It's stupid to think short term. You hand over Celly and get a lil payout now, then what's gonna happen next winter? And the one after?"

The Snapper— Haji— twitched. "Maybe they'd take our cooperation into account..." she muttered, her face a twist of resentment.

"You think them upstairs are gonna grow a soul if you sell yours?" asked Allegro, softly. "Hajira... C'mon. You're desperate, not stupid. You know there ain't no point in sitting around hoping Imperium change their minds. A company's not a person; it ain't got no sympathy and it ain't gonna learn none. Not while there's no profit in

196

it, anyway."

Hajira deflated with a sound of pure frustration, the FelonyFreezer flyer a crumpled mess in her hand. "I just- I can't take it," she grated out, as Allegro patted her on the back. *"I hate this.* I hate not knowing what to do."

"Don't we all, sis," whispered Allegro. In the silence that followed, they nodded towards Ms Cellanea, still seated in the corner. "Well, the ol' gal here thinks she's got something. Might as well hear her out."

Mr Roberts took back his place at the head of the table, straightening his rumpled tie. After a reluctant nod from the rest of the room, Hajira included, he addressed Ms Cellanea. "The council will hear your proposal."

Pulling herself to her feet, she bobbed a sincere curtsey before the table. "My thanks to my fellow council members," she said. "To you especially, Allegro. Though I grant you permission to lose the *old* from the old gal."

The club owner arched one perfect eyebrow. "Always gotta push your luck."

"That is my job, yes." Ms Cellanea smiled. She stepped up alongside Roberts, her own greying head a clear foot lower than his, and faced the room at large.

"My proposal for you, my friends, is a simple one. Survive the night. Do what you can for those in need. And by tomorrow." She shrugged, "we shall see what has occurred."

At her words, an uneasy ripple of hopeful mutters fluttered about the room. Roberts frowned. "So you *do* have a plan, then?"

She waved away the question as though it were bobbing by on a light breeze. "I think it would be best to not burden this council with the details. Let us simply say that if all goes well, we ought to have a merry Christmas indeed."

#

Once the meeting came to a tense close, Renji and Melody emerged from their hiding place. The council had filed out, taking their ruckus with them and leaving the pub's basement seeming far emptier than it had from the other side of the wall. Minjun had also reappeared to take his place by his boss' side and leading in Weaver, who seemed far lighter on his toes than before.

"How's the leg, old man?" asked Renji, watching Weaver bending his knee experimentally.

"Better," was all he said, but the difference was apparent. His back was straighter, a far cry from the way his shoulders had hunched in pain with every step. Even that knotted frown had been ironed out by Auntie Septic's quick work, though he kept his expression steady as Cellanea smiled in his direction.

"Seemed kinda intense for local politics," Weaver muttered, apparently eager to change the subject.

"Yeah, where was all the dull admin shit we were promised?" said Renji, throwing himself into one of the plastic seats around the central table. "The paperwork! The amendments! I came out here for tedium, not high-stakes debate! Management, I'd like a refund please." The last was addressed to Minjun, who ignored it in favour of putting the kettle on.

"Oh, the amount of shouting was rather standard, though usually it is not quite so directed towards myself. Still, ce qui est fait n'est plus à faire. It ended well enough, and if we have our way, we shall not have to go through that again." Cellanea sighed, handing her assistant her empty coffee cup with a look of deep gratitude. "Please, do not think poorly of Hajira. She runs the shelter in Temperley, and they are sorely pressed at the moment."

"Desperate people do desperate things." said Weaver, propping himself up against a wall.

"Quite, though she is of a stronger sort than most. She will see sense, I am certain of this." Ms Cellanea settled in, her age-lined hands knotted on the table before her. "To be perfectly honest, I am glad you all saw that little display. It demonstrated the stakes at play rather well."

"How much we could bugger up, she means." Grabbing a mug from the table, Melody gave it a quick wipe with her sleeve before handing it to Minjun. "If you're brewin' up, I'll have one."

With a tut, he plucked the mug from her outstretched fingers, and took it over to a small sink in the corner to give it an actual clean. "How exciting to hear that I am also *your* assistant now, though I'd swear I hadn't put in an application for the role."

"Pleeease may I have a cuppa?" she half-sang, swinging on the back legs of her chair.

A damp tea towel landed on her head.

"Since you asked so nicely." The now-sparkling cup was ferried back to the tiny tea table.

As Minjun set about preparing the somewhat more polite coffee and tea requests from the rest of the table, Ms Cellanea opened her second meeting of the day with a gesture towards Renji. "Mr Hayakawa, I believe you are rather eager to share with us the details of your plan, and I believe we should very much like to hear them."

Renji sat up straight as though he'd been called on by teacher to present his homework to the rest of the class. Unlike during the majority of his school life, however, he'd put in the effort this time.

"Sure, yeah! Okay, so I've been to like a million of these Christmas parties. I know what they're gonna look like, who's gonna be there, and what they're gonna get up to, right? It's the usual corporate event; whole buncha schmoozing, too much wine, bad decisions in front of your boss, pretty standard; except for one thing. Cus it's meant to be this charity event, there's these big ol' sacks going around, right, and the idea is that you throw in some huge cash donation in front of everyone so they can see how generous you are. Paper money too, the only time you see it— uh, up there, at least. It's some real show-off bullshit."

From the shadows, Weaver cleared his throat.

"Uh, bull… stuff," corrected Renji impatiently. "Whatever, you get the point!"

"Hang about." Melody frowned, "they just pass the cash around? Couldn't anyone just…" She aimed a dipping motion into an imaginary sack of loot with a whistle.

"Take it?" Renji shrugged. "I suppose, but they're not gonna."

Minjun hummed in agreement, just audible over the straining hiss of the small travel kettle's pathetic attempts to boil. "The amount in there is nothing to them. Besides, the point of this type of event is to raise your reputation, not lower it."

"Yeah, you wanna show everyone how charitable you are. Not that they give a shit which 'charity' it's going to. Ain't like it's a legit one anyway, right?"

"Not according to our data," Minjun confirmed.

"Tax evasion," muttered Weaver.

"Yeah, that kinda thing!" Renji leaned back into his chair, finding he was settling into this idea, gaining confidence the more of it he said out loud. "Anyway, everyone makes a huge show of their donations for a couple of hours, then they take these sacks away and a bunch of other shit happens like a buffet and a dance and a guy dressed as Santa drives about in a little sleigh to give stuff to the kids, blah blah blah, none of that matters. All we gotta do is grab that cash before it vanishes outta the building and into some Swiss bank account or whatever."

"Do you know where in the building it would be taken?" asked Ms Cellanea.

"Nah, not exactly the sorta thing they advertise. And they change the venue every year anyway, besides. This time it's some hotel that just opened this year, uh…" Tapping the table in irritation, Renji tried to dig out the name from its hiding place in the middle of Jeremy from Marketing's blather. He snapped his fingers as the memory unearthed itself. "Il Coccodrillo!"

Ms Cellanea blinked in surprise. "The Crocodile? A strange name. Crocodiles are not known for their hospitality."

"I've heard of it." Minjun placed a mug of milky coffee on the table before a grateful Cellanea, and flipped open the cover on his phone. "The name is something of a tacky gimmick. As is the building."

After a moment's searching, he scrolled through what seemed like one of dozens of articles packed with extravagant praise to show a picture of what could have been any given nouveau hotel restaurant combo among the Court's glassy spires, if it weren't for one standout feature; partway up the building an infinity pool jutted out of the side of the building like a crystalline aquatic balcony, its water catching the light in a manner that the photographer must have been very pleased with indeed, and within those shimmering depths swam a dark, dangerous, and very reptilian shape.

"Goddamn." muttered Weaver, breaking the stunned silence.

"Yeah, seriously." Melody muttered. "Enclosure's not wide enough for a crocodile that big. Should be at least twice the length of the adult reptile."

The stunned silence was now aimed in a different direction.

"What? I worked in a pet shop for a bit." she shrugged. "Point is, that's just cruel, that is, putting a living thing up like a bloody billboard just for publicity. Why would you do that?"

Cellanea observed the picture, her smile grim. "Perhaps your answer is within your question, my dear."

"Ugh." Melody shuddered, taking her newly delivered mug of tea and cradling it, her mechanical fingers poking above the pulled-up sleeves of Cadence's jacket. "These swag bags though. Could drop a tracker in there, that'll do the job."

"Hell yeah!" Renji beamed at the hacker in delight. "Sounds like a plan!"

"Aye." She took a sip of tea; black, one sugar. "Just pop it where you want and follow it on a paired phone. If I boost the range on the signal a bit you could follow it around the building. Easy as."

"Alright, we can work with that! Guess that means you're my plus-one, huh?" He dumped his bag onto the table and pawed through it until he pulled out the suit he'd stashed away. Could hardly turn up to an event like that in jeans and sneakers, after all, and if he could only grab one outfit on the way out of his previous life it may as well be one with the nice red inlay.

Melody, meanwhile, had frozen. "Um. What?"

"You're coming in with me!" Pulling a favourite hairbrush out of the bag, he span it around his finger and threw the mortified girl a wink. "How else are you gonna get close enough to set up your bug, genius?"

"But. Uh." Melo seemed to be still stuck in place, as though trapped in a loading screen. It seemed that the simple prospect of entering a party had rattled her more than the airship jailbreak and the ongoing blackout combined. "You, uh. You could just drop the tracker in yourself…"

"And if the money's all stashed away in some safe with a crazy electric lock then what am *I* gonna do, talk it open? I need my computer witch!"

"Can't you break into their network like on the ship?" asked Weaver. "Do it all remote again?"

She mumbled something into her tea. It didn't sound especially positive.

"That was a stroke of luck on our part." translated Ms Cellanea, watching Melody with concern. "We cannot guarantee their network will have such an opening as that one did."

"It's no problem, I'll be on the list! You can just pretend to be my date." Renji reassured her. "And it's okay if you don't have a dress or whatever, I lifted one of Aunty L's for you! Might wanna take it in a little, but yeah." He pulled the silky length of ivory and gold fabric

202

out of the bag, and Melo inhaled a lungful of tea.

"Doesn't look like the lady wants to step out with you, kid." chuckled Weaver, over the sound of her coughs.

"I mean it's not an actual *date,* I'm not even—" Renji paused, then shook his head. "Look, just don't worry about that, okay?"

"It's not that." Melody coughed, as Cellanea patted her on the back. "I'm just not very… chatty. And the rich people and the pretty dresses and that, it's… not my scene, is it." She shifted awkwardly, seeming to shrink deeper into the beaten leather of her sister's jacket.

"I am certain you can turn your hand to anything you choose, dear girl." Ms Cellanea told her. Her sincere smile met its match in the face of a wretched lip wobble of pure misery.

"Couldn't someone else do it…?" pleaded Melo.

"I mean I *could* show up there with the old man on my arm, but that's gonna raise a couple of eyebrows, y'know?" It had occurred to Renji that him showing up in female company would also probably lose a few quiet bets between the more gossip-hungry hangers-on, but he kept that to himself for now.

"Perhaps if your sister were to step in—" Cellanea began, and there was a moment where everyone pictured Cadence in a roomful of executives. In this image, she was cracking her knuckles. "On second thought, perhaps not."

"It's gonna be simple, anyhow." Renji grinned. "I'll handle the talking!"

"I'm sure you will," Minjun said quietly, passing over a coffee.

Renji grabbed the mug, dumped three sugars and too much milk in it, and had another shot at being encouraging. "It kinda sucks, but you could just play dumb, y'know? Bat your eyelashes, smile, and if someone asks a question just giggle at 'em."

"Giggle." Melody took a deep breath and held it in.

"Yeah, giggle!"

"Fine." She exhaled. "I could... giggle."

"You giggle for the good of your city, my girl." Cellanea beamed at her.

"So you track down the cash and crack the safe. How d'ya move it out?" Weaver asked, taking a black coffee from Minjun with a nod of thanks. "Ain't gonna fit that amount in your pockets, y'know."

"That's where you come in, old man!" Renji flipped Weaver a lazy salute that made his eyes narrow. "Il Coccodrillo's one of those places that's like ninety-nine percent window, so they got them platform things on the outside to send some poor bastard up to give the glass a clean."

Those grey eyes narrowed further. "Lemme guess. I'm the poor bastard."

"You got it! If you can jack one of those outdoor death-elevators and meet us on the right floor..."

"He could take the money and bring it down to street level along the outside of the building," said Minjun, taking a seat with his own mug of lightly sugared tea in hand.

"Hell yeah he can. Then me and Melo just stroll on outta there and meet you in the getaway van! ...Uh, there *is* a getaway van, right?"

"I can find one," said Weaver, without a trace of doubt.

"Alright! Getaway van!" Renji raised his mug in a joyful toast. A fully formed plan and a getaway, this was all coming together even better than he'd hoped.

Leaning back in her plastic chair, Cellanea gave a thoughtful nod. "Not bad, not bad at all. Now, to address the weaker points of this little affair."

"Weak points?" Renji blinked. *"What* weak points?"

"To take a van up to the Court, you will each require an ID that will allow All Tier Access, and will work on a freight elevator."

"Oh. Um…" Renji halted, mid-protest. The idea of someone not having open access to all three tiers of Unity wasn't something he'd even considered.

"I believe Melody is still Steelepool Tier, I suspect Mr Weaver may only go so high as Central Commons, and I am afraid that we are not in possession of anything more at the moment."

An outstretched metallic palm slid into Renji's view. "Gimme your phone." He handed it to Melody before he could think better of it. It was a sleek new model, one he was rather fond of. He hadn't even cracked the screen on it yet.

"Uh, isn't that trackable or whatever?" he asked, hoping she wasn't about to rip the thing open.

"Not when I'm done with it." As she powered the thing on she rolled back the sleeve of her mechanical right arm, withdrew a wire, and connected the two. After a minute of tapping at her own phone and waiting for several installs to complete, a few dozen lines of code popped up, and Melody let out a low whistle. "Cor, you're on better than All Tier, mate. You're on Open Access. One step down from root."

"That's good?" asked Renji, feeling a little lost. He rarely used his phone for anything more complicated than paying for drinks.

"That's bloody brilliant, is what it is. Never had my hands on one of *these* before." There was a hungry glint in her eye, all concern about dresses and parties vanishing as she scanned row upon row of nonsensical symbols with quiet glee. "Mm. I can piggyback a couple of falsies off of this, no worries." She looked up from the screen and towards Renji. "If they check back in their logs it'll be obvious that it's your ID we're using, though."

"Yeah, well…" Renji stared at the screen of a phone he'd thought he was pretty damn familiar with as she ran her safety scan, stripping away various apps he'd never interacted with. The names on them had always seemed benign enough. "That's fine," he said, eventually. "Go ahead."

That got him another of those serene little half-smiles. "Sound."

Cellanea nodded, satisfied. "Next, I should like to know if you are up to this task, Mr Weaver?"

"Reckon so," said Weaver, with a glance down at his temporary yet far-improved leg. "So your docs say, anyhow."

"Can you drive a van?" Minjun asked.

Weaver snorted dismissively. "Drove a Commons bus for years, a van ain't nothing."

"Wait, no, hang on!" interjected Renji, who had all but dropped his coffee. *"You're* a bus driver? *You?!"* It seemed impossible to picture the knife-wielding airship-scaling guy who had taken out the biggest guard on AirCast Two taking tickets from cross-town commuters.

"That so unbelievable?" grunted Weaver.

"You just seem kinda murdery for a bus driver, is all."

"As someone who has frequently taken a Commons bus, I can assure you that it is entirely believable," Minjun said.

"Very good." Cellanea's warm smile flashed in Weaver's direction for the briefest of moments before she placed her drained coffee back on the table with finality. "Now, there is one last point to discuss. Mr Hayakawa, you seem rather certain that you are not in trouble with the Forces, yes?"

Renji shrugged. "Well, yeah! Aunty L said she took care of all that."

"And no others who saw you escape AirCast Two shall be present?"

He had already given this angle some thought; the only ones who had seen his mid-air escape were Sergeant Flood and his shitty little cronies, all of whom were far too unimportant to be strutting around a soiree of that level. "Absolutely not," he confirmed proudly.

Cellanea nodded. "And your aunt. What is it that she expects you are doing tonight?"

"Dunno, she usually just lets me do whatever."

An unreadable look was exchanged between Cellanea and her assistant. "So you're sure," said Minjun carefully, "that when she sees you appear at the party unprompted, this won't raise any alarm bells?"

Renji paused.

"Well—" he began, but didn't get much further.

"The commander's gonna be there?" Weaver had glanced up sharply enough to spill a few drops of coffee.

"No no, it's okay…!" Renji's protests went ignored as Minjun let out a deep sigh and Cellanea clicked her tongue in irritation.

"Whoops," Melody whispered over her tea.

"Woah hey, everyone calm down, it's *fine!"* Renji insisted. "She absolutely won't be going! Aunty L's never met a company party she can't dodge, she *hates* 'em! Hell, she doesn't even like Christmas! She was already racking up an excuse to skip it when I saw her today!"

"Mr Hayakawa…" Ms Cellanea leaned back in her chair, her customary smile replaced with the do-not-mess-me-about-sunshine glare favoured by schoolteachers and head nurses everywhere. "This is very, very important. I need to know that you are certain this will not be a problem."

"Fuckin' A, one hundo percent! Aunty L will *not* be there." Renji said. "No way in hell is there gonna be a problem."

He was pretty certain that if he repeated it enough times, it would have to be true.

CHAPTER 15

WHAT COULD POSSIBLY GO WRONG?

The elevator pay station's card reader chirped in satisfaction. *Open Return Off-Peak Rate (Steelepool Freight 358- Imperium Court Freight 358) x 3: Fare paid successfully! Have a nice day!* agreed the ticket app on Renji's phone, and he let out the breath he'd been holding onto as the elevator doors opened with a welcoming *ping.*

"Told you it'd work," muttered Melody.

"Didn't say it wouldn't," Weaver muttered right back. "Just said it was difficult."

Tucking his phone away, Renji kept his expression serene for any hidden cameras as the gate before them slid open. "Can we try a little less suspicious mumbling, folks?"

With a final dark grumble and no flair for performance, Weaver rolled the van forward into the waiting freight elevator, which turned out to be a bare space with no delusions of being anything more than a bland, inoffensive container to wait in while rumbling upwards to one's target destination.

The van Weaver had managed to source— it seemed best not to ask how or from where— was a standard white transit van of the kind that formed a majority of the vehicles on the roads of Central Commons, a smart choice for when the time came to slip away into the crowd. As a bonus it even had a rack of ladders on top, which was the sort of touch that ought to help sell the window washer facade. The inside of the vehicle was empty aside from Weaver's bag of mysterious tactical crap, Weaver himself, Renji, Melody, and the awkward silence that had descended between them once the lift had begun to climb.

Silence! Renji hated that shit. Usually he had no trouble pushing it away with some distracting chatter, but what the hell was someone meant to say in this kinda situation? *Hey, how you enjoying the heist so far? Pretty nice huh, d'you think they'll have good snacks at the place we're about to fuck over cus hoo boy am I starving.* It seemed a little insufficient. He'd also rejected the standard ice-breaking tactic of throwing out a compliment on Melody's new ensemble; it couldn't be clearer than she wanted to rip the whole thing off, throw it into the river, and find a nice keyboard to hide behind. Since they'd entered the van she'd barely spoken, aside from the occasional discomfited hum, sitting all bunched up in her seat as though she could make herself vanish into the gaps between the cushions with enough effort.

Considering the hurry they'd been in, Cellanea had done an excellent job with Melo's hair, tucking away the too-recognisable dyed ends into an elegant and neat low bun that covered the cranial port in the base of her neck, and Minjun had done some quick, neat work with safety pins to draw the dress in to better fit its new, far shorter owner.

Since the gown had belonged to the pragmatic yet stylish Aunty Lissa, it was a practical affair in clean ivory and gold trim, styled without much in terms of frill or excess, with an agreeable neckline and a drape that fell to skim the ankle without much fuss. The look was completed with a clutch that Melo complained was too small, a pair of elbow-length prosthetic-hiding gloves that she tugged at in irritation, and Flood's ornate golden sword belted at her hip, which she clearly hated in every way it was possible to hate something.

("Don't see why I have to wear this bloody thing and you don't," she'd grumbled as Renji had handed her the blade.

"Cus it's the style, and cus I can't fight for shit!" he'd told her, not adding that it was also because he found it funny to bring Flood's sword to a party the man himself wouldn't be invited to.)

Renji was wearing his favourite black suit, the one whose cut had always been the most flattering, having carefully adjusted the buttons and tie in just the right way to ensure they appeared careless. The tie was loose, the cufflinks were forgotten, and the shoes pinched in that way that expensive shoes always did. As he'd slipped on the tailored jacket with its crimson silk lining, he'd found himself idly trying to remember just how much this outfit had cost. He couldn't. That sort of number hadn't been so important at the time he'd bought it.

The silence remained. Weaver sat with his arms folded, staring resolutely at nothing. Melody glared out of the van's window at the safety information pinned to the elevator's walls as though it had done her some great injustice. Restless and fidgety, Renji fiddled with the tiny earpiece he had been told would enable communication between the three of them, though it was evidently not doing its job at the moment. A near invisible comms device sounded useful and cool until it was painfully clipped in place, plus the range on the things was restricted to avoid detection, meaning it couldn't reach down to Buried and summon any help from Cellanea, if it was needed.

Or hear any conversation from her either.

Which brought him back round to the silence.

Fuck it. Renji kicked the door of the van open, stomped around the side of it past the signs requesting that all passengers wait inside their vehicles, and located the carriage's sole tiny window. A moment later, there was a quiet rustle as Melody joined him in staring out past the glass.

Outside and below them, Buried stretched out like a dark, mottled blanket.

"Doesn't look how I thought it would." she said eventually.

"You haven't been up here before?"

Rather than give an answer she shrugged one shoulder, standing on her toes for a better look. "Wish Cade could see it too."

"She'll remember *you* seeing it though, right? Shared memories, or whatever."

A gloved finger dragged along the glass, tracing the black line of the River Steele, running from the port to bisect the city below. "Not the same."

How long had it been since the two sisters had shared a room rather than sharing a body? How long since they'd even been able to speak to each other? Renji had a lot of questions, but he wasn't certain he'd earned the answers quite yet.

"Dark out there." he said instead.

"Yeah."

"Darker than it was yesterday."

"Mm."

Immense supports and girders slid into view, smothering the landscape before them, until the entire window gave way to a blackness suggesting they'd reached the underside of Central Commons. As it was on its express route their elevator continued to rise through Commons without stopping, and the inside of the carriage was flooded with amber streetlights and the ambient glow of the city—all the bustle of a standard Friday evening.

Neither Renji nor Melody said anything more as they passed the steady rows of bright, burning lights. Advertisements winked alongside the buildings that ran parallel to their own bursts of electric colour, millions of LEDs working in brilliant symphony.

"Hell of a view, huh," murmured Weaver, who had silently joined them by the window.

"If you're about to tell me I've got another last chance to reconsider this, you're wasting your breath." Renji smirked.

"Nah. Too late for that."

"Oh." The smirk withered. "Well… alright then. Good."

After several more long moments of silence, the view from the window vanished into blackness one last time, and the elevator doors slid open with a *ping.*

The approach to Il Coccodrillo was pretty much as Renji had expected it to be; the red carpet had been rolled out, a lavish display of Christmas lights were twisted into elegant arches leading towards the hotel's entrance, and a queue of the Court's finest and better-connected snaked out and along the pavement for some distance. Several storeys above, the crocodile that gave the place its name swam a lazy circle in the too-small enclosure of the lidded balcony pool, unconcerned with the chattering crowd below that was making use of the great selfie opportunity it was providing.

Melody's frown deepened as she pulled the pretty crocheted shawl she'd borrowed from Cellanea about her shoulders in an attempt to keep out the cold. It didn't seem especially up to the task. They'd hopped out of the van by the elevator, leaving Weaver to get himself and the vehicle into position, and in the time it had taken for her and Renji to walk the two blocks to the venue the hacker had already decided she'd had more than enough of this.

"Didn't know there'd be a bloody queue," she complained, squinting with annoyance at the cloudy night sky where light flakes of snow had begun to dance on the breeze. "Should've brought a proper coat."

"Lucky for you, I don't do queues." Renji linked her arm with his, and walked them straight past the line to the front.

"Sir, ma'am, you need to be on the list to—" began the doorman, and before he could even finish the sentence Renji's ID was already in his face.

"Pretty sure I am, bud." He winked at the startled doorman.

"Y-yes, sir, Mr Starkweather! Right this way, sir."

Beside him, Melody cringed at the scandalised stares and outraged whispers from the waiting crowd as they sauntered by. Renji didn't quite understand why; to him, that had always been one of the better parts of these evenings.

The party was taking place in the hotel's ballroom, located halfway up the Court-levels of the building; a perfect height for an excellent view of the city and, more importantly, of the crocodile. The elevator leading to this floor stopped there, meaning that if a guest's destination was further up the hotel they would have to walk across the ballroom to be suitably impressed by its grandeur before they could reach the upper floors lift on the other side.

Both elevators were of that retro New York apartment style, the kind that came complete with visible beams and even a metal grille that pulled over the front, all rendered in gleaming, classy brass. As the grille pulled open, they emerged into a huge space so spacious and modern with its high ceilings and wide windows that it reminded Renji of Aunty Lissa's flat, leading him to wonder if Jeremy from Marketing or some other, similar, Jeremy had chosen it that way on purpose to appeal to the commander. All of the guests were in lavish overpriced formal dress, some in Forces dress uniform, many carrying fashionable duelling blades ranging from delicate little pearl-handled daggers to full bejewelled cavalry sabres. Large tables lined the walls, laden with pricey yet tiny food and a tower of champagne glasses, an open bar that the partygoers were very much taking advantage of. A man in black tie was seated at a great grand piano cased in transparent plastic, the workings visible as he played an inoffensive soft jazz version of 'Jingle Bells'. To his credit, the guy was doing a pretty good job of keeping his concentration considering that a feral pack of unattended kids were darting about and under his piano's legs playing a loud game of who knows what, yelling and skidding on the floor and scuffing up their best dress clothes in the manner of little kids everywhere.

However, that was all just detail. The real centrepiece of the ballroom was a huge Christmas tree, decorated with baubles in I.I.'s blue and silver-grey, strung with dozens or possibly hundreds of delicate spun-glass lights. A great golden chandelier crouched above it, its own equally absurd quantity of fragile lights like stars dipping so low and the tree reaching so high they almost seemed to form a pillar of light, an immense crystalline fixture around which the guests milled and mingled and laughed at their bosses' jokes and networked and drank and ate as if there was nothing wrong going on below their very feet.

It used to be that all of this flashy grandstanding excess bored Renji but today, it made him feel a little ill. Glancing across at his 'date', he could tell from the scowl on her face that she wasn't holding up much better.

"C'mon, you're excited to be here, remember?" He jogged her arm, dialling up the brightness on his fake smile as he scanned the crowd for someone to make nice with. So far, he seemed to be correct about the attendance; there was no sign of either Aunty L or Sergeant Flood, and thus a pleasing lack of people who may blow his cover.

"Haaaate this," Melody growled through her teeth, glowering at the tree.

"Cheer up!" He beamed. "Try some of that rich people food. Foie gras or caviar or whatever."

She wrinkled her nose. "Ergh, no. Vegetarian."

"Huh. I didn't know that."

"Worked at McDonalds. That'll turn anyone."

He blinked, wondering if there was an establishment between here and Manchester she hadn't been employed at. "Listen, I know this sucks, but til those bags of cash start circling we gotta look like happy normal guests who aren't trying to kill the decorations with laser vision— Oh hi, Captain!" Renji waved to a Forces Upper Manager he vaguely recalled and began a course of gentle schmoozing around the room, greeting people he recognised and some who recognised him. There were more than a few faces missing from the usual crowd in the wake of the firings and reshuffling Harlow's broadcast had caused, and a definite air of low-key uneasiness, which Renji couldn't help but savour.

Several times he ran through the standardised acceptable conversation script; *No I haven't seen you in a while, yes the venue does look fabulous, of course I'll pass on your regards to my aunt,* peppered with the right jokes, laughs or nods of sympathy where appropriate. He'd always been good at playing this particular game, and tonight he was on fine form, even managing to draw enough attention that Melody was able to stay lurking silently on the edges of conversation, hidden behind a distant look of neutrality and a plate of expensive cheese on sticks.

By the second glass of champagne Renji had begun to relax into the role of Dutiful Nephew, and was listening politely to the world's most boring accountant's pitch about the benefits of offshoring funds and by the way does your Aunt need anyone to review her finances when a sharp elbow nudged him in the ribs. Excusing himself, he turned to find Melody squinting across the room.

"Look," she said, around a mouthful of imported French brie. There they were, on the other side of the ballroom's dancefloor, circling by the piano; the donation sacks, in the care of a gaggle of interns dressed as Santa's elves. They had the pointy hats and the shoes with bells on and everything, the poor bastards.

"Now there's a job," she remarked, nose wrinkling.

"Probably one they had to fistfight twenty other applicants to get." Renji cocked his head. "You ready?"

Opening her clutch to peek inside, she nodded. "Let's go."

Slipping his arm through hers, Renji had begun to lead them towards their target when—

"*Mr Starkweather?!* Oh, haha, so glad you could make it!"

That empty laugh shot across the ballroom with terrible clarity. Squeezing his eyes shut, Renji considered pretending he hadn't heard the remark, but such a faux pas could draw the sort of major social attention they very much didn't want, so instead he spun on his heel with a smile and clicked his fingers in recognition. "Jeremy from Marketing, right?" he smiled, over the sound of Melody's groan of complaint.

"Yes, yes! That's right!" Jeremy from Marketing cleared the space between them with the speed of a sprinter. "Haha, um, I wanted to extend my apologies if I misspoke earlier, I- I didn't mean to—"

"Oh please!" Renji waved the apology away magnanimously. "Forget about it! Hell, if anything, I should be apologising to you, huh?" He dipped his voice to a conspiratorial whisper. "Just between you and me, I've been trying to quit smoking, and well; ya caught me mid-cig!"

"Oh!" Jeremy from Marketing's eyes lit with delight at the prospect of being let in on a little secret. "I've always heard that's a difficult habit to break, haha."

"Got kinda pissed at myself for slipping, but I shouldn't have taken it out on you, man. That's on me."

"Well, your secret's safe with me!" He smiled, miming the old zip across the mouth motion.

Renji very much wished that zip was real. "Well nice to catch up, Jer, but we gotta be on our way to—" But already Jeremy from Marketing, the perennial networker, had decided to go ahead and do what no-one else in the room had bothered doing yet, and addressed Melody.

"I don't believe we've met yet, Miss…?"

She blinked at him in stark horror, the pause between his simple question and her lack of answer extending for far too long.

C'mon, Melo, you can do this, Renji urged her on silently as the hacker's grip on his arm tightened into a vice. *Just make up a name and pretend it's yours!*

But rather than saying *hello I am Susan Smith, a pleasure to meet you*, Melody instead took the terrible route of trying to follow Renji's advice.

"HAHAHA." was the noise she made.

It took him a moment or two to even realise that was meant to be a giggle. The alien noise had creaked out of her as though she were an under-oiled robot, her face bearing a frozen expression resembling someone's last-known photo.

216

Jeremy from Marketing's eyebrows practically hit the ceiling. Even by his standards, that was a hell of a fake laugh.

Attempting an emergency rescue, Renji shuffled in front of her. "Ah, what she means to say is—"

A delicate little sniff and a shiver sounded behind Renji. A gloved hand fell on his shoulder, moving him aside.

"Oh my gawd, I'm like, *soooo* sorry! Silly me, I always forget the bubbly stuff goes straight to my head!" his 'date' giggled. Actually *giggled,* a real giggle, rather than a sound like a lawnmower that had run over a sprinkler head. "I'm Janey! It's so nice to meet you, Mr Jeremy! My gosh, isn't everything here just *beautiful?"*

"It is, isn't it!" Beamed Jeremy from Marketing, visibly grateful to be back on solid ground. "I designed the centrepieces, you know."

"No waaaay!" she gasped in mock surprise, one hand flying to her mouth as the other tugged on Renji's arm. "Babe, wasn't I just saying how pretty those flowers were? With the big silver leaves and the sticky-up things and the glitter? *Soooo* pretty!"

"Y-yeah. Real pretty," he stuttered, watching flabbergasted as 'Janey' tittered and simpered and twisted a loose lock of hair around her finger while Jeremy from Marketing explained the finer points of choosing winter-appropriate blossoms while remaining faithful to the brand's colours.

"By the way, while I have you Mr Starkweather, there's someone I'd like you to meet!" Jeremy from Marketing enthused. "Do you know Delaney, in sales?"

The sudden question jolted Renji out of his stunned trance. "Uh, no, I don't think so."

"Oh he's a real up-and-comer, just lighting the whole department on fire! You'll simply love him, haha!" Jeremy from Marketing was all but giggling himself, now. "I'll go fetch him, excuse me a moment!" Stopping only to give 'Janey' a nod that dipped so low it nearly became a bow, Jeremy from Marketing scampered off.

This was the sort of move Renji had seen before; people would be all too happy to introduce the commander's nephew to someone they wanted to impress, thus making themselves look well-connected and earning a favour to repay at the same time. It seemed that Jeremy from Marketing fancied a chance at being Jeremy from Sales.

Renji could not begin to care about that, however, not after what he'd just seen. Already the false Janey had shifted off the dancefloor and over to a quiet little corner of the buffet table, where she was pretending to survey the bread rolls with deep interest.

"What the heck!" whispered Renji, hopping over to meet her. "That was *amazing!* Where the hell did that finesse come from?!"

"I hate this," she growled, snatching up a bread roll like King Kong might snatch up a blonde. "I hate your plan. I hate you. But we're here now, everyone's waiting for us, and Melo's out of her depth when she isn't behind a keyboard. So, if a giggling idiot is what we need, then I'll the *most* giggling," she jabbed her fingers into the bread roll, "most *idiot* you ever flippin' saw." With a tearing motion, Cadence disembowelled the hapless roll. "Cus *I* know how to get the job done. Got it?"

"Hang on a fucking second, how come you're the angry one when you literally tried to kill me last night?" retorted Renji.

"Didn't try it, just suggested it. If I were proper trying, you'd have known about it, mate." Cade stuffed the lump of bread innards into her mouth and chewed savagely. "Anyway, you're the one who legged it and made a scene."

"Oh yeah, next time I'm running for my life I'll keep it more subtle," he grumbled. "This is bullshit. Here I am bringing you an amazing cashgrab on a silver platter, and you still don't trust me."

"Nope. Like I said, I don't like you."

"Why not? Melody likes me."

"I'm not Melody, am I?"

A petty little notion struck Renji, and he seized it with both hands. "Hey, no worries! These things take time," he grinned. "Mark my words though, soon enough you won't know how you managed without me!"

Cadence threw him a suspicious scowl over the hollowed-out remains of her bread. "The hell do you mean by that?"

"Oh, you know, since I'm going to be around you guys so much now, you'll see me all the time. Pretty much every day! We're gonna be working real close with each other, y'know!" He chuckled. "Yeah, I can tell already. Give it a little time, and you and me are gonna be *good friends.*"

She snorted, a mix of annoyance and shock that sent loose crumbs tumbling to the floor. "Fuck that."

"We'll see..." Her nose wrinkled in disgust, and Renji went in for the kill. "...soon-to-be-bestie!" He winked, as obnoxiously as possible.

The look that now darkened Cade's face was similar to the one he'd seen on the crocodile earlier. He savoured her aggravation; a little vengeance for the fright she'd given him back at the leisure centre. "Anyway," he smirked, "we'd better go track down those bags before we have to deal with—"

"Haha, thought I'd lost you two for a minute there!" With impeccable timing once more, Jeremy from Marketing Who Wanted To Be Jeremy from Sales was pushing through the crowd in their direction.

"Piss," muttered Cade, dusting the last of the breadcrumbs off her front and plastering on her vacant Janey smile. Renji glanced around, but the buffet table corner offered no suitable paths for escape. It seemed that this useless little encounter with some random berk from sales was inevitable.

Oh well, might as well get it over with. As he took a deep, steadying breath before facing his fate, Renji caught a surprising edge of a familiar peppery scent; one that reminded him of warmth and red leather, and the instant he looked up to introduce himself to the couple trailing behind Jeremy, all of the pleasantries he had lined up died in his throat.

"Mr Starkweather, Chance Delaney." beamed Jeremy happily. "Mr Delaney, this is Renjiro Starkweather."

"Is it, indeed…?" An all-too familiar handsome stranger leaned forward to take Renji's unresisting hand. "Well, well. What a delight."

CHAPTER 16

CRISIS MANAGEMENT

The handshake felt as though it lasted for three hundred years, yet somehow that still wasn't long enough for Renji to process what was happening. The stranger from the club— the one whose jacket he'd stolen, the one who he'd been making out with only hours ago, the one who was apparently Chance Delaney— had a tall red-headed woman on his arm and what sounded like a burgeoning career in sales to his name. Renji wasn't sure which was throwing him off more.

As he released the handshake, Chance had already managed to smooth the surprise out of his own expression. "A pleasure, Mr Starkweather," he said cordially. "You'd be the commander's nephew, then…?"

"Yep. That's me," Renji managed. "Renjiro Starkweather," he was forced to add, because Jeremy had pronounced it wrong.

"Fascinating," hummed Chance, in a tone that could not have been better calculated to send a shiver up Renji's spine. "Then it's an honour to meet you, Renjiro."

He pronounced it well. He pronounced it *way too well.*

With some effort, Renji pulled himself together and turned towards the beautiful woman whose arm was twined around Delaney's. "And you are?" he asked, attempting to keep the accusation out of his tone.

"My fiancée, Annisette." Chance said, his practised smile betraying not a hint of shame.

"Ah, haha, Ms Accardo's in accounting, am I right?" chimed Jeremy. The woman gave the barest of nods in reply. Unlike Chance, she hadn't even bothered with the polite false smile; her expression

221

was cold and distant, as though her mind and her body were in entirely separate places. All the same, the redhead was the picture of icy composure, her free hand resting on the formidable silver blade hanging from a delicate belt at her hip. Between the sword and the general air of dangerous glamour, this woman couldn't have seemed less like an accountant if she'd tried.

"I'm Janey!" exclaimed Cadence, who was unable to keep out of a situation for long. "Woooow, accounting! That's like, numbers and stuff, right?"

After hearing that pearl of wisdom Annisette checked out of the conversation, staring off into the middle distance as Jeremy and Janey fake-giggled back and forth about the difficulties of doing basic sums. Yet even if Renji had wanted to follow their conversation, it would have been impossible to concentrate on anything except the look Chance was giving him at that moment. While the man had been interested in Renji back at Static Void, it hadn't seemed like anything more than a passing curiosity, one that would have been unlikely to last past breakfast in bed. Now, however, those cunning green eyes were alight with intrigue.

Typical. Like any other ladder-climber he'd met, once they heard the surname Renji became nothing more than a walking shot at a promotion, and he'd gone and given this beautiful asshole the perfect blackmail material. Aunty L had always told him to avoid the sales department, and while he doubted this was what she had in mind, he could see what she'd meant.

As the conversation nattered on around them he could still feel the man's burning, persistent stare. Renji risked another glance in Delaney's direction, intending to meet him head-on with a look of his own to suggest that any attempt to leverage their brief little tryst would be a very bad idea indeed; but it was apparent that promotion was not on the man's mind. Chance Delaney's gaze was sliding over every inch of Renji, deliberate yet eager, his lips slightly parted in quiet appraisal. As their eyes met, a wry quirk of one dark brow was enough to suggest the sort of conclusion he'd come to, and it didn't seem to involve blackmail. Narrowing his eyes, Renji shot a pointed glance towards the disinterested fiancée, posing a silent yet pertinent question. The reply came in the form of a nonchalant one-shouldered shrug; whatever was happening there, it was no big deal, apparently.

"—isn't that right, Mr Starkweather?" Jeremy from Marketing asked.

"Of course, yes," replied Renji without skipping a beat, wondering what the hell he'd just agreed to. Whatever it had been, it was enough to prompt a fresh round of laughter from both Jeremy and Janey.

"Ohhh look babe, they're coming over! It's the thing with the bags that you told me about, isn't it?" She jogged his arm, pointing at the approaching interns with a gasp of delight. *"Soooo* exciting!"

Thank fuck. That meant a natural end to the conversation was presenting itself, one Renji accepted with open arms. The intern in the dismal elf costume jingled their way over to dutifully hold up a sack, a traditional burlap affair stamped with jolly letters reading *EXPRESS DELIVERY FROM THE NORTH POLE!*

Delaney flipped open a money clip, and with only the briefest glance to make certain he was being watched he tossed more than a few notes inside, then stepped aside to make way for Renji with an overwrought bow and a look that had far too much smoulder in it.

Aware of the multitude of eyes on him Renji opted for a showy approach, reaching into his jacket and withdrawing with a flourish the a stack of cash that represented the majority of what had been in his bank account. Just as he'd been hoping, a ripple of gasps went through the nearby crowd. With everyone staring at the stack and trying to calculate the total of that charitably huge chunk of change, that ought to mean it would be simple for Cadence to fish the tracker out of her clutch unseen.

"If you'd do me the honour, my dear?" Renji said, syrup-sweet, handing his 'date' the bills as they'd planned. With a joyful squeal Janey dumped the fistfuls of cash into the sack along with the tracking bug, to a round of polite applause from the oblivious guests.

"Haha, fabulous! Thank you Mr Delaney, Mr Starkweather! What kind donations!" bleated Jeremy from Marketing, who was holding out his phone to take pictures. "Looks like you're both in a generous mood!"

Chance flashed Renji a smile. "I do love to give."

"Well it's been lovely, folks," began Renji before his face could finish turning scarlet, "but if you'll excuse us, me and Janey have an appointment with the dessert cart."

Their excuse saw them across the ballroom, where they took up a strategic position behind the gateaux. This suited Renji just fine; after what had just happened, he needed to catch his breath, though the chances of that happening with Cadence around seemed slim. Sweeping up a dessert spoon with a scowl, she was about to say something when their earpieces crackled.

"I'm in position. What's your status?" The gravelly tones of Weaver were just audible over the party's constant sounds of chatting and music.

"All good, old man!" Renji responded, perhaps too quickly.

Squinting at him, Cadence drew her phone out of her clutch. "Donation's paid in, sir." she said, tapping at the screen. "Looks like we're online. Just have to wait til they're done with their stupid show-off parade, then they'll take the bags to their safe room."

A grunt of affirmation. "Good. You maintaining your cover?"

The squint aimed in Renji's direction intensified. "Yep. We're in the clear," he replied, keeping a wary eye on the spoon Cade was wielding.

"Roger. Send an alert when we're moving to the next phase."

"You got it."

As he turned back to the dessert cart, he was relieved to see that Cade was digging the spoon into a pile of profiteroles rather than his own liver. She'd scraped her chosen pastries onto her plate from the bottom of the stack, collapsing the artfully arranged pyramid that had

224

probably taken some poor chef hours to set up. With a loud sigh at the state of it all, Renji snagged one for himself from the sad heap of choux and popped it into his mouth.

"So. Is he going to be a problem, then?" Cadence asked after a moment.

"Hm?"

"That sales fella. He *is* the one you were having it off with in the club, isn't he?"

Swallowing the dessert awkwardly, Renji opened his mouth to deny everything; then closed it again. *Well, shit.* It had been years since he'd been caught with his hand in that particular cookie jar.

"Y-yeah," he muttered, his mind racing through the grimmer possibilities of where this conversation might be heading. "Yeah. I, uh... didn't know you saw that."

"Melody's got a good view from the DJ booth." Cadence shrugged. "She told you about the shared memories thing. And don't give me that look, I don't care that you like blokes, it's only rich arseholes that have enough free time to get weird about that."

"Oh." He paused, took stock. And grabbed another profiterole, this time from her plate. "Well, alright then!" he grinned, relieved.

"Bloody hell." She gave him a sharp frown while shielding her plate from future invasions. "You met Allegro and the Aunties, and you still think we'd care about something like *that?*"

"The Aunties? What about the Aunties?"

"They've only been married for like, twenty years, mate."

"Married?!"

"Not legally, but that's whatever, isn't it."

"Huh...!" Renji chewed the pastry thoughtfully.

"Is he going to grass you up, though, is the thing?"

"Nah, I don't think so." Whatever was going to happen with Delaney, Renji was certain he could string it out for at least a little while. Perhaps a night or two, if he was lucky; and going by what he'd seen so far, luck was on his side.

"Right. Good." She twiddled her spoon between bites. "You've no taste, mind you."

Renji frowned. "Whaddya mean?"

"Please, look at him. He's even worse of a blagger than you. He looks like he's gonna sell you life-coaching advice through the internet."

"Does not."

"Does too. He's a budget vampire. That's a bargain bin Dracula, that is."

"You are not being a very supportive friend right now."

"I'm not supportive. Or your friend. Besides, *actual* supportive friends would tell you when you're dating an evil executive from a shitty Robocop sequel. He looks like he's going to have his plans to bulldoze the zoo foiled by some plucky teenagers."

He rolled his eyes. "Point made. Can we just move on and—"

"Don't get me started on that flippin' name either. *Chance Delaney.*" Cade bisected a pastry puff with a savage dig of her spoon. "No way is that a real bloody name. Chance is either a heroic cartoon dog or a fake name you'd use to write embarrassing books about sexy Vikings."

"Alright, that last part seemed oddly specific, and I'd like to know more."

"Whatever," she said, not so much dodging the question as barrelling straight past it. "This isn't about sexy Vikings, it's about you and Discount Dracula."

"Give it a rest, will you?" he said, irritated at her persistence.

"Shan't. He's got a wife and all."

"Fiancée."

"Bloody hell… Aren't you meant to be smart? Just because he's got a nice arse doesn't make him a nice person, you know," she said smugly. "Dunno how you can't see it. I can spot a wrong'un from a mile away, me, and that one? More red flags than a golf course."

"Alright, jeez, lay off! It's not like I'm trying to marry the guy or anything, it was just a bit of fun." Renji snapped.

"Worth thinking about how *his* idea of fun involves picking up lads on the sly down in Buried instead of up here."

"That's— it's different in the Court. You can't just… do that here. Be open, y'know? People make judgements."

"Bet you found a way though, right?"

"That's not the point!" Renji was getting frustrated now, and keeping his tone flat enough that they didn't draw any attention was becoming difficult. "You just don't get it, do you?" he muttered.

"I bloody well don't, thank you very much," she said, taking the final bite of her dessert with relish. "Doesn't it strike you as creepy that he went after you thinking you were some cute little waif who'd swoon right into his bed as soon as he whips out his big ol' wallet?"

Renji snorted in protest, aware he had been on the verge of doing exactly that. "Get fucked."

"You first, apparently."

"Kids, d'you need to have this discussion on the mission frequency?" came a weary voice over the radio.

Cade nearly dropped her spoon. "No, sir. Sorry sir," she said, dabbing away the chocolate at the corners of her mouth with a napkin.

"Sorry, old man," muttered Renji.

"Hrm."

After parking their plates down on the nearest table, they retreated to a less crowded spot between the grand piano and a placard where a cartoon reindeer declared this year to have been I.I.'s best yet, which had been getting some rather venomous glances from those whose departments had been worst hit by the reshuffles.

It would have made sense to wait out their remaining time in relative silence, passing the minutes until the elves and their bounty had completed the circuit of the ballroom. But that would involve leaving well enough alone, something that Renji was in no mood to partake in.

Cade was already slouching up against a pillar, picking at the guard of the sword strapped to her hip with malice. He matched her slouch on the pillar's other side. "Look, I know I was being a dick earlier, but I *am* out here to help," he muttered.

Her reply was a short bark of harsh laughter.

"I really am trying here, y'know," he said, annoyance ticking up a notch.

Another rough chuckle. "You're *trying,* alright."

Another notch. "C'mon, we're all working together here. Would it kill you to be a bit nicer?"

"Nicer." Cade's laughter died abruptly in her throat. "Nicer to *you.* Aye, yeah, cus this is all about *you,* isn't it. We have to be nice to *you* because we just need *you* so flippin' much."

"I mean, you did tonight, didn't you? Kinda sounded like you'd all be sat down there in the cold if I hadn't come along."

"Yeah, that's right. Where would all of us daft poor people be without some great man descending from on fuckin' high to guide us, eh?" Her voice was low, dangerous, the glower she was shooting him from the other side of the pillar threatening to bisect the marble column at any moment. "Like a fuckin' missionary. Aren't we blessed, the gods themselves have sent us their own perfect idiot!"

Exasperated and running out of good arguments, Renji resorted to bad ones. "That's not what I meant! Look, I could've just stayed at Aunty L's after last night— you know, *when you tried to kill me,* but I didn't, did I?"

"You only came back because you're too thick to understand what's at stake here. Someone like you's never had to deal with a single consequence in your stupid little life."

"The hell do you mean by that?"

"Oh please. Look at all of these idiots here." She slashed a gloved hand through the air in an arc, indicating the rest of the partygoers. "Last night you deserted, you aided in the escape of political prisoners, and you assaulted your boss. How many of this lot know about that?"

"Like I said before, none!" Renji snapped.

"Exactly. If anyone else had done it, they'd not exactly be enjoying the fucking canapes right now, would they." Folding her arms, Cadence regarded him again for a moment before shaking her head. "Nah. You act the big rebel, but I'd put money on the fact that any shit you've ever kicked up was buried by your dear old aunt before it ever got close to touching you."

"That's not—!" Renji began, yet was forced to hesitate. She wasn't incorrect. "I- I never asked her to—"

"Knew it." That same look of triumph was back on Cade's face, though this time there was an edge to it, something harsh and unforgiving. "Yeah, you're out here, and yeah, you're helping us pull this off, but you're only doing it because it's *fun*. You're just playing at being a hero, like it's all just a big game to you. A bet you don't even have a stake in. We're risking everything, you're risking your bloody pocket money. And *that's* why I don't like you, mate."

Before he could respond she had already whipped around and begun stalking back in the direction of the buffet table. The sudden motion dislodged part of her pinned-back hair, allowing the briefest flash of the jagged metal at the base of her neck before her hand slapped over it, covering the obvious, out-of-place augmentation. With one last glare in his direction as though her problematic hairdo was his fault too, she diverted her furious pace towards the bathrooms, leaving Renji to seethe alone.

"She got you there, kid."

"Shut up, old man," he grumbled, poking irritably at his earpiece.

What the hell was all of *that?!* Of course Renji knew what consequences were, for fuck's sake. Laughing in the face of danger was an easy thrill that he'd been picking at for years now! All he'd ever done his entire life was push his luck, flip the metaphorical finger to authority and rebel in hundreds of tiny ways every damn day. Was it his fault if Aunty L kept sweeping up his little indiscretions? And last night, that was hardly nothing. He'd broken out of prison! Hell, Cadence hadn't been the one fifty storeys up out on the side of an airship, had she? No, that had been him, because he'd had enough, because he needed to take a stand, because—

Well. Not because of what had been happening in that back room, he hadn't known about that at the time.

And not because of the price-gouging gas bill in Buried, he hadn't known about that yet either, had he...?

If he was being honest, all Renji *had* known was that he didn't fancy going another round with Sergeant Flood, and so it had suited him to leave. Were he a better fit for the Court's expectations, or even if he'd been given a cushier position to doss away his time in, one with a sergeant who'd been less quick with his fists, would he have even discovered those terrible truths? That thought was an uncomfortable fit, one that left Renji squirming in agitation. *Goddamnit,* Cadence.

He swept his restless gaze across the crowded ballroom for something to stop him from poking the problem further; and spotted the perfect distraction standing alone by the windows, with a drink in one hand and a beckoning glance in Renji's direction.

"Fancy meeting you again so soon," smiled Chance Delaney, as Renji approached.

"Yeah, fancy that," he grated out, surprising himself with how much irritation remained in his voice.

"Why Mr Starkweather, you seem a little vexed. Care for a breath of fresh air?" Delaney flashed him a smooth smile, tweaking open his jacket just enough to reveal the pack of cigarettes tucked away in his inside pocket.

Discount Dracula. Cade was going to hate this. "You know what," said Renji, with a surreptitious scratch at his ear that happened to loosen the radio within, "that sounds really good right now."

And as they walked by the buffet table on their way to find somewhere more private, Renji flicked the earpiece into one of Jeremy's floral displays.

#

"So when you said that your position was a little complicated," Chance slid the cigarettes out of his pocket with an amused little smile, "you weren't joking, were you?"

It hadn't taken long for the two of them to find a balcony all to themselves, the quiet spot ignored by the other partygoers due to it being outside in the cold, and on the opposite side of the building to the crocodile. The urban beauty of the Court stretched beyond the balcony's edge to run in perfect steel grids, its crystal and metal spires dusted with a scattering of the light snow still drifting by on the lazy winter breeze. With the blinds closed over the windows behind and the sounds of cordial workplace merriment dulled by distance, they seemed to be somewhere else entirely; somewhere quieter, and despite the countless anonymous eyes of the city, somewhere less observed.

In other words, the perfect spot for a smoke break, no matter what the brass *No Smoking* sign attached to the wall may say.

"How'd you know I smoke?" asked Renji, accepting the offered cigarette.

Chance laughed, pressing a finger to his lips. "You left me something of a hint when we last met, if you recall."

Renji tutted, glaring at the cig in his hand. "Been meaning to quit."

"And yet, here we are." Producing an elegant silver lighter, Chance lit Renji's cigarette, then his own. "Though if there's something else you'd rather be doing, that rather fine room I mentioned is just upstairs. Silk sheets, marble bathtub, room service…"

"I literally just met your fiancée."

"…door lock," he finished blithely.

Renji gave Delaney and that smooth smile of his another critical glance. Sure he might be a cheating asshole, but it had to be said, the guy wore a suit well. And unlike others Renji had known, he more than stood up to inspection when no longer under the dim lighting of a club. Hell, if anything, their first encounter hadn't done him enough justice; he was a little taller than Renji had assumed, shoulders a little broader too, all adding up to a frustratingly perfect score. Back in Static Void that thick mane of dark chestnut hair had fallen into natural waves, but now it had been swept back into a relaxed sort of order, formal with just enough casual to stay interesting. The scattering of stubble had been allowed a stay of execution, presumably due to being on trend, which wasn't helping matters one bit.

"Always heard everyone in sales is shameless," Renji said, leaning on the balcony's railing.

"Only when our interest is piqued."

"That fiancée of yours doesn't do much piquing, then."

Frowning up at the clouded night sky, Chance drew in a deep breath. After a moment, he exhaled it as a sigh, the warmth of it hanging in the air to mingle with the curling smoke from his cigarette, disrupting the tiny snowflakes and disappearing into the wind. "Annisette and I have less of a relationship, and more of an… arrangement."

"Yeah, sure," Renji scoffed, flicking ash over the edge. "Never heard *that* one before."

"If you'd like, you could go and ask her permission." Delaney's smile widened. "Though I can't guarantee you'll enjoy the experience."

"I'll pass, thanks."

"Are you really so upset with me for being a little sparse with the details when you were doing quite the same thing, Mr *Starkweather?*" Each syllable of the name was weighted with meaning.

Renji winced, holding up a hand. "Nope. You don't get to call me that when you're trying this hard to fuck me. Renji, it's just Renji. And yeah, so I didn't introduce myself, big deal. From what I remember it wasn't like you were asking for ID."

"All I'm saying, *Renji,* is that it sounds like we were both indulging in a little light fakery."

"Not telling you my family tree on sight isn't on the same level as picking up guys while engaged, *Chance.*"

"And if we were to ask your Janey her opinion on the matter?"

Renji met Delaney's smirk with a glower. "I- Ugh. She's just a friend. If that. I owed her a favour and for some reason she wanted in at this goddamn shitty party fulla useless fucks, so hey, her loss."

Chance's dark brows shot up, and Renji instantly realised his misstep. In his attempt to paper over the crack in his story he'd pushed it too far; he'd insulted I.I. at a company event, and worse, to someone who might want to turn careless words into a weapon.

Chance raised his cigarette to his lips. "Not exactly what I expected to hear from the commander's nephew."

"Yeah, well—"

"The truth, I mean. It *is* a shitty party. And I can personally attest to the high quotient of useless fucks." He leant beside Renji on the balcony's railing. "I'm reasonably certain that the head of my department couldn't tell her arse from her elbow without an instructive email and three assistants present." A little of the rigidity had dropped from the way he held himself, a little of the polish gone from his tone. The warmth of him so close by cut through the night's chill, and a captivating roughness had begun to show itself around the edges of those flawless good looks.

Renji nearly inhaled his cigarette.

"She'll be on a six-figure salary anyway, I bet." he managed after composing himself.

"Absolutely." Delaney's laugh was a bitter one. "The only people who end up in senior management are wretched at any task beyond working out whose arse to kiss."

"Fuckin' Jeremy."

"Jeremy."

"Could be worse, though." Renji sighed, taking a drag. "Lotta nastier bastards out there than Jeremy."

"Oh, most certainly. Take me, for example." Delaney tapped his cigarette, sending a few embers spiralling away on the wind.

"Hm?"

"As you said, mine is a shameless line of work. Nothing is off the table. I say whatever I must to build a rapport with an unsuspecting client, establish a promise, gain a level of trust; then exploit that trust for all it's worth. Once I discover an enticing lead I'm to chase it down until it's brought in, pushing the absolute limits to get what I want." He shot a sly look in Renji's direction. "There's very little room for decency. So I make do without."

"Uh huh." Despite the breeze and snow, Renji loosened his tie a little; he could swear the temperature had risen a few degrees. "You, uh... don't exactly seem torn up about that."

Another light laugh. "I'm not."

"Why not? All you're doing is lining the pockets of some asshole in a boardroom somewhere. Seems like it'd feel pretty... I dunno. Hollow."

"Oh no, no." Delaney's smile was ruthless. "I'm *good* at it, you see. And my own pockets go rather well-lined too, I should add. It may be a shallow game that we're forced into, but at least I have a winning hand."

Renji snorted. "That only matters if you play by the rules."

"And you don't, hm? Going to throw your cards off the table, lead the revolution?" The city lights danced in those aloof, emerald eyes. "You'd be in the Forces, I suppose."

That hadn't been a question. "Mm. Kinda." Renji shrugged.

"And how has that been working out in terms of rebellion? I seem to recall mention of a 'job interview' when we last met." When he received no answer, Chance took one last puff of his diminishing cigarette and nodded, satisfied. "There's nothing for it. Whether we like it or not, we're all playing the same game here, raising and bluffing as suits our needs. I certainly do. Annisette too, for what it's worth." He tossed the smoking remains over the railing. "You, also."

"Yeah, right." Renji laughed the notion away, despite the comment ringing true now more than ever.

Chance seemed to catch him hanging on that thought, quirking an eyebrow in amusement. "Oh? So you're a rarity, are you? The one honest man in Imperium Court."

"I never said *that.*"

"Mm. I think you might be a rarity all the same." In a quick motion Delaney plucked the cigarette from Renji's lips. "Though perhaps not for your honesty." He flicked the stub over the balcony's edge. And as Delaney leaned in, eyes full of intent, it occurred to Renji that since his lips were now unoccupied it was only right that he should put them to good use.

Their previous kiss in Static Void had felt audacious, but it had been a stolen thrill in the indifferent dark, no real risk at all. This time however, with the judgemental eyes of the entire Court's upper brass so close by, the effect was nothing short of electrifying. Evidently Delaney was feeling the same way, his kiss full of an intensity that hadn't been in their last encounter, one that left Renji eager to match that fervour with his own. Their lips met again and again, kiss after demanding kiss, and he raked his fingers through Delaney's hair almost vindictively, brushing it free of formality. Now Renji had been allowed a peek beneath the cloak of respectability Chance was so wrapped up in, all he wanted was to see more; to seize that tantalising loose thread, tug it free, and watch this glorious bastard *unravel*.

Breathing out a chuckle with a savage little glint in his eyes that suited him far too well, Chance tugged Renji's tie loose, and as the man turned his attention to the sensitive skin along Renji's neck he found himself almost lost in the sensation, gripping the expensive fabric of Delaney's shirt as those clever hands slid around his back, his waist, down, *down;* and then, with his head so full of down, everything shifted into focus. The reason he'd come here, those night-black houses waiting in the city's cold depths, waiting for him to stop talking shit and start breaking some fucking rules already.

Gently, firmly, Renji pushed himself out of the embrace, quietly cursing his sudden attack of responsibility. Between longing breaths hanging heavy like clouds in the frozen air, Chance shot him a questioning look.

"Look I, uh… gotta get back to my date." Renji muttered, turning away to fix his tie. "About time you did the same, I bet."

He'd expected disappointment, perhaps annoyance, either would have been understandable. Instead, Delaney laughed, running his fingers through his hair to tousle it back into place. Tilting his head, he gave Renji an appraising look, as though weighing some unknown quantity. "You still owe me a jacket."

"Better come to the club and collect it sometime then, hadn't you." Renji replied, and the satisfied chuckle that followed him as he left suggested it had been the answer Delaney had hoped for.

#

Rejoining the bland ceremony of the Christmas party after *that* was a lot like dunking his head into a bucket of ice, yet Renji plunged back in all the same, trying to ignore the lingering edge of pepper-dark cologne that still hung about him like a taunt.

Perhaps it *had* been a little impulsive to take a little break mid-mission, but that didn't mean Cadence had been correct when she'd said all that shit before. Hell, if anything it had made him more certain she'd been wrong; anyone who could turn their back on that balcony was more than committed to their cause.

Now, if only he could find her to make that point.

A quick scout of the ballroom for any hints of an ivory dress containing a furious bruiser turned up nothing. Perhaps that was a good thing; if Cadence had been in the bathroom this whole time attempting to re-pin her hair she might not have noticed he'd removed his earpiece. If he could retrieve it before she got back, then at least she couldn't give him shit for his brief lapse in judgement. As he studied the floral centrepieces trying to remember which of the ugly messes he'd tossed the damn earbud into, something else caught his eye. A small crowd had formed by the front window, full of furtive whispers, all trying to snatch a glimpse of something down in the street below.

Something uncertain sank into the pit of Renji's stomach. Cautiously, he approached the window through a sea of excited murmurs; only to find himself once more face-to-wretched-face with none other than the centrepiece maestro himself, Jeremy from Marketing.

"Isn't this exciting!" he bleated. "You could have told me earlier, you know!"

"Told you what?" Renji asked, that sinking feeling turning leaden and dropping even deeper. Standing on his toes, he peered over Jeremy's shoulder so he could see what everyone was looking at.

A long, gleaming white car had pulled up alongside Il Coccodrillo, and stepping out of it in her dress uniform and sabre came a sight that froze Renji's blood.

"She's missed most of the presentations of course, but there's still the departmental awards, and the sleigh ride," Jeremy prattled on happily, "and maybe later, I don't know, if you could perhaps introduce me—"

Renji's teeth gritted into the approximation of a smile. "I'll get right on that, Jer. If you'll just excuse me." Without waiting for a response, he turned on his heel and strode away as fast as he could before his knees gave out.

Shit fuck fuck shit fuck! Why would Aunty L have picked now, of all times, to get over her lifelong hatred of the company Christmas party? Could she somehow be on to him? Where the hell was Cadence? *Why did he throw away his radio?!*

Head spinning, trying to keep his shaking steps at steady pace so he didn't draw attention, Renji did the only thing he could think to do, pushing past the bag check lady and an affronted waiter and making for the closest of the ballroom's great brass elevators. It ought to take Aunty Lissa a few minutes to make her way up to the ballroom, and that could give him time to move to a different floor and give her the slip.

As Renji got close enough to the cage doors he realised that in his panic, he'd run to the elevator descending from the ballroom to the ground floor rather than the one that went further up the building. That was fine, he thought as he jabbed the button to call the carriage, it could still work. He'd just have to be faster about it, is all. Hop in after the lift stopped here and get out on a lower storey before Aunty L could even make it inside, then she should go right past him on her way to the ballroom, never knowing he was there. The elevator arrived with a *ding,* and a harried Renji fell in through the doors the second the grille opened— and fell back out again as he realised what was waiting for him in there.

One large hand clamped onto Renji's shoulder and wrenched him forward, pulling him off his feet and dragging him inside before he could even think about escaping. An unpleasant smile spread across the face of Sergeant Hugo Flood.

"Still feeling clever are we, cadet?" he leered.

And as the heavy brass cage doors came together behind him with a sickeningly final *clang,* clever was about the last thing that Renji was feeling.

CHAPTER 17

A FRIENDLY CHAT

The worst part about this was that Cadence had been right.

If Renji was being honest with himself, the most terrible outcome he'd thought he might face from tonight's little caper would be his aunt's disappointment, and the scorn of the Court; nothing more than some closed doors that he'd had no interest in going through anyway. Despite everything he'd encountered over the past few days, perhaps, as the furious Mancunian had said, his idea of danger had in fact not been quite on the same scale as most.

All this to say, the fact that he'd ended up bound to a chair beside a crocodile enclosure had come as something of a surprise.

The room itself was a practical sort of concrete affair with all of the charms of a serial killer's basement, and as it was supposed to go unseen by the public it was decorated with little more than some loose supplies and the stink of fish guts. Still, despite its low ceiling, bare walls and ominous stains, that half of the room was the preferable side to be on, as it was meant for humans. The other half very much belonged to the crocodile.

Melody would be pleased to hear that the beast's enclosure was larger than it appeared from the outside; the floor-to-ceiling windows that made up the exterior wall of the room offered a perfect view of the glass-lidded infinity pool 'balcony' protruding from the side of the tower, but once inside the building the pool opened out into a large, shallow pond. There was even a sandy bank for the croc to rest on and presumably enjoy its grim dinner. Still, even with a ten-foot drop between it and the rest of the room the stink from the dank, swampy pool water was evident, lending the air a cloying texture. The only thing that stood between Renji and that sharp drop to sharper teeth was a thin safety railing, which in his opinion didn't seem nearly safe enough.

Trying to not panic and failing, Renji tugged at the ropes binding his wrists behind his back for what must have been the tenth time in the last minute. The knots remained stubbornly in place.

"Any chance we can talk about this...?" he asked, and while the fist that connected with his sternum in reply didn't come as a surprise, it hurt like a bastard all the same. The blow shifted his chair backwards, bringing it several inches closer to the railing and what lay below. Shuddering and gasping, he fought for breath while trying not to consider the noises in the water behind him, and by the time he'd managed to clear the stars from his eyes Sergeant Flood's glower had taken on a twist of triumph.

"Business as usual then," Renji wheezed.

Lurking in the shadows behind the sarge were three equally unwelcome figures; the hulking shape of Perhaps-Yates, the sharp grin of Maybe-Carter, and of course Probably-Simmonds, who was nursing a broken nose and the horrible grudge of a man who had googled the word *helium* since their last encounter. There was no sign of Cadence here whatsoever. Renji had no idea if she had been grabbed too, or if perhaps she was back in the ballroom eating round two of dessert and wondering where the fuck he'd gone. Either way, thanks to his smart and great move with the earpiece there was no way for her or Weaver to know where he had vanished to, which meant that rescue wouldn't be coming any time soon.

"Cocky little brat," the sergeant rasped, cracking his knuckles. "I knew you'd be trouble from the minute I laid eyes on you."

"Oh but you were right there, sarge! I've got it all written down, every last offense!" piped up Probably-Simmonds, pulling out his cursed notebook with the usual glee. *"Partaking in banned substances, attempted bribery, disrespecting the forces (multiple occurrences), desertion, aiding in escape of a—"*

"That's enough, cadet." Flood held up a hand.

"No no, let him carry on!" said Renji. "Maybe you could rank them? Like a top ten list of my best infractions, that could be fun."

"Well, actually—" began Probably-Simmonds, who was clearly considering the statistical possibilities of a points-based system.

"Perhaps a graph? A six-month report of shenanigan production over time, with a projected bullshit forecast for the coming year."

"Don't you dare." Maybe-Carter's warning elbow caught her pensive colleague in the ribs.

Flood didn't seem to appreciate the routine, however. "Ridiculous." he sneered, that perfectly groomed moustache bristling. "What an embarrassment you are to the Forces, and to the Starkweather name. Though I suppose that's hardly a surprise, not with that mixed blood of yours."

Renji's breath caught.

"Been all kinds of rumours about this one from the start." Maybe-Carter hummed through her pearl-white teeth, twirling her baton around her fingers. "Bit of a deviant, they say."

Probably-Simmonds nodded, with a sniff. "From what I hear, I don't have even *half* of it written down yet."

"Embarrassing." echoed Perhaps-Yates.

"Yeah, you lot would know all about *embarrassing,* wouldn't you?" Renji snarled, no longer interested in playing around. "Nice nose, you snap it in your shitty little notebook or break it off in some Upper's arse?" Probably-Simmonds snorted in rage, his hand flying to his bandaged face. Renji jerked his head towards Perhaps-Yates. "Or what about Mr Taken-Out-By-A-Limping-Old-Man there? And I dunno what you're laughing at, lady, it ain't like you had a great view of the action from whatever fuckin' cupboard you hid in!"

Renji knew he was likely making things worse, but the terrified, agitated high he was running on wouldn't let him stop before he'd finished the job. "And you, sarge." He snickered at Flood, "you must've got a real good look at *embarrassing* when that ship docked

242

and Aunty L found you passed out on the floor in your pyjamas."

As soon as the words had left his mouth he realised his mistake, the same one he'd made time and time again on AirCast Two; he'd handed Flood the excuse the man had been waiting for. The sarge's hand slammed into Renji's shoulder, and in a sudden blur of stomach-churning movement the chair he was bound to was tipping backwards over the railing, balanced only on its back legs. He yelped in terror as the ceiling flashed past his eyes, but before he could finish the sickening plunge down into the pit Flood's hand knotted in his shirt collar to bring him to a bone-jarring halt, and he was left hanging over the edge with nothing but the sergeant's mercy between him and what waited in the water below.

The look on the man's face was one of brutal gratification. Renji had to work very hard to hold back a whimper.

"Not so cocky now, are we?" sneered Flood, his grip tightening ruthlessly.

"Y-you can't hurt me!" Renji stammered in desperation, playing the last card he had left. "The c-commander—"

"The commander." The sergeant laughed. "Yes, that's the only way a scrawny little insubordinate like you could infiltrate our hallowed ranks, isn't it? *Connections.* That sort of thing can even blind a woman as noble as our commander. All you'd have to do would be to show up to work once in a while, and before long they'd have made you a bloody lieutenant! They'd have *me* saluting *you!"* The jealousy was all but radiating off the sarge at this imagined scenario, as though Renji had any interest in rank or saluting whatsoever. "Useless brat. It's leeches like you that give the Forces a bad name."

"Me?! I'm not the one threatening my cadet with a croco—" Renji's words vanished into a wail as Flood's grip loosened, sliding from shirt collar to red silk tie, allowing the chair to tip another nauseating few inches backwards. Unable to stop himself, Renji peeked downward, and regretted it at once. Scales glistened in the city's lights as an immense, rough shape broke the surface of the water beneath him.

The crocodile blinked slowly. The crocodile moved with purpose.

"If I were to let go, I'd be doing the commander a favour, really. Cleaning up the Forces," Flood continued, evidently very pleased with himself. "Eliminating a problem. Correcting…" another inch of tie, another dip downwards, "…a mistake."

Too terrified to even breathe in case the movement caused the perilous chair legs to lose balance, Renji hung there helplessly, squeezing his eyes shut. Below, he could hear the sound of thrashing water, could imagine those jagged jaws yawning wide, could feel the sarge's grip slipping for the final time—

From the back of the room, Perhaps-Yates gave a meaningful cough. Suddenly Flood tugged Renji forward, causing all four chair legs to land back on safe ground with a clatter. Drawing in a shuddering gasp of relief, Renji wrenched open his eyes just in time to see Flood's nod of approval towards the large cadet, who had been peering out into the corridor. Flipping a smart little salute, Perhaps-Yates opened the door, and as the new arrival stepped into the room Renji couldn't tell if the wave that hit at the sight of her was relief or terror.

"Thank you, sergeant." Commander Starkweather's smile was ice. "I can handle the rest from here."

Renji watched in wary silence as the sarge and his cadets were dismissed from the room, leaving him alone with his aunt. The commander cut an imposing figure; the Starkweather family had always produced strikingly tall women composed of severe angles, and Aunty L was no exception. The reading glasses and casual wear from their last meeting were gone, replaced by a crisp dress uniform and neat, slicked-back hair, all elements of her manner snapped into what Renji had always thought of as Commander Mode. As she approached her nephew however, she relaxed into that casual, exhausted slouch that was far more familiar. She flipped off her hat to hang it on a nearby mop handle, then tousled her white-blonde hair into its usual messy spikes with a heavy sigh. A spare folding chair was leaning against the wall; she snagged it, kicked it open and placed it across from his.

"Well, here we are." said Aunty L, taking a seat. "Anything you wanna tell me, Peanut?"

"Yeah, that sergeant of yours is a fuckin' psycho! He just tried to kill me!" Renji struggled against the ropes biting into his wrists again. "C'mon, let me outta here before he comes back to finish the job!"

She held up a hand. "Just a sec. We're gonna have a chat first, you and me. You can go once we're done."

He stared at her in slack-jawed shock. Wasn't she going to untie him? "Wha—? Didn't you hear me?! Flood, he was gonna—"

"Don't overreact, Renji. No-one's going to hurt you."

No, she was not going to untie him. Resting her chin in her hands as though they were chatting over coffee like they'd done so many times before, Aunty L continued. "So! What's put you in the party mood this evening? You've never been a fan of these things, and you've sure as hell never come along to one without me dragging you."

"I— how did you know I was here?"

"Oh, that? Well you see, I was enjoying my evening off when some absolute nobody in marketing tagged me in this godforsaken promo post." Retrieving her work phone from her pocket, she proceeded to open an app that showed I.I. Marketing's official media account; and there was Renji, standing by beaming as Cadence/Janey deposited cash into a tired-looking elf's bag. *Goddamn it, Jeremy.*

"When I saw that, I couldn't help but wonder what exactly you were doing here. Specifically, why you were throwing what looks like the majority of your savings into a charity box while accompanied by a… date." Her eyebrows rose on that particular note. "A date who happens to be wearing my best evening gown. Now, we both know that none of that is very you, is it Peanut? Not your style at all. So I called your sergeant, and we agreed it would be best to look into it."

Renji squirmed in the uncomfortable seat. "Maybe I just felt like a party. I party."

"Not like this, you don't. Another curious little thing; your phone's been invisible all day."

Ah. Weaver and Melody had been right on that one, then. "I just put it on battery saving mode, is all."

"You did more than that. It was entirely off the grid, until a few hours ago when your ID was used to access an elevator."

"So?"

"A freight elevator. One you boarded in Buried, with two other people. I assume this 'date' of yours is one, so…" There was a sharpness in her tone now, a note of urgency as she leaned towards him. "Who's the other?"

Renji hesitated. Best to not give anything away. "Hey, maybe I just wanted to show off for a cute girl or two." He shrugged as casually as the ropes would allow.

Aunty L regarded him for a long moment. It was a bad, desperate bluff, he knew; she was aware he had no interest in girls, the both of them having endured a long awkward conversation after he'd been caught getting a little too close to a classmate after school. The eventual conclusion had been that she would continue to not ask, and he would learn a thing or two about subtlety.

"I see," she said eventually. "Then when we catch up to your *dates*, we will have a lot to talk about together, won't we."

He felt sick. It hadn't ever been a secret that I.I. were the law in Unity, but he'd never quite realised what that really meant before. If the Forces did find Cade, Melo and Weaver, they would all die in the jaws of that terrible machine as inevitably as Kiki had. Neatly, legally filed away, in the name of justice.

As distant as though it were a hundred miles away Aunty L's phone began to ring; not her work phone, but her private number, the one he'd helped her set the ringtone for. It sounded so ridiculous now, the

Unity City anthem rendered in cat meows, a stupid joke they'd once laughed at together now echoing against the cold concrete walls. Aunty L winced.

"Oh, Peanut... Look at us." There was a genuine sadness in the slump of her shoulders as she regarded him. "This is just ridiculous, isn't it? You aren't a criminal, and it's ridiculous that you're making me treat you like one."

Renji blinked, stunned. "But— No, I *am* a criminal, Aunty L," he said. "You know that. You know what I did yesterday!"

"Don't be ridiculous. You're my nephew, not some hoodlum. All that's happening here is that you're falling in with a bad crowd. It'd hardly be your first little phase, would it?"

"I broke out of prison!" he blurted it out desperately, as though he were defending himself rather than the opposite. "I knocked out my sarge! I broke out some convicts! I—"

"Enough. God. Just... please try to keep up, will you?" The melancholy vanished, replaced by the sort of exasperation she'd employ when admonishing the cats for scratching the furniture. "This is so much more dangerous than you could understand! I know you like to play about on the edge, but what you need to get is that the people you've been hanging around with? Those are *real* criminals. Serious ones. Terrorists like that, all they want is to destroy everything we've built here, everything Unity stands for... And when we catch up to them— not if, *when*— they will be dealt with in the most serious of terms."

She exhaled, as though catching herself at the peak of some cold crescendo. "But... it's not too late. We've still got more than enough time to get you back on the right path, Peanut. All you have to do is tell us who put you up to this little stunt, and where we can find them. Then I'll deal with the rest, okay?" She gave him a hopeful smile. "It'll all be over, and you can come home."

The word *home* rang hollow as Renji winced at a twinge of pain from his raw wrists. "And if I don't tell you? You gonna pull my brains out like you did with Kiki, huh?"

The private phone's ringtone started up once more, and Aunty L rolled her eyes in exasperation. "You're still hung up on that? Let's just move on, get back to normal."

"Normal?! How am I supposed to believe anything's normal when you're out there ripping people's heads open?"

"I already told you, the Imagers are an unfortunate necessity."

"They're *murder!* And you're—" His words guttered out as he searched his aunt's expression for remorse, and failed to find even a hint. "You're okay with that, aren't you...? Just like you're okay with this." He nodded down at the chair, tugged at his bindings again.

Aunty Lissa received the accusation like a slap to the face, the force of it raising her from her seat as though to strike him in return. "Do you think I'm *enjoying* this?!" she snapped. "As if questioning my own goddamn nephew is something I'd *ever* want to do! Renji, you're my sister's kid! My *family!* I fucking care about you, you little dumbass!"

He'd heard her angry before of course, but never quite so... raw, agitated. It was difficult to not feel a tug of guilt; ever since he'd ended up on her doorstep Aunty L had always been there for him in her own easy-going kinda way, helping to steer him through some seriously dark waters; and now she was looking at him as though he was tossing every year she'd spent on him straight into the garbage.

"All I had to do was keep an eye on you. Keep you out of trouble." She raked her fingers through her hair in frustration once more. "I don't understand why you have to make that so bloody difficult!"

"I'm not—! This isn't..." Renji stuttered, unable to grasp the whole of what he wanted to say. The words were too much, the weight of them too complex to arrange into the right order; especially over the goddamn ringing phone that had started up again. Not many people had her private number, so the call must have been an urgent one. All the same, she hissed in annoyance and stabbed it into silence with her thumb without a glance at the screen.

"Listen, I—" he again tried to get his thoughts in order, failed, and simply let the words come rushing out. "I-I'm not trying to make problems for you, it's not about that! I just… I can't *deal* with this! I can't deal with the shit you do, how you think it's okay to murder someone just cus you've decided they did something wrong! How that's like… legal, for you to do that! I can't deal with this place being how it is! We're letting people freeze to death down in Buried while we got foie gras on the table up here!"

"That nonsense with the unpaid bill? Oh please, you're overreacting again. They'll be fine."

"How can you tell?! You're not even looking! No-one up here does! None of this is fair, nothing about this *entire fuckin' city* is fair!" he yelled, voice cracking with desperation.

Aunty L stared at him, stunned; then her eyes narrowed, as though she were studying him, reconsidering something important. "Fair…?" All signs of vexation had vanished, leaving the commander's gaze a cold, unyielding one. "Since when did you care about fair?"

"Since I saw what *unfair* looked like!"

"I see." Her mouth was a thin line of barely suppressed fury. "This is because of him, isn't it."

Renji found himself caught off-balance. "Him? Him who?"

"Oh please." She rose from her chair, the low light of the room casting her face into shadow. Even though he couldn't see her expression it was clear that there was something else in her manner now, something sharper than he was used to seeing. "Do you think I don't know that rat bastard is involved in all of this?"

"Aunty L, I- I dunno what—"

"I don't know how he found you, or why, but…" she paused, a low growl escaping her lips. "That was his plan all along, wasn't it? That's why he broke into your airship! He's using you to get to me! To make me give back Harlow!"

"Wait… Harlow?" Renji said slowly, as he attempted to put the pieces together in his mind. "Are you— are you talking about *Weaver?*"

She gave him a long, cool look; and when her phone began to ring again, the commander had had enough. Snarling, she jabbed at the green icon on the screen as though she could shatter it into a thousand pieces.

"Whoever this is," she threatened the caller, "you'd better speak quickly while you still can."

"Hello, Lissa."

Even over the phone's tiny speaker, Weaver's gravelled tones were unmistakable. The commander stiffened, rigid with fury. *"David."*

"Seems like we got a thing or two to discuss. Wanna be adults about this?"

Her fingers tightened around her sword's hilt, knuckles as white as her face. "Nope."

A soft chuckle. "Shoulda known. Third floor hallway. I'll be waiting."

And before an astonished Renji could even process what had just happened, the call had ended, and Commander Starkweather had turned to leave.

"What the *hell?!*" he yelled, almost tipping over his chair. "What was that? Where are you going?!"

"To deal with this." Her thin blade shone as she withdrew it from its scabbard. "Directly."

"Hey, wait! Aunty L, wait—!"

But already, she was opening the door to leave. "You!" she barked at Flood, who had been waiting outside in the corridor obediently. "Take over here."

The sergeant snapped off a quick salute, both of them ignoring Renji's continued howls of protest.

"Yes, commander! Orders, commander?"

"Let him go."

Renji's mouth snapped shut in surprise. For his part, Flood seemed equally taken aback. "C-commander? Surely he's under arrest, after everything he—"

A cold look silenced him in an instant. "Do not presume to tell me how to do my job, sergeant."

"My apologies, commander," Flood grated out, "but are you sure that's a wise move?"

"Oh please. He'll come back before long. He always does." And without even a backward glance, she pushed past her sergeant and made her way out.

"No, hold on!" Renji yelled desperately. "Aunty L, you can't leave me with—"

But it was too late; she was gone, and the hulking broad-shouldered shape of Flood filled the doorway.

"Fuck!" finished Renji, with feeling. What had that call from Weaver meant? Was there help on the way? How did Weaver's daughter figure into this? All important questions, none of which he had time to contemplate as Flood strode back into the room, trailed by his cadet groupies.

Squirming against the ropes, Renji could only watch as Perhaps-Yates and Maybe-Carter took up positions behind him, one by each of his shoulders. The third stooge of the trio, Probably-Simmonds, was absent; a fact that wasn't as reassuring as it might have been.

Well, it was worth a shot. "The commander says to let me go," he said. "So go ahead, then. Let me go!"

Maybe-Carter snickered. "Oh, so *now* he cares about following orders."

"Don't you have some boots to go lick?" snapped Renji, unhelpfully. Flood nodded at Maybe-Carter, and with a cackle of glee the vicious cadet's baton thudded into Renji's already-bruised ribs.

"N-now what, you're gonna beat the shit outta me and hope Aunty L just doesn't notice?" He coughed, over the dull pain throbbing through his chest. "Gonna tell her I fell down the stairs, huh?"

Another nod from Flood. This time it was Perhaps-Yates' turn, the big cadet taking the opportunity to cuff Renji about the head so hard his vision blurred with the shock of the blow. He was left reeling for a moment, until strong fingers with neatly clipped nails seized his face, yanking his chin sharply upwards.

"Now, here is how this is going to go," sneered Flood, leaning in far too close for comfort. "You're going to be a good little cadet, and you're going to tell me exactly where those prisoners of mine got to. If you can follow your orders, then perhaps I'll consider following mine."

Of course that was what this was all about. If he could recapture Sugar and Trig, maybe even Weaver too, the sergeant's damaged reputation could be mended, or at least left somewhat less dented. Frankly, that didn't suit Renji one bit. "Or else what?" he spat.

A terrible grin split Flood's face. "I'm so very glad you asked."

Turning on his heel, he marched to the door and threw it open. There was Probably-Simmonds, his weasel face twisted into a smug approximation of a smile, and on the trolley he was wheeling in front of him—

"No way…!" Renji breathed in mounting horror. "You *can't* be serious!"

The machine, a Limbic Imager as he now knew it was called, seemed like nothing more than a snarl of wires and connectors in the centre of which sat a compact terminal; but with the grim knowledge of the purpose of the largest connection plug, the jagged pins of metal along the thing's edges seemed like nothing more than brutal violence. It looked just like the one from AirCast Two. Perhaps it even was the same machine.

"The latest in Imperium technology!" Flood chuckled, patting the top of the nightmarish device as though it were a beloved pet. "You see, I don't plan on leaving here without the information I need. And I don't especially mind how I get it."

His breath hitching, Renji realised that below the Imager, on the trolley's shelf, lay that same vicious style of input plug that he had last seen implanted so cruelly in the base of Kiki's neck. It was surrounded by an array of surgical implements. They didn't seem like the type that were especially good at doing things with care for the patient.

"Y-you can't!" he stuttered, "You *can't!* You think the commander isn't gonna care that you killed her fuckin' nephew, huh?!"

"But I followed my orders and released you already, as these witnesses can attest. Whatever happened to you after that is hardly my problem, is it."

"She'll look for me! She'll—"

"—never find you. Not when we have such a helpful means of disposal at our fingertips." Flood waved a hand, the broad, theatrical motion indicating what lay behind the safety railing. The sound of reptilian movement in the water sent a chill up Renji's spine.

It was a bluff. It *had* to be. His nerve began to waver, all the same. Flood, who had always been far too observant at the worst possible times, chuckled at his discomfort. "Besides… The commander seems a little distracted lately, doesn't she? A little off her game. Burned out, you might say. And with the weight of a missing family member on her shoulders, perhaps our good commander would not remain in her position for long."

The stream of creative cursing he received in reply didn't budge Flood's radiant poster-perfect smile an inch. "Of course, if you'd like to save her the anguish, and us the clean-up," Maybe-Carter sniggered at that, "then you could simply tell me what I need to know, and we'll let you go safe and sound. If not, well…" Again, he tapped the Limbic Imager's terminal.

It was clear now; the sarge really was stupid enough to try it. Aunty L would find out in time, no doubt, and she would eviscerate him, but it wouldn't matter to Renji at that point because he'd be fucking dead already, wouldn't he. Reduced to data and an empty shell. Nothing more than a file on a disk, just like Kiki. His entire being, everything that made him himself ripped away like that, torn to shreds, stolen, *deleted*.

The information the sarge wanted, everything that would lead the Forces straight to The Loose Ends, rose in his throat. The bastard would be getting what he needs to know either way, why shouldn't Renji tell just them everything and save himself from that hellish machine? Yet… the words wouldn't come out. Something in him wouldn't allow it, a part of what he couldn't bear to have torn away by that machine; that core of stupid stubborn bone-deep defiance that had sent him sneaking out of the damn airship window in the first place, that had brought him to The Loose Ends, that wanted more than anything to believe that a way out of all of this was somehow possible.

Renji wasn't certain when he'd started trembling, but he managed to lock eyes with the sarge all the same. "Go fuck yourself."

"Ah. What a shame." Flood reached into the tray of surgical tools, and withdrew a scalpel. That perfect smile widened, and it couldn't have been clearer that the bastard never had any intention of letting him leave this room alive, no matter how much he'd given them.

Maybe-Carter and Perhaps-Yates descended, seizing Renji's shoulders to hold him steady, and as though he had been waiting for this moment all evening Flood was already in motion, barking out a stream of sharp, pointed commands which were rendered instinct and muffled to Renji under the sound of his own terrified heartbeat. Tools were produced. The trolley rattled closer. Everything and everyone seemed to move with a terrible slowness that at once ran far, *far* too fast. A vicious hand knotted in the back of Renji's hair, and as his head was roughly pushed down to expose the vulnerable base of his neck he yelled and squirmed and strained against his bindings for all he was worth because no no *no* he couldn't die, he wasn't ready to die, he'd not had enough time, not yet, not so soon, *please*—

All at once, the sound of shattering glass exploded from behind them. A blast of cool air rolled over the room, taking the cadets by surprise long enough to allow Renji to twist about to see what was happening. Cadence, one mechanical hand outstretched and still crackling with electricity, stepped off the window cleaner's platform and into the enclosure through the smashed glass, her evening gown whipping in the wind about her as though she was some kind of furious gift from above.

"That's *our* idiot," she snarled. *"Hands off."*

CHAPTER 18
WITH A FLOURISH

Not even the crocodile had time to react as Cadence sprinted across the edge of the enclosure's shallow pool. Ignoring the ladder that led up to safety in favour of scaling her way up the ten-foot-high drop via bouncing off the corner like something out of a Jackie Chan film, she landed amongst the stunned cadets where, presumably in order to clear up any confusion about her intentions, she proceeded to slam the heel of her palm into Probably-Simmonds's already broken nose. The hapless lackey's howl of pain seemed to be enough to break the shock that had paralysed the room, and both Perhaps-Yates and Maybe-Carter let go of Renji to advance on their new, far more threatening problem. The sight of two trained cadets barrelling towards her didn't seem to faze Cade, however; from the look that flashed across her face, it seemed to be what she'd been hoping for.

Crouching low, she waited until the last possible second as Perhaps-Yates' meaty fist was only centimetres from making contact with her face; and then with one quick kick against the floor she was gone, sliding between her assailants before they could do anything to stop her. Coming to a stop beside a slack-jawed Renji's chair, in one fluid motion she drew the ornate sword from her hip and brought it down to slice through the ropes at his wrists.

Renji toppled forward, wildly glad to be free of the hated metal chair. Cadence pressed the hilt of the golden sword into his hands, and he stared at it, bewildered.

"Shouldn't *you* have this?!" was all he could think to say.

Curling her fingers into a fist, she snorted. "Swords are for arseholes."

And with that she was already darting back to rejoin the fray, leaving Renji attempting to work out if he'd just been saved or insulted, when an unwelcome voice cut over his thoughts.

"That," snarled Flood, his bloodshot gaze fixed on the sword, "is *mine.*"

The sergeant drew what must have been his second-favourite blade from the scabbard at his belt. It was far plainer than the high detailed golden-hilted affair Renji was clutching, but more than sharp enough.

He desperately tried to recall a single goddamn thing from that week of fencing lessons he'd taken as a teenager. Nothing seemed to want to present itself, which meant he'd have to try a tactic he was far better trained in.

"Are you sure you want to fight me? I should warn you, my family are very good at this." Renji flourished both the sword and his widest grin, hoping either gave the impression that he knew what he was doing. "Why not back off now and save yourself the agony of defeat, hm?"

"Back off? Why would I do that when I've been waiting years for a chance to duel a Starkweather." The sarge gave a dark chuckle. "I suppose you'll have to do." Slipping into a perfect duellist's stance, he brandished the blade with a determined grimace and tapped it against Renji's in a rigid, sportsmanlike gesture that didn't quite match the bloodlust in his eyes. *"En garde."*

Renji's grin faded.

Meanwhile Maybe-Carter, who had been aiming her baton at Cadence's nose, was left rather surprised when her target ducked out of the path of her wild swing and even more so when a metal fist proceeded to connect with her solar plexus. Wheezing, the cadet dropped to the floor, but as Cadence rose triumphantly and wheeled around to locate her other foe she was already too late.

Perhaps-Yates had scooped up what was becoming Renji's least favourite chair in the world, and with a grunt he brought it crashing down across her shoulders.

In the weak lighting of the room it was impossible for Renji to follow what happened next. All he could see was the shape of Cade crumpling, then disappearing, swallowed up behind the wide shadow of Perhaps-Yates. Already, the cadet was hoisting that goddamn chair for a second shot. Gripping the sword hilt, Renji lunged forward in an attempt to do something, anything to help— but was forced to skid to a halt as Flood's blade slashed through the air, only centimetres from his nose.

He raised his weapon just in time as the sergeant launched himself forward with a flurry of blows, every cut and slash forcing Renji backward, away from Cadence. In a panicked flurry of cursing and barely remembered sword work, through some miracle he managed to get the gilded burden into position to block one attack, two; then the third struck home, slipping past his defences to tear through the sleeve of his favourite suit jacket and leave a thin score of blood in its wake. Renji yelped, the sudden sharp shock of pain almost causing him to drop his weapon.

"One point to me!" Another flash of Flood's steel, another stab of agony, this time to Renji's shoulder. "And that makes two." The sarge snickered, his delight at his opponent's pain as sharp and terrible as his blade.

Panting, Renji clutched his bleeding shoulder and tried to remember how many points were in a duel. Twelve? Fifteen? The thought of taking over a dozen more hits like that made him seriously consider taking his chances with the crocodile instead. Looking about the bare concrete room for another way out, Renji caught the edge of a brief movement from the dark corner where Cadence had fallen, a familiar pale purple glow; and then there came a great clattering of metal on metal followed by an abrupt crackling blast of electric.

The steel chair that Perhaps-Yates had been hoisting sailed over the safety railing to splash down into the crocodile enclosure, and with an almighty thud, Perhaps-Yates hit the concrete floor, smouldering a little. Cade was back on her feet, the light panel along her robotic right arm picking out her silhouette against the darkness; with Perhaps-Yates down, she now found herself facing only a furious Maybe-Carter and a sniffling Probably-Simmonds.

In a rare burst of good luck Flood had turned to see what the noise was, giving Renji a second to assess the duel he'd landed himself in and come to the very important conclusion that he was utterly fucked if he didn't do something drastic. Yet, while the sarge had several decades of fencing experience on his side, Renji had one advantage on his; namely, a complete lack of interest in playing by the rules. And so while his opponent was distracted he took the opportunity to employ a move that had not been covered in fencing class, and kicked the man square in the bollocks.

The sarge exhaled sharply; then folded, swearing and spitting and withering, collapsing into a furious heap on the cold concrete.

"Two points to me!" Renji crowed as the victory registered. "Hey, Cade! I think I just won a fight!"

"Gis a sec, mate." she replied as she stepped around Probably-Simmonds and his inexpert baton swings. With a snort of laughter she swatted him in the nose again— but then choked out a gasp as Maybe-Carter's nightstick drew across her throat. The ever-resourceful cadet had allowed Probably-Simmonds to make his sad little attack first and used him as a distraction to slip around behind Cadence, pulling her into a savage chokehold with the baton crushing her victim's windpipe in a perfect display of one of the Force's favoured suspect incapacitation methods.

It might have even worked, too, if Cade hadn't been in evening wear.

She brought the pretty kitten heel of her borrowed shoes down on Maybe-Carter's foot with a snarl, avoiding the uniform boot's steel toe cap in favour of the bony ankle joint. Hissing in pain, Maybe-Carter fumbled her grip just enough to allow Cadence's shoulder to slip under her own, and before the cadet even knew what was happening she was airborne, flung straight towards the bloody-nosed Probably-Simmonds. The cadet-on-cadet collision took the both of them out, leaving them in a stunned, useless pile beside the equally insensible bulk of Perhaps-Yates.

Catching her breath, Cade swept her messy hair out of her face. "What did you say, sorry?" she asked Renji.

"I said, I think I won a—"

Her eyes widened. *"Look out!"*

Renji span on his heel just in time to catch Flood's lunging attack, messily blocking the blade before it could reach him; so messily, that with a hiss of delight and a flick of the wrist Flood was able to twist the blade enough to wrench the golden-hilted sword from Renji's grasp with one hand and catch the fucking thing with the other.

Finding himself disarmed, discomforted and now facing a frenzied sergeant with not one but two deadly weapons, Renji scuttled backwards out of sword range, putting the Limbic Imager's trolley between the two of them.

"C'mon sarge, can't we just forget all this happened?! I'll not tell Aunty L how you tried to feed me to a crocodile and you'll— uh, not do that, and then we just can move on from all of—"

He ducked just in time, and the overarm slice intended for his face instead caught the Imager, cleaving into the thing's terminal and leaving the plainer sword tangled in the wreckage. Snorting, Flood kicked the trolley out of the way and switched to the golden blade, which seemed to fit his hand perfectly.

"Stop. Talking." he growled, each syllable a threat.

For once, Renji listened to that advice and instead made an attempt to retreat further; but to his mounting horror he realised his back was now quite literally against the wall, pressing into stone that seemed as bleak and unforgiving as the sarge himself. Flood drew his arm back to raise the gilded weapon high, then with a savage roar he brought it down at full force in a vicious strike intended to split Renji's skull; until something shifted lighting fast between him and his target, and his blow once again struck metal instead of flesh.

Cadence grunted in effort, her false fingers curling and twitching and wrapping around the sword and the deep furrow it had cut into her robotic right palm where she'd caught the blade. Tugging and wrenching with all his might, Flood tried to free the weapon, but even as sparks shot out of her hand's damaged components she hung onto the thing with a death grip, seemingly powered by sheer stubbornness alone. With an almighty effort she pushed back against him and sent the pair of them spiralling in dizzying circles, locked together in a chaotic battle of will that brought them up against the enclosure's safety railing. Cade winced as the pale purple light along her forearm flickered and dimmed, a final spray of dying sparks spitting out from the capacitor in her palm; from the look of it she'd attempted to fire her electrical pulse, to no avail. Neither willing to be the first to give, it seemed as though the struggle could continue forever; until the sergeant's nostrils flared in that way Renji recognised all too well as a sign that the man was about to do something violent. Flood thrust his free hand into his dress uniform's jacket, and Cade's eyes rounded in indignation at the sight of the gleaming pistol he withdrew from his inside pocket.

The smiling bastard clicked the safety off, and aimed for the dead centre of her chest.

Which was when Renji and the Imager trolley came clattering across the floor at full speed, ramming the thing and its wretched cargo straight into Flood's side, jarring the gun out of his hand and leaving him teetering and flailing and snarling at the edge of the safety railing, that golden blade whipping uselessly through the air. If he'd have been a smart man, he could have dropped the heavy weapon and perhaps regained his balance, but no-one had ever accused Sergeant Hugo Flood of being a smart man. Cadence and Renji exchanged the briefest of glances and came to the same conclusion. Each took a hand on the trolley, and gave it a solid, final shove.

Howling, the sergeant toppled over the railing and into the enclosure below, landing on the sandy shallows with a bone-crunching *thud*. That terrible splashing of water that had been filling the room intensified, the dark shape flitting through the balcony pool curving to head back to its shallow beach with shocking speed.

"Come on." said Cadence, tugging Renji away from the edge.

"But—"

"Trust me, mate. You really don't wanna see this." She scooped up the fallen gun and made for the door, hopping over the pile of unconscious cadets.

Hesitantly, Renji shuffled a single step back from the railing; then span around and bolted as the sounds from the enclosure started to become decidedly worse.

#

Having scrambled out into the halls and run in whatever direction seemed as though it would take them the furthest away from whatever was happening back in the crocodile enclosure, it became clear from the decor that they'd made their way to the hotel portion of Il Coccodrillo. While busting into a random room in the hopes of finding a spare luxury suite in which to properly finish off this ongoing panic attack was more than a little tempting to Renji, Cadence instead threw open a door marked *Employees Only* and proceeded to stuff the both of them into what turned out to be a housekeeping supply closet full of stiff hotel towels and fresh white bedsheets.

Flexing her damaged palm in annoyance and pacing as much as was possible in the tiny, cramped linen-lined cupboard, Cadence tried to hail Weaver on her earpiece. Judging from the swearing emanating from her general direction, it wasn't going well.

Renji, for his part, was also not doing well. Every bit of him hurt; not just the still-bleeding wounds ruining his best suit, but every frayed nerve in his body seemed to be furious at him, leaving him so uncomfortable he could scream. Aunty L had always said that taking ten calming breaths helped her keep it together when she was on the verge of losing it. While it hadn't looked like she'd remembered her own advice today, Renji gave it a shot all the same.

"Fuck," he exhaled, on the tenth. "Fuck fuck fuck *fuck*. I- I can't believe what just— They were gonna—"

Cadence shook her head. "Focus, mate. We're still on the job."

"Oh my god. Oh shit." Renji stared at her in realisation. "Did we just kill the sarge?" he said hoarsely.

She heaved a sigh of irritation. "I mean… kind of? Maybe. He had a sword, he might be fine."

"Sword-fighting a *crocodile?!*"

"Alright, so it's a bit unlikely, I grant you…"

Renji didn't find this thought comforting. "Fucking… *fuck!*" he moaned.

Cadence eyed him warily as he slumped down into a morose pile, surrounded by towels. "Look, *he* started it!" she snapped, as though she'd been asked to explain something terribly obvious. "You're allowed to get someone if they're trying to get you. That's self-defence, innit?"

"Yeah, well. I think it goes a bit past self-defence when you feed people to a crocodile."

"We didn't make the croc do anything. Whatever they got up to down there isn't our fault!"

"I mean… it *is* though, isn't it."

"He's the one that did for Kiki, right?" she said, fiercely. "So, whatever. Bastard got no more than he deserved."

"I just didn't… I've never actually hurt anyone before, really, let alone—" From his linen heap, Renji started up at the tiny, bare bulb in the closet's ceiling, head too full of churning thoughts to focus on any one of them for long. "Guess you were right, huh? I wasn't ready for any of this."

Halting in her pacing, Cade stared at him as though waiting for the punchline. When one didn't appear, she seemed unsure what to do about it.

"You're not— I didn't mean—" she tried, then gave up. "Ugh, fuck's sakes. I'm not meant for this stuff. Hang about."

Cadence closed her eyes, and a shiver and a sniff later, Melody opened them. The hacker stared around the cupboard in confusion for a second, until everything seemed to click into place.

"Oh." Melo looked at her mangled hand, then at Renji. "Ta very much." she grumbled to no-one present, then flopped onto the sad little improvised towel-nest next to him, wriggling in until she was comfortable. Finally, she turned to face him.

"Hi."

"Hi." He wasn't sure where to start. "So, we maybe killed a guy…?"

"Yeah yeah, I saw. Shared memory, remember." Melo touched her throat, the bruise where Maybe-Carter's baton was already beginning to bloom, and hummed a note of discord. "So, yeah. I know it feels bad to have done that, but that's how it's supposed to be. You're *meant* to feel bad. What it is, right, is that the bloke who was gonna turn you into a zip file, how d'you think he was feeling about what he was about to do?"

"Uh… good?" Renji stuttered out a nervous laugh. "Probably *too* good. He always was a creep, that guy."

"Exactly. So that bad vibe you've got right now is the best way this could go, actually. Feeling that's what makes us not like him. But you still have to do for the bastards before they do for you." She traced one of her few remaining non-mechanical fingers along the gash in her ruined palm, testing the wrecked hand's fingers one by one with a twitch. "So you put that feeling away, til there's less arseholes with guns about the place."

"A-away?"

264

"Yeah. Shove it somewhere safe, and don't look at it yet. If ever."

Renji frowned, but her words did make a kind of sense. He was used to playing a part, he could handle the role of Guy Who Isn't Freaking Out for a couple of hours. Another ten breaths later, he gave it a try. "Alright, yeah. Okay. I'm fine."

"Sound." Nodding in satisfaction, she gave her fingers one more wriggle. "Good job in there, by the by. Solid. They didn't get owt from you."

"Wait, how d'you know I didn't tell them anything? Cadence only came in *after* that."

"Mm..." She rolled her shoulders, wincing. "Yeah. About that. Cade actually might've got there a little earlier, then kinda like... waited a bit. And listened. She wanted to see what you were going to say."

"She *what?!* Jeez!"

"Yeah, but it's whatever, isn't it? Worked out fine. Anyway, point was, most folk woulda told them everything."

There was a strong temptation to bluster it off, scoop up the praise and breeze past it with an *obviously I'd have never let them break me because I am very cool and also strong* type of swagger, but it turned out that a languid hacker reclining in a heap of hotel towels was a difficult person to lie to.

"I wasn't really thinking properly, if we're being honest. I only told him to fuck off because that's what came out of my mouth."

"Good instinct." She nodded again. "Keep your radio next time though. Plonker."

Next time, he noted with a jolt of satisfaction. "How did you find me without it, anyway?"

Rolling up one of the towels to make herself a sort of rudimentary pillow, Melody explained that Cade had returned from the bathroom to find Renji wasn't in the ballroom, but before she could track him down and drag him back to the mission, from outside on the window cleaner's platform Weaver could see trouble incoming, in the form of the commander's car. Both tried hailing Renji on the radio to no response, and agreed that something had gone terribly wrong. Weaver said he could distract the commander, Cade and him switched places so she could ride the window cleaner platform...

"And what, she looked for me in every window of the place?"

Melody exhaled. "Not exactly." she said, reaching over. It took him a moment to recognise the thing she retrieved from his jacket pocket; a tiny device, almost identical to the one that had been placed in the bags earlier. A GPS tracker.

"She bugged me?!"

"Mm..."

He squinted at Melody, who was twiddling the tracker between her fingers innocently. *"You* bugged me."

She shrugged. It wasn't a no.

"Oh." Renji couldn't help but feel a little stung. "Damn, okay. I thought you were the one that liked me."

Her gaze stayed fixed on a shelf of pillowcases. "Liking someone isn't the same as trusting them." Stretching her damaged hand towards the ceiling, she tensed her fingers, curling them into a fist. "Me and Cade, we don't... We don't trust easily."

Renji examined that unreadable expression. "Soooo, after all of *that, "* he wheeled a hand, trying to encompass everything that had just happened, "how's my trust level looking now?"

While she remained as laid-back as ever, this time there was a hint of something genuine in that half-smile. "Better."

It was a small note of approval, but it sparked a warm glow in his chest all the same. "Heh, I'll take it." He grinned. "And Cade?"

She shook her head, unwilling to tell. "Her feelings, her business."

"Fair enough." Everything about the two sisters was a puzzle, one whose pieces seemed difficult to earn. He hoped to be able to solve it, one day. "Still though, I heard her in there... *Our* idiot, she said. That's gotta be a good sign, right?"

"Set your standards higher, mate." Popping her earpiece out, she fiddled with it a little before attempting to hail Weaver again. She wrinkled her nose at the lack of response, until a sudden pop of static from the tiny speaker made the both of them jump.

"You find him?"

Weaver's voice was strained, breathless, yet strong. Renji sat bolt upright. "Holy shit! What the hell's happening down there, old man?!"

Melody waved him away and set to answering Weaver's question. "Got him. What's your status?"

A grunt, and a clatter. "Still giving Lissa the runaround."

"Can you lose her?"

"Reckon I can make it to the van from here, yeah."

"Then we'll see you out front. Radio when you're in position."

"Roger."

"Don't get killed!" added Renji, helpfully.

"I'll take it into consideration, thanks."

With that, the line went dead.

Renji huffed out a breath of relief. There were about a hundred questions he had for that ex-Forces mystery man following that little phone call he'd witnessed, none of which Weaver would be able to answer if Aunty L cut his head off first.

A similar thing seemed to be going through Melody's mind, too. "What's going on with him and the commander, d'you know?"

"No idea! I knew they were both in the same squad as my mom, but I dunno why Aunty L wants him dead so bad." He paused, as a vital piece of information almost lost in the rush floated back up to the surface. "It's weird, though… When we were talking back there, she did mention Harlow. I think she has her."

Melody blinked in surprise. "Did she say where?"

"Nah. Sorry."

"Right. Okay. Yeah." Exhaling, she drew herself to her feet, smoothing out the rumpled evening dress as best as she could. "Theft first, think later."

Renji felt a jolt of something electric course through him at her words. The job was still on, then. He *hadn't* ruined everything. "You reckon we can still do this?"

She consulted her phone. "If Weaver keeps buying us time. No security alerts up yet."

"Hell yeah!" He struggled upright, freeing himself from the linens in a burst of renewed energy. "Then let's fuckin' go!"

Melody tilted the phone one way, then the other; then nodded as she picked up the position of the GPS tracker, sending its silent signal from the depths of the bags of perfectly filthy cash.

"This way."

CHAPTER 19
CHRISTMAS SPIRIT

It turns out that even when someone is bleeding and their suit has more stab holes than would be proper for a formal event, they can still get through a crowd without drawing much attention if they walk as though their multitude of problems simply did not exist. Wielding only a confident stride and a neutral expression, Renji was able to lead both of them through the hotel's halls without any of the scattered guests or staff seeming to take note of the frazzled state they were in.

The signal seemed to be indicating that the cash was stowed somewhere on a higher floor towards the hotel's peak. As they were still on the crocodile floor, which wasn't far off street level, thanks to the inconveniently located ballroom elevators getting up to the floor they wanted would mean passing straight through the hordes of I.I. Christmas guests. Confident as it was, Renji wasn't so certain that the stride would be enough to get them across a party full of gossip-hungry revellers without at least a couple of questions, so instead, much to Melody's complaint, they took the stairs.

"You could just swap and let Cade do the walking," Renji offered.

"Bugger that." she huffed, without offering further explanation.

The security room they were led to offered no outward sign of what lay behind its door other than a compact keypad lock over the handle.

"Tsch, easy. Have this open in a jiff."

Melody fished through her purse to withdraw a bundle of wires and keys that unrolled into a compact keyboard and, true to her word after mere moments of typing and fiddling with her phone the lock gave an enticing little *click* of assent.

"Witchcraft," snickered Renji.

"Just code," she hummed, rolling away the keyboard with only the faintest air of self-satisfaction.

When they slipped into the formerly secure room, Renji was more than a little relieved to find they had no need of the *whoops, wrong door* excuses he'd been lining up, as there was no-one else in there. Rather, the place was little more than a haphazard pile of party supplies; loose decorations hung from the shelves, scraps of centrepiece and spare seating placards littering the floor, as though everything had been assembled in a hurry. Much of the room was occupied by that odd artifact of Renji's childhood memories, the I.I. Santa Sleigh, which had been jammed into the middle of the room where its long gold-painted handles and big slatted runners could block easy access to most of anything.

Her phone held aloft and searching, Melody gingerly stepped onto the sleigh to clamber across it. "Oh. More solid than I reckoned. Thought it'd be plastic or summat."

"Nah, this thing's been around forever. Hand-carved wood and all that shit." Renji rapped on it with a knuckle. "They actually drive it around at the end of the night. See, all the Santa outfit's in there too."

Melo bent to examine the carriage. "Huh. Looks like it's built over something... Kind of an electric go-kart, style o' thing."

"A go-kart?"

"Yeah. Cade used to work at a go-kart place. Doesn't look too different to the ones from there." She lifted a panel of the wooden sleigh-shell to indicate a couple of pedals and a craftily hidden steering wheel.

"Man. Is that all it is…?" While he'd rather get back in the crocodile pit than admit to being a fan of the stupid sleigh, he couldn't help but feel a little disappointed in how mundane the magic was.

"That and the invisible reindeer, yeah."

"Very fuckin' funny."

Just behind the sleigh lay their target. Evidently, no-one at Il Coccodrillo was used to dealing with this quantity of physical money, as the sacks of cash had been dumped unceremoniously in the corner, covered by a disdainful little heap of jingle-bell hats and pointy shoes. Presumably the interns had re-joined the party in an attempt to leverage as much networking as possible out of the rest of the evening. Scrambling over, Renji rustled around in the bags, withdrawing a handful of cash with glee.

"Holy shit! Merry goddamn *Christmas!*" he breathed, grabbing another handful just for the novelty of it. "You ever seen this much paper in your life?!"

"Don't think there's this much in all of Buried." Melody pulled open another bag. "Cor."

"Wonder which stack was mine."

"Why, d'you want it back?" she asked mildly.

He shook his head, letting the bills flutter back into the bags— and almost leapt out of his skin at the sound of a crackle of static.

"I'm clear." came Weaver's voice from the tiny ear radio. "Back at the van now."

"Goddamn, that was quick." Renji scrambled to his feet. "You okay, old man?"

"Mm." he grunted, strain evident in his tones. "Remind me t'thank that engineer. This leg's a lifesaver."

"And Aunty L…?"

"Hasn't lost her edge since I saw her, that's for sure. Won't take long for her t'notice I ain't in the building anymore." The van's engine sprang to life in the background.

"Well, shit! How're we gonna move these bags through the party without anyone noticing?" asked Renji, looking from them to Melody.

"Was hoping you'd have an idea." she shrugged, slumping down on the sleigh to have a think. "You can't get to the window cleaner platform, Mr Weaver?"

"Not since your sister left it halfway up the hotel."

"What if we put it in suitcases, then walked it out like we were guests…?" mused Renji. "Nah, that's no good. Too many people know me, then they're gonna notice the, uh… *this.*" He picked at his ruined suit jacket in frustration.

"Find some cleaning staff uniforms. Put it in laundry trolleys."

"Nah, any of those party planners are gonna flip out if they see cleaning staff in the room. Could shove it out the window?"

"Too many pedestrians around."

"Worst comes to worst, we fill our pockets." Melo patted the sides of her dishevelled dress. "Uh, *your* pockets."

"I guess… Ugh, we'd leave so much behind, though!" Renji glared at the bags in frustration. There had to be a way around this, there just *had* to; they'd come too far for this sad little detail to trip them up now.

"Whatever we're going to do, we need to do it now." Melody frowned at the clock on her phone from her perch on the sleigh.

And as Renji turned to her to reply, that was when it hit him, crashing into his brain like a truck loaded down with a full delivery of pure, blissful *stupid.* Sure, getting themselves and the loot out without making a scene was impossible; but what if the scene they made was one the crowd had been expecting to see?

Melody eyed him suspiciously. "You've got something, haven't you."

"Yep."

"I'm not going to like it, am I."

"Nope."

#

The brass elevator's cage doors rattled open, and the pleasant ambient party sounds of the ballroom took on a note of excitement at the sight of what came rolling out to greet them. At last, the beloved great wooden Christmas sleigh had arrived, complete with sacks of goodies and a perfectly festive Santa; perhaps one that seemed somewhat younger and skinnier than the standard, but nevertheless he greeted the party guests with appropriate amounts of festive joy. The somewhat nervous elf at the sleigh's wheel manoeuvred the rather bulky vehicle into the midst of the welcoming crowd.

"Cannot honestly tell if this is tragic or brilliant." muttered Melody, the bells on her hat jingling with a cheer that didn't register on her face.

"I think we both know the answer to that." Renji winked from behind the big fake beard, then got back to the prescribed Santa business of bellowing like a right jolly old elf. *"Ho ho ho! Merry Christmas!"*

The sleigh crept forward, progressing at an agonising rate into the centre of the ballroom and picking up a low orbital chain of children, all of whom were apparently doing their very best to get under the damn thing's treads. The helms-elf cursed under her breath, forced to a stop by the barrage of a dozen or so incoming infants in tiny designer formalwear, all of whom began to swarm the sides of the sleigh like rosy-cheeked termites. Standing firm against the onslaught of moppets Renji held his nerve and kept up the act to the best of his ability, chortling and bringing the Christmas cheer while attempting to push away some of the snottier specimens. The nearby parents seemed to be taking the brief window of opportunistic childcare to grab themselves extra drinks, which was understandable.

"Santa! *Santaaaaa!*" wailed an alarmingly red little girl on the verge of apoplexy.

"We've been waiting *all* evening!" demanded a cross child who had a bright future in middle-management. "Where's our presents?"

"Yeah, presents!"

"Pressies!" came the resounding cry from the horde.

Renji was lucky the false beard was fluffy enough to hide the wince that crossed his face. "Ho ho ho, uh… give Santa a sec, will ya?"

Shit. He'd forgotten about the presents. There hadn't been a bag of the usual goodies waiting on the sleigh in the safe room, and the kids were already close to rioting just from sugar intake alone; if he told them there were no damn gifts, there'd be a stampede. This cosy Christmas scene had to play out as expected for the escape plan to work, and a dozen wailing children ripping Santa apart wasn't quite how this was supposed to go. He eyed Melody. She shrugged. His plan, his problem.

In desperation, Renji dipped his hand into one of the sacks and turned to the nearest kid.

"Merry Christmas!" he chortled, handing the tiny round-eyed boy a twenty. "Um. Don't tell your parents, okay?"

A gasp rolled up from the assembled tots, their eyes fixed on the cash, and just as Renji was starting to think he'd performed an irreparable fuck-up the kids surged forward as one eager crowd.

"Me next!"

"Gimme! Gimmeeee!"

"He's five years old and I'm ten, so I should get twice what he got!"

Breathing a sigh of relief, Renji slipped a few notes into each grasping hand, his gaze darting around the room to make sure none of the adults noticed their kids were being handed cold hard cash rather than gingerbread. While Renji had no interest in parenting, on an instinctive level he suspected that handing a ten-year-old a hundred bucks wasn't the sort of thing he was meant to do. Still, it seemed to have mostly worked.

Mostly. Because only metres away, sipping a sherry and watching proceedings with apparent interest, was Chance Delaney.

Renji groaned, his heart sinking. But… Maybe Delaney hadn't recognised him. Maybe he was smirking like that because he thought Santa bribing children is funny. Maybe everything would be just fine.

All in all, it shouldn't have been a surprise when, with that innate comic timing of small children everywhere, a pudgy hand grabbed at the fake Santa beard and pulled it hard enough to dislodge the damn thing. With a jolt of speed he hadn't known he'd possessed until that very moment Renji managed to re-cover his face and fling a defensive fifty into the kid's face before anyone else took a good enough look— but already Delaney's gaze had caught his own, a ripple of amusement spreading over those fine features. One of his dark eyebrows rose in a questioning arch.

"A-alright kids, Santa's got stuff to do, uh… at the North Pole, or whatever!" Renji stuttered, attempting to dismiss the kids in as jolly a fashion as was possible. "Ho ho ho, it's time to *go!*" The last word was a plea, directed at Melody.

"I'm not going to run them over, am I?" she said, jingling her bells at the mob of children still pressing in around them. "If you want us to move, you'll have to get 'em shifted."

"How?!" Renji had barely ever interacted with kids, let alone tried to shepherd them around, and it was proving impossible to get the rowdy little bastards to listen to what he was saying. The gang of children remained rooted to and around the sleigh like adorable wheel clamps no matter how many times he tried to excuse himself, and he was just about to attempt a more impolite method when a voice cut across the clamour.

"Whatcha got there, kids?"

Every child's face flushed with the unimaginable horror of being caught doing something naughty. While they couldn't have been aware *why* they shouldn't have fistfuls of cash they damned well seemed aware that it was contraband.

"Presents from Santa, huh." Chance addressed the kids with all the pleasant menace of an older brother on the verge of telling mum. "Wanna go show your parents what you got?"

They did not. In one quick flurry of motion the mob scarpered, their loot disappearing into sleeves and pockets as they dispersed into the party crowd.

Renji blinked at his unexpected saviour. "Not that I don't appreciate it, but... why?"

Chance eyed the sacks of cash. "Frankly, I want to see where you're going with this."

"Out the door, preferably."

He let out that light laugh again, the one that seemed to be extremely good at making something inside Renji shiver in just the right way. "I admit it, you may be a little more of a renegade than I'd assumed."

"So you're not gonna turn us in?"

"No, I don't believe I will." he smiled over his glass. "Let's call it a Christmas gift."

Renji hopped back up onto the sleigh. "And here I didn't get you anything. Yet." He threw one last wink over his shoulder at an amused Delaney before the sleigh's engine ticked back to life. "Merry Christmas!"

Chance raised his glass in a mockery of a salute, and with an exhale of relief, Melody finally began to ease the thing forward again in the direction of the elevator.

"What was that...?" she whispered in disbelief.

"Sales negotiation!" He readjusted the beard and jolly hat to hide the wild, stupid smirk on his face. "C'mon, gift horse, mouth, who cares! Just drive!"

Inch by slow inch the sleigh approached the big brass gated lift doors, and as the carriage rose to meet their floor Renji thought his heart was going to burst out of his chest with excitement. Despite all of tonight's mistakes and near misses, the sheer delight of walking out of here under everyone's noses was incomparable, a thrill unlike any other he'd ever experienced. Glancing down at Melody it was plain from the set to her laconic half-smile that she was feeling the same way.

That was, until the elevator doors before them pinged open to reveal an incalculably livid Aunty L, drawn sword still gripped tight in one shaking hand. Her dress uniform, formerly an immaculate series of folds and creases, was now a rumpled mess, her breathing was heavy, and despite the December chill a trickle of sweat beaded on her forehead. She looked at Renji, still hidden behind the Santa outfit; then down to Melody; and then back to her nephew, her eyes widening with furious understanding. Suddenly, he knew just how the pack of children caught with their hands full of stolen cash had felt.

"I can explain…!" he said, even though he couldn't, and from the sleigh's driver seat there came a now-familiar sniff and a shudder— followed by a crunch, as Cadence jabbed her hand into the guts of the go-kart beneath the sleigh, pulling something loose and tossing it aside. She did something violent to the controls and with a sudden gut-wrenching jolt the sleigh barrelled backwards and span left into an abrupt J-turn away from the elevator doors and Aunty L, sending shrieking party guests scattering out of the way.

"Arrest them!" roared Commander Starkweather, pointing her sword in their direction. It took a moment for the assembled guests to shake off the shock from both the sudden burst of movement and hearing the order to arrest Santa and his elf, but several people Renji recognised as Senior Forces Upper Management were already recovering, reaching for their own weapons with intent.

"Get the van beneath that stupid reptile balcony, *now!*" Cade barked into the earpiece, withdrawing Flood's gun from her clutch.

At the sight of the shining pistol the path ahead of them cleared of shrieking partygoers, leaving a straight shot between them and… Well, *nothing,* except one of the ballroom's great, tall windows, the one that offered the best view of the crocodile. Heart pounding, Renji stared at the weapon in Cade's hands. "What are you—"

Leaping to her feet, she threw Renji into the driver's seat in her place. "Floor it!"

"At what, the fuckin' window?!"

"Just do it!"

As if the intent in her voice wasn't clear enough, the click of the pistol's safety release as she lifted the gun to point it directly ahead acted as rather convincing punctuation. And so before the Uppers pushing through the crowds at their sides could reach the sleigh, Renji did as he was told and stomped on the accelerator. *Hard.*

The wheels of the go-kart beneath the sleigh strained and screamed along the polished ballroom floor as the engine sprang to life, tearing across the room faster than he had ever assumed the bulky old thing could go. The pane of thick glass making up one of Il Coccodrillo's floor-to-ceiling windows loomed before them, large and implacable; then at once it shattered with a thunderous blast, splintering into a hundred thousand glittering pieces as a snarling Cadence emptied every last bullet she had in its direction. With nothing left between it and the cold night the sleigh shot through the destroyed window like a chaotic wooden rocket, bouncing along the suspiciously crocodile-free covered balcony with a horrific creaking, splintering *crack,* and the last thing Renji remembered was a howl of exhilarated, joyful terror bursting from his chest as the sleigh ramped off the shining water-filled platform to sail through the frozen December air in a beautiful, uncontrollable freefall into the darkness below.

CHAPTER 20

THE DEEP END

After several seconds, minutes, hours; however the hell long it had been, Renji stirred, cracking his eyes open with a groan. All about him was a confusing blur of movement, streaks of light zipping through the darkness, the wind whipping about his face and roaring in his ears.

Ah yes, that was right. They were falling. Surely they'd have to land soon. Maybe he could keep his eyes closed until then.

At the sudden blare of an angry car horn the world seemed to jerk erratically, accompanied by the unmistakable squeal of rubber on road, as Renji began to realise that the roar wasn't the winter gale at all; it was an engine.

Seized by a sudden jolt of energy and a rather pressing need to know what the hell was going on, Renji was finally able to remember he had limbs and used them to prop himself up, balancing shakily on his elbows. They had landed alright, landed right on the top of Weaver's plain, indistinguishable transit van, which was looking a lot more distinct than it had before as it sped through downtown Imperium Court with a stoved-in roof and the wreckage of a Christmas sleigh tangled in its ladders. The sleigh itself was more intact than it might have been— thanks, whoever had insisted on solid carved oak rather than chipboard— but the go-kart beneath was now more of a gone-kart. Yet, the dozen or so sacks of cash were still with them, tucked away in the covered sleigh bed.

Kneeling at the destroyed helm, her hair whipping about in a brown and teal tornado, Cadence risked a questioning glance over her shoulder at Renji. He gave her a dazed thumbs up.

"He's fine." she shouted down to the transit van's open window, and an answering grunt that could only have come from Weaver drifted up from the driver's seat.

"It worked?!" Renji asked, an elated disbelieving grin creeping across his face.

"Ask us in ten minutes." Hanging onto one arm of the sleigh for support, Cadence scanned the road behind them. "Fast as you can, sir!"

Fast, it seemed, was Weaver's speciality. The van zipped between lanes of Friday night traffic, ducking and dodging without fear to a medley of furious car horns, never missing an opportunity to slide into the smallest of gaps between vehicles with the iron spine that comes of having a tight bus schedule to stick to. While the sleigh lurched on the corners, the tangle of destroyed go-kart and ladders had formed an anchor point that held together well enough to allow Cadence and Renji to remain on their rooftop cruise, the Court seeming to fly by around them almost as fast as it had when they had been in freefall; until at last, they reached the freight elevator they'd arrived on just a few hours ago.

"Piss. They're here." Cade squinted at the road behind, where the ghostly sound of distant sirens and flashes of red and blue had begun to creep their way towards them.

A breathless Renji fumbled his phone out and tossed it to Cade, who dropped it into Weaver's hand. With a muttering grumble the old man ran it over the pay station's card reader— and just as it occurred to Renji that Aunty L might have already disabled his ID, the thing let out its merry chirp of approval.

Open Return Off Peak Rate (Imperium Court Freight 358-Steelepool Freight 358) x 3: Return successfully redeemed! Have a nice day!

Tyres screeching, Weaver jolted the van into the elevator, and the doors rolled shut, blocking out the approaching sirens with a welcoming clang.

"Ho ho *holy shit!* We did it, *we did it!"* Renji crowed, punching the air as the elevator began its descent. "I told you it'd work! We're the best at this, number one, primo, top of the fuckin' line!"

Slumping back into the sleigh's seat, Cade flicked one of the elf costume's bells out of her eye in irritation. "You're lucky, is what you are, mate. If I hadn't been there they'd have hung you from the flippin' Christmas tree."

"But you *were* there." He winked at her. "The hell did you do to that go-kart engine, anyway?"

"Tsch. Just knocked the speed suppressor off. Kids'd do it all the time at the place I worked at." She shrugged nonchalantly, but a flicker of amusement played about her lips. "Did the trick."

"Yeah it damn well did! See?" Renji clapped in delight, the sound only slightly muffled by the Santa mittens. "Perfect! That's what I'm saying, we got my great plans, Melo's skills, your muscle, and old man Weaver on the getaway! We're a *team!* A goddamn unstoppable one!"

"Nope. You don't get to declare me on your bloody team. Not when you and your shitty 'plans' are responsible for *this. "* She gave a bell a savage flick.

"Oh I'm sorry, Jingle Bells!" Spinning on his heel, Renji dropped into the sacks at the back of the sleigh, sending several bills flying. "Please, join me in the *giant freakin' pile of money we just stole* and let's discuss in detail the shittiness factor of my ideas."

"Quit horsin' around up there, you're gonna knock the damn thing loose," warned Weaver from the van's driver seat. He wasn't wrong; while the sleigh was still tangled in the rooftop ladders, the whole structure had begun to creak alarmingly when they moved.

Renji inched towards the edge to look down at Weaver. "Hey hey, old man, what was that up there, the stuff with you and Aunty L? She *hates* you! I've never seen her that pissed before."

The lights of Central Commons rumbled by, reflecting over the man's pensive expression as they continued their descent. He drummed his gloved fingers on the vehicle's wheel for a long moment before responding. "Not til we're done here. Gotta deliver the goods first, and that ain't gonna be so easy."

Renji frowned; but before he could voice his argument for why he needed the gossip now actually, thank you, Cadence's hand flew to her ear in a crackle of static.

"Ma'am, can you read me?"

Through the tinny speaker, Ms Cellanea heaved a genuine sigh of relief. "Ah, what a delight to see you are back in radio range, darling girl. Did all go well?"

"It… didn't exactly run to plan." Cade admitted, then began a quick rundown of events, leaving out the details of some of the evening's bigger fuckups.

There was a pause, and then, to her credit and Cade's apparent relief, Ms Cellanea chose to forego any chastising in favour of getting down to business. "The Forces will be assembling. They shall be waiting for you at the station, my dears."

Weaver grunted his agreement. "I'll try t'shake 'em off, but this ain't exactly a peak performance vehicle we're looking at." He patted the van's door, almost apologetically. "Best bet is we drop the cash someplace, then ditch the van in the backstreets and lose 'em on foot in the alleys."

"Drop it where?" said Cade. "We can't let them follow us home!"

"Absolutely correct," agreed Cellanea. "But I believe your, ah… unique situation could lead to an equally unique solution."

"Oh yeah?" Renji leaned in, deeply interested.

"Indeed," she replied, and despite the distance between her and them, the smile in her voice was evident. "You are not the only person around here with clever ideas, Mr Hayakawa."

#

The scene outside Steelepool Freight Elevator Station 358 was not quite everything it should have been.

If all had gone by the book, as soon as the baffling alert came in from upstairs that a rogue Santa and accompanying criminal elves were on their way down to Buried in a transit sleigh and must be detained unharmed, the station ought to have been surrounded by every local officer, Upper and cadet alike. All armed units in the area should be present and mobile, all exits from the station ought to be blockaded with tyre-shredding spike strips, and all Upper Management assigned to Buried should be alerted and on-scene. Tonight, however, the vast majority of those Upper Managers were still upstairs in Il Coccodrillo, several glasses deep in the Christmas spirit and staring blearily at a hole in the window where the crime got out.

By the time the freight elevator touched down, the on-duty lieutenant— a woman already sore about her lack of overtime pay for skipping the company party, and even sorer that the alert had come in just after she'd poured herself a nice hot cup of that fancy French imported coffee she liked— was already on edge. All the same, as annoying as this was, she felt confident the blockade of Forces vehicles they had assembled around the elevator's doors ought to bring this issue to a nice, quick resolution. Perhaps they could even make it back to the station before her coffee cooled off.

So when the suspect vehicle and its roof-rack sleigh came shooting out of the freight carriage like a cork out of champagne, knocking aside the patrol cars without so much as slowing for an instant, the lieutenant was not best pleased. The solid wooden sleigh runners that had been lashed to the van's front to be used as impromptu bull bars shattered to pieces, spraying out over the tarmac as the van shot off into the distance; and not for the first time tonight, the on-duty lieutenant found herself wishing she was an off-duty lieutenant.

The van tore through the cramped streets of Buried like a creaking, rickety comet, drawing bewildered stares and shouts from pedestrians who hadn't been expecting to see a roof-rack sleigh careening along the road, especially one complete with a scowling cybernetic elf and a Santa joyfully flipping off the Forces vehicles in pursuit.

"Three on our tail." muttered Weaver, his gloved hands gripping the steering wheel as though it was about to try to get away from him.

"Four!" said Cadence, eyeing the lights of the Forces cars screaming up the road behind them. "Hey idiot, you ready for this?" she asked Renji.

"Are you kidding?!" He beamed, adjusting his fake beard and red hat. "I've never been more ready for anything!"

Clinging onto the side of the sleigh, he dug out a fistful of cash from one of the sacks; and as the sleigh-van rounded a corner and skidded past a Chinese takeaway, Renji flung the bills into the air to rain down over the queue of people huddled outside.

"Merry fuckin' Christmas!" bellowed Santa, and the bemused muttering of the crowd turned to squawks of surprise as cash was grabbed from the ground and out of the air. Car horns began to honk all about them as Cadence upended a bag in the direction of a bus shelter, where an old lady who had been huddling in a patched sleeping bag, using the shattered glass siding as a shelter looked stunned as hundreds of bills fluttered into her lap.

"Y'know, I think I could really get into this whole *giving back to the community* thing!" Renji snickered, dropping a few thousand on the roof of a taxi and causing it to screech to a sudden halt.

"Where to?" Weaver shouted through the growing clamour of honking and cheering.

Cade scanned the streets ahead. "Take a left, sir!"

By now the sleigh and its valuable confetti trail had gained followers; at least half a dozen cars sped along in their wake, some with open windows and passengers leaning out to grab what they could, getting between them and the pursing Forces vehicles, who had no idea what to do with the situation. After Renji dropped a nice large sum on a group of late-night commuters one of the cop cars veered off and screeched to a halt, the cadets within leaping out in an attempt to seize the evidence that was all too quickly vanishing into dozens of pockets in dozens of jackets. The lack of lights in the press of streets and pitch-black buildings didn't seem to be helping matters much either.

Their convoy led down a street full of shops that seemed familiar to Renji, though it wasn't until they reached the open door of The Arms pub that he remembered why. As they passed by, Cadence threw an entire sack of cash to land at the feet of the pub landlord who filled the doorway, his phone pressed against his ear.

"Many thanks, Ms C!" chortled a redder-faced than usual Arthur into the phone, stowing the bag and its contents in the pub before the Forces could catch sight of it.

"Where next, ma'am?" Cadence asked, fingers on her earpiece.

"Allegro is ready!"

Renji cackled, nearly overbalancing in the rickety sleigh as he threw a handful of money at some people sheltering for the night in a shop doorway. "Hell yeah! To the club!"

The next sack of cash vanished down the stairs leading to Static Void to a hollered whoop of thanks from the nightclub owner. Just for good measure, a hefty sum also landed on the doorstep of the late-night barbershop above it, where one customer yelped as the wide-eyed barber ran the clippers a little close to his ear in shock.

"To the Aunties!"

This sack was thrown in through a TransGrid Station entrance, where two shapes lurked in the shadows, one scrawny, one large, both cackling with glee as they stowed away the goods.

"Over to Hajira!"

A diversion through the park saw two bags thrown onto Temperley Sanctuary's doorstep, a perplexed Hajira in pyjamas and slippers with her phone dangling from an emergency battery pack dashing out to meet it just in time. They flew past the food truck circle in a cloud of loose money, causing Chips Darren to shout in annoyance as he was forced to swat loose tenners away from his deep fat fryer. The other cooks piled out of their stations to hoot in delight, snatching the bills out of the air alongside their customers.

Tearing out of the park, Renji spotted a familiar cramped alleyway in the darkness, and directed Weaver to head towards it.

"Why here?" yelled Cadence.

"I owe 'em one!" he bellowed at the darkened windows of that anonymous block of flats, and as the unknown residents within slid their windows open to see what the fuss was about he pelted them with as much cash as he could manage.

By the time they were reaching the end of the sleigh's cargo, the van had reached the outskirts of town, their protective civilian convoy having dropped behind the press of Forces vehicles that had muscled them out of the way. While several of their pursuers had either stopped to launch futile attempts to recover the stolen money or become lost in the twisting and turning streets of the great sprawl that was once Steelepool, the backup had arrived in the form of half a dozen gleaming Forces cars, their Imperium Blue lights flashing in time with the screaming of their sirens, doggedly speeding along on the van's heels.

Before long Weaver's erratic driving brought them through the lines of industrial parks and onto a closed road for goods vehicles, one which ran alongside the high banks and litter-clogged waters of the River Steele. Some twenty feet below them, the water reflected a glistening mirror of their headlights, distorted and warped by the depths on their way out to sea.

Then, with the flat seaside horizon and the looming husk of Buried's inert port rising into view, a shape detached from the darkness and drew up alongside the van; a black motorbike, the many scrapes on its paint covered by stickers of cartoon bunnies. The driver's hands were glued to the throttle, her neon-pink helmet drawn down to hide her face, but there was no mistaking the rider for anyone but Sugar. Behind her and clinging on as though his life depended on it, Trig shouted a nervous greeting up to Cade and Renji.

"Ready?" Cade hefted the final two sacks.

Trig's bike helmet bobbed. "A-as we'll ever be!"

Sugar flashed a thumbs up, bringing her bike close to the van. Cadence leaned down to hand over the very last of their loot— the sleigh swaying alarmingly with the movement— and the bike peeled off, zipping into a tiny cobbled alley between two rows of terrace houses and clattering away into the night with a fading wail of protest from her terrified passenger.

Another lurch rocked the sleigh as Weaver righted their position, and Renji found himself needing to cling to the wooden siding to keep from being tossed into the streets like the bags of cash; or worse, bouncing off the railing into the river below.

Cadence steadied herself in the frozen sea wind that had begun to howl around them, losing her jingly bell elf hat in the process. "It's done!" she yelled down to Weaver. "Get us out of here before this thing falls to bits!"

The old man grunted out a strained response. It seemed negative. Renji, who had never driven in his life, stared at the straight and empty road ahead in an attempt to work out what about it had Weaver so concerned. He didn't have to wonder for long as a tell-tale blue flash glinted off the steel fencing at the end of the road; and then they there were, two Forces cars screeching to a halt to block off the exit. They were trapped.

Renji looked around frantically. The only way out of the alley now was a bridge coming up fast— *too fast*— on their right, but they'd be past it in seconds. "Shit!" The vehicles behind kept up their speed, harrying them towards an inevitable conclusion. "Fuck!"

"Language," muttered Weaver, his hand finding the parking brake; and before Renji knew what was happening the van span into a dizzying, horrible handbrake turn, a graceless and desperate lunge to make the turnoff for the bridge.

Taking a corner on two wheels is never ideal at the best of times, even more so when the vehicle in question has a few hundred kilos of solid wood and swearing fool attached to its roof-rack; and with a snarl from Weaver and a sickening heave that was beginning to feel far too familiar to Renji, the van, the sleigh and all within shot straight through the bridge's railing, plummeting like a stone into the icy waters below.

#

Renji slammed into the river hard enough to knock the breath out of him, which felt somewhat unfair considering he was about to need it. Too panicked to do anything else, he twisted in the freezing water, his world reduced to nothing more than a swirling chaos of dark shapes in darker water, a confusion of motion and terror. A stringy, vile mass covered his mouth, and his too-heavy limbs were tangled as though some unknown something had him snared, intending to drag him down into the inky depths.

The Santa costume. Of course, he was still wearing the heavy bastard thing over the top of his suit! Desperate to not get killed by a fake beard and several yards of crushed red velvet Renji struggled for all he was worth, shucking the thick robe off and letting it drift down to the river bed.

Now free enough to float and with a better idea of where *up* might be, he began moving towards what his aching lungs were desperately hoping was fresh air; then froze, horrified, as a long dark shape passed him by. For one primal moment of terror, all he could think of was scales and bone-white teeth and yawning wide jaws— but the water turned her gently as she drifted downward, and the pale purple light of Cade's arm flickered in the murk. Her mechanical limbs hung useless and heavy, and while her long hair was a black and teal tangle about her face, enough was visible in the weak glow to show that her eyes were not open.

With a wild kick Renji hurled himself forward to fumble his arms around her waist, and using the very last remains of a strength he was reasonably sure he didn't even possess, he dragged the both of them upward in a frantic paddle towards the surface.

288

The first gasping lungful of air was a relief to Renji, but hearing Cadence splutter and cough the instant they reached the surface was even more so. The look of pure disbelief she threw at him was a nice bonus, too.

The river had brought them further downstream, the bridge from which they'd taken a sharp exit now some distance away. The flashing lights of the Forces vehicles played over the ruined railings their van had torn through. There must have been a dozen officers there now, fanning out around the area in confusion, peering into the river with torches. Searching for them.

His body aching from the strain of keeping both himself and Cade afloat, Renji cast about for the quickest way to get out of the river without being spotted— and had to bite back a yelp as a hand seized him by the back of the collar.

"Shh." hissed Weaver, tugging him and Cadence into the shadow of a nearby pedestrian bridge. There they hid while a patrol with radios crackling out short, angry bursts passed overhead, Weaver treading water steadily enough to keep all three of them afloat. Neck-deep in freezing water, all Renji could do was stay quiet and hope the chattering of his teeth didn't give them away. Back over by the bridge a long white car had pulled up in a screech of brakes, Aunty L bursting out of the door like a category-five hurricane, and while Renji couldn't make out the words exchanged between his aunt and her officers, he could guess at enough to feel more than a little guilty about it.

After what felt like far too long the patrol on the bridge moved along, and Weaver allowed them to bob further down the river until they had drifted out of sight. Then with an almighty kick of that brand new leg, he dragged Renji and Cadence to the nearest riverbank, where they were able to flop out of the water with all of the grace of a frozen fish. All three lay on the silt for a moment, exhausted and rumpled, clothes stained a concerning greenish-brown from the river water, catching wheezing breaths that disappeared into the frozen night as clouds.

"Th-thanks, old m-man." Renji managed, through the shivers.

The reply came in the form of a grunt and a dismissive gesture, which suggested Weaver had already done about as much moving as intended to do for the rest of the evening. This seemed fair enough to Renji, who with great effort, propped himself up on his elbows to face Cadence.

"G-gotcha." he grinned, weakly.

"Get l-lost." She struggled to pull herself upright, snarling at the muted jingle from the still-present bells on her elf shoes. Her right arm remained motionless at her side, the large rend across her cybernetic hand from Flood's attack oozing water. Since her other arm contained less electronics besides those in her palm and several digits it seemed to be in better working order, thus she was able to use it to wriggle into a sitting position enough to give Renji an unreadable look that could have been gratitude or disgust or anything in between.

"For what it's w-worth," he said, "this absolutely makes us f-friends, y'know. Best friends, even."

"W-why are you like this."

Renji aimed his most obnoxious finger-guns at her. "Hey, you're w-welcome, *bestie.*"

"Nah. I'm not d-dealing with this," she muttered darkly, closing her eyes. The motion of her change was almost lost in the rest of the shivering and sniffing that was going about, but the satisfied hum she let out afterwards could have only belonged to Melody. She allowed herself to slump backwards, sprawling in the chilly riverbank mud.

"N-nice." she whistled in satisfaction, despite all evidence.

"Yeah." grunted Weaver, from the ground. "Nice."

Since it wasn't as if he could get any muckier, Renji flopped back into the mud beside them. The underside of Central Commons hung far above, its electronic billboards glittering in the dark like market-tested constellations.

The commotion of their little money parade stunt rang throughout the darkened streets, the scattered Forces trying to split their attention between searching for the criminals and regaining the evidence, failing at doing either, and leaving plenty of time for three soggy figures to eventually slip away unnoticed into the night.

CHAPTER 21

GETTING AWAY WITH IT

It was around 10 p.m. on Saturday when the blackout was lifted from Buried.

A muted cheer went up from the assembled crowd in Temperley Park as the strings of lights flickered to life above their heads. It was meant to be a small gathering, but the bonfire crackling away on the hill overlooking the shelter had drawn something of a crowd, and no-one was about to tell them to leave. Besides, thanks to the recent windfall, there was more than enough drink, food and Christmas spirit to go around. With the power back on, the speakers Allegro had dragged into the park's small plaza sprang to life, and the gathering settled into a comfortable atmosphere.

Apparently, Kiki hadn't been the type to want a funeral. Trig had been quite clear on that. While she hadn't been part of the group as long as others, she'd once mentioned that the notion of people stood around wearing black and wailing her name sounded far spookier than the actual idea of dying, so what was happening here wasn't a funeral; it was a wake, one buzzing with music, laughter, and life. A celebration. And going by the way more and more people were filtering into the plaza, one which was very much welcome.

Since they'd stumbled back into the railway Roundhouse dripping wet and sneezing several hours ago, Renji had managed to grab a hot shower and a deeply satisfying snooze. Auntie Biotic had been more than delighted to take a crack at tending to his injuries; it seemed that stab wounds were a favourite of hers, especially when they'd been doused in filthy river water. Now, he was all patched up and back in his favourite T-shirt and stolen leather jacket, feeling far closer to human again.

Feeling quite aware of the fact that he'd never met Kiki, he'd taken up a seat on the dead grass in a cosy spot near the bonfire rather than join in the conversations, most of which were about small, happy memories of pinball contests and drinking games and her attempts to learn guitar, which had never gone quite as well as she'd have liked. Sugar and Trig perched on the edge of the fountain, her head on his shoulder, chattering away happily enough despite having to wipe away the occasional tear. Allegro and Melody sat with them, the right sleeve of the hacker's shiny pink puffer jacket pinned back above the elbow. The rest of her arm had already been presented to an apoplectic Auntie Septic, who was taking her time to attend to what she saw as careless misuse of one of her masterpieces. The DJ didn't seem to be letting the missing limb bother her however; one-handed, she tapped away at her phone to set up the music, selecting some low-key, serene beats for the occasion.

At one of the tables beside Riley's coffee stand Ms Cellanea and Weaver were deep in conversation about something or another, her hands in expressive motion as they often were when she was intent on something. Not one for conversation, Weaver seemed to be contributing little besides grunts and nods, but the small flick at the corner of his mouth suggested he was enjoying himself; at least, as much as he was capable of doing so. That salt-and-pepper stubble of his had gone unchecked for another day, Renji noticed. He suspected the old man was making a play for that rather handsome beard Ms C had suggested the other day.

Ms Cellanea… Once they'd finished their little heist, the leader of the Loose Ends had very much lived up to her title. While she never claimed credit for the crime, that obscene power bill for the community had been paid in anonymous cash gathered from the dropoffs they'd made to her allies, along with a strong suggestion that any further bills of that nature would be dealt with in a similar manner as this one had been.

Someone must have picked up on her hint, as this very morning the news broke that going forward, Imperium International would be offering a lower energy rate on winter bills, as their way to give back to their citizens in these trying times. All day long the media had been praising their unprecedented act of generosity towards those in need, with only a few quiet souls in Buried understanding the true reasons for the move. It had been a good media day for I.I. in general, in fact; much acclaim was heaped on the apparent theatrics that had taken place at their Christmas party last night, a jolly good caper involving a real flying Santa sleigh, as the reports told it. The kids had loved it.

Downing the last of his beer, Renji pulled himself to his feet and wandered back towards the food trucks, past Minjun attempting to wrangle the correct pizza order from Speedy Pete's with desperate politeness. He strolled by The Steelepool Fish Shop which was beset by a solid quantity of punters waiting with cash in hand, with Chips Darren working at a steady pace behind his counter. Despite the press of the crowd the large chef caught Renji's eye, regarding him for a moment; then gave an aloof tilt of his head that could only have been approval, before turning back to his fryer. A little surge of delight shot through Renji, and he scurried away before the redness rising in his face became noticeable.

Humming a little nonsense tune to himself, he dipped around the side of the Roti Queen truck with a cheerful wave to its proprietor Sarasi, who was out front ladling generous amounts of curry into people's bowls. He'd already had a bowlful earlier in the evening at her insistence, and while the level of spice did threaten to knock his head off, it would have at least been a delicious way to die. Sliding the truck's door open, he fumbled around in the kitchen until he found the ziplock baggie of rice that, on Melody's suggestion, he'd stuffed his phone into. After their little dip in the river Steele the device had taken in almost as much gross water as Renji himself had, and while his usual fix would be to buy a newer model, the fact that all of his cash had been dispersed throughout Buried meant any spur-of-the-moment shopping sprees had ceased to be an option.

Rifling around in the baggie that Sarasi had so kindly donated he fished out the phone, brushed a few soggy rice grains aside and with fingers crossed, hit the power button. A long two seconds later, it sprang to life. Sliding down to sit on the floor of the truck's kitchen, Renji breathed a sigh of relief— one that caught in his throat as the missed call notifications began to flood in. Dozens and dozens of messages, all of a similar tone, all from the same number, choked the screen. His stomach grew sour as he scrolled through the more recent ones.

L. Starkweather (Private number, emergencies only):

Answer your phone, Renji.
Answer me immediately.
I'm calling your mother if you don't answer. I'll tell her everything.
Please pick up your phone, Peanut.
Please
I'm not angry, I promise. I'm sorry if I scared you.
I don't care about what you did, it's just money. It doesn't matter. Hardly anyone even knows it was you who did it.
i can fix this
i just need to know you're okay
please answer

It would be foolish to respond, he knew. His fingers moved across the screen all the same.

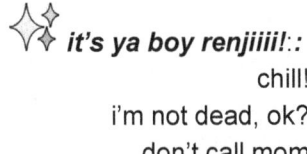 **it's ya boy renjiiii!:**
chill!
i'm not dead, ok?
don't call mom

Almost instantly, the phone buzzed with her incoming call.

Rubbing at his still-raw wrists with a sigh, Renji turned his phone off and slipped it into his pocket. He'd let her know he was alive. And right now, surrounded by mourners and friends of a person who neither he or Aunty L had ever met, that seemed like the limit of what he owed the commander.

Hopping out of the Roti Queen truck, Renji peered around until he found the exact sight he'd been hoping for; Weaver, this time without company, arms crossed and eyes closed as though taking a nap. Catching Melody's eye, he gestured in the direction of the old man's table and made his way over, stopping to buy a round of beers with a damp tenner he'd found in his shoe earlier.

Taking a chair felt too simple, so Renji instead opted for sitting on the table. "Wake up, old man! I gotta talk to you."

Cracking an eye open, Weaver regarded him critically. "Do you."

"I promise, this sh— uh, *stuff* is important." Renji handed him a beer. "Hear me out, huh?"

Heaving a sigh, Weaver accepted the bribe. "Uh huh." he grunted, unconvinced, as he snapped the bottle cap off on the edge of the table.

"It's about your kid."

That permanent frown of his eased as his heavy brow lifted in surprise, but before Weaver could ask for more information there was a scrape of chair on floor as Melody came to sit beside them. Renji looked between her and Weaver questioningly. After a moment's contemplation, the old man nodded. Beaming, Renji tossed her the last beer and she popped the lid off between her metallic fingers, settling in to listen.

"So look, back at the hotel, Aunty L said something weird." Renji fiddled with the cap on his own drink, attempting to mimic Weaver's bottle opening manoeuvre and failing. "I mean, she said a lotta weird somethings, but this one in particular, something about Harlow—" He halted, cursing, as his attempts took a small chunk out of the table rather than opening the stubborn bottle cap.

Weaver took the bottle and popped it open for him. "Get to the point, kid." he said, handing it back.

"I dunno why, but… I think Aunty L has your daughter."

A hiss escaped through Weaver's teeth. He slumped back into his chair. "Makes sense."

Renji frowned. "Alright, you don't exactly sound surprised about that."

"Mm." Weaver took a slow sip of his beer. The look on his face was almost one of… relief? "Means she's alive. Safe."

"Safe?" asked Melody. "With the commander of the Forces?"

"Lissa isn't gonna hurt her. She's…" Weaver exhaled roughly, as though forcing the words out. "Lissa is Harlow's mother."

"Are you serious?" Renji almost dropped his drink. "Holy fuck. *Fuck!*"

"Keep it down, willya?" muttered Weaver, glancing around, but Renji was too spun to care if anyone was listening in. The very idea was unreal. Never once had Aunty Lissa made a single mention of having had a child. She never even seemed to know much of what to do with one; from the moment Renji had ended up at her place, she'd left him to his own devices, as if he were a tiny adult roommate rather than a kid who needed a parent. But if she was Harlow's mother, then—

Renji stared at Weaver. "You and Aunty L were like… a thing?!"

"We were married for a while, yeah." He shrugged, as though he hadn't just said something entirely unhinged.

"Married?!"

"Gonna guess she didn't mention us."

"No! What?!" A few pieces clicked together in Renji's mind. "Damn, is that why she hates you so much?!"

Looking away, Weaver didn't respond, besides a wordless grunt and an uncomfortable shift in his seat. That answered that, then.

Renji pointed his drink at Melody accusingly. "Hey, did *you* know about this?"

Eyes fixed on Weaver, she took a long gulp of beer before responding. "Nope."

"It'd been a long time since either of us saw Lissa." Weaver's sullen gaze seemed to be fixed on something far away. "Wasn't sure if she'd even recognise Harlow since she, uh- Hm." He stuttered to an apprehensive stop.

"Since…?" prompted Renji, waving his bottle.

"Since Harlow transitioned?" said Melody, finishing the sentence for him.

Weaver nodded, his broad shoulders sagging with relief. "Yeah. Didn't know if you knew about that, either."

"She's always been pretty open about being trans. That's how she met Minjun, she helps people get a hookup for their meds. It's no secret." Melody tapped the lip of her beer. "Didn't think she was much for secrets."

"Means your boss doesn't know about her mom either, then." Weaver mumbled, thoughtfully. That made sense; most of Ms Cellanea's information seemed to come from Melody, who seemed as surprised about this as the laid-back hacker was capable of being.

"Can't say I blame her for not telling Ms C." Renji said, dazed at the stream of new information. "Fuck knows I tried to not mention Aunty L either, and I'm just her nephew."

Melo shook her head. "You haven't met Harlow, mate. S'not like her to keep something quiet."

"Must've been a reason she didn't tell Cellanea about Lissa. A good reason, at that." Weaver said. One by one, all of them found Ms Cellanea in the crowd. She was at a table with Minjun and Hajira, sneaking a slice of her assistant's pizza while he chatted with the shelter owner.

"So let's keep it that way." Weaver finished. "Til we know why."

"Sure thing." Renji nodded.

Melody's answer came less easily. As far as Renji could tell, both sisters had staked a lot of that precious trust of theirs in Cellanea, and the thought of keeping something from her must have rankled. She took another quiet sip of beer, then nodded, once.

"So like... What happened?" asked Renji.

"Me and Lissa broke up when Harlow was young. Found I didn't take to the whole Forces thing, and she didn't... didn't really take to the whole parent thing. Lissa didn't want custody, but we had to stay in Unity anyhow, cus Harlow didn't have papers for anywhere else. She didn't— she didn't visit much. Ever," Weaver continued, hoarsely. "Last time they met, Harlow was just a little kid. Wasn't exactly, uh... herself yet. And when she grew up she didn't care much to keep her mom updated on her life. Thought that might mean when she got arrested she'd fly under the radar, end up in the same place as the others. That's why I broke into the airship." He shook his head. "It's my fault she's wrapped up in this in the first damn place. Taught her too damn much. Enough to get her into trouble." He took another swig of his beer, not quite hiding the crack in his voice.

"C'mon, old man." Renji said. "People are gonna do whatever they want if they wanna do it hard enough, no matter what their family says. Trust me on that one."

Melo nodded in agreement. "Harlow always knew what she was risking. She did it anyway."

"I don't—" Weaver began to croak, but Renji rolled right over him with positivity.

"And hey, now we know who has her, it's gonna make finding her way easier, right? Like, I know about a couple of places Aunty L owns."

"Gimme the addresses. I'll look into them." said Melody, without hesitation.

"See?" He reached out his bottle, and Melo clinked it against hers in salute. "We're a team now, remember? And I wanna meet this extremely cool secret cousin of mine!"

"Aye. We have to get Harlow back," she confirmed. "She owes me a tenner."

Weaver looked from one of them to the other and exhaled, as though letting go of something deep within. He ran a scar-knuckled hand across his face; then clinked his bottle against each of theirs. "Alright then."

"Holy shit, is that a smile?!" Renji exclaimed.

It disappeared. "No."

Melody elbowed him in the ribs. "You scared it away."

"Aw, I'm sorry, Uncle Dave." said Renji gleefully.

"Call me that again and I'm throwing you back in the river."

Before Renji could think of something even more infuriating to say he felt another warning poke in his side from a metallic knuckle. The small figure of Ms Cellanea was bobbing towards them, wrapped in a thick woollen coat and so many layers of scarves that she seemed twice her usual width.

"Ah, here you are, my dears." She smiled, finishing the last of her purloined pizza slice. "Melody, David. I was wondering if I could perhaps borrow Mr Hayakawa for a moment?"

"Absolutely." glowered Weaver, moving to push him off the table in her direction.

Cackling, Renji dodged the shove and rolled away, hopping over to meet his new boss. "What's up, Ms C?"

"I was wondering if you might care for a game." she said evenly.

"Always! What're we playing?"

"Excellent answer, dear boy. Come this way, and I shall show you."

Ms Cellanea led him to a spot a little closer to the bonfire— to keep her old bones warm, she insisted— and took a seat at a picnic table, retrieving a deck of cards, a small paper bag covered in napkins, and a plastic knife from the cavernous pockets of her coat. She motioned for Renji to sit opposite as she unsheathed the cards.

"Vingt-et-Un. You would know it as Blackjack. Are you familiar?" she asked, shuffling the deck with an expert hand.

"Kinda, basically." Renji shrugged. "It's the one where you gotta get to twenty-one, right?"

"Correct. You must play against the house to decide how far you shall push your luck. Would you like a try?"

While the Court held a casino or two Renji had never been much of a gambler; though having met the type of people who did like to play the tables, he reasoned it couldn't be so difficult as all that. "Sure, why not."

"Excellent." Smiling, she tore the paper bag apart to reveal two large slabs of brownie, then turned her attention to the deck of cards, cutting it and setting a stack aside.

"Uh, I gotta ask, what's with the cakes?"

"What is a game without stakes?" Taking the plastic knife, she divided both brownies into cubes. "And these, dear boy, are Riley's famous salted caramel brownies. As they are made by hand, they usually sell out of these quite quickly, you see, but I asked them to put some aside for today. What with all of the goings on, it seems I caught them in a generous mood."

He had to admit, the brownie looked fantastic. The cake gleamed in the way that suggested it was at that perfect level of gooey chocolatey goodness, topped with thick strands of golden caramel. It took all of Renji's admittedly lacking willpower to not scoop them up and eat them at once, napkin and all. "Goddamn."

"God would consider himself lucky to be damned for one of these." Setting out two napkins, she placed six of the cubes on each, and slid one set over to Renji. "That is yours. And these are the house; or in other words, mine."

"For now, sure."

Ms Cellanea chuckled. "That is the spirit! Place your bet, my dear, and the house shall meet it." She said, setting a napkin in the centre of the table.

"Alright, I'll go in on a couple of these guys." He dropped two brownie cubes onto the napkin.

"Two it is." She matched his bet with two pieces of her own, then dealt the cards; one face down for the house, she explained, and one face up. For him, two face up cards. He would make his play to get his total closer to twenty-one than hers, though going over that number would mean instant failure. "Now… Shall you draw another, or stick with what you have?"

Renji considered the cards he'd been dealt, a nine and a three. Twelve seemed low, in the good kinda way. Lots of room to make up on, right? The house had another nine, though he wasn't sure what to make of that, exactly. Probably it was good. "Draw!"

She dealt him a two. Fourteen, total. He could push his luck on a fourteen. "Hell yeah. Gimme another!"

The next card flipped to reveal a Jack; a ten.

"Alas, twenty-four! That is a bust, my boy."

Renji cursed, scowling at the little red bastard on the card like it was his fault.

"Which means, these are now mine." And before he could protest, Ms Cellanea swept up the two chunks of brownie and ate them, her dark eyes twinkling in the bonfire's light with a mischief that seemed to be at odds with her years.

"Again?" she asked between bites.

He snorted. "I mean, yeah! Gotta win some back before you eat the lot, haven't I?" He dropped two more cubes in the middle, then slouched in his seat as she prepared to deal again. "So... Why The Loose Ends? Sounds kinda like a hair salon."

"The answer is quite simple." She dealt for the house, drawing an eight. "We are, you see, a result of the carelessness of Imperium. Each of us is a problem that fell through the cracks. A loose end yet to be tied. No matter how much it may pretend otherwise, a business so huge as Imperium International shall always be an imperfect machine. It amuses me to remind them of this." Flipping two cards for Renji, she revealed a seven and a three. "Draw, or stick?"

"Draw!"

A seven. He hesitated, contemplating what the correct move might be.

Leaning in, Ms Cellanea lowered her voice to a conspiratorial whisper. "If you would like my advice, I should play it safe. Seventeen is a good place to stick." She winked at him.

That did seem to make sense. There were way more high numbers than low in the deck, right? Renji's brain, unused as it was to caring about maths, wasn't offering much help on the odds. "Mmm... sure, okay. Guess I'll stick." he relented.

"A seventeen for you, and for the house..." A four, followed by a nine. A perfect twenty-one. "Aha! Vingt-et-Un!"

"Aw, what?! You tricked me!"

"I simply advised a safe play." She took her winnings and popped them into her mouth. "As the English are so fond of saying, 'it is what it is'." she concluded, once she had finished chewing.

Renji had never liked that phrase. "Can I ask you something?"

"Of course, though I cannot promise an answer."

"You were Court once, right?"

He'd been expecting shock, or anger. What he got was laughter. "Interesting!" she chuckled. "Most interesting. Why do you presume this?"

"Well for one, you just answered a question with a question. That's pretty classic."

"You see me dealing in the boardrooms, perhaps? Or cracking the skulls with your Forces, hm?" She mimed a little *bop* with one hand, as though to underline the ridiculousness of it all. "A difficult picture to place, is it not."

That wasn't a no, but... perhaps much like with Melody and Cadence, he could earn an answer in time. And Court or no, he couldn't help but like the old lady, with her mysterious ways and calming presence, even if she was hustling him for the last two pieces of brownie. Deciding that the chances of him being a secret blackjack prodigy seemed rather low at this point, Renji considered his options carefully, then decided on the careless one. "Let's make this interesting," he said.

"I am listening."

"How's this; I wanna go all or nothing! I win, I get to keep what's left of my brownie and all of yours. You win," he snapped his fingers, "and I get nada."

The audacity of it earned him a peal of laughter. "Yet you have so very little left to lose, and so much to gain! These stakes are a little unbalanced, are they not?"

"Ah, but I can't play for shit, so that evens it out!"

She snorted out another sincere laugh. "Very well. I accept your ridiculous bet." All six cubes of brownie joined his last two in the centre of the table, and the deal began. The house drew a King, a ten; and for Renji, a four and six.

"Oho, it seems that we are even. What shall you do, dear boy?" Ms Cellanea asked, that patient schoolteacher smile of hers taking on a mocking little turn.

"Hit me!"

She flipped the next card, a seven. "Seventeen again, Mr Hayakawa! Would that I too could be as such." She chuckled. "Once more, this would be a sensible place to stick."

He shook his head, determined to play this one to the hilt. "Gimme another."

"A risky play," she hummed, tapping the top of the deck. "Are you quite sure?"

"Yeah. Risk's worth the reward sometimes, right?"

Ms Cellanea drew in a breath, passing him a card…

…and revealing a four. Twenty-one, right on the money.

The howl of pure dumb joy Renji gave out obliterated any possibility of appearing cool in the moment, but he couldn't care less. With a smirk so wide he was at risk of losing the top of his head, he reached over and flipped the house card. An eight.

"Eighteen." Cellanea murmured. If he'd have taken her advice, he'd have ended the night thoroughly brownieless. "Well, well… My congratulations. It seems you are a lucky creature indeed." With her smile back in place, she slid the napkin of his winnings over the table. "I must admit that when we met I was not so certain, but now I feel you shall prove to be quite the loose end indeed."

"Weird compliment, but I'll take it!" Renji flicked a chunk of brownie into the air, catching it in his mouth. It tasted exactly as good as it looked, if not better.

"Luck is a wonderful thing to have, as long as one understands that like any resource, it can run out." She gathered up her cards, reshuffling the cut deck back into one. "Today we have dealt with the problem before us as well as can be, yet another will be along shortly. Another after this, and another, another, *another*. This fight you are choosing, it does not end in victory; at least, not our own." Placing the pack down, she locked eyes with him, solemn in the firelight. "Understand that there is no way to defeat this dragon, dear boy. We can only bar our gates, and pray that they hold."

Minjun had said the same earlier on their trek through the long-dead tunnels of the Steelepool grid; that Imperium was the heart of this relentless city, and a city could never be stopped.

Ms Cellanea was studying him now, watching his face carefully. "You once told me, Mr Hayakawa, that you wanted *in*. Now that you have better seen what that means, that it is an unwinnable bet indeed... Are you still in?"

#

Renji kept half of the remaining brownie. The rest was spent on a bribe.

While he knew he should have been grateful to have the bedding Arthur had dug up for him from fuck knows where, having to physically lug a mattress through the Grid tunnels to the Roundhouse proved to be something of a trial. Still, if he planned on getting any sleep tonight it needed to happen, and Melody was willing to carry the duvet and pillows in exchange for the salted caramel treats.

The heavy bastard mattress barely fit into the train carriage, though after Renji had cannoned into it a few times both he and it flopped through the doorway and onto the chilly floor. From the doorway, the duvet was thrown onto his head.

"No smoking in here."

"No problem, I was gonna quit anyhow!" By the time he'd untangled himself from the sheets, Melody had already turned to leave. "Hey, wait up a sec!"

She paused. "Hm?"

"Before I forget to ask, whose place is that?" Renji waved at the next carriage along, the one whose window was stuffed full of leafy green plants bathed in an ultraviolet glow; the only greenery he'd encountered in all of Buried. "Cus I kinda ended up with this one plant, and I have no clue what you're meant to do with it. Was

306

wondering if I could talk to your gardener there, find out how to keep from killing the thing."

He rifled through his bag, withdrawing the somewhat battered houseplant he'd stolen from AirCast Two what felt like three hundred years ago. While he'd been out robbing parties and whatnot, some of the poor thing's round rubbery leaves had already begun to wrinkle, taking on a tinge of yellowish brown about the edges that didn't seem especially healthy.

Melody looked from the plant to him, and shrugged. "Fine. Can't guarantee she'll help, though." And with that, she closed her eyes.

"Hang on, you can't mean—"

A shiver and a sniff, and Cadence was stood in his doorway, giving him a blank stare for just a moment until her usual scowl settled into place.

"Uh, hey, Cade." he said, a little more sheepishly than he'd have liked. "Soooo... I got this, uh, plant—"

Without a word she lunged forward to grab the plant out of his hands, and in a swirl of Melody's pink puffer jacket, she was gone.

Oh well. It'd probably be better off with her, anyway. Renji kicked off his sneakers and arranged the bedding into something like a nest, wrapping himself in the plain duvet and settling in for what felt like a well-earned rest.

He'd almost drifted off to sleep by the time a knock rattled at his door, jolting him awake. Untangling himself from the duvet, he rolled over to the door and cracked it open, only to find no-one there. Except, on the metallic step leading into his carriage, there sat his plant, repotted into a larger container that sat in a shallow dish. A small battery-powered UV light apparatus had been attached to the pot, bathing the leaves in a gentle, pretty purple. Even the soil was new, its damp surface mixed with little flecks of some white substance.

A plastic drip feeder labelled Jade Plant Food had been worked into the mulch, and attached to the pot was a post-it note, with a biro-scribbled message:

Water once a week only.

Idiot.

Only was underlined. So was *idiot.*

He found a spot for it on one of the carriage's seats, where it seemed rather at home. Relaxing in the calming light of his little plant friend, he fished the napkin of remaining brownie bites out of his pocket and settled back into his blankets.

On the rare occasions that Renji had thought about his future, he'd never expected to spend any part of it on the floor of a draughty old train, snacking on gambling winnings and wearing a stolen jacket; yet here he was all the same, and he was pretty damn okay with that. Sure, the rusty carriage was cold and kinda dirty, and maybe the bedding didn't even have linens, but that feeling of unease he'd woken up with at Aunty L's apartment had left him entirely, replaced with a keen sort of pride in what he and the others had achieved yesterday. Even the silk sheets and room service Delaney had offered didn't seem quite so necessary any more, not if they meant being forced to hide beneath a layer of false respectability as Chance forced himself to do.

Squishing a chunk of brownie between his fingers, he considered Ms Cellanea's words about the unwinnable bet that was joining The Loose Ends. He wasn't so sure she was correct. Having lived in Imperium Court his entire life, he knew the people there weren't some formless power, some inevitable beast that could never be defeated. They were just *people,* like Flood or Jeremy or even Aunty L, all with their own foibles and problems, compromising and squabbling and infighting to either maintain their comfortable position or claw their way up to a better one.

Looking around the plaza tonight and seeing the gathered crowd of revellers who only yesterday had been huddled in fear against the cold had been proof enough that not only was it possible, it was necessary. It would take careful planning, and fuck-damn was it going be dangerous, but for Renji it had never been clearer that Imperium could be defeated. *Would* be. And he'd be there to help make it happen.

Lying back in his makeshift bed, Renji ate his last piece of brownie. And grinned.

ACKNOWLEDGEMENTS, AND ALL THAT

Well, here we are. Not sure how this happened, to be quite honest, but it appears I wrote a whole book, and you have read it! I'm as surprised as you are. I very much hope you enjoyed your time with the gang, and if you did, I hope you'll consider leaving a review on Goodreads or Amazon or social media or tell a friend who might enjoy it, pass them your copy of the book, whatever suits you best– I know the "word of mouth" spiel is one you've heard before, but reviews help new authors more than you'd expect. I believe the magic number on Amazon in particular is fifty (!) reviews before the dread algorithm starts churning in a book's favour, so deal with that information as you will.

While I'm here, I'd just like to thank a few folks who, whether they're aware of it or not, helped make this whole thing happen. My best friend and husband John, who encouraged me a lot; this is largely all your fault, I make no excuses. Our besties Simon and Laura; what can I even say except *hello* and thank you for everything, especially the various amusing noises Laura made whenever I sent over a new draft. And a special shoutout to Jan; it was a pleasure to rediscover writing with you over the helltimes! Keep going, you're honestly incredible.

And thank you, the one who is reading now! I hope to see you again whenever I hurry up and write another one of these.

-Kate